NIGHT SKY
BURNING

For more information about H A Walker's work, visit @h.a.walkerwrites on Instagram or email h.a.walkerwrites@gmail.com

Cover Design Paperback: David Gardias

Cover Design Hardback: Emiliya @_silentium_art_

Map Design: Rahma

Edited by: Melissa Smith

CONTENTS

CONTENT WARNINGS

Night Sky Burning is a new adult fantasy novel that contains the
following:
Animal cruelty and death
Themes of anxiety, loneliness, and depression
Descriptions of torture, death, and sexual assault
Kidnapping

*This tale contains scenes of violence from the outset. Tread with care
through the Boreals and, as always, keep an eye on the skies.*

NAME GUIDE

Humans:

Destry Kivisto Des-tree Kiv-ee-sto

Silvano Coen Sil-va-no Co-en

Jaryn Adacus Ja-rin Ada-cus

Amadea Machimaja Ama-day-a Match-e-mar-ja

Aalto Thorra Al-to Tor-ra

Rekorious Niemi Rek-or-reeus Nee-em-ee

Animals:

Orrin Oar-rin

Ebrel Ee-brell

Gracien Gray-sea-in

Spearian Spear-ree-in

To Nora and Rob, for lighting the way through the dark.

And to those who just love horses, who collect Breyer's and doodled ponies in their schoolbooks.

PART ONE

THE SWIFT

CHAPTER ONE

ASHER

The Pegasus colt knew he was about to die.

A thin, crisp layer of ice clung to the beast's whiskers, and he exhaled warily, creating a billow of cloud around his flaring nostrils. He looked to be carved from the winter mountains, a brutal force in a coat of ash, black and silver.

Ears twitching back and forth, the colt cast his head about, trying to locate my father and me in the snow-covered birch trees. His eyes were white-rimmed pools of ink.

He was terrified.

A forehoof the size of my outspread hand pawed at the powder in frustration. Hock deep in snow, he knew he wouldn't be airborne in time to dodge our bolts. A young and muscular fellow like him had only recently been kicked out of his maternal family band, and he was yet to find the refuge and safety of the bachelor herds further north.

A large and easy target.

Supposedly.

Grounded whilst searching for food, he had left tracks to follow through the snowdrifts.

My calloused and frozen forefinger twitched on the trigger of my crossbow as I trembled with anticipation.

The huge, feather-clad contraptions that were his wings arched over the colt's back. Muscles in his hindquarters bunched, and his hocks sank low toward the ground, nostrils flaring with every ... last ... billowing breath.

This colt was mine. This was what I had trained to do for the past ten years. I had watched my father shoot down countless others without a second thought. Now it was my turn. *Just pull the damn trigger, Asher.*

But I didn't fire. *Couldn't* fire.

Hesitation gripped my bones fiercely in a sudden jolt, and darkness tunneled my vision. My aim was perfect; the colt was right there. It would be a perfect shot, effortless really. My gaze raked over the creature once more, taking in his sheer beauty.

I ... I can't.

I should, but I lowered my finger from the trigger. Doubt thundered through my body as my stomach roiled.

We can find another. It doesn't feel right to—

A deadly bolt fired from the opposite direction and seared itself into the colt's thoracic cavity.

The effect was immediate. I flinched and shuddered as if it had struck me instead.

Crumpling like a falling sail, the colt dropped to his knees with a guttural groan. His hind limbs followed suit, and the Pegasus sank into the snowdrift with a muted and heavy thud.

Blood, startlingly bright against the white ground, seeped from his chest. Steam began to rise from the scarlet pool.

No new ballads would be written today of how Oban Field's only son failed to shoot down his first Pegasus. No, the other hunters would not be singing my name or swaying over their fiddles about this.

I shuddered, chilled to my core. The wind cut across slices of my exposed, sun-kissed skin.

That colt could have gone on to become one of the Great Stallions. He could have indeed had stories written about him and even gone on to be a man killer. They commanded sheet-white fear and the deepest respect—a hunter's greatest challenge.

Yet now he was a broken mess of feathers, pelt, and dreadlocked mane, never to fly or fight again. His fate now rested in one of the market squares in Aarine as parceled sections of dried meat, feathers, and bone.

I felt my chest cave as I tried to quell the growing panic that stirred there. *What have I done?*

My father was the first to break cover from the snow-drenched trees. Shouldering his crossbow, he cut through the powder as silent as a waif. The duck feather-covered snowshoes strapped to his boots and mine made the going slightly easier. Pausing at the colt's head, he dutifully laid a hand, kept warm in seal skin mittens, onto that muscled, iron-gray neck.

Oban Fields. Debated to be the Boreal's most experienced Pegasus hunter. He looked up and fixed me with a disgraced glare. I was a failure.

Removing one of his mittens, he reached across the colt's huge, twitching wingspan and wrenched a long primary feather free. The rachis that ran along the feather's spine had already paled with the colt's death, but the ebony barbs glistened brilliantly still. In a well-practiced motion, he tucked it alongside the countless others in the band of his leather hat.

As a boy, I had seen the hunters marching around the guild mansion, their cloaks and wide-brim hats bedecked with feathers from their fallen quarry. How badly I had wanted one of my own. Just one feather to tuck into my hat, to mark my place amongst the toughest men in the north.

My crossbow was a hard, heavy weight in my arms.

I moved lithely, yet slowly out from my hiding place of close-growing birch trees and walked over to the creature my father had slain.

My ten-year-long apprenticeship was not over, and I would not be taking my hunting vows in the shadowed guild hall next week on my twenty-fifth birthday. Would I ever be one of them, one of the hunters, a true predator?

An anger-filled silence held space between my father and me. I wouldn't be surprised if he disowned me entirely because of this. Confusion made my mind feel like I was wading through oil. Why hadn't I pulled the trigger? I had dreamt of this moment for years, imagining the glory and awe I would feel. Yet now...

As my father and I set about preparing his body for transport on our sledges, I felt less and less like a proficient hunter and more like an accomplice to murder. The snow seemed to quiver where it fell, as if the frozen kisses sent down by the water spirit, Merevis, resented being so close to the atrocious death.

The moment I had anticipated for so long was now burned into my memory for all the wrong reasons.

His gaze fixed skyward; the colt stared at the heavens in which he now roamed only as a spirit on the harsh winter wind.

"So ... tell me. What's more likely to kill you up here, Unicorn or Pegasus?" asked my uncle, Edgar Fields. He had ridden north to help us carry the colt off the mountain with his string of five sturdy hill ponies and wooden sleighs.

Well, at least my uncle was talking to me. Hell, I was surprised they even allowed me to share the same campsite as them. My father was probably inclined to leave me at the killing site for all he cared.

Lesser men might have scoffed at my uncle's question, yet I knew this was a test. Yes, it was pure fantasy to try and track, kill, or even coerce a Unicorn, but you still had to appreciate the risks.

To step foot into this mountain range was to also sign your death warrant.

I did not want to be tested right now. I wanted to run off the Andun Mountain Range as fast as I could, find the nearest tavern, and drink until the sun rose and sank again.

To never see a Pegasus again would have suited me just fine.

I imagined the black feather on my father's hat burning his skull like a brand.

"Pegasus," I replied, my voice weary.

My father glanced at Edgar with unwilling approval.

Of course, I was right. I'd worked too damn hard to be wrong now. I had been absorbing their expertise since I could walk, talk, and ride. Entering my apprenticeship aged fifteen, I had been more experienced than any of my year mates.

Yet for what? For *what*?

I could be the first man in my family to be an ordinary, run-of-the-mill hunter.

Yeah, my father would rather disown me than let that happen. He wouldn't be able to bear the shame of it.

Glancing at the hulking mounds of canvas and linen-wrapped bundles not far from our campfire, I could still feel the colt's hot blood on my skin. Hastily, I looked away and swallowed harshly as my meal of burnt rabbit stew battled to resurface.

Our little trio sat huddled beside a giant rock fissure, precariously positioned at one of the highest points of Jacob's Pass, the only route into the Anduns from the south. Once the pass ended, it was just untouched forest, mountain cliffs, and valleys, with no clear tracks between any of them.

Beyond the mountains and the star-dusted horizon, lay war-torn Petowin to the northwest. Once home to fearsome clans, Petowin no longer had its own population of Pegasi.

A sharp winter wind whistled down the fissure, while a cluster of stars twinkled in the gap high above us. We were seventy miles south of the highest peak in the range, Mount Serebo, a place where summer did not venture. The mountain was a hulking mass of ice and dark violet stone against the winter night.

Despite the clear skies, no ethereal lights danced across the heavens. The Petish called him *Wings of Fire*. Colladonians simply named him the Night Pegasus. His blazing feathers illuminated the dark as he flew by. He was clearly resting tonight, or maybe his business was needed elsewhere in the spirit realm, rather than in the skies above the Boreals. It was a good omen to see him the night before a lynx hunt.

I pondered as to whether it was indeed an extremely *bad* omen to not see him after slaying one of his mortal brethren.

Edgar chucked another small log onto the fire. "Explain your answer."

Oban took a deep pull on his smoking pipe, his only other pleasure in life, besides hunting.

Despite our matching short black hair, we looked nothing alike. He was squat and barrel-chested, but strong. I, apparently, for I don't remember her, looked like my mother, a refugee from Petowin. I'd inherited her smattering of freckles across my nose, along with her brown eyes and the famed bottled wildness of Petowin descendants. Wildness that liked to surge forward whenever I got into a brawl, which was more often than I could count. More like Edgar in build, I was lean, honed by countless hours spent training and climbing.

People had mocked my father, slated him even, for making a wife of Airin. She had not only been Petish but a Turunin at that, an ancient clan that was feared nearly as much as the Kivistos. Maybe he had seen the wildness in her, a feral quality I now possessed and wanted to try and tame it for himself.

I leant toward the flames, warming my hands. "Unicorns are secretive, and their family herds are tiny, maybe one or two mares to a stallion. They evade rather than engage with any potential dangers. They are born with a set amount of magic that doesn't grow in power as they age. Once it's gone, it's gone. Besides ..." I shrugged, tiredness and darkness tugging at my bones. "The majority of Unicorns died alongside the Petish Pegasi from the Nijinxes slaughter. Pegasus stallions will seek out potential dangers that roam within a ten-mile radius of the herd. Then they will either lead you away from the mares or, most likely, kill you."

Inching back from the fire, I willed the winter night to envelope me like a shroud, so I could contemplate the utter shit show of a day. Darkness, older and deeper than that of the night surrounding us, pressed against my skin.

How long would I carry that gray colt's blood on my hands? Maybe I would carry it forever. I balked at the thought.

The battle cry of a Pegasus stallion boomed through the still night air and echoed off the rock that sheltered us.

We were all armed and ready within a heartbeat, listening intently as we tried to source the direction the sound came from. A second later, another war cry was bellowed into the expectant and chilled night air.

The second challenge had been louder, deeper, emitted from the lungs of a larger beast.

My father relaxed a fraction and lowered his crossbow. "They're a good distance west of here. Rare for two stallions to challenge each other at this time of night. They'd be foolish to fight in the dark with more predators around."

Fools or not, the stallions' cries and squeals rolled out over the valleys, stone, rock, and ferns. The ground readied for blood to be spilled.

On and on, the noise echoed, and we had little reprieve that night. Not until dawn, as the skies began to blush with the rising of the sun. There came a horrendous sound, followed by an abrupt silence, and the cry came from neither of the two contenders who had fought. This was the haunting chorus of a third animal, a female. It pierced my eardrums and sunk deep into my heart.

Somewhere to the west, a mare was dying.

My father sucked down a deep breath. "Have you ever heard of such a tragedy?"

"Never," whispered Edgar.

"Who was that?" I peered into the meek, pink horizon.

I knew of the Great Stallions, of course. Some had proper names such as Rosken, Thadeus, and Cassaden; whereas others held titles like *the Blazing Star* and *the Silent Blizzard*, all passed on through stories my father, uncle, and fellow hunters had spun.

But none of us had ever heard an almighty roar such as what brought the mare down.

Edgar stood stiffly. "They're all dangerous. Every dratted feathered one of them, but there's one ... one who the men talk about the most, to try and scare each other out of the job, I guess. I've never crossed him, thank God."

"The scarred gray one?"

I knew that look on my father's face—his need to hunt and kill—but the Great Stallions were completely off-limits.

"Aye, *the Oncoming Storm*, they call him. A huge brute." Shouldering my pack, I looked across to my uncle. He looked wary. His gaze met mine. "He killed five men last year alone."

We broke camp quickly, and as we did so, the haunting bellow of a mourning stallion washed over the frigid mountains.

The weather was agreeing with us, for now, with little cloud and no fog, which was deadly when it came to Pegasi. They used it as a cloak to dive down from. Yet today, there was a sky so blue you could lose yourself in it, stretching from east to west, fractured in places by those snow-cloaked mountains.

Edgar led us through the wilderness, while my father and I held our crossbows ready. The weapon was usually a reassuring weight in my hands, but not this morning. Before us, the plateau dropped down into a mass of jagged granite, forming another snow-covered plain below.

We had picked up the tracks shortly after dawn, a small bachelor herd of four young stallions, heading south in search of better grazing.

My father wanted to try his luck at snagging one. We had a spare pony, so we had the power to bring it off the mountain.

I refrained from mentioning that he was merely being a gluttonous show-off. He simply wanted to conquer: stags brimming with pride, Pegasus colts, my mother. He wanted to tame them all and snuff out the light of their souls.

The bachelor herd was dangerously close to the established herds of the Great Stallions, some of whom held territory near here. If they were close, then we were borderline idiotic being within a ten-mile radius. My father had quashed my uncle's objections, and we had trudged along this plateau.

Each year, hunters rotated where they were allowed to prowl. This year, we were shadowing all the colts east of Jacob's Pass. The most notorious Great Stallion around here was Rosken. Revered and feared throughout the guild, the eleven-year-old stallion was a brown, black-winged barbarian who had killed ten men in his lifetime so far.

We dismounted and tethered the ponies, then I set about making the trap. Despite a small, yet growing louder voice in the back of my head that whispered, *Don't do this.*

The trap was simple. I was the bait, and I was to be as loud and obnoxious as possible, luring the Pegasi in; all the while my father and uncle slipped into hidden positions atop the cliff faces. As potential protectors of a herd, the scent of a man close by made the young colts wary and want to seek out the danger. A remnant of the Trinitor curse.

Despite the countless seasons I had spent up here, my body still barked in protest as I waded through the snow. Something gifted down by my mother gnawed at my consciousness. Maybe ancient Petowin instinct, if you will. I wanted to be off these mountains. *Then just leave,* said the voice in my head. I fought against the temptation, desperate to salvage whatever fatherly-son relationship I had left.

I ventured down the cliff edge, recalling the hand and foot place-ments from memory. Climbing had been my very first love, the pure and simple nature of it, placing total trust in your body. I had spent many a summer in these parts, edging my way up the cliffs, powdered chalk clinging to my sweat-soaked body.

Those sweet memories foundered and froze in my mind as I stalked down the plateau and set about making a small campfire, cold nipping at my face. Apprehension clung to the marrow of my bones and this feeling had never come when I was hunting other animals, only since yesterday. I could still feel that colt's dark eyes burning into my soul.

Sitting cross-legged before the little fire, I brought out the small wooden carving of a swan from my shirt pocket. My father had no idea I owned it, bought discreetly from an outlying Aarine village. He only believed in what he could hear, touch, and kill. A typical Colladonian.

It was a Petish belief, however, that your soul could be lured away while you slept or worried aimlessly. Despite being raised practically Colladonian, I had spent enough time in the wilds to catch fleeting feelings of something, not human or animal, and more than a change of wind or a shift in temperature.

The spirits the Petish worshiped still prowled the land. Most were good, like those tied to the land and the water, but those who drifted and held no purpose taunted unaware humans instead.

They believed that feral spirits feared the long-necked water birds and having a carving of one kept you safe and benevolent forces at bay.

Countlessly, I ran my thumb down the swan's now smooth neck.

I had just placed another birch log on the fire when I heard a ptarmigan call. The plateau was rimmed with gold as dusk crept closer.

Rising to one knee on the snow-topped grass, I propped the stock of my crossbow against my broad shoulder and peered down the sight.

Three more calls sounded.

Four colts were making their way down the plateau toward me.

Deftly, I cocked the crossbow and added a fresh, chilled bolt to the flight groove.

Feeling like a fool, yet knowing it was necessary, I started singing softly to myself. I was a siren luring the Pegasi to their deaths amongst the rocks. They were tempted by the scent of a man, even more so if they could hear one.

"Gonna catch me a Pegasus, the horse upon the air.
Gonna catch me a Pegasus, a feathered treasure I will share.
It's feathers to market, its pelt to the king,
I'll save enough money and buy my maiden a golden ring.
Hair to the weaver's and bones to the buil ..." I trailed off, stunned into silence. I had never seen a Pegasus like this in the flesh.

Rounding the stone corner of the plateau came the most beautiful creature I had ever seen. It was the sun-given flesh. Tavaris, the fire spirit, in Pegasus form. Leader of the bachelor band, his white wings were as pristine as the winter snow on which he walked. Those wings half extended over his back as he scented me keenly.

A palomino Pegasus, a thing of beauty, a rare creature that was woven into the tales told to children.

The three other Pegasi shadowed the golden one, and they stepped cautiously forward.

My crossbow trembled in my hands.

A black colt jarred to a halt as it spotted me in the snow and tall, dead grass. He huffed loudly and flung up his head, ears pricked forward. The others followed suit and pinned their molten gazes on my frozen, still body.

My father would no doubt shoot the palomino. In his career, he had never gotten a golden.

Heart hammering in my chest, I ground my teeth, the muscle in my jaw clenching. Something roiled under my skin at something so glorious being dead upon the snow.

Back up, I thought frantically, *you're about to die.*

Knowing my father, being the greedy bastard he is, he'd try his luck with the black too. My gaze flicked upward to the lip of the cliff, where a bolt head glistened, ready to be fired.

Four pairs of intelligent eyes followed suit and stared at the two barely moving hulks of winter camouflage that were Oban and Edgar.

The palomino reared, whinnying a warning call, and all four scrambled backward and upward in a winged mass of black, gold, brown, and chestnut.

A blur of movement atop the granite revealed Oban ditching his white cloak as he raced to get a shot at the palomino.

Years of training had me bracing and re-aiming the crossbow.

Above, the gold and white colt launched himself up and up into the air, glowing in the dusk light like a newly minted god. With his wings ablaze with sunlight ... I understood why we hunted them.

We were utterly inferior to them. The flight, the speed, the strength, we would never be able to master and own such abilities. So, we had taken one jealous look and decided to conquer it instead, stripping the beasts of all that they stood for.

The Petish had dropped to their humbled knees whenever a herd flew overhead, murmuring thanks to the air spirit, Ilmari, for the good omen.

The golden colt dived.

Mouth open in a silent scream, the palomino hurtled downward, straight at me.

A doomed, falling star.

My aim was perfect as I fired. Efficient and ruthless.

Time slowed as the freezing air bent around the bolt head.

The *crack* of my bolt smashing into and destroying my father's crossbow echoed over the plateau. A breath later, I loaded another bolt, swiveled on my knees, and fired again.

My uncle cried out as his crossbow splintered apart in his hands, spraying him with wooden shrapnel.

I felt the huge draught of air as the golden colt swept downward.

A blazing bearer of death.

Tossing my crossbow far out of reach, I flung myself aside, the air smacking out of my lungs as I wrenched myself around to face the colt.

Barely a foot above the snow, the Pegasus swept upward to land forcefully on the snow. Pinning his ears, he flung up his head and leapt forward.

I gasped harshly like a freshly plucked fish as the colt pinned my neck between his two iron-strong forelegs.

His hot breath billowed over my face in a cloud of steam. Wings arching over him, he lowered his gray muzzle to a mere inch above my nose.

I was about to die.

The rest of the world, the violence and cruelty, filtered away to nothing as I gazed up, my lungs racking for air to look into the eyes of the colt.

They gleamed like liquid amber under glass. His dark oval pupils staring straight into my tarnished soul.

And ... and f-for a moment, a heartbeat, I could see directly into his too.

Sentient emotion tumbled through those eyes, an emotion that warred with fire, darkness, and rage.

At least ... at least this would be peaceful. He could crush my skull, and it would all be over.

I could hear my father and uncle yelling and cursing, but none of that mattered.

The veins that ran on either side of his head beneath the facial crest pounded. His heart rate clearly matching my own.

Another breath swept over me, slower this time.

I would happily look into those eyes forever, content if they were the last thing I ever saw. Blood roared in my head, and I could feel the weight of my daggers digging into my hips, yet my frozen fingers didn't reach for them.

The colt blinked, breaking off his stare. He raised and turned his noble head to his right wing, muzzle reaching forward, and plucked a lone primary feather free. Clasping it gently in his velveteen lips, he stepped back a pace, then another.

In the darkening air, I could hear men screaming and Pegasi roaring.

A colt the color of embers whinnied in warning.

Time seemed to slow even further as the palomino pressed that gleaming white feather into my bare right palm.

Willing my stiff fingers to move, I clutched it in my sweat-soaked hand, and the world around me burst into voices of a different kind. It felt like my eardrums were being cleaved apart, as my mind tried in vain to comprehend the magnitude of what it was hearing. And behind it all was a heat, a fire so intense it claimed everything in its path, a warping darkness sweeping down in its wake.

"Murderers."

"Colt killer."

"Raiden died because of you!"

They ... they could talk to each other?

I blinked at the insanity of it.

The palomino exhaled loudly over me, a nicker sounding deep in his throat, and in a voice that was harsh and guttural like forest on fire, he murmured, *"Use it wisely, human."*

My vision blurred, and the air turned to cracking ice in my lungs.

Arching his wings, the palomino launched into the air in a billowing updraught of snow.

"Fly now! Fly brothers!" The golden colt's voice hurtled through my head.

My fingers scraped along the frozen earth, snow crusting under my nails. Heart beating wildly, I tried desperately to suck down air into my lungs and get my body under control.

I was alive. By some utter spirits-forsaken miracle, I was alive.

Lurching over in the snow, I hauled myself to my knees and vomited.

As I got to my feet, the feather in my hand trembled furiously.

Utter silence descended over the plateau, and I gazed up, up, up, to the cliff tops now bathed in auburn light.

Chest heaving for breath, my mind still reeling, I willed my legs to walk, then I saw what made the winter air so quiet and laden.

The Pegasi may have let me live, but my father and uncle were dead.

CHAPTER TWO

DESTRY

"The Heir Lord of Moray and his envoy have arrived, my lady." The footman smiled and bowed deeply before the round table, believing he was spreading happy news.

I really wished he hadn't.

The five ancient councilmen around me blanched in their seats and did a sterling job of studying the notes they had just jotted down. Doing anything other than looking at me. They would end this meeting early and withdraw to their own private rooms, abandoning me to my betrothed. It made everyone on edge whenever the Heir Lord visited Aarine. My father would find solace with his wine, happy to hide away until the visit was over, and my mother ... I clenched my fists and passed my sheaf of paper to the councilman on my right.

Lord Torkell gently took the notes from my shaking hands. "Best of luck, my lady."

I gave him a meek smile and stood, smoothing down my dove-gray woolen dress. I'd need all the luck I could get. This was the Heir Lord's last visit before the wedding. Each day that passed felt like a noose tightening around my neck.

The footman left the open doorway and walked toward where I stood at the table, dimly lit by the torches along the granite stone walls. Even on the brightest summer day, Reckforton Castle was dark and damp, like some ancient cave. I half expected to find moss growing along the corridors. He gave a small, hesitant smile and leant in toward me. "The Heir Lord wanted me to let you know that the Duchess is in the very best of care. You needn't end your meeting early."

It was an effort to stay standing. "He said *what?*"

The footman, Alder, blinked and straightened. "The Heir Lord, he ... he said that his medic would take over your mother's care." I paled, and I must have looked like death as the footman grimaced. "I'm sorry, my lady. Have I done something wrong?"

I placed a shaking hand on his forearm. "No, of course, you haven't. It's not your fault. Is Narve's guardsman here too?"

Now it was Alder's turn to blanch. "Lonan is here, my lady."

I withdrew my hand.

And broke into a run out of the meeting room.

The castle hallways seemed to press in all around me. The dark, gray stone cutting off any air. I had to move, run, run, *run* in this stupid, spirits-forsaken dress. The castle was empty, courtiers scuttling away, hiding from the far northern presence that had arrived here.

The guards standing by the doorway barely shuffled aside in time as I burst into my mother's bedroom. In a heaving breath, I slammed to a halt and assessed the utterly quiet room.

In the darkened corner opposite the fireplace, her lady's maid, Rose, leapt to her feet.

But the stranger who sat beside where Damara lay did not so much as flinch as I stalked toward him.

I walked to the end of the bed, taking in every detail of my mother: her sallow skin barely illuminated by the candles in here, the sips for breath, how her closed eyelids fluttered endlessly.

The cloaked Colladonian finally turned to face me as I towered beside the bed, my hands clenched into fists. His worn leather medical bag sat open on the navy velvet coverlet, filled with vials and glass syringes.

I barely recognized my own voice as I hissed through gritted teeth. *"Get away from her."*

The black-cloaked medic removed his wire-framed glasses and rose slowly, yet he kept one pale hand on my mother's frail forearm. He glanced up at me, his black hair peppered with gray, but he was young, late twenties at least, certainly not old enough to be a noble attending medic.

He did not bow to me.

"I said, *get away from her.*"

"The Heir Lord of Moray gave me clear instructions to attend to the Duchess as soon as I was able. I thought you would be appreciative of my services, *young lady.*"

Palpable tension descended upon the room and shock jarred through me.

My gaze raked over him once more, reassessing the threat of him.

I braced my fists upon the bed. "I do not know you. I don't know where you trained or *what* you trained in. The fact that you are my betrothed's medic does not grant you immediate access to my mother. Now. Get. *Out.*"

The medic cocked his head, smirked, and bowed deeply, but it wasn't me he was suddenly showing respect to.

I kept my gaze locked on the medic as Narve and his guardsman, Lonan, entered the granite-walled bedroom.

A large, black-gloved hand gripped my elbow.

I half turned, trying to rein in my panic, as I took in Narve.

Rugged and weathered, like most men from Moray, his dark eyes matched the scaled eel sigil on his cloud-gray tunic. At twenty-five, he was the same age as me, but once again, I was glad of my apparently "unladylike" height of just under six feet. He barely had but an inch on me, and it brought me a small dose of courage.

He noted the sleep-deprived circles under my eyes, and he gripped my elbow a little tighter. I ground down on the part of me that wanted to tear the Heir Lord apart with my bare hands.

"We weren't expecting you for another two weeks, Narve." I tried to step back but he held firm.

His words were soft, coaxing. "The Duchess is terminal. We feared she would not see out the week. So, I brought our plans forward."

I placed my free hand on his forearm, unable to ignore the unyielding strength that lay beneath the gray cloth. I had learned months ago that he trained every day with Lonan, wielding swords and axes. Yet Narve was famed for none of those things. No, the Heir Lord of Moray was known throughout Aarine for his knife-fighting skills. I couldn't see it, but I knew his beloved seax was strapped along his lower back, shielded by his knee-length, black cloak.

But it was the sight of Lonan blocking the door that made dread shiver down my spine.

He was no more than a tense and lethal shadow behind Narve. His head was clean-shaven, his warrior body clad in muted black leather. The glinting of steel caught my eye. Lonan's blade, *Kathkar*, hung at his hip; the onyx stones in the hilt flashing in the low light like a spider's eyes.

Narve angled his head, gave a subtle nod to his guardsman, and Lonan slid the deadbolt into place across the door.

The night sky seemed to press in against the ice-gilded windows.

Rose did not seem surprised by the locked door and neither did the medic.

Subtly, I readjusted my stance, bracing my legs.

I had no weapons on me, not a single, dratted one. Luckily, I had done some training with my stupid woolen court dress on to *try* and move in a fight.

A green light tinged with deep violet pulsed across my vision.

Fighting to restrain my panic, I forced myself to breathe.

Breathe. Breathe.

"Medic Wylmar, how fares the Duchess?" Narve's hand shifted from my elbow to rest against the small of my back.

It was impossible not to flinch at the contact, hating how his fingers dug into the fabric of my court dress ever so *slightly*.

The medic was professional with a sincere smile for his Heir Lord. "I fear her Grace is in a far worse condition than I anticipated."

"A shame." Narve shook his head, yet there was no remorse in his lilting voice.

Wylmar tightened his grasp on my mother's arm, and my gaze flicked to the open and empty vial on the coverlet, half shrouded by the man's cloak.

I stepped closer, my face glacial. "What did you give her?"

The medic closed his leather bag and threw Damara a distasteful look. "The Heir Lord did not tell you what I trained in, my lady?" His gray eyes met mine, and my blood turned to ice. "I trained in poisons."

"No!" I lunged for him.

I'd kill him and rip that smug smile off his wretched face. Wylmar simply chuckled.

My nails were a hair's breadth away from his neck when a pair of battle-scarred hands wrenched my arms back behind me. Kicking and pleading, I was heaved away from where Damara lay dying.

I cried her name over and over.

Her fingers twitched on the bed, the only movement she had strength for.

A distant war drum hammered in my head.

They had poisoned her, ensuring she would never wake up from the fever that had held her prisoner for the past week.

Narve went to stand beside his medic as Lonan struck his boot into the back of my knees. With one hand in my loose hair and the other wrapped around my wrists, he knelt me before the Heir Lord.

I bared my teeth at the pair of them, my breath coming in sobbing pants.

Lonan hissed softly in my ear, "She was as good as dead anyway. The medic did her a kindness."

"Your sources were right, my lord; she is a snow-born feral wretch indeed," Wylmar murmured, his face cast in shadow.

Frantically, I ran my gaze over Damara. How long did she have left? *Let me say goodbye, please, please.*

Narve was practically brimming with satisfaction. A mountain cat playing with a mouse. Rose stepped forward and bowed, a dark wool bundle in her grasp.

I blinked, horrified. They had gone through my things.

That was *mine*, and they had no right to put their filthy hands on it.

"Quite protective of this little item, aren't we?" Narve waved a casual hand to the prize proffered to him. He reached forward and clasped it to his iron-strong abdomen. "The color of the wool is the most ... precious thing, isn't it, Destry, my love?"

The cloak was my most treasured possession. Dyed with cherished flowers that only bloomed for one week in a secret fell in Petowin, it made me a threat to this pathetic joke of a province. Even Ilrair, far to the south, would check themselves at the sight of that wool.

My scalp ached with pain as Lonan tightened his grip on my hair.

Narve stared down at me. "You will come with me back to Moray lands. There, you will use your power under our direction."

"I have no powers," I lied. The ice-cold granite floor bit harshly into my scraped knees. My whole body trembling with rage and fear.

The Heir Lord scoffed and reached into his tunic pocket.

I tried to scramble backward and away, but Lonan was an immovable force behind me, wrenching my body back down.

Dropping fluidly to one knee before me, so different from when he had proposed to me three months ago, Narve elegantly twisted his wrist to show his upturned palm and the oval-shaped lambent stone that lay there. It shimmered in the low light, blue and gray iridescence banding across its polished surface.

My lips parted as I sucked down a deep breath.

I had never allowed myself to get this close to a lambent stone, never.

The green light that tinged the edge of my vision bucked and wreathed, fighting to free itself. It had called the female line of my family home for generations. It was the reason Damara had banned all lambent stones from the castle.

"I've held suspicion for some time now, Destry." Narve flipped the stone expertly in his hand and laughed softly. "Just one look between you and Duke Cormac ... what with your hair, which I'm sure is near black underneath all that white dye. Your brown eyes and dark tan skin. Damara hid you in plain sight, didn't she? The Ilrarian witch." His gaze leveled with mine. "No, you're a true purebred Petowin heathen, after all. You have nowhere to run if you try and fight. Ilrair will not have you, and you'll never make it to what's left of Petowin. We will hunt you down like the wild animal you are."

He inched closer, our breaths mingling.

Light danced and pulsed across the surface of the lambent stone, my skin stippling in response.

"What will the Petish people think when they find out their beloved *Koskivarri* has been in hiding all these years? They will offer you nothing but hatred." Narve's gaze ran over my face, and he gripped my chin with his free hand. "One of your rotten ancestors fucked a magical horse, and here we are."

"That is not what happened, you bast—" Lonan wrenched back my head, exposing my throat. "I'll kill you," I seethed. The lambent stone shimmered and flashed in response. "You and your little medic."

Lonan tugged harshly at my hair. "I've hunted down your kind for sport for years. I'll have little qualms in ending you, *winny*."

"The King wants her alive, Lonan," snapped Narve.

The guardsman tensed but remained silent.

Beyond the bedroom window, tendrils of silver light snaked across the black night sky.

A corner of the glass window cracked.

I could see a green vein of light before Narve's face. I tried to blink it away, but it pulsed there, waiting. It was a gift bestowed by the most primordial of beings, born of darkness and fire.

Outside, those silvers of light bloomed into broad banners of violet.

"I wonder what else prowls under your skin," whispered Narve as he leant toward me, his breath warming my bare neck. I trembled as he placed the cool surface of the lambent stone against the hollow of my throat. "I'll still have the King make you mine when this is all over."

The first kiss of the stone against my skin set my nerve endings on fire. My heart galloped frantically as the window beyond the fireplace splintered apart in a shower of glass.

A crackling *boom* twined with an ancient beast's guttural roar sounded throughout the room and ripped over the castle, deep into the world beyond. What felt like an avalanche of light roared over my body and soul as violet streams striated through the window and into the room, illuminating it with the energy of a newly forming star.

I yanked my chin free from Narve's grasp, shifted my feet underneath me, and lunged upward, smacking the back of my head into Lonan's scarred face. To his credit, he still tried to hold on as he snarled, spitting blood.

Narve, Wylmar, and Rose tried in vain to shield their eyes, but it did little to help them. A scrap of human flesh wouldn't stop it. At such close vicinity, they would be blinded for an hour or so. Even I was struggling with the intensity of it, despite being used to it since birth.

I twisted in Lonan's grasp and swept my booted foot across the flagstones, kicking his feet out from under him. Flailing to keep his balance, he let go, but not in time to save his head from smacking into the floor.

Rising to my full height, I let the light wreath around my body. It felt glorious to be wrapped in it, to feel it caress every pore, like a sensual touch from a lover, electrifying and daunting all at once.

Narve stumbled toward the locked door, and I prowled after him. Cloaked in undulating waves of lavender, my hand snaked forward, and I ripped the lambent stone from his grasp. The precious gem pulsed against my skin once more, and I shuddered before pocketing it.

Then I turned toward Damara, willing the curtains of light to part as I approached. It danced around the carved four-poster bed, whispering and crackling over the Duchess.

She was still, her lips parted for a breath that would not come.

The woman who had been my mother was gone.

Grief tore through my blood and bones. I had felt its chilled embrace many times before, and I knew its texture like some old childhood blanket.

The only mother I had ever truly known, Damara had saved me from freezing to death in the wilds of Petowin, shielding me from those who may harm me.

But she was gone.

Standing at her side, I placed a kiss on her still-warm forehead. Her hair spread out around her like a glorious nebula of gold. Even in death, she was beautiful. I twined my fingers with hers and committed her scent to memory.

Damara Furia Orcatain.

I hated my brief goodbye, but my rage and sadness would have to wait.

Wylmar screamed and pounded the door.

Stepping away, I picked up the wool bundle from where it lay abandoned on the floor and turned to face Lonan, his body prone on the flagstones.

Kathkar gleamed in the contained light of the Night Pegasus, and I felt little remorse as I relieved the guardsman of his most prized possession. The blade's hilt felt solid in my grasp. There would be a small justice at least, to wield it against those who had harmed my countrymen.

Those onyx stones in the hilt glinted up at me. *What now, thief?*

The bedroom door buckled inward as the palace guards rammed into it.

Lonan, Narve, and Wylmar would die, but not today.

I ran for the window casement.

Glass shattered and sliced at my exposed skin as the horrendous feeling of free-falling filled my bones.

I flung the sword away from me as the ground surged up to meet me. The snow-topped gravel smacked into my boots, and I hurtled into a forward roll in the castle gardens. Splintering pain lanced up my legs and hips.

Then I was up, sweeping up the sword and the cloak, and I ran painfully, like a doe from a hunter's sight. I galloped through the winter-encrusted rose beds and tore into the shadows, while the lights of the Night Pegasus convulsed overhead.

CHAPTER THREE

ORRIN

The small brown rat visited me again, clearly unperturbed by the yelling and shouting of men in the dark. He came nosing through my stale, ammonia-soaked straw with the hope of finding any spilled grain.

Just like myself, he'd go hungry tonight.

I paced the stable, my well-muscled frame churning the dank and soiled bedding as I circled. My desperate whinny rang off the stonework and wood, which kept me prisoner.

Another castle, another leaden cage.

Small silver scars riddled my body. This new place was strange and truly awful.

The men here were even more scared of me. At my first home, the soldiers had been scared too, but smart enough to stay the hell away.

I was not a Pegasus, gifted with that deathly fear factor, or a Unicorn armed with magic. I was a Mountain Horse. Speed, that was my curse.

And day after day, I would seethe and roil until I was rage-given flesh.

The day I arrived at Reckforton Castle, I had savaged a man, and nobody had come near me since. That had been two days ago. Two days of diminishing water and moldy hay.

My lack of visitors was about to change.

A man dressed in simple stable clothes, with a gold clasp at his shoulder signifying his rank as chief groom, walked down the central aisle of the stables. He smelt heavily of ale. *Charlton.*

I snorted, shaking my head in distaste at the strong smell, and pulled away into the farthest corner of the stable. It only gave me a mere two-meter distance yet left me within easy striking range.

Men turned into heathens once the drink was inside them.

I bore enough scars to prove it.

The chief groom drew level with me and pulled back the wooden and metal door.

I bared my teeth at his ruddy, middle-aged face. It was he who had sanctioned my capture from the wild and ordered that I be brought south to the province's capital city.

Abandoned days after my birth, I had stood little chance in evading capture, but I would have preferred a quick death from a wolf than be hauled to this spirits-be-damned place four years later.

My molten gaze appraised him, hate seeping from my skin.

"We need to move you," he stroked the leather of a whip curled at his left hip.

I understood Charlton's words perfectly. I understood every word uttered or usually cursed to me. We didn't know why we couldn't reply. It was a curse to not be able to converse with the humans but to understand them so clearly.

I whipped my blond tail from side to side and raised my dark brown head to gain more height over him. The muscles in my neck and hindquarters bunched under my chocolate-colored hide.

Two more grooms, strong and able men, appeared further down the passageway, ropes in hand.

"They say Lady Destry is on the run?" one of the grooms asked Charlton.

"That's why we're moving this brute. I want him somewhere more secure. With all the extra law enforcement officers around, I don't want anyone getting any smart-arse ideas," the chief groom chided.

The other groom twirled his rope. "Destry won't get far, not in this winter."

Charlton turned back to face me.

I stared the man down.

I would not yield. Not to him, to any of them.

A life of domestication, of men on my back and iron in my mouth. *No.*

With my instinct to flee inhibited, a fight it would be. My soul screamed at me to leave this wretched place, to flee north, to return to where I was born.

I had a clear memory of loamy, leaf-covered ground and unending forest.

Strength riddled my bones. I wanted to rampage and fight, to tear into the chief groom with every ounce of energy I had left.

The warrior instinct of a colt primed to become a stallion, a remnant of the Trinitor curse, the pure need to end a foe.

A low, rumbling sound echoed in my chest, and a lumbering threat escaped my blackened, velveteen mouth, resounding around the stone barn. The horses housed in the stables across from me nickered nervously to one another.

They had tried to persuade me to submit, to stop fighting, but I would not. Could not.

The three grooms crept forward, ropes in their gloved hands.

I had fought with ropes before. I knew not to pull against them, which would make the pressure so much worse.

In unison, they cast them out. I tried to dodge them, but I was roped expertly and harshly around my neck and head.

I reared and the grooms pulled tight, heaving their body weight against mine.

My ears snapped back to my skull, and I charged forward straight into Charlton's path.

The chief groom swore and launched himself out of my way, the other two grooms losing their balance as the ropes slackened. My sweat sprayed Charlton's face as he rolled away, and I brought myself back down onto all fours, a hand's width from his rotten face.

Limbs bunching beneath me, I careered down the barn passageway, only one groom holding on now in vain. Charlton yelled obscenities in my wake as I raced for the open doorway ahead, snow vortexing in the night beyond.

I skidded to a halt in the cobblestone stable yard, searching wildly for the gates I had been dragged through two days ago. There, tucked against the shadows and torchlight of the far wall.

Charging forward again, I yanked the last groom off his feet, and the rope swung free.

The winter wind blew, and I smelt the creature a moment before I reached the gates.

I knew that scent, recognized it deep within my core. My body knew to instinctively fear and dread it. Hind feet sliding beneath me, I shuddered to a stop once more, scanning the dark for the threat.

The concoction of fully grown Pegasus mare lay heavy on the cold air. It swirled into my flaring nostrils, but I couldn't see the source.

There was a soft movement to my left, one of light filtering into shadow ... then I saw her, penned behind a massive grill of iron bars.

Her scent was so strong, it masked everything else. It was her and me now. Fear, raw and strong, trickled down my spine. The only Pegasus I had ever known had been my mother, but she had abandoned me.

This was a stranger and, therefore, a death threat.

She was huge. A creature of feather and muscle.

Her coat was the color of ink, but it was lackluster and dull, dust caking her stomach and limbs. The mare paused beyond the bars as she tested the air with a nose that was just as sensitive as mine.

Turning her neck in increments, she looked directly at me with eyes the color of a dying fire.

I froze, my muscles trembling, as I focused every sense I had onto the mare.

Her body language changed, ears flattening to her skull and ever so slowly, she expanded her immense wings. She could have blocked out any source of light with those wings and could have flown free from this granite prison. But confinement and isolation from her kind had led the mare to self-mutilate.

Gone were the luscious and plentiful feathers that had once adorned her lightweight yet iron-strong bones. All that was left were ripped and shredded pinions that made the mare look like the harbinger of death.

A scream of rage screeched over the courtyard. The iron sang shrilly as the mare slammed and clattered her teeth and hooves against it.

My heart hammered in its bony cage.

"Half-blood of Gracien," she hissed in my mind. She half reared, whipping her head from left to right. *"You should be dead. Didn't Spearian have it in him to execute you as well?"*

I snapped my teeth at her, inching toward the open gates, my mane a tumbling golden wave down my neck.

"Those blond locks won't save you, forest prince. Beauty is a prison sentence here." Her eyes glowed like embers in the dark.

My gaze roved over the bolts that kept that huge prison closed. *"I could free you?"*

"I would rather die than have you take pity on me, half-breed," she spat.

"As you wish, mare." I lowered my head and pawed the snow at my hooves.

She clenched an iron bar in her teeth and ground down on it. *"Spearian will kill you, forest prince, if the humans don't get to you first."*

Men shouted from the barn, and I bolted from the chaos and confusion, pivoting to gallop through the gates and onto the snow-covered grass beyond the castle.

The sound of a roaring Pegasus mare soon became distant, then fell quiet.

I burst into the late winter night. Soldiers yelled and waved their arms, but I wheeled away from them toward another set of open, curving black gates on fringes of the castle grounds.

Long legs extending and unfurling beneath me, my body moved at speeds that could not be surpassed. The sky turned ashen, and I flew without wings toward my home.

It was the hour before sunrise, and winter mist was beginning to twine around the base of the trees.

I was out of my depth.

My breath came in deep lungfuls, and steam rose from my sweat-covered pelt.

Every whisper, snowdrop, and mist whirl were so prominent to me. Every sense of mine was heightened.

I could no longer hear the heavy breathing of the hunter's horses, rugged types that were used to this terrain. But the smell of people was still in the air, mixed with sweat, leather and iron.

It wasn't just me they were hunting for. A young woman had also escaped tonight.

The air was so still now, as if the night spirit, Iltavorn, was giving me a moment of peace, of calm. Cold moisture froze where it fell from the snow-laden trees, and the faint moon cast a beacon of bluish light.

I was a large black shadow under those trees, and I shifted my weight from one hind leg to the other. My head hung between my knees in exhaustion. The tendons and ligaments in my legs locked, keeping me upright as I slept fitfully, waking every now and then to a real dreamscape of myth and nature.

It was because of my tame upbringing that I didn't realize I was being watched.

CHAPTER FOUR

ASHER

The ground had been too frozen to bury them.

So, I had built a large pyre of birch, moss, and fir and had laid my father and uncle upon it. The smoke billowed high into the air before the cold wind whipped it across the evening sky.

The Night Pegasus had been violent that night, thrashing and sweeping across the heavens for hours, glowing above my grief-torn body that sat slumped before the pyre. It was the strongest light show I had ever seen, the air crackling with untold power.

They were dead because of me. I had destroyed the weapons that they could have defended themselves with. And now, four Pegasi roamed the Boreals alive and free in their stead.

I couldn't return to Aarine. No one would believe what I told them, and truthfully, I hardly believed it myself. I would be charged with murder. Under normal circumstances, no Pegasi would spare the life of a man whilst killing two others. My only options would be to roam the wilds, carving out a living here, or trudge north to Colladon.

I twirled the white feather in my hands. Every Pegasus feather I had ever held had come from a dead one. This feather, however, had been gifted from a living, breathing, furious creature, and it seemed to have acted as a bridge between minds of man and animal.

Is this how the Ilrairians tamed their Pegasi? Their aerial cavalry held some of the finest and most brutal fighters ever seen. Would their cavalry fail if they knew they were sentient? Maybe Ilrair knew they were and just didn't care.

Standing slowly, I brushed the fresh snow from my warm hunting coat and looked down at the mound of ash and coal that simmered before me. My body felt like an echo chamber of confusion and loss.

I had placed a few things onto one of the sledges after turning my uncle's hill ponies loose on the mountainside. If I disappeared, it would make it look like an accident had taken place out here, and the Pegasi would get a new notch in their reputation for savagery. Yet what happened yesterday was no mistake; I had condemned my father and uncle to death. Grief and despair clawed at me, gouging deep into my soul.

I bent down, donned my snowshoes, and braced the strap attached to the small sleigh around my waist. My stomach growled with hunger; I had stashed some supplies, but I couldn't think about eating right now. Any thoughts of food were making my stomach feel sour.

Leaving the smoldering pyre behind me, I trudged slowly north-ward. A branch of birch attached to the back of the sleigh swept the rail tracks away, hiding my path deep into the Serebo foothills. I barely felt the snow and wind pulling on my body as I walked. Darkness pulsed in my head and radiated along my bones.

The terrain was changing.

The miles upon miles of alpine forest in hibernation was becoming sparser. I was entering true Pegasus territory now. High plateaus of snow and dead winter grass, sheltered by crags, cliff faces, and vast open tundra circled by the dusky blue and brown mountains.

Mount Serebo was a faint, light gray incision into the sky, flanked by her sister peaks on either side, Ghel to the north and Bronzo in the south. The trio created an almost impenetrable circlet of stone, snow, and ice.

Whereas the two smaller mountains had been successfully explored and mined in areas for precious metals, Serebo remained unbroken. Her snow-crested summit remained free from the touch of man. She was a true primitive and wild place that acted as a constant reminder to mankind that not all nature was conquerable. It was said to summit her was to enter heaven and be blessed with immortality and magic.

Countless men and women, determined to conquer her, had perished on her flanks. Some ancient races and people from Petowin to this day worshiped Serebo, calling her their mother spirit, the most powerful of all the spirits they prayed to. With her icy, timeless gaze, she saw everything. Caves littering her foothills were filled with time-worn finger paintings depicting mighty battles in the sky, storms, and Trinitors: creatures possessing magic, speed, and flight.

How the first families from the far northeastern country of our continent, Colladon, had managed to get over the mountain range hundreds of years ago is almost unimaginable. Petowin, their westerly neighbors beyond the Scarp, refused to aid them in their quest to explore and conquer the Anduns and did not want to step foot within the mountain range.

Centuries later, the Petish would have no choice but to flee their homes and venture south.

The Colladonian settlers had contended furiously with the wilderness, lured there by rumors of countless game. They claimed the land for their king and country, declaring it a province of Colladon.

They soon discovered the Pegasi, and a steady stream of Northerners poured into the mountains and the forests beyond. The tales and legends those families left behind were told and retold again over the years, stories of battles, hardship, and mythical creatures.

My father loved, *had* loved, those stories, retelling them over and over around our worn dining table at the tavern with friends and with his brother while they prepared for hunting trips.

I'd never hear those stories again from him. All my life, I'd wanted to be out and away from him, finding solace in my solitude, but now that he was gone ... I desperately wanted those stories, to sit down with him and hear them all, my uncle chiming in with anecdotes.

My tears froze before they fell as I walked.

Fog was coming thick and gray down the mountainside, curling toward the sparse tree line on my right.

The weather was a lore unto itself on the mountains, but the fog would be a small blessing, hiding and tucking me away. I hoped it would help block the smell of burning bodies still clinging to my nose. The silver sky had bleached the land of any bright color. The tall, hibernating ferns I traversed through were cut off again by a birch and fir forest several meters away.

I tracked toward it until I was fully ensconced between the papery trunks. Beard moss, shaggy crystallized clumps of it, hung off the higher branches of the trees, leaving the lower ones bare, eaten by hungry deer.

From deep within the fir trees came a glint of gold and brown. A few feet along came another flash. Something moved through the trees.

Only one creature had that coloring.

They were thought to be extinct. One hadn't been sighted in years. Yet Mounties were nearly as elusive as Unicorns.

I shook my head, desperately trying to clear it of the leaden sorrow. Maybe I was just imagining things in this fog-stained light. I moved slowly through the frozen ferns, dead grasses, and meter-wide firs.

Silence had descended over this side of the mountains, not even a bird called. The fog crept lower and lower on the ridge opposite, slowly diminishing what light there was. The ferns stirred up ahead, and I halted, withdrawing a dagger from its worn scabbard on my left hip. Silently, I stepped out of the sleigh strap.

Almost immediately, I heard a crash in the forest.

My sight adjusted to look beyond the trees near me and into the darkness. The sound of breaking wood and crunching leaves was distant, but it was growing louder.

I took a breath and waited.

Then came a sound that made the blood in my veins turn to ice as the fog rolled over the valley floor and brushed the forest. I prayed to the spirits that the fog would mask any sounds and scents coming from me.

Through the trees came the ear-splitting roar of a Pegasus stallion, followed by an abrupt silence. Cold sweat trickled down the groove of my spine.

Any light there had been now diminished. Fog swirled around my boots as I listened intently to the sounds of the forest, or the lack of. All around was a maze of darkness, fog, and columns upon columns of snow-coated silver birch and fir.

Once again came that almighty, deafening roar. Closer, so much closer this time.

Instinct thrummed hard through my body, a warning.

I shouldn't be here.

From deep within the gloom, the air frozen and still, a flash of gold moved from left to right. The sound of galloping hooves grew soft and then fell silent.

My body was taut as a bowstring as my heart pounded.

Waist-high, ice-gilded ferns shook to my left, and I pivoted toward the movement.

The ferns stilled.

The fog grew thicker, trees that were only ten feet ahead disappeared. The forest felt sullen, muted, no longer the living thing it had been minutes ago.

Thudding footsteps sounded behind me, and I turned slowly.

Coming face to face with a fully grown Pegasus stallion. He towered over me, his hot breath clouding over my skin.

The stallion was the biggest creature I had ever seen. He was immense and the color of an oncoming storm. His muzzle was dark gray, stubbled with whiskers, and his eyes were black, white-rimmed glass.

Reflected in which was my ashen yet awed face.

He was a titan. *The Bringer of Storms.* His nearly charcoal-covered mane fell over an arched neck that twitched with tension. Heat radiated off him. Silently, he unfurled his wings, arching them. It was a posture meant to intimidate. It did the trick. My left hand reached for the white feather in my tunic pocket.

His head rose higher, his jaw opening to reveal white and yellowed teeth, ears snapped back to lie flat against his skull.

I had studied my father's papers; I knew Pegasus body language almost as well as him.

"That white feather in your pocket won't save you, hunter. Your father killed my son, Raiden, and I'm going to return the favor." His voice ravaged my already battered mind.

I closed my eyes, and I felt the huge intake of breath from the stallion. The air around me shifted as the Pegasus rose onto his hind legs, ready to bring his forehooves down on my head.

Like the palomino should have done to put me out of my misery.

Then came a male cry of a different kind. A deep and powerful roar of rage and the deadly blow never fell. Instead, I was knocked sideways as a horse just as big as the gray smashed into the side of the Pegasus.

I scrambled backward into the ferns, recognizing the sounds, and suddenly, I put the events together. This was the pair who had battled on the mountainside days ago, and now here they were, restarting an assault that had clearly gone unfinished, and the death of a beloved mare unpunished.

The two stallions came at each other in a clash of noise that sounded like deafening thunder. Their bodies, one the color of storm clouds, the other of earth and gold, smashed together in a tangle of hooves, legs, wings, and teeth.

I clutched the white feather in my hand like a shield.

The traditional pre-battle dancing did not occur for this pair. The arching of necks, comparing heights, and prancing were usual precursors for stallions to settle a disagreement and avoid conflict. Yet these two were far beyond a war dance.

The stallions bellowed at one another, landing ferocious bites on the opponent's neck, withers, and knees. They were more than a match for one another, huge and baroque creatures whose simple aim was to kill the other.

I watched on, sickened yet awed.

A black shadow moved to my right, and a second Pegasus came high, stepping toward the others, and my gaze met his. The palomino's comrade, the first colt who had spied me on the snow yesterday.

He bobbed his head. *"Why are you here, hunter? The golden one spared you for a reason."*

Then a fourth equine trotted into the small clearing. Paler than *the Bringer of Storms*, this Pegasus mare was smaller and nimbler. She burst from the trees and launched herself at the black colt.

It was outright war between them all.

I hauled myself backward against the snow, my muscles trembling.

"Murdering bastard," yelled the Mountie Horse as he raked his forehooves down the gray stallion's neck. *"Take your wretch of a mare and get the hell out of my forest, Spearian."*

The Bringer of Storms, Spearian, laughed a horrible, haunting sound. *"Shall I take young Carter with me, Gracien? I should kill him, too, and remove the last remnants of Nessa from the face of this earth."*

"Fuck you, Spearian. I'll kill you myself," roared Carter, the black colt, as he bucked and wheeled on the gray mare.

Spearian threw his head up high, dodging Gracien's lunge. *"I am here for Ebrel. She is a banished loner. You have no right to shelter her here. Where is she?"*

"I have every right to offer her refuge here. This is my forest and I rule it. That mare has been through enough. You killed Fintan, then Nessa," Gracien reared. *"You made a pact with that abhorrent wild ward to have Ebrel branded. If my heart beats, Spearian, you won't harm her again."*

Spearian bounded across the ground, teeth snapping together. *"Good thing your heart won't be beating for much longer then, Gracien."*

In the dense foliage, the Mountie, Gracien, had the advantage. He was nimble and agile, the quickest horse I had ever seen, quicker than the Pegasus mare. Spearian was foundering. His huge wingspan, normally a lethal advantage in the air, was his undoing in the forest. They were cumbersome, burrs and ferns latched onto his feathers until the snow was carpeted in them.

The Mountie was using brute strength and speed to win the battle. His lunges were insistent and always found their target. Red began to stain the pristine white feathers and snow. Spearian's roars were becoming weaker and hoarser. His strength waning, a king of the skies yielding to an emperor of the forest.

"Do you yield, Spearian?" roared Gracien.

The gray snaked his head. *"Never."*

The mare must have realized they were losing. She dodged Carter's attacks and withdrew, calling out to Spearian.

Spearian arched his wings in defiance, and the Mountie saw his opportunity. He wheeled on his front legs and barrelled Spearian in the ribs, both his rear hooves smacking into the rival stallion's massive chest.

There was an audible crack, and Spearian let out an anguished squeal of pain. He stumbled backward, withdrawing into the trees, snapping his teeth, and snaking his head from left to right in frustration and submission.

The gray mare whinnied again and darted after him.

The Mountie stood victorious before me. His sides were heaving, his veins standing out beneath a coat turned black with sweat. Blood trickled down his noble head, leaving a trail of red from his right eye, down to his flaring nostrils that quivered for breath.

I beheld the rarest creature in the world. A full-grown Mountie stallion, trembling with power and conquest over a flying nemesis, *the Bringer of Storms* no less. Spearian wheeled on his hooves and cantered into the trees, crashing through the ferns and bracken until he was enveloped by fog; an apparition vanishing into thin air.

The Mountie stamped the ground with a forehoof and tossed his beautiful head.

Suddenly, his left ear twitched, and his noble head turned to fix on me, with glorious molten gold eyes.

Carter stood stock still and waited for Gracien to make the first move.

Now there was a peculiar picture. I had half expected the black colt to flee with Spearian, but here he was, standing shoulder to shoulder with a cursed enemy.

I swallowed hard, my fingers digging into the snow and decomposing pine needles.

From somewhere in the forest, an owl screeched. The Mountie froze and made no move toward me, his hindquarters and neck twitching with fatigue. The great beast sighed, his huge chest expanding, and he suddenly looked exhausted and wearied, his adrenaline now receding. He swung his neck away from me and ambled toward the tree, his golden tail flicking to fracture the fog with long, blond tendrils. A champion leaving a bloodied arena. The fog engulfed him in a cloak of silvery air, and he was gone.

Carter squealed in frustration and leapt after him, no more than shifting shadow.

Despite the Trinitor curse, despite everything, a Pegasus and a Mountie had worked together?

The forest yielded no answers. It just watched on silently as I stumbled to my feet.

CHAPTER FIVE

DESTRY

I t was just over seven hundred miles to the outlying towns of Ilrair, another fifty to the capital, Orman, then ten more to the palace, the Adacus Residence. A twenty-day trek if you were walking quickly. There were two main routes that led to it from Aarine, the North Road and Selmon Pass.

Being the dead of winter, trade between Ilrair and Aarine was conducted on the better maintained Selmon Pass, leaving the North Road pretty much deserted, bar the odd traveler and poor pilgrim.

I had never been to Ilrair, and even if I had wanted to go, or had I tried to accept their king's proposal two months ago, I would have never been allowed.

My body resented each step I took south. My light was banked, barely there in the fringes of my soul, nearly extinguished from the surge I had used yesterday. It had never flickered in my mind during the day, only when the sun descended beyond the horizon and only ever as a faint, subtle glow.

The road was a quagmire, entrenched with divots of frozen, muddy water created by endless wagon wheels and hoof prints. Beyond the sides of the road, as far as the eye could see, was miles upon miles of untouched moorland, covered in a thick blanket of snow. I had roughly followed the fringes of the road south, remaining hidden beyond the large expanses of gorse, heather, and strands of hares-tail cotton grass.

My fingers and toes were numb, and I trembled with the cold. Mud and grime coated my skin, especially on my lower legs, where I had hacked off the bottom of my dress to have better freedom of movement. The excess I had wrapped over my head and around my neck in a makeshift hood.

I had never been so cold.

But I was alive.

The lambent stone was a tingling weight in my dress pocket, yet I couldn't feel its power like I had last night. I was drained, utterly spent.

I peered north, where the road disappeared into darkness tinged with a pale sheen of moonlight. To the east, beyond the moorland that undulated like a frozen sea, the sky was beginning to blush, fire returning to the ink-washed heavens. One by one, the stars began to soften and disappear as the largest of them all rose higher and higher, coating everything to the color of amber and gold.

High above, skirting over the reaches of the snow-soaked heather and gorse, its fan-like tail lancing the dawn, a hen harrier soared.

I blinked, doubting myself. I had never seen one so far south.

The national bird of Petowin, it was highly revered and worshiped by Petish as a messenger of Ilmari, the air spirit. Small offerings of meat scraps used to be left for them under known nesting sites in springtime to bring good favor and weather for the coming year. The athletic and agile bird of prey banked smoothly toward the northeast, its tail twisting to gain a more severe turn upon the air.

Then I saw what the hen harrier was flying toward.

A pack of horsemen, too far off to be heard yet moving at speed down the North Road.

As the sun breached the horizon, I heard the thundering of the horses' hooves, and the earth beneath my feet began to groan and rumble in anticipation.

A high-pitched, piping screech echoed across the moor. The hen harrier. It banked sharply, wings arched and began to race the ever-fading night.

I wasn't about to question its sense of direction.

I dived into the gorse, its thorny tendrils whipping at my snow-soaked skin. The most dominant vegetation bar grass for miles around, the gorse and heather sheltered me as I ran, and my breath came in freezing heaves as I put as much distance between myself and the North Road.

Harracombe Moor was vast, spreading to at least half the length of land that separated Ilrair from Aarine. To the untrained eye, the land was barren, awash with a sea of nothing. But these sloping and rolling hills held treasures. The hen harrier knew it, and so did I; Harracombe was remote, old, and wild.

The hen harrier raced across the winter morning, and I sprinted after it.

On the road, the horsemen were cantering. From the corner of my eye, I spied their banners. Not Orcatain colors, but the pale blue of Colladon whipped in the wind. The riders were casting their heads wildly about, searching, hunting. They had halted their search late last night when I had lost them beyond the Harracombe crossroad.

I wondered if Lonan and Narve rode with them.

A shout went up among the men. They slowed, their horses fighting against the command to halt, their legs splattered with mud.

The earth beneath me dropped away sharply, yielding rounded towers of rock that had been excavated from the sandy ground after a millennium of wind, rain, and ice. I dived down between the stones and listened intently to the sounds the men made upon the road. Their voices were hoarse upon the frigid air.

Peering above the snow-topped parapet, I spied the harrier. It was gliding over the tallest rock spire to my right, and it unleashed another short screech.

The Colladonian men clearly didn't see the omen of the harrier, as it fluttered and hovered in the dawn sun. They did not worship the spirits, only their singular, ancient God. They yelled back and forth to one another, then pushed their horses onwards, cantering south in the hope of cutting me off further down the road.

Trembling, I removed the dusky blue bundle from my sweat-soaked back and sank with relief against the gray and black-streaked rock. My breaths came in frozen gasps, the exhaled air billowing out before my wind-whipped face.

A blur of movement and the hen harrier dived to land on a small outcropping of stone before me. Its avian gaze was direct and protracted, black pupils narrowing within its yellow eyes as it focused on me. A crown of pale gray feathers dispersed into dark shades of smoke and silver at the wing and tail tips. A male hen harrier. The bird of prey appraised my shattered, torn, and injured form. Its gaze made all the more intense by the narrowing of its skull toward its deadly beak.

"Thank you," I said softly, my voice broken.

The harrier twitched its head to the right, its black talons clenched against the slick rock.

I frowned.

That's when I noticed the jesses.

Someone, somewhere, owned this bird. It wasn't the Colladonians. They preferred Harris hawks for their falconry. It looked unhurried to return to its master. If anything, it seemed quite happy upon the moss-ridden rock.

I compressed my knees to my chest, teeth chattering, cold creeping and slithering down every limb, numbing every pore. I couldn't dare start a fire, and I had little else on me, bar *Kathkar* and the lambent stone. I could don the cloak, but it was ornamental rather than for warmth, and the color would paint a target on my back.

I gazed down at the cloak.

Dusky blue, with a silver trim around the hem and collar, it was the last surviving one of its kind.

Loneliness crushed me like a ravaging wind.

Just like the Mountain Horses, I was a dying species, doomed to extinction.

The desperation of it, to be the last one in my family, savaged my crumbling soul.

The ice-cold temperature made me want to hunker down and sleep for an eternity. But if I fell asleep out here, I would never wake up. I had to get moving again, but I was utterly spent.

My gaze drifted upward to the serene sky above.

The Ilrair aerial cavalry did patrol the moors, but not often, and certainly not in the dead of winter. These frozen months were spent training new recruits in the capital and in the distant, tropical lands of Jaryn's growing empire.

With my dark tan skin and brown eyes, I highly doubted Ilrair would let me walk straight up to the royal palace. The white dye that had been placed on my hair, that I usually replenished in secret every night, had already begun to fade, my black hair starting to show through.

I wondered what my family would think of me if I did set foot into the most southern city of our continent. We weren't exactly welcomed with open arms there.

That's if I even made it that far.

A whinny sounded across the dawn sky. The hen harrier unfurled its black-tipped wings and took flight.

I scrambled to stand and peered over the stones.

Someone was walking through the gorse.

Drumbeats suddenly roared in my skull and chest as I gathered my things and pelted from my hiding place.

The arrow came from nowhere.

I was running, then I was on my knees, blood pouring down my left calf. Not a direct hit, but enough to hinder me.

Biting down my scream, I crawled forward, seeking shelter under the gorse.

This was it then.

Fighting back a sob of pain, my frozen fingertips reached out to brush the soft woolen fabric of the cloak. I clutched it close to my chest and dragged my body through the undergrowth.

Boots crunched on the snow toward me, following the bloody trail I had left.

Flipping onto my back, I held *Kathkar* across my trembling body, the snow beneath my legs stained red.

A tall male figure appeared to my left. He was uniformed with a storm cloud sigil on his chest, a recurve bow strapped to his back. His face was cast into shadow from the felt hat atop his head.

I snarled up at him. I was not going to be dragged back to Narve alive.

He didn't approach. He merely stood several feet away and watched, his gloved hands clasped in front of him.

Watched, with that shrouded gaze, as I realized the arrow had not been loosed to kill.

With every shuddering beat of my heart, a sedative spread until I lost all sensation in my limbs and spine.

The soldier inched closer, his body wary.

I hissed weakly, my vision tunneling.

Slowly, he withdrew a short sword from a leather scabbard at his left hip and closed the distance between us. With a predator's grace, he knelt on the snow next to me. He raised his sword.

"I'm sorry," he murmured, his voice rough but calm. "He didn't make it in time to find you."

Then came the final blow to my head. Cold and sharp, it fractured me into silence and then I felt no more.

I was utterly weightless. Wind tugged and tore at my clothes and body. I couldn't move my hands, arms, or legs.

Yet the wind felt too real, too cold. I had not passed through Serebo's gates and into eternal paradise beyond our world. The wind burned and bit at any exposed skin, and I could feel the pain in my left leg from where the arrow had clipped me.

I blinked, and my right temple seared with pain.

My vision became blurred as I urgently tried to gather my wind-torn senses.

Flying.

I was *flying*.

I looked up, as fright and wonder gripped me fiercely.

My hands had been bound at the wrists and my legs tied to the Pegasus rider that sat behind me. The man was a solid wall of heat and muscle at my back. His arms wrapped over mine as he lightly held the reins in front of me.

The wound to my left calf muscle had been tightly bandaged, yet it throbbed viciously as I peered down. I had been tucked into an Ilrairian rider's coat of knee-length, wool-lined leather. But *Kathkar*, my cloak, and the lambent stone were gone.

We sat astride a liver chestnut Pegasus, its huge wings lofting us through the air at a speed that left me breathless and my eyes watering.

All around, the dawn-lit sky expanded for miles, filling the horizon with glinting amber gold. Harracombe Moor stretched beneath us far below, a carpet of rolling snow, pocked by rocky pits and spires.

I squinted to the right, and my chest caved.

Ilrair was famed for its aerial cavalry. The men, women, and Pegasi who served and fought were to be feared and admired. They were ferocious fighters and elite aerial combatants. Up to forty Pegasi and their riders were flying with ease in three triangular formations.

They were majestic. A scene from some famed war tapestry.

The now rising sun glanced off what little traveling armor they wore. At the head of the closest triangle was a male rider with a black tricorn hat firmly secured onto his head. His mount was a gleaming palomino Pegasus. Its golden coat was so sleek, it blazed under the sun's rays as if it, too, were a glorious star in the heavens.

North or south? Frantically, I tried to gauge the position of the sun and the fleeting shadows beneath the cavalry.

I felt a small flicker of relief down my spine.

South.

Peering over my shoulder, I tried to speak to my captor over the sound of the wind, but my words were whipped away from me. All I could see was the hint of a sun-kissed, stubbled-jaw, and ear-length, bronzed blond hair.

I resigned myself to silence and watched the world slip away beneath me.

All day we flew, and the soldier behind me did not utter a word, not that I could have heard him anyway.

My body was lanced with pain and cold despite the rider's coat.

I took a closer look at the tack the Ilrairians used on their Pegasi. Our liver chestnut mount wore a bridle of fine, brown leather, the wide noseband engraved with clouds and lightning. A supple and padded breast collar kept the high pommel and cantle-backed saddle in place whenever we ascended, and a crupper wrapped around the base of the tail stopped us from slipping forward when we banked and dived. The leatherwork was of the highest order, the craftsmanship perfect. It gleamed with hours of polishing, as did the coats of the Pegasi.

The sun began to set, casting the sky was cast into a wash of amethyst. Snow clouds roiled in the north. We would have fresh snowfall in a few hours.

Slowly, the platoon began to descend from the skies.

Then, huddled in the distance against a series of flat-topped hills, I spied our destination. We were approaching Saltfen, a small settlement that had accepted Ilrair rule. A tiny place, consisting of a few clusters of thatched, whitewashed buildings and a tavern, surrounded by acres and acres of farmland.

Torches burned around a large field on the outskirts of one of the farms.

The farthest triangle of riders descended first into the field, landing fluidly and with sheer skill in the oncoming dark. The formation led by the palomino Pegasus landed next, and then my rider gave a slight squeeze on the reins, the smallest pressure of his calf muscles and we dropped.

My stomach rose to my throat, thunderous wingbeats drowning out all other sounds as the liver chestnut Pegasus sank toward Saltfen, landing lightly beside the flickering torch lights.

The calvary riders began to dismount and led their Pegasi into one of the two barns beyond the field. Grooms appeared, bearing buckets of warm water, hay, and grain.

In another paddock beyond, rows of army tents were pitched.

Why come so far north? In the dead of winter at that. They had been here for weeks, it seemed, to have their camp so well established.

The rider behind me sat in tense silence as darkness washed over the camp.

I peered around me as I tried to control my shivering.

A meek shaft of torchlight revealed the cavalryman wearing the tricorn hat. He strode toward us. His sun-kissed features, lighter than my own, could easily be admired, but his gaze was thoroughly displeased as he peered up at me.

I sat utterly still, my silhouette cold and waiting. A doe weighing up a lynx.

He wore a rider's coat like mine, complete with an elbow-length leather cape, over a pair of brown knee-high boots and loose, gray breeches. Gold embroidery of three inverted *V*s on the cuffs, topped with an Ilrair crown, displayed his rank as platoon commander. The name *Coen* was stitched onto a badge over his right breast, adorned with a storm cloud. He clenched the dagger in his right hand, and he walked closer, carefully cutting me free from my rider with calculating and deft strokes.

He stepped back, sheathing the dagger. "Get down."

His voice was harsh but cultural, clearly a pure-blooded Ilrairian, with his sea green eyes and dark blond hair.

I waited in wary silence as the soldier behind me dismounted first and went to stand by the head of his Pegasus. His gloved hand stroked the liver chestnut's nose gently as he looked across at me.

A recurve bow and full quiver were strapped to his back, and a short sword hung at his waist.

I glared at him. This was the man who had shot me down. His copper eyes met mine, his full lips set into a grim line. *Farrow* was stitched into his name badge beneath his sergeant's symbol. He was handsome, prettier than the other Ilrairian soldiers dotted around us.

I quirked my head. Copper-colored eyes? In an Ilrair soldier? That was unheard of.

My ankle and wounded leg twinged in agony as I stepped onto the snow-hardened grass. I couldn't remember the last time I had graced a saddle, and neither could the muscles in my legs and hips it seemed.

Farrow stepped aside as his mount was led away by a groom, and I cast my gaze around guardedly.

The sky was now a deep violet. Smoke wafted through the settlement as the villagers set about making supper, and the army cooks prepared food for the cavalry's return.

I clutched my elbows and stood tall before the Commander.

Another soldier, a female Lieutenant named Kramer appeared, her wavy golden curls cut short under her felt hat. All three of them closed rank around me. All three of them were armed.

Coen folded his arms over his chest. "You're a long way from home, *winny.*"

My spine stiffened. The Petish nickname was once used fondly, but not anymore. "No thanks to *you*," I snarled. As much as I wanted to try my luck at heading south and talking with the King of Ilrair, they had shot me down. "Why did you take me?"

"King Jaryn requests an audience with you."

"And you had to shoot me down to do that?" I hissed, glaring at Farrow, who stared unflinchingly back at me. Surprise gnawed at me though. Jaryn knew I had fled Aarine already? There was no way the news could have traveled so quickly to him; no messenger was that fast.

"After the reports from Aarine, I wasn't going to take any chances," snapped Coen.

"You took my things from me."

Coen laughed. It was one of the most joyless things I'd ever heard. "You think I didn't recognize the color of the cloak when we found you? I know your kind. I'm well versed on what your true family is capable of." He stepped closer, anger burning in his eyes. "You're all just thieving, cowardly murderers."

A muscle in Farrow's jaw ticked as he crossed his arms over his broad chest.

My own grief coiled under my skin like a serpent. Coen understood nothing. Not a damned, dratted thing. He clearly believed the lies that had been spun about what happened with the Kivistos at Lake Wylda.

Lips curling back, I snarled at him. *"Hypocrite."*

"Would you rather be in the hands of Narve? Trust me, I can gladly oblige you."

I would have understood a slight undercurrent of hostility from Coen, but aggression poured off the Platoon Commander in waves.

"I'm surprised it wasn't you that fired that arrow," I spat.

Coen strode forward and grasped my right elbow with a vise-like grip. I tried to hide my jolt of shock at the contact. I could feel his hot breath on my cheek and neck. His eyes were suddenly cast into the shadow of his hat.

Farrow made to step forward to intervene, but Kramer shook her head and the Sergeant backed down.

"If it were up to me," Coen whispered harshly. "I would have left you in the fucking snow to die." He thrust me away from him, and I stumbled backward. "Shackle her in the far end of the groom's barn."

"Not the tents, Commander?" asked Farrow.

Coen peered across at me as I regained my balance. It took every ounce of what strength I had left to not send my fist flying into his jaw.

"She's a wild creature as feral and probably as dangerous as their own Pegasi. She can stay in the barn. I'll sleep more soundly if she's chained to a solid structure, and I want her out of sight from *that* thing." Coen gestured up to the snow-cloud-covered sky.

With that, he turned on his heel and walked away, headed for the mess tent without a backward glance.

I hobbled after him, hands clenched into fists, and slammed into the iron-strong shoulders of Farrow and Kramer.

"Don't." Farrow's voice was deathly low in my ear.

"Point proven," gritted Kramer, shoving me off her.

"The Night Pegasus doesn't fly this far south," I whispered, retreating, wishing I could throw real daggers into Coen's back, and not just my glare.

"He did last night," said Farrow softly, his tarnished blond hair whipped up by the evening breeze. "We had reports of sightings as far south as the Cape of Kitrinos."

Shit. That was Ilrair's southernmost border.

Kramer motioned toward the stone barn on our left. Her gaze was cold and unflinching. "You set him loose upon us last night."

Not waiting to be told, I turned and walked heavily toward it, my leg pounding in pain.

"I can't control the Night Pegasus," I muttered as I limped.

"Jaryn thinks otherwise," warned Farrow from behind me.

Currently used for storage, stacks of hay and straw were laid out on the right side, whilst packs and food were laid against the opposite wall. On the gable end, a fire burned in a grate, well away from the flammable straw. The air smelt of beeswax, iron, and sweet meadow hay.

Several pallets had been set up close to the warmth of the flames. Two grooms, both young girls in their early teens, looked up in alarm at my approach and glanced at the soldiers behind me.

"She's sleeping in *here?*" piped one of the girls, her tanned and freckled face pinched with worry.

"Commander's orders," shrugged Kramer at my left elbow.

The freckled girl looked at me with unease. I gave her a small smile, and she quickly glanced down at the bridle in her hands.

I was told to sit by one of the barn's support beams, and I was shackled to it via manacles and a long chain. A latrine pot was shoved under a new pallet set out for me, and the freckled girl threw me a thick woolen blanket to sleep under.

My whole body throbbed, but I made myself sit tall on the rickety pallet. Kramer, happy that her work was done, stalked from the barn. Farrow watched her walk out into the snow that had begun to fall.

I stared up at the Sergeant, and his coppery gaze met mine. He sighed, a hand on the hilt of his sword, his classically pretty face gilded by torchlight.

"Your cloak, sword, and lambent stone are safe. The girls will share the food once it's ready."

I dipped my chin in the smallest of thanks. "You said he didn't find me in time? Who did you mean?"

A muscle in Farrow's jaw twitched. "No one."

He strode silently from the barn. I blinked after him, thinking I'd imagined his words, and I tugged my knees to my chest on the pallet, awkwardly wrapping the blanket around me, trying to dodge the manacles. The cold iron scraped at my wrists.

The freckled girl's friend, a teen with a shock of tight, blonde curls, brought me a bowl of hot cauliflower soup and a pitcher of water before scuttling back to the safety of the fire. Ten other grooms, boys and girls, joined the first two, and they talked amongst themselves as they eyed me with suspicion.

Tired. I was so bone tired.

Why were they camped so far north?

It seemed I had traded the granite prison of Reckforton Castle with a colder, harsher, more hateful one.

I turned away from the whispering grooms and huddled on my side on the bed, facing the now closed barn door. The wind howled amongst the snow outside.

It took hours, but I slowly drifted into snatched moments of sleep. My exhausted mind struggling to place the darkness of the barn with the darkness in my body.

That's when I felt him. He was no more than a whisper of gray light over me. A silvery thread that ran a primitive touch over my wind-tousled hair.

My light, bestowed by him, shivered in response. Yet it didn't have the energy to curl up into that caress like it wanted to, like *I* wanted to. Without the lambent stone as an amplifier, I could only lie here, listen, and discern that power.

I felt no fear, only a sense of relief at his presence.

I had never sensed him so strongly before. I had noted he was there, in the fringes of my world when I lived in Aarine, but after last night, it was like a doorway had been opened between us, a floodgate.

That touch ran over the length of my body, gently studying my injuries, and I felt the flicker of his disapproval against the ice-hewn barrier of my mind.

"They thought they could hide you from me," that primordial being in the dark snarled. *"I would never abandon you, my darling light."*

Eyelids flickering open, I panted silently, my chin turning into the gossamer filament that cradled my cheek. There was only the dim glow of the fire in the grate, and that overwhelming sensation of him, a whisper of radiance crafted from a time when only the spirits roamed the Earth. A strand whispered over the shell of my ear.

"I will always look for you, no matter where they try and lock you away." His coarse and celestial voice filled my mind, skimming over my skin.

My heartbeat racketed as I lifted my chained hands up to trail a finger down that convulsing ligament of light. It curled around my fingers like a cool mist. The Petish called him *Wings of Fire*. Most knew him as the Night Pegasus, but I doubted we were even close. Our mortal words barely slicing the surface of what he knew about him. I didn't dare to speak, terrified of waking the grooms sound asleep behind me.

"Stay strong, for you are glacial, unconquerable, and mine. Just know that I am here in the darkness beyond the clouds. I will visit you again soon, I promise."

I bolted upright on my pallet; the light bannering over me before snuffing out into glooming darkness, leaving choking loneliness in its wake.

CHAPTER SIX

ORRIN

The sun began to sink beyond the jagged peaks of the snow-capped mountain. They cut through the crimson dusk, casting gargantuan shadows upon their foothills, dowsing the land below into darkness.

Having sought a rocky plinth that still sat bathed in light, the sun warmed me and turned my blond mane to the color of fire, my coat burnished bronze. The shadows elongated, slowly encasing the rocky outcrop.

All day the forest pressed in around me, brushing against my sides with ice-covered boughs, and I had welcomed it. That tangible feeling of being home. Inhaling deeply, I took in the scent of spruce, pine, birch, fox, rock, and young Pegasus mare. My head shot upward, black nostrils flaring as I tried to source the origin of the smell.

She almost disappeared into the sunset; her coloring matched it so perfectly. I nearly lost sight of where the slabs of bare, red stone ended, and her earth-colored limbs began. Her head was dainty, covered in brown and rose-pink flecks. A pair of wings upon her back expanded, the massive pinions slicing the light. She looked like she could pull the sun below the horizon and into the next dawn.

Turning, I faced her head on, my body tensing.

She blocked any escape from the plinth. The mare tilted her head, her brown nostrils quivering as she took in my scent. A concoction of colt, Pegasus, and Mountain Horse. Her ears twitched with unease.

Stamping the snow with a forehoof, she eyed me with honed caution. *"You can't stay here, Prince."*

I bared my teeth. *"Who are you, feathered one? And you haven't tried to kill me yet? That's a new trick."*

The strawberry roan mare blinked, her manner defiant as her gaze roved over me. She was taller than me, probably stronger, too, but she was my age. *"I'm not here to kill you, Prince."*

There was that word again. Prince. I was a prince of nothing, no one, an orphan.

"Surely your instincts are clawing at you to kill me?" I stepped forward and she retreated, her wings arching.

She swallowed and her feathers quivered. *"I've never possessed that drive to kill equines different from my own kind."*

I snorted. *"That makes one of you then."*

"No, it doesn't." She glared at me. *"We're not all monsters."*

"I'd beg to differ."

"I mean you no harm. I swear it."

I could never trust a Pegasus. The instinct to run from her clawed within my blood. I gained another foot of ground as she backed up. *"And where's your herd? Lying in wait?"*

Her silence was reply enough. She was a loner.

She turned her muscle-hewn body, revealing the silvery cross burnt into her left haunch.

My breath caught in my throat as I froze mid-step. A *brand*. *"Who did that to you?"*

Who in their right mind would *brand* a Pegasus? I hoped to every spirit living that the mare had killed them for it. The soldiers had tried to brand me once with white-hot iron singing with heat, but I had broken the man's back instead. This mare was physically stronger than me and had been branded anyway. The power that would be needed to ensnare her, to hold her still ...

"I'll tell you on the way. I need to get you to your father, Gracien; he rules this forest."

My heart stuttered. My father? I had given up all hope that I had any family left, that I was the last one, the last Mountain Horse. Yet my father was alive, and this was *his* forest. No wonder the place felt like home. Gracien. That name settled deep in my core, like a rock reaching the bottom of a calm pond.

She folded her wings over her short, strong back and led the way off the plinth into the shelter of the trees. I stood frozen, unwilling to follow her into the shadows. She admitted to knowing my father, but if she was lying and this was a trap ... the mare paused and looked over her shoulder.

"I promise I won't hurt you. My name is Ebrel."

I shifted uneasily. *"I'm not going to follow you to spirit knows where. We're cursed enemies."*

She rolled her eyes but turned to face me properly. *"Ah yes, cursed enemies, but I haven't killed you, have I? If it's proof you're after, then let me tell you this. I got my brand for loving your older brother, Fintan."*

"What?" I said, aghast.

Her wings pressed closely against her sides, and the feathers trembled. *"Spearian, my old band stallion, caught wind of us and killed Fintan in a fit of jealous rage. He had his lead mare, Hex, bring the wild ward in to have me branded and cast out as a loner."* She took a deep breath. *"I loved your brother very much, and I bear this brand and exiled as punishment."*

The sorrow in her words made it feel like my heart was fracturing apart. Any unease or lack of trust I harbored for her slowly started to melt away.

"I ... I'm so sorry."

"The loneliness of losing him is worth the joy of loving him, for what little time we had together." Her voice was velvet soft against my mind.

I tilted my head and assessed her with fresh eyes. Sadness clung to her body like a second skin, but she watched me with an urgency. If she had truly loved my brother, kin that I never knew had existed, then maybe she truly didn't intend to hurt me. My mind stumbled over the rare possibility that Pegasi and Mounties could be amicable to one another, even love each other.

Cautiously, I stepped toward her. *"You say a wild ward branded you?"*

"She's a witch, an abomination. She siphons the soul out of the earth for her own power. She has stone circles within Glentay, this forest." Ebrel's entire body thrummed with hate. *"Which is why I need to get you to Gracien, to keep you safe."*

I inched forward until I was within touching distance of her. She kept utterly still as if trying to reassure me that she wouldn't strike.

"My father lets you live here?" I cast my gaze over the forest and valley. Gracien ruled this land? Such a vast territory seemed unattainable, yet my father held kingship over it.

"He offered me sanctuary after Fintan's death. Please, follow me. I'll try and get you to Gracien."

My steps were silent upon the drifts of snow that lay under the canopy as I carefully followed her into my father's kingdom. There was a beat of silence as we walked, the forest watching on. The pink-flecked mare and I kept a watchful eye on our surroundings. The air damp, cold, and clinging to every living thing. What little winter evening sun there was struggled to pierce through the heavy, ancient canopy. The deer trail widened, and I walked up beside the young mare, noting the battle scars on her withers and neck.

Ebrel climbed a small knoll, the trees growing sparser, allowing a snow-topped glade to appear. We skirted around the open space carefully, sticking to the shadows. The forest seemed to press in closer, reaching out with ice and moss-ridden limbs to touch us. I grappled with the idea that I was an heir to this land, that the song of this place was what had kept me sane during those years spent caged.

It had been calling to me since my earliest days, a chorus of ancient wild music, and now I walked amongst those notes, a song murmured by fir, ash, stream, and birch. My father's home ... and now mine. I wondered if my father had known of my existence, and if he had, why he hadn't tried to rescue me years ago.

I glanced across at the brand on Ebrel's haunch. *"You didn't kill the wild ward for what she did to you?"*

Ebrel bared her teeth. *"Not yet. She grows more powerful by the day, too many other animals protect her now. Gracien lost kingship over them when she cast her dark net of magic out, but the forest will not yield to her. If Gracien and you live, the forest spirit Tellervo is strong enough to stave off her magic."*

"Why would Tellervo need us to live? The spirits are laws unto themselves."

"Every spirit has a scion, a living being that it siphons off some of its power to, for safekeeping. After the Trinitors were cursed and cleaved apart, the spirits thought it best to seek out scions in case their magic was challenged next. The mountain sisters have the Unicorns, the forest has his Mounties, the water has her Orcas, the air has her Pegasi. Not that she answers any of my prayers."

A step ahead of me, Ebrel flinched.

I halted as the mare sucked down a hissing breath. She turned her head to look at the brand that had been burned onto her right haunch. It glowed red against her dusky brown pelt.

Horror coated my senses. It wasn't glowing, it was *burning* as if the scorching hot iron had just been applied to her skin.

I felt an archaic whisper against my mind, a blend of a hundred voices, a song that had been sung since Tellervo had first whispered over the land.

He's coming.

Storms ride on his wings.

Ebrel whipped her head to face east, her wings brandished in pain and loathing.

"Spearian is coming. You have to go," panted Ebrel. Her body quaked in fear, but she stepped in front of me, and she beat those mighty wings, once, twice, warming up for a fight.

"I won't leave you," I said sharply.

I could hear him then, a mighty thundering gallop over the tree roots and frozen, damp earth.

"I will not stand by and watch another Mountain Horse be slaughtered. Fintan died because of me. I will not damn his brother to the same fate. Now go!"

"He'll kill you, Ebrel."

"He'll kill us both if you don't run. Go now, before he calls the wild ward here."

"I'm not leaving here without you. We can both run."

Spearian crashed through the undergrowth, a hulking creature of gray and black. He skidded to a halt before us and reared, his fore-hooves raking the still air. He neighed, the sound carrying deep within the trees. Fresh battle scars laced over his withers, knees, and chest. The ground shuddered as he returned to all fours and his head lowered, ears pressed flat against his skull.

My body mirrored his, and a snarl ripped from me as I sidestepped Ebrel.

"I look forward to seeing your corpse rot in the snow, Princeling." Spearian stepped forward, his tail whipping against his flanks. *"As for you, my dearest Ebrel, I'm going to cleave you apart piece by piece until there's nothing left, even for the crows."*

Ebrel didn't grace him with a reply. She merely stepped forward to my side and pressed her velveteen nose to my quivering neck. *"Go, please. Find Gracien. Let me lure this monster away from here. Please, Prince."*

"I'm not leaving you."

"Fintan said the same thing, and now he haunts my dreams. Run, Orrin. I'll find you again."

Spearian roared at the pair of us and charged, his dreadlocked mane billowing behind him. I cursed, turned on my haunches, and ran as the clash of hooves, teeth, and flesh echoed behind me.

CHAPTER SEVEN

ASHER

I wormed my way out of my small snow cave just before sunrise. My stomach sated with the last of the rabbit jerky in my supplies. The white feather had remained clutched in my hand throughout the freezing night, and voices that belonged to the creatures of the forest had filtered to me in the dark. Lynx squabbling over a rotting deer, a stag murmuring to his brother over the men encamped in their territory, and the whispers of a Boreal fox to her young ones.

Trekking northward, the air was icy cold in my lungs, cooling in wisps of gray before me. Winter was a season the forest bore well, the trees lying dormant and still, readying themselves for the warmer months to come. The little creatures tucked deep inside their burrows and nests, only the skittering of rabbits over the brush could be heard.

Grief was a numbing shroud over my body, and I welcomed it, along with my bewilderment that my world had turned on its head. I had stuffed my crossbow at the very bottom of the supplies on my sleigh, happy to never touch the damn thing again. I'd even considered using it for firewood.

Repeatedly, I could hear my father and uncle's weapons splintering apart, their deaths coming moments later under Pegasi hooves.

On and on I walked, stopping only for water and food, but the heavy feeling in my bones didn't leave. It just settled deeper, seeping into the very marrow of my being.

I glanced up to check I was heading in the right direction, due north, then snapped my head back up again. My body grew wholly still, quieting into a hunting posture I knew on instinct. Not even the wind stirred.

Across the bare space between tree lines, about thirty feet away from me, was a woman, her cloaked silhouette dark against the snow.

Silently, she walked toward me.

I ditched my sleigh strap and stepped forward, a dagger in each hand.

Despite the lack of wind, I felt the pulse of power from her as she approached. She looked utterly human, if it weren't the metallic tang of magic that radiated from her with every step.

She halted not far from me.

I raised my right hand, flicking the dagger to hold it at its tip.

Her lips were sinfully red, vivid against the paleness of her skin. Clumps of moss clung to her bare collarbone, the rest of her concealed beneath a cloak bedecked with feathers. A hunter's cloak. She looked ethereal, a maiden of sweet savagery, but who knew what spell altered her skin.

My hand aimed for her chest, and she simply shook her head.

"I wouldn't do that if I were you, Asher."

"Or what, witch?" *She knows my name. By the holy spirits, how does she know my fucking* name?

"Or it won't be me that tears your eyes from your skull." She motioned her pale hand to the fringes of the trees, where, through the shadows, countless pairs of brown and amber eyes lurked. Lynx, wolf, owl, and bear, all still, all silent, waiting for her command.

She took a step forward. "Unarm yourself."

"No," I snarled, clenching my left fist around the worn hilt of my other dagger.

Another step closer. Her voice was low and whip sharp. "Don't make me tell you again."

From the trees came the snarl of a wolf and the yowl of a lynx. My gaze ripped from them and back to her as my fingers trembled with restraint.

"It's clearly a habit of yours, isn't it? Not taking orders," she hissed. "We'll have to break that."

It was my turn to snarl then, and the dagger in my right hand flew for her face. Her eyebrows shot up in surprise, yet she remained calm and collected, barely flinching, as she swept the hurtling blade aside with a plume of gold-brindled magic.

The dagger fell to the snow with a silent thud, and I braced myself. Slowly, not taking my eyes off her, I crouched and placed my remaining dagger atop the snow. She smiled faintly as I rose again.

"You look a little like your father, Asher Fields," her voice was smooth yet distant, totally unfazed by the fact I had tried to kill her. Any other mortal would have had my dagger embedded into their windpipe from my throw, but not her. "Yet you have your mother's eyes, her nose too. Airin was indeed a beautiful woman to produce such a handsome son."

"You weave pretty words, witch. What do you want with me?" I glared at her, refusing to acknowledge how she knew so much about me, what power prowled in her body.

"I know of everyone who passes through this forest. I hear their words, their hopes, dreams, and nightmares. Blood clings to your hands. Not Pegasus blood, but that of your father and uncle. You failed them. Failed in the simple tasks given to you."

She crept forward and I retreated a step, angling my body to create a smaller target for the weapons she surely carried under her cloak. Her full, sensuous lips parted, revealing straight, white teeth. "You could avenge them, your father and uncle. Bring down the Pegasi that killed them. The guild hall would be filled with the sound of your name."

"Tell me one more of your lies and I will rip out your throat," I snarled.

The woman halted, her eyes darkening in a satisfied smirk. "I speak the truth, huntsman, and you know it. I've watched you for years, training in my territory, finessing your skill to end lives. But I will not stand by and watch now, to leave you in your sorrow and guilt. For it is guilt you feel, isn't it?"

My fists curled and I straightened to my full height. "You know *nothing.*"

"I know there is still a bloodlust in you beneath your darkness and despair." Her green eyes were cutting, glacial. "I can take all that pain away, hunter."

"No," I cut, my voice lethally quiet. Fear pricked at the base of my spine, but I willed it to go away, as I placed my laser focus on her, calculating how I could end her, swiftly and brutally.

Her lips tilted into a savage smile. "I know there's a killer in you still. A wild beast that prowls in your heart. *A predator.*"

Deftly, she parted the fold of her cloak, a rough-hewn dagger in her right palm. I recognized the color of the stone; I had passed the huge monoliths where this piece would have been cleaved. Gray with brindling of gold. A wild ward stone.

"I have a gift for you," she murmured.

"I don't want your fucking gift. I don't want *anything* from you, *wild ward.*"

Her smile was victorious, and I hated it. "Such rage and grief and darkness."

She gave a simple wave of her hand, and the creatures on our periphery began to stalk forward; predatory gazes fixed on us.

"I said *no*."

"I have need of you, huntsman. By abandoning your career, you were always destined to be mine. Had you shot down Raiden, I may have let you go on to be one of the finest Pegasus hunters the Boreals had ever seen, even surpassing your father ... but you didn't kill him, did you? And now your fate brings you to me."

A brown bear charged forward, its huffing, grating breaths coming closer as it barreled over the snow.

Turning on my heels, I tried to run.

The first blow against my back sent me flying forward, knocking off my hat. I had no time to catch myself as I slammed into the shin deep snow.

I yelled, falling onto my chest as claws shredded through leather and skin. Then the bear was pressing down, down, against my spine. My cursing turned to screaming as it snapped one rib, then two, then—

The wild ward knelt beside me and grappled for my right hand.

I hurled every insult I knew at her and roared and roared as the bear shoved down harder. With utter patience and grace, she tried to pry open my fist, which now gripped the white feather with all my strength.

"And what do we have here?" She wrenched my fingers free with a power she shouldn't have to pluck that glistening white feather free. Her long, pale fingers clutched it and in my next shuddering breath, she unleashed a howling scream of pain. She flung the feather against the snow, clutching the wrist of her injured hand.

The bear huffed against the back of my neck. My body screamed in pain, but I forced myself to turn my head and look up. The wild ward's gaze seethed with hatred.

"You *wretch*," she hissed, her gaze feral. "You *dare* use spirit magic against me."

I looked down at her right hand; the flesh singed and peeling. Her eyes glinted as she whispered. "It won't save you, your little magic trick. You're mine now, hunter."

The fingers of her burned hand clenched in my hair, and she wrenched my head back. Like an artist wielding a brush, the wild ward struck my open palm with the wafer-thin dagger, until blood dripped onto the snow.

Icy spears of magic punctured through me like shards of glass, breaking and slitting me bare. Her magic tore at my mind, trapping and holding it. I screamed once more.

Darkness, archaic and cold, gilded my bones, and feasting alongside it was her wild ward power, seeping deeper and deeper until it entered my heart.

My cries became feral, snarling, my entire body shaking. Predator, hunter, assassin, I was all those things, the wild ward magic disturbing the core of my soul. The Petowin blood pounded in my veins, hating the alien feeling writhing in my body.

The carved swan in my pocket turned to ash, as did the gifted feather upon the snow. Somewhere beyond the darkness that consumed me, I felt her lyrical voice echo through my mind. "We can't have such a talented and skilled hunter wasted."

CHAPTER EIGHT

DESTRY

The grooms shuffled past me before dawn into the gray-washed light to tend to the Pegasi, wrapped up warm in layers of wool and fur. I peered up from my bundle of blankets.

Illuminated by what light there was filtering into the barn's huge entrance was Commander Coen. With his arms crossed over his broad chest, he stood talking to two male flight riders and a female flight medic. All three looked at their Platoon Commander with complete and utter adoration. They laughed at a joke he uttered, their breaths fogging in the air. Coen's smile completely changed his features, softened him. He seemed utterly relaxed yet confident, totally at ease within his uniform.

Then his head turned, and he looked into the depths of the barn to where I sat huddled on my pallet, and his smile disappeared quicker than a winter sunset. The female flight medic, a red cross stitched onto her cuffs and felt hat, hovered by Coen's shoulder, and she followed his gaze to peer at me.

Her hair was cut short under her dark green hat, a lighter shade of blonde than Coen's. She was lithely built, her uniform hugging her lean body, yet her face, although pretty, was drawn and weather-pinched, her cheeks flushed with the cold.

Slowly, like two wary wolves, they entered the barn and approached me.

I sat up straight and monitored their every move.

"This is Corporal Terra, our flight medic. She's here to check you over and see if you're fit to fly to the capital." Coen's tone was curt, and his gaze was icy cold as it had been yesterday.

Terra gave a tight, professional smile and knelt before me. She grasped my right wrist firmly and glanced down at a pocket watch pinned to her leather coat pocket. Surprisingly, her hands were warm upon my chilled skin, and she was gentle yet deft and efficient as she probed my skull and my fading black eye.

Pain lanced across my forehead, and I fought back my wince.

"Can you feel any pain? Besides the wound to your leg from the arrow?" she asked, as she inspected the cuts and grazes upon my collar bone and shins.

I had managed to remove the remnants of glass that had sliced my skin open during my window jump at least. I loathe to admit any other weakness in front of them, but ... "My back, they got in a few hits."

"Who's *they*?" asked Coen, his features darkening.

"Aarine law enforcement."

Terra's gaze snapped from me to Coen, then back again. "Stand up."

I glanced down at the manacles.

Coen strode forward and unshackled me with astute silence.

Standing slowly, shifting my weight to my good right leg, I tried to hide the wave of pain that ran from my shoulders and down my back.

Terra didn't miss it and she turned me with that same surprising softness, but then she grasped the back seam of my tattered court dress and ripped it open. My shoulders hunched under her scrutiny as the medic emitted a hiss.

Her voice was quiet in the chilled air. "I doubt she could have run far from you yesterday, Commander, even if she had wanted to."

I couldn't guess if she was being sympathetic or sarcastic. My jaw clenched as I envisioned what she and Coen were seeing on the freezing skin of my exposed back. Coen took a deep breath, and from the corner of my eye, I could see him running a critical glance down my body.

Reckforton Castle had a reputation for their ruthless law enforcement units. Some were moral, most were not, and when it's three against one outside the city walls, they're going to land a few punches and cuts to your blind side.

A painful bruise, likely as dark and unforgiving as Coen's disposition, ran from my lower left ribs down to my waist, where several, luckily shallow, lacerations crisscrossed my right hip. The sorest part was a large fist-sized bruise over my right kidney.

Terra released the fabric of my dress and I slowly turned back around to face them, shivering, clutching the bodice to my torso. She tilted her head, and she assessed me silently for a moment.

Coen stood, watching her, not me, his body tense.

"I'll need to clean and bandage the cuts on her back, and I have arnica in my stores for the bruising. Her leg will need re-bandaging too. Once I've addressed that, she can fly. The Residence medics can take over once we reach Orman." The medic looked at Coen, who nodded.

"Very well. We take off in thirty minutes." The Commander turned on his heel and strode from the barn. The fact that he had left me alone with Terra gave me no doubt that she could take me down if I tried to flee. Not that I would get very far.

"Follow me," said Terra and she took the lead from the barn, headed toward the giant medical tent in the next paddock.

I swept up my loaned rider's coat and hobbled after her, point blank refusing to acknowledge the stares thrown my way, until I saw Farrow walking toward us down the laneway. His gaze snagged on me, though he kept walking, but as he drew level, he half turned his head and his steps faltered. My eyes met his for a heartbeat, then he looked at my back and his jaw clenched. An emotion I couldn't place flickered across his sun-kissed face, though it left as quickly as he did, striding toward where the Pegasi were assembling in the flight field, the half cape of his rider's coat fluttering behind him.

Still trying to decipher what I saw in Farrow's expression, I kept up with Terra as she opened the flaps of the canvas entrance to the medical tent aside and ushered me in. Lit and heated via oil lamps on the ground, the tent sported three empty patient pallets. Trunks containing medical supplies sat across from the beds. The structure was solid and well built, like it had been here for months.

Terra motioned for me to undress and lie on my front on the nearest pallet. Ever the professional, her gaze remained resolute as I discarded my filthy court dress and undergarments. I lay face down on the pallet, my bare skin stippling with the cold, despite the heat from the lamps.

The medic threw a blanket over me, and her hands were methodical and calming as she smeared arnica ointment onto my bruises. She did not utter a single word when I flinched, as she went on to clean out the long cuts across my hip and re-bandaged the arrow wound to my leg.

If she felt any sympathy for me, she didn't show it.

I swallowed; my arms crossed under my chin. "Does the Commander hate all of those from Petowin?"

Terra paused in her bandaging. "The Commander has a hard time controlling his feelings when it comes to winnies." Her tone was harsh, defensive, and she gave the bandage on my leg a sharp tug to tighten it. "I can't say I blame him."

I sat up warily, hugging the blanket around me, as Terra fetched a bundle of clothing from her stores. A flight rider's uniform; simple, comfortable underwear, warm dark gray breeches and shirt, moss green waistcoat and brown leather, calf-high boots. Terra passed them to me silently, then picked up my old, ruined clothes, stalked outside the tent and threw them into a burning grate.

And just like that, the last remnants of my old life went up in smoke and embers. Panic coiled in my stomach about what unknowns lie ahead, and I wondered if I would ever find any allies or friends in these southern lands. I had not a penny to my name, a name that harbored resentment and hate wherever I went.

We flew throughout the day, the platoon split into three triangular formations once more. Coen was not taking any chances, and I sat bound once more in front of Farrow. The Sergeant hadn't uttered a word as Kramer finished tying my bonds. Farrow's thighs a solid, warm weight against mine. He remained a muscled wall of heat at my back, which I was thankful for, as it was so cold up here. My left calf pounded in pain still, despite Terra's mending.

Freezing air nipped at my skin as the Pegasi battled through a snowstorm that had swept south during the night. The Ilrair Pegasi were a sight to behold. Sleek, elegant, and powerful. They gleamed as they flew. No savagery lurked in their muscled bodies, no hints of wildness. They were well groomed and cared for, each one at the peak of fitness. None of them struggled as they cut through the falling snow.

Every mount wore a leather breast collar, stitched onto it were the Pegasi's name and their rider's name and rank. Farrow's liver chestnut mare was called Corrach.

They were so different to those that lived wild and free in Aarine and beyond. The northern Pegasi were nimbler, rugged, and more brutal, as harsh as the environment they lived in.

Snowflakes clung to my lashes, and my face felt frozen, but the feeling of flying, to sit astride a Pegasus, did not fill me with fear. It awed me. It felt right to be up here, soaring through the flurrying snow.

Yet with every mile south, something sputtered in me and fell quiet. I felt no sense of the spirit that had visited me last night, and the male voice that had whispered over my skin. All I knew was that I longed to see him, hear him, and feel him again. Deep within my bones, my light hid, quiet and still. There was no crackle or tendril to be felt. Just unnerving dark silence.

Gradually, as we ventured further south, winter began to yield and loosen its grip on the land. The moors were overtaken by vibrant forests, and the air around us began to warm, snow yielding to soft rain.

Breaching the final swathe of cloud, I finally saw Orman.

Penned between the azure sea-fed Fal Lagoon and thick masses of forest, Orman sprawled out between outcroppings of chalky, yellow rock. Hulking stone ringed the northernmost fringes of the city, rocks that had been bleached on their southerly faces by millennia of wind and rain.

Beyond the cresting lagoon lay the Cape of Kitrinos and further still lay the vast open ocean, miles upon miles of it. The Adacus Residence dominated the rolling hillside, the evening sun glinting off its many glass windows. The lagoon lapped the King's home on its eastern wall, and irregular slivers of beach ringed the small blue waves.

Houses, halls, and market squares blended seamlessly with the forest. From the air, the city looked veined with trees.

As one, the platoon banked to the west, Coen at the helm.

The largest outcrop around loomed ahead, its sheer sides free of foliage. Crowned by slim oaks, a finely built limestone fortress had been constructed atop it. No human could ascend those sheer and slick limestone cliffs. The only way someone could gain entry was on the back of a Pegasus. Enemies could be shot down with ease from the walls and watchtowers that sat at each corner of the monumental mass of rock.

I swallowed, my mouth paper dry. Steam rose from my rain and snow-soaked body.

Orman alone was twenty, maybe even thirty times the size of Aarine. A cultural, thriving, and chiseled epicenter that was the pounding heartbeat of Jaryn's empire, which extended beyond the cape, over the Hortulis Sea, to the Alsida Archipelago and colossal twin islands Omichar and Omivarra.

Four large harbors filled with sea and river-worthy ships flanked the capital's southern edge. Even with the setting of the sun, they were alive with activity. Yet it was the fourth, southernmost harbor that drew my attention. Warships, primed and manned, bobbed within the protection of the harbor wall.

Corrach's wings arched in response to Farrow's gentle squeeze upon the reins, and the mare dropped. Wind whistled through my hair as she cleaved through the pink-washed sky, heading for the rear of the fortress.

There, cut into the rock, was a smooth, sandy section, once more ringed with torchlight. The platoon landed fluidly, and the Pegasi called out to one another, answering neighs resounding from deep within the limestone.

Coen dismounted and his palomino stallion was led away. Farrow's entire body tensed behind me as the Platoon Commander walked over and cut me free with his dagger.

I wondered how much he wanted to sink the blade into me.

My body was stiff with fatigue and hunger. My clothing damp and cold as Coen escorted me into the awaiting mammoth fortress. The Commander didn't utter a word, he just kept a gloved hand on the small of my back as we delved lower into the depths of the limestone. The scent of hay wafted through the torchlight, and hooves clattered on the stone floor above.

Deeper and deeper, we descended into the belly of the outcrop.

Finally, Coen paused before a solid oak and iron doorway. He took a deep breath, knocked twice, then pushed it inward.

I shielded my eyes as sunlight blasted through the room, chasing away the shadows of the hallway.

With that large, capable hand, Coen pushed me over the threshold.

My sight finally adjusting, I quickly took in the cavernous room ablaze with the evening sun. Floor-to-ceiling glass on the three walls showed me a panoramic view of Orman. The view took my breath away.

Blinking, my gaze shifted from the exterior to the interior. A table big enough to seat twenty people sat in the center of the flagstones, and at its head was a male figure I knew all too well. I had to refuse his offer of marriage three times.

It was probably high time I met him in the flesh. The portraits I had been given of him, in an attempt to sway a decision that wasn't mine to make, did nothing to contain and capture the beauty of the man.

King Jaryn Adacus of Ilrair.

He did not stand to greet us as Coen ushered me toward him. Dressed in polished, calf-high boots, cream breeches, white shirt with the sleeves rolled to the elbow, and a green and gold vest, he silently assessed me as I stood before him.

No crown in sight.

His head was completely free of hair, although he had a hint of stubble on his carved jaw. He had those familiar green eyes that I had grown so used to seeing now, although they were far colder than even Coen's. The hair on his honed forearms was bleached from countless hours spent in the sun.

I never did find out his age, but I guessed early thirties.

"Please, take a seat, Destry." Jaryn gestured to one of the chairs at his right-hand side as he filled an empty glass with wine from a crystal cut decanter.

Like Coen, he had an educated and velveteen voice.

Saddle sore, I hesitantly sat down and leant back in the leather-covered chair, my damp clothes chilling my already clammy skin.

Jaryn smoothed down the fabric of his vest and his gaze was cutting as he apprised me. I really wished I had the chance to wash and change before meeting him. Slowly, he took in my wild, wind and rain tossed hair, dust, and mud-covered skin, before pausing on my fading black eye.

I wanted to recoil, to duck and hide. My light tucked itself deep within my bones. I could barely feel a flicker of it.

"Duke Cormac and the Heir Lord of Moray have *instructed* me to have you arrested and flown back to Aarine, should you be found within my borders." Jaryn laced his fingers over his stomach and tilted his head inquisitively.

I glanced down at my knotted fingers, then back up to his sun-freckled face. "And why haven't you?"

He sighed, bitterly. "I should. Cormac's council has informed me of the events and circumstances, but I want to hear your side of the story." What he didn't say was, *you have one chance here, Destry.*

To tell this stranger my life's story went against all my instincts, every single one of them.

The King must have seen the doubt on my face as he pushed the glass of wine closer to me. "It's why I had the wine brought up here. Drink, then talk. You owe me that much."

Any other king would have thrown me over his borders and been done with it. But there was more to this than just me. The encampment at Saltfen was too permanent to be a coincidence. I looked up at Coen standing guard by the door.

Jaryn followed my gaze. "Pull up a chair, Coen."

"What?" I glanced between them, panicked.

"It will do well to have a witness here. I trust the Platoon Commander with my life, as do many in my court." Jaryn moved his seat over to one side as Coen walked over.

Settling in beside the King, the pair sat back and waited. They were too casual together to simply be king and commander. Coen removed his hat and placed it on the table.

"Why head south?" asked Jaryn. "Why come here? Was it merely to seek refuge?"

"I would have never made it to Petowin alone, not during this time of the year, and I don't know if Nijinxes still roam there. Ilrair was my only viable option."

Coen darted a glance to his King but remained silent.

Jaryn looked over his Commander and me before inching the wine closer.

Hesitantly, trying to hide my shaking hands, I took a sip, testing it. I had to be careful. I hadn't eaten anything since dawn and spirits knew if they had spiked the wine ...

The King's features darkened. "I haven't fucking poisoned it, Destry. *Drink*."

I took a mouthful, swallowed, then took another. "After taking a poisoned arrow, you would forgive me for being cautious."

I glared at Coen, who happily returned the favor.

"Explain," ground out Jaryn.

"It was meant to die with us, the secret Damara and I carried, of what she did the day after the Nijinx massacre at Lake Wylda," I said softly.

The lake was one of the largest bodies of water in Petowin, situated mere miles away from the southernmost border. A small detachment of soldiers from Aarine, along with Damara and her sickly two-year-old daughter, had been sent north for aid.

Yet they had arrived too damn late.

"Her grief was raging; she had gone mad with it. Maybe it was luck, or just the spirit's will, that she buried her daughter in the snows, lost to a fever, and then found me amongst the devastation close by." I took a shaking breath. I couldn't bring myself to look at Coen or Jaryn. I tracked my memory back, back to those first blurry few, of snow, screaming, and then sudden comfort from a stranger.

"She was a fool to take the child along with her," spat Coen.

I ignored him, leashing my rage. "Some people have held suspicions for a while, and as I matured, a few of them decided to take their chance and see if I really was the daughter of Cormac and Damara."

"Narve perchance?" asked Jaryn.

I glanced up at him and frowned. "How do you—"

The King simply waved a hand. "He's well known in this court. Please continue."

"I think Narve's father had been there that day, at Lake Wylda, when Damara claimed a miracle had occurred and held me in her arms. She had me well covered in blankets to hide my still dark hair." Narve's father must have taken one look at me and had questioned my existence ever since that fateful day. My fingers absentmindedly brushed the strands that lay over my left shoulder, the ends still clinging to the white die Damara had placed upon it ever since she found me.

I often thought of Damara's true daughter, the poor little girl who was buried in the wilds of Petowin. The name I bore was hers, and I had never discovered my own, it was lost along with my people. I had always loved my name until I discovered that it wasn't really mine at all, when Damara had told me the truth on my eleventh birthday. It gave me a small sliver of comfort that my adopted mother now rested with her true daughter in the afterlife, and they had found each other again.

It was I who was now utterly alone.

"When Cormac told me to accept Narve's proposal, it gave the Morays greater access to the castle ... and to me."

Jaryn dipped his chin. "What would you have done if your secret had remained a secret?"

"I would have tried to take Petowin back at some point. I didn't want to marry Narve, but I hoped to use the men at his disposal to rid the land of the Nijinxes."

"I think the Reck has driven you mad, cloistered up there away from the real world," snarled Coen. "No lord would let his wife control his armies, especially one like Narve."

"Don't worry, Commander, I came to that conclusion as soon as I met him, but at that point it was too late, the proposal was made official," my voice was as cold as a glacier.

"There are many Petish refugees in Aarine and Colladon who would support a Nijinx cull so they can reclaim their homeland. They would stand behind you, I'm sure, if you finally revealed the power that hides in your veins and the family name you hold so close to your heart," murmured Jaryn, his gaze fixed on my face.

Beside him, Coen was motionless, rigid in his chair. He gazed down at his gloved hands that were curled into tight fists. "And there are many Ilrairians, my king, who would slaughter her the moment they heard her last name on her tongue."

"My family was *innocent*. They did not murder your peo—"

"Don't spout your lies to me, *winny*." Coen's face was livid.

"That is enough, Commander." Jaryn took a deep drink from his own wine, then leant forward toward me. My spine pressed into the back of the chair as I fought for space between us. "Petowin lies in tatters, barren of its people. You may be their *Koskivarri*, even a queen, but of what? Of whom? You have no one, no supporters, not even a fellow clan member that bears your name or anyone who could vouch for you."

The King's words struck deep.

He was right.

No one.

No family or friends or allies.

No one.

Jaryn wasn't finished, his words lashing my soul. "My spies tell me of a Petish warlord currently stationed in South Colladon, Rekorious Niemi. He is making it very clear that he wants the Petish throne and is rallying those of Petish blood to his cause. Many are flocking to him;

I'd say he has a greater claim than you." Niemi. Once a large fishing clan along the Scarpa coast. It had been large enough to be noted on the maps I'd sourced at the Reck. "Some would even go so far to say that you are a fake. An imposter, desperate to find a way out from the noose around your neck."

It was Coen who uttered, "She is in possession of a Kivisto cloak, the last surviving one."

I sat a little taller in my chair.

Jaryn brooded, his gaze not leaving mine. "I have a proposition for you, Destry."

I froze. "Of what nature?"

The King was world known for his heavy-handed bargaining. He had won countless territories with it, the original occupants yielding on bended knee to the King, rather than see their people be slaughtered. Aarine was a prime example of that. Colladon may have kept the province, but Ilrair siphoned off nearly all of its goods to its own people.

"You want to remove Njinxes from Petowin and take back your home?" Jaryn captured my brown-eyed gaze in his cutting, cold green one.

"Yes," the word was a balm against my battered heart.

"I could vouch for you, even give you some of my men to claim back what is yours. I could influence the fall of this Rekorius fellow and sway the people to support you instead."

I held my breath, my bones feeling brittle.

"On one condition."

Forcing myself not to tear away from those stalwart green eyes, I held my shoulders back. "And that is?"

"Enlist."

"What?" Coen whipped his head to stare down at his King. "Your Majesty, we did not discuss—"

I gaped, the air rushing from my lungs. "Enlist into *what?*"

"Jaryn, please—"

"My aerial cavalry. Bromtide Platoon, if you want specifics."

"Jaryn," Coen ground out through gritted teeth. "She has no military training. I will not let her waltz into *my* platoon just because she's a supposed *Koskivarri*. Her family murdered mine and that *beast* crawls under her skin."

I bared my teeth at Coen, that light in my bones flickering in response.

Jaryn wholly ignored his friend. "Enlist in my cavalry, help me take Aarine, the Anduns and Colladon, and I will give you any resources I can to help you reclaim Petowin."

Those warships, the Saltfen camp. Jaryn had been preparing for war for *months,* if not years. Aarine had received no word or warning.

"She has no mount," Coen's voice was guttural.

"So, you take the Boreals while I have Petowin? It would be no more than a puppet state." My hands were trembling. "I have nothing to offer you to help you take those territories."

"After your little light show the other night, I beg to differ. I know the women in your family have played *host* to that power for generations. You will use that power under my orders." Jaryn's features were as hard as granite, unyielding.

"It is not designed for warfare, my king. She's no more than a fucking insurance policy to that *thing* in the sky." Coen ran an exasperated hand through his finger-length, tousled blond hair.

A flash of rage speared down my spine. I glared at Coen, but he was right. "This light is not something you can wield in a battle, so whatever plans you have for it, I suggest you shove them—"

Jaryn snarled. "*I* will be the judge of its use, *Destry*. My wife is a water wielder. She can help teach you how to direct it under my orders."

I couldn't hide my surprise. Jaryn had married? Another thing that Aarine hadn't heard of. My gaze snapped, the gold wedding band glinting on his left hand.

"Cavalry soldiers are bound to the crown until the ruling monarch decides to release them." My brain scrambled for sense.

A cruel smile played on Jaryn's lips. "Help me, and I'll *decide* to free you of your military obligations. Petowin will be yours, but you will still answer to me."

It felt like the rock was closing in, sealing me down here. Surely it wasn't just luck they had found me in the moors. They had been looking.

"Coen is right." The Commander blinked, shocked that I had agreed with him. "I have no military training. I have limited hand-to-hand experience at best. The soldiers will know I don't belong there."

Coen gave the tiniest of nods, his arms crossed over his broad chest.

"Enlist or our deal is over. I will have no qualms in sending you back to Aarine to face lawful judgment, nor will I feel sympathy as I count you amongst the dead when the city falls to me. Or I could hand you back to Narve? He seems *quite* keen on getting you back." The King braced his forearms on the table. "Or I could move you to the Residence and keep you there for my own personal use. The choice is yours."

I sat frozen, my nails digging into the flesh of my palms. The snake, the ruthless fucking snake. "I have no *choice*."

The King slowly sat back in his chair. "It's the only offer I'm willing to make."

Coen swore harshly under his breath.

"I'll do it," I said quietly, barely restraining the rage in my voice. "I'll enlist."

CHAPTER NINE

ORRIN

The forest enveloped me, ushering me deeper into its ancient depths. Strength waned in my limbs, and I knew I was too tired to gallop much further. A few days without decent food and my escape from Aarine had used up any energy reserves I had stored up.

My stride began to shorten, my nostrils flaring wildly with each of my harsh breaths. The ferocious gallop my species had inherited, had been cursed with, slowed to a canter, then a jarring, lengthy trot as I covered the shadowed ground of Glentay. Meter-wide tree roots interlaced over the ground, the canopy too thick for snow to fall through. It was just damp, moss, ice, and darkness in here now. The sun had long set.

Veins streaked and stood out over my body, and steam rose off my skin as my trot finally crumbled into a walk. My body screamed at me to stop. The tendons in my legs pounding with the effort I had exerted on them, but I couldn't stop. I had to keep moving.

Ebrel. I had left her to die. Pain scorched my heart. I had run, abandoning her to that feral beast. The same monster who had killed my brother. I felt no sense of my father, couldn't detect if he was near or far. Did he know his son walked his forest? Did he really care about me or Ebrel?

My breath came in guttural grunts as I walked, and the forest felt utterly still around me. No birds called. No rabbits stirred in the chilled undergrowth. I paused for a moment, my large eyes taking in the pocked patches of moonlight amongst the gloom. The forest was quiet. Unnaturally quiet.

Up ahead, through the gnarled trunks of pine and fir, was a huge monolithic stone. It sat half bathed in darkness, shifting streams of moonlight flickering over its gray and bronze-brindled surface. Five times my height, it towered beside the forest surrounding it, and it seemed to draw in every ounce of air to it.

From the corner of my right eye, I spied movement.

Ebrel?

A meek ray of moonlight revealed the creature. A person was moving through the frozen ferns.

Exhaustion gripped my body. I couldn't run; if I risked it, I would never run again. My tendons would snap, and it would all be over. So, I turned slightly, the wide pan of my vision unveiling more of the human gaining ground on me.

A cloaked woman wove through the undergrowth and stalked toward the monolith. On a dead, beard moss-covered tree beside me, a great gray owl landed and peered its burning orange gaze over my trembling body. Then it turned its head to look over its speckled wing, so it could watch the woman.

She appeared to be a creature of the forest. The delicate features of her face half hidden by the cloak that she wore. A cloak bedecked with every feather I could think of: owl, pheasant, wren, dove, goshawk, Pegasus, a ceaseless cascade of feathers that ruffled and gleamed in the low light.

A few meters before me, she halted, and the huge owl swooped down to land on her shoulder. Its talons didn't pierce her skin.

My tail lashed against my flanks, as my ears flattened and nostrils flared. A metallic tang coated my tongue, a taste and smell I couldn't place. It was alien.

Her red-lipped smile flashed. "Prince."

The word was suspended between us, no more than gossamer floating on the still air.

This was the creature that Ebrel had warned me about. The woman who had held a red-hot brand against the mare's skin. A warning rumbled deep in my chest as I glared at her.

"*Wild ward,*" I snarled in reply.

"Indeed, I am, and you are the son of Gracien. Heir to the Forest. I'm here to help." Her hand reached up to stroke the plumage of the great gray owl.

"*You weave a web of lies.*" I backed up a step and stamped a fore-hoof. "*I know what you did to Ebrel.*"

The wild ward whispered to her owl, and the bird took flight, disappearing silently into the darkness. With a flick of her hand, she folded back the hood of her cloak, revealing tumbling dark blonde dreadlocks that ended below her shoulders. Again, she smiled at me, yet it reminded me of a viper's hiss.

"That mare was branded a loner for a reason. She's an outcast, just like her mother was." The woman stepped closer, her hands now hidden by her cloak. "I'm not here to hurt you, Orrin. Follow my wishes and this forest will become yours."

"*Lay a hand on me, and I'll break your back.*" That warning rumble echoed in my throat as I bared my teeth at her.

"I've tamed beasts far more wild than you, Orrin. You won't be a challenge." She stepped closer and my head swung up, teeth snapping. "I think you will find it will be *you* that is broken, if you don't come with me willingly."

"I'll shatter your bones for what you did to Ebrel." My head lowered again, my heart hammering in my chest. I wasn't going to go down without a fight, not to this spider. Not for all the pain she had caused.

"I heard the soldiers at the Reck couldn't even get a bridle on you, let alone a saddle. You had to be roped every time." She moved her right arm out from beneath her cloak, her wrist twisting elegantly as gold-brindled light danced across her fingertips.

"Try to break me, viper, and I will be the one that kills you."

The forest heard the proclamation and siphoned it away, deep into their heartwood.

Her laugh was soft in the midnight air. "Nothing is strong enough to kill me anymore."

She lunged, her right hand hurling her abominable magic straight at my head. I reared, forehooves raking, but the golden light streaked upward, whipping behind my ears, and clamping down hard over my nose. Wrenching my head, I bucked savagely, tree limbs scraping against my pelt as I snaked my head, doing anything to relieve myself of the pressure that bore down against my skull.

Yet with every rear and kick, the pressure only worsened, grinding down along my poll and nasal bones, its touch like a flame against my skin. My vision cleared for a fraction, and I roared, diving, teeth bared at the wild ward. Her throat was mere inches away, but she simply held up her right palm, and that vicious magic yanked down hard against my head, pinning my nose to my chest.

I backed up, away from her, until my hind legs knocked into a pine tree, and I halted, my legs trembling. The pressure around my head eased, yet it kept a tight hold. Breathing hard, I desperately tried to contain my panic, to focus on anything but the vise-like feeling against my head.

The wild ward stalked after me, a smug smile on her face. She stopped just to my right side, her chin lifted in victory. Her right hand came up again, and I fought to bring my head around, to clamp my jaw down onto that slender wrist, but she hissed, and my nose was wrenched back to my chest.

I flinched as she laid her cold, white palm against my sweat-soaked neck. "What a fine mount you will make for my hunter."

No, no, no, no, *no*.

My heart rammed into a frantic pace, panic lacing my every breath. I would rather die than have a man on my back.

"You won't be dying anytime soon, my darling." The wild ward ran her fingers through my long, blond mane. "You have a far greater purpose. Come this way."

Her right hand unfurled again, and a rope of her magic looped around either side of the dreadful headpiece. *Reins.* I tried to bolt forward, but she clucked in disapproval and yanked me back, that pressure around the top of my head nearly making my knees buckle.

I couldn't resist her orders; they were whip sharp against my mind, and I stepped back beside her. Her left hand moved to rest on my hindquarters, while the other wrapped itself in the reins. My entire body trembled with shock as she took a deep, settling breath and jumped in one fluid movement onto my back.

Instinct so strong it speared through me, had me twisting my head down and bucking, just like I would do if it were a cougar. But this predator was cunning. She sat deep, those long, slender legs clamping around my sides, and she pulled hard on those horrible reins.

My hind legs skidded beneath me with the force of it, and I threw up my head, hoping to knock her out. Her hands moved to her knees, and she drew my head down, down. I staggered, my vision blurring.

"Yield, Orrin," she snarled.

Her death will be ours, Prince.

A pine bough brushed against my neck, stilling me.

We have foreseen it. We have heard her screaming.

I stood square, head hanging uselessly by my knees, my heart beating so fast I thought it might give out with fright.

Her calves squeezed against my sides, and I stumbled forward a step. I felt her smile.

"You all break in the end," she whispered. "Come on, there's someone I want you to meet."

There was a cave, lit only by a fire that burned at its rear, which cast long, horrid shadows around its entrance. My first glimpse of the hunter was that of a tall silhouette against the winter moonlight outside. I battled and fought against the mental stranglehold that the wild ward wielded, but to no avail.

We had been walking slowly for what felt like hours, the wild ward knowing not to push my legs any faster.

The hunter stepped away from the cave, and I jarred to a halt.

A predator, that's what he was. A sliver of rock had changed his abilities to be like that of the animals, and with that, the wild ward had taken full advantage. She now controlled him just like she did with every other animal here.

His movements were sinuous, lethal, a taker of life. Dark brown, almost black hair, framed a rugged face and his earth-toned eyes were lanced with silver. The pearl-like wisps that now resided in his irises were the wild wards doing. His pupils expanded as he adjusted his carnivorous gaze to the gloom.

"Asher, I believe you have already met Gracien? Well, this is Gracien's last living offspring, his son, Orrin," said the wild ward as she gathered her cloak and slid down off my back, keeping one hand pressed against my neck.

I ripped my gaze from her to look at Asher, a Pegasus hunter. He stood in strained, agitated silence, the light of the fire dancing across his tan skin. The dim air of the cave crackling with tension and engulfing magic.

He couldn't speak to me, not in the way I knew he could. My mind screamed at him to run, but his booted feet remained locked in place, and we gazed at each other.

"The horse the Duke took from the wilds?" said Asher, his voice rough and iced. "Why do you have him?"

The man stood covered in dirt, his leathers and reindeer hide worn yet well made. His gaze darted everywhere, taking the whole scene in like a true hunter.

He watched the pair of us like a hawk.

I felt the wild ward shift her weight as she grasped the dagger hidden within the folds of her cloak. "To introduce him to you, of course. You're going to make a wondrous team."

I frantically fought against her grip on me, yet I remained as motionless as a mountain. "Team?" Asher looked sidelong at the wild ward.

"Orrin, here, is Heir of the Forest. When you kill his father, all of Gracien's power will transfer to his son. What better mount for the finest hunter in the Boreals? You will be lethal, unstoppable." Her voice was practically euphoric with the notion.

I had battled and fought my entire life to stop myself from being broken. The witch's nails dug painfully against my pelt, and my eyes rolled in their sockets in pain.

Rage flared through me. I wrenched my neck away from her touch, the action causing blinding pain to rip down my head and spine, as Asher strode forward and grasped a handful of my golden mane.

I met Asher's fearsome gaze head-on.

My roar of rage remained sealed in my chest. Trapped.

You'll die beside the wild ward, hunter.

Steely determination danced in the hunter's eyes, twinned with icy hunger. His lips rose in the smallest of smirks.

"He shall give you no trouble, once you are astride him," instructed the wild ward coolly.

I tried to buck, to rear, to wreak havoc. My very being yelled at me to break the hunter's back, to bring my forehooves down on his head. Muscles and flesh trembled with the effort, sweat glistened on my flanks.

No ... please no ...

Please.

In one fluid motion, Asher hauled himself onto my back.

I jerked and froze at the weight of him, as his legs clamped against my ribs and his fingers picked up the golden, glistening reins.

I could feel my free will crumbling, disintegrating into fragments, as the wild ward's magic flowed through him, then into me, into my soul.

With a final puff of silken soft magic, my spirit splintered and disappeared.

Yet one shard, one tiny shard of glittering will remained. It withered and pulsed with hatred.

I'll kill you for this.

CHAPTER TEN

ASHER

Darkness flared along my bones.

It was a darkness before light graced the heavens, before planets circled the sky. It was ancient, and it rested in every pore of my skin. Writhing above it was the wild ward's magic, gray and gold light that sluiced through my blood. I had no beginning and no end, just this darkness and death.

Now and then, a vision of leathery wings and hollow eyes flitted across my mind, and I welcomed the sight. I wanted to see it, hungry for more. I wanted to see those black-pelted creatures for real, and not just fleeting images.

The wild ward's magic pulsed beneath my flesh—cold, suggestive, and blood-thirsty. The wild ward had hammered her wishes home until those demands rattled through my brain, and I could think of nothing else. I was a weapon bent to her will.

I was hers, her huntsman, tasked with two simple goals.

Firstly, kill Gracien, the King of the Forest, and destroy the Pegasi, all of them. *Every last dratted, feathered one*. The Mountie couldn't be killed by magical means. The wild ward's magic had failed to control him. He was protected by Tellervo, the forest spirit. Only a man-made weapon could bring the stallion down.

Not even Spearian would be able to escape me. The stallion had failed her, the wild ward had told me. He, too, would be killed alongside his herd.

I was to do her bidding and not question it.

Orrin shifted beneath me as I sat astride him.

The young stallion walked steadily onwards through Glentay, the cave miles behind us now. I could not hear the Mountie talk, yet I had to merely squeeze my legs or the reins, and he would spring into action.

Just as I was the wild ward's, Orrin was *mine*.

My vision had shifted to that of black and white with her magic, as we traveled westward, the way the wild ward had instructed us. We were headed for Gracien's personal domain within the forest.

The ground turned rocky under hoof, as Orrin began to climb a steep embankment pitted with rocks and pine needles. The forest enveloped us, coating our senses with the scent of pine and the sound of sighing branches as they moved against one another. The bitter gloom that lay under the tree's canopy was endless. Creatures who also called this place home stopped in the daily tasks to stand still and wary as Orrin walked sedately past them. Red squirrels straightened their tails and owls peered from the treetops, their large eyes cutting through the darkness.

Trees grew so densely that Orrin had to maneuver carefully to pass through them. The Mountie clambered upward and topped a ridge.

The brooding darkness suddenly ended.

Before us was a forest glade that blazed with blue-tinted sunlight. The trees that circled it had been worn down in such a way that they created a curved roof of pine needles and leaves, giving covered shelter from any Pegasi that may fly overhead. The grass was hidden beneath inches of snow, which refracted and danced the sun's rays across the glade. It was the white crown of the forest, bejeweled and gilded with icicles and frost.

The home of a forest king.

Flinging my booted leg over Orrin's neck, I dismounted with lethal grace, crossbow armed and ready in my gloved hands.

Gracien did not await us in the glade; the only signs of him were hoofprints embedded deep in the snow. I knelt, sizing the prints against my hand. My outspread fingers barely touched the half-moon shapes.

Behind me, Orrin stamped a forehoof.

I looked up and rose from my crouch.

The gigantic firs did not stir in their winter-coated slumber; only the fallen pine needles were pressed to the frozen earth as Gracien walked from the depths of his realm and out into the winter daylight.

His pelt changed from black within the shadows to dappled and burnished copper as he crossed the glade. He towered over Orrin, and the lustrous strands of golden mane veiled the crown of his neck. Silver-colored scars crisscrossed over his withers, and the huge muscles of his neck, shoulders, and hindquarters rippled as he paused in the center of his home.

The stallion snorted warily, his exhaled breath billowing between us.

I stood a good ten meters away, within easy range of my crossbow.

Gracien's molten and alert gaze ripped from my crossbow to Orrin standing stock still behind me. I could feel the young Mountie straining against my leash on him, but I clamped down hard on it.

"So, the wild ward holds my son hostage and sends you to kill me?" said Gracien, his voice as rough and coarse as an ancient valley.

Whatever magic the wild ward wielded, it clearly had little effect on Gracien; he was immune to it. His voice cut through my mind, yet I stood steadfast, my crossbow ready.

Gracien strode forward, his black-tinged nostrils flaring. The Mountie stallion snapped his teeth in front of my face. I swung up the weapon; Gracien's head was in my sight. The tiny x of the magnifying glass hovering between those brown, dulcet eyes that burned with rage and bitterness.

"You will not kill me, hunter," seethed Gracien. His words were snarling and burning as they pierced through my skull. *"You can tell that bitch that I'm coming for her. I will shatter her ribcage and crush her blackened heart."*

Violence erupted in my veins. The wild ward's magic.

Gracien bellowed a stallion's war cry.

I pulled the trigger and the bolt shot from its bearings toward his skull.

It landed in empty, crumpled snow.

Gracien was gone, like a coppery wraith upon the breeze. The stallion had vanished.

The glade was still once more.

Orrin breathed hard behind me.

I had underestimated the speed of the stallion. He had sired the fastest creature ever born and had disappeared faster than I could pull the damned trigger.

I loosed a chagrin-filled snarl.

Then I felt it, the forest.

The very trees themselves were watching, waiting, silent sentinels. The wild ward may have stolen control of the creatures who lived in Glentay, yet her power did not extend to the vegetation. The ancient trees rasped against one another, whispering about the hunter in the forest who wanted to spill blood.

CHAPTER ELEVEN

DESTRY

I lay awake atop the plush double bed; the sun having long since set. The apartment was one of several located in the largest tower of the Roost, the large fortress on the outcrop. The air smelt heavily of sweet, fresh hay, despite the lemongrass candle that burned on the dresser. Appointed with pale cream linens and geometric patterned, turquoise blue china, the guest room was lofty and light, so unlike the dark and dank Reck that I was used to. I supposed this room was to make me feel welcome, at home, but the locked door that remained under guard said otherwise. It was a prison, just an opulent one.

The bedroom window room sat open, the pale wood shutters folded back, and a soft, warm breeze ruffled the white sheer curtains. The drop below the tiny balcony was vertigo-inducing. There would be no escaping. I gazed at the fluttering fabric, my knees tucked to my chest as I lay on my side, not bothering to change out my rider's uniform and into the long, gauzy night dress Jaryn had laid out for me. The mere thought of him had my stomach roiling with nausea.

Somewhere within the fort, a faint bell rang eleven times.

Tomorrow afternoon, I would take my military vows, leashing me to that snake until he deemed otherwise. I gripped my knees tighter, my breath taut. What would Damara say of all of this? Had I made the right choice?

It was a living, breathing thing.

The grief.

To call it just that one word was atrocious, the five letters incapable of capturing and containing the feeling, a feeling that raged against the cage of my mind. Yet it was the loneliness that ate at me the most. It would sit in the corner of whatever room I was sitting in, curled in on itself, a whirling shadow, and watch. It yielded no company, no feeling of comfort, just a yawning hole where those things should be. And it was quiet, so utterly still, and quiet. I would sit and stare at it, pleading with it to move, to speak, to engage with me. But it would only watch me, and I would watch it in a silence that encroached on my every pore.

The night sky beyond the window glittered with a thousand stars, yet I knew I wouldn't see the Night Pegasus this far south. After my outburst against Narve, I hadn't felt that kind of power within me since, and with the lambent stone gone and being away from the north, I figured I wouldn't again.

I rolled onto my other side, blocking out that taunting night sky.

Would my ancestors curse my soul for treading so far from my homeland? This was the land of Damara's birth, where her family still lived. Would she be proud or sickened at my choices? I took a deep, shuddering breath.

The lone candle on the dressing table across from the bed flickered, sputtered, then went out entirely.

Slowly, I sat up, bracing my hands against the duvet, ignoring the dust prints I left on the pristine cream sheets. The sense of relief was all-consuming, as a mist-like hand cupped my cheek. I nestled into that touch; my eyes closing as tears threatened to fall. None of his light flickered over me, against me, and it confirmed my suspicions. I was too far south. But his power, albeit dimmer here in Orman, was still detectable, brushing over every part of me.

He didn't speak in my mind like he had in Saltfen, but as if he sat opposite me on the bed. Yet there was only all-consuming darkness in the room. His gravelly voice, no more than a lover's whisper, brushed over my exposed skin. "I told you; they could never hide you from me."

"He's locked me in here," my own voice was barely there.

That touch shifted to gently curve around the nape of my neck as it simultaneously wiped away a falling tear. "My powers are too weak this far south, especially without a lambent stone. But I promise, you will be free again."

"Is it true what Coen said? That I'm just your insurance policy?"

His snarl echoed quietly over the room, and he cradled my face between night-washed hands. "You hold a piece of me, yes. You will always hold my magic in your heart, but it was a gift and will never be something I tear away from you for my own gain. I will need your help before this is all over to defeat the evils at work here, but that power will come from the both of us." I felt a thumb run over my lower lip and I trembled. His touch shifted to gently caress my fading black eye. "When the wild ward is gone and my powers fully return, I'll rip out their throats for what they did to you."

"The wild ward? She's not a myth?"

"She's the biggest threat this continent has ever faced. She threatens to bend every living thing to her will. Once the spirits fall to her, it will all be lost."

"Promise me you're not just in my head, I'm not just imagining all of this." I was desperate to reach out my hand, to brush my fingers over his cheek, if he could even be a man at all. But those invisible hands on my skin, the sense of power coming off him, he had to be. "You *are* the Night Pegasus?"

His cool breath swept over my neck, and I inhaled deeply at the sensation of it. My own light stirred in my veins, and I felt a wave of comfort. "I have many forms, but that of a Pegasus or a man are the ones I utilize the most. As for my name, the Night Pegasus is one of them. And I promise you ..." Those broad hands moved to cradle my face once more, and his voice dropped an octave. "I am very real."

My heart pounded in my chest as I breathed, savoring the sensation of his hands on me. I had met him only once before, but again, I felt no fear, only comfort, reassurance. With him here, I wasn't alone. "Why do you visit me?"

"I have only ever interacted with two mortals. The first being your great ancestor, who freed me from my prison hundreds of years ago ... and you. When Petowin fell and your family was slaughtered, I thought the bloodline was lost. Then I sensed you that night in the castle when you blinded them all and stole that bastard's sword." His words were coated with pride. "So, I decided to step down from the skies that night in Saltfen and make sure you were ok. I thought I lost you once, I'm not losing you again."

His power in the room flickered, just like the candle had.

"Stay," I whispered.

"I will visit you again, I promise." Cool, full lips pressed against my forehead in a tender kiss. "You are unconquerable."

And then he was gone. Hollowed silence settled over the room, over me, and I laid down on my side once more, hugging my knees and praying for sleep to take me away.

A soft, mid-winter dawn peeked through the bedroom window, the cool air smelling heavily of the sea. I stepped back from the large, gilded, oval-shaped mirror that hung above the dressing table and surveyed my appearance. My ebony hair was now free from all the dye after I had scrubbed it down in the huge iron-cast bath in the adjoining bathing room. I had been cleaning myself before dawn, having given up on sleep entirely.

Hanging in shallow waves down my back, I resisted the urge to tie my hair into a knot. My training with Amadea wasn't to start till this evening. My hands clenched and unclenched at the thought and anxiety left a tangled lump in my chest. I shrugged myself into a new, clean set of rider's clothes, the freshly laundered uniform smelling of sweet citrus. The sigil stitched over the left breast was that of a storm cloud. Bromtide Platoon.

A brisk knock on the door sounded, and I gingerly pulled it open. Jaryn stood in the shadowed corridor beyond. Two guards flanked him, and they looked suspiciously at me, at my skin, the uniform.

One actually blanched.

Jaryn's shoulders were thrown back, and he stood poised as if he was ready to enter into battle. His green gaze swept down my figure, then back up, slowly.

"The uniform fits ok? I had my quartermaster draw it up for you," he asked. Today he wore his crown, a weave of golden strands glinted atop his bare head.

"It fits ... fine," I said quietly. It was hard to hold his gaze.

"Had you said yes to my proposal all those months ago, then you would be in silk gowns and finery, not a uniform."

My skin bristled and I recoiled a step. I had never wanted such things anyway.

The King blinked and had the decency to look abashed. "Forgive me. I've made you uncomfortable. Please, let us forget I said that. You must be hungry; I've had breakfast laid out downstairs on my private patio." He straightened and gestured to the vast corridor.

I exited my room and fell into step beside him, keeping a healthy distance between us. The guards brought up the rear, and I hated the feeling of them at my unprotected back.

Jaryn ushered me down the wide corridors that blazed with early morning light. Winter, it seemed, could not touch this place. Maybe it was the Lady's gift upon the land that kept it locked in this mild heat and kissing, cool breezes.

We entered the lower levels of the Roost. Servants, footmen, and courtiers swept past us, offering deep bows to their king and shocked, wary expressions to me as they walked by us. From the corner of my eye, I even saw a few pause and stare at my retreating back.

A pure-blooded Petowin in Ilrair uniform.

I felt as bewildered and threatened as they did. I would feel a lot more comfortable if I were armed.

Walking down an expansive, open-air walkway, Jaryn paused beside a guarded metal door and allowed me to enter first.

The muffled voices of many people below indicated that the soldiers were well into their structured day in the rooms beneath this one. Stone busts of former kings and queens adorned the limestone walls, and the glassless windows looked out over a small courtyard filled with olive trees and a sparkling fountain.

Onwards we walked, until the walls opened out onto a lush, vined-filled veranda which offered uninterrupted views of the gleaming Adacus Residence and Fal Lagoon. I searched for the source of trickling water, and there to the right of us, was a three-tier fountain with the Lady of the Cape atop it, the deity the Ilrairian's worshiped.

Carved from glistening marble, the sun glowed against the curve of her cheeks, braided hair, and the ripples of her pooling gown. Crystalline water flowed from her upturned palms as she looked serenely down at the tiers at her feet.

Movement dragged my gaze to the white table, where Coen sat waiting, uniformed once more. A silver, curved sword hung from the back of his wooden chair. He rose and bowed. I didn't miss his disapproving glance at my attire.

Jaryn took his place at the head of the table and gestured for me to sit between him and the officer.

Water was now in the place of wine. A small bowl of winterberries sat before me, along with wicker baskets full of sweet-smelling breads, pastries, jams, and more fruit. Breakfast was far from my mind, however, as Jaryn plucked a sheaf of paper from his waistcoat.

"Your vow." He laid them upon the table and thrust them toward me.

In the late afternoon sun, I stood in the Royal Quadrant of the Adacus Residence before a towering statue of the Lady of the Cape, whose beauty was spellbinding, even in statue form.

Coen, Farrow, Kramer, and some of their fellow officers sat behind me upon limestone-tiered seating. I could feel their heated stares burning into my shirt-clad back. Jaryn stood just before me on my right, bedecked with his golden crown. Medals festooned the gray uniform he wore. He held the rank of Commander-in-Chief over the Ilrair army and personally swore in all new recruits.

Amadea, his new Queen, whom he'd wed just a month ago, stood beside him in a silver gown that complemented his uniform. A Queen who could wield water. She met my gaze and gave a warm, comforting smile, the sun bronzing her dark brown skin.

With a shuddering breath, I placed my right hand over my frantically beating heart. Stealing a moment to compose myself, I gazed up at the Ilrair deity, so different to the countless spirits I paid homage and respect to, and I swore my Vow of Allegiance.

"I, Destry of Petowin, hereby pledge my loyalty, faith, and true allegiance to His Royal Highness, King Jaryn Adacus of Ilrair. I pledge to defend, protect, and shield His Highness and his family from harm. I swear to help protect Ilrair from anything that may threaten her borders and citizens." The words felt foreign and unwanted on my tongue. "May the Lady save us all."

And as I uttered those words, the light in me recoiled and shuddered, as if it had been struck by some invisible force.

I shivered in turn as I gazed up at Jaryn, and he smiled savagely down at me.

CHAPTER TWELVE

ASHER

With the glade now abandoned by Gracien, I decided to make it my temporary base. I started a fire beneath the frosted canopy of trees and allowed Orrin to dig for grass under the snow, although my leash on him tightened if he tried to stray too far.

I sat cross-legged beside the flames, closed my eyes, and let the wild ward's magic wash over me. Our minds weaved and connected through chilled blackened tendrils, speckled and striped with bronze, that spread outwards from my head down to my chest. The claws of her magic sliced into my will.

I felt the wild ward's rage a second later.

She was pacing in her cave like an estranged wild cat, hissing and spitting in fury.

"Huntsman ..." she seethed. *"Why has Gracien's blood not been spilled?"*

"He is faster than I believed possible," I replied darkly.

Her nails dragged across the walls of her lair. *"Time is of the essence ... the Koskivarri has been found. I felt it a few days ago. The faintest flicker of magic that was not of my own making. The night you buried your father and uncle."*

The wild ward realized her mistake the moment those last words left her red lips. At the mention of family, my throat constricted as a torrent of memories battled against her magic: huntsman hats, seal skin mitts, a Pegasus dead upon the snow, a white feather burning, burning, *burning*, singeing flesh—

I jolted backward from the fire, the flames flaring brighter, the memories scrambling and flinging themselves against the barrier of my mind. For a second, my free will tore at the wild ward magic. My own darkness and flame ripping and clawing at her web, but she stamped down, hard, like a boot on a beetle. That fire was snuffed out, and the magic pounded anew in my blood, smothering the memories in oily blackness.

"Only this ... your task, matters now. Do this for me, huntsman, and I shall reward you beyond your wildest dreams." The wild ward's voice dripped with seduction and second by second, I felt myself relaxing against her restraint.

"That's it," she whispered. *"Do not fight me, Asher."*

I succumbed fully, and her magic infiltrated every artery, every valve of my heart until it coated my entire core. Bronze brindling danced behind my shut lids.

There was no beginning or end to me, just here and now, these tasks I had been assigned. To end life. Yes ... my heart breathed. Yes.

Bloodlust danced across my vision.

Across the glade, the campfire smoke cloaking him, Orrin pawed at the snow in frustration, the magical bridle on his head glowing harshly.

"Tomorrow night, I will watch with joy in my heart when you bring the King of the Forest to his knees."

The next night was shrouded in clouds and the half-moon remained hidden from sight. Fog crowned the mountains and not one star peeked out from the heavens. The Night Pegasus did not want mortals to see him flying tonight.

I slunk through the undergrowth to the campsite the wild ward had warned me about. Tucked beside a huge, curved granite cliff, a cavalry unit bearing no sigils had hauled a great wooden and iron cage into the mountains with a team of draft horses with one goal in mind. To capture Pegasi. Soldiers milled around, mending hook nets, tending fires, and smoking pipes. From the huge wagon came the sad, frightened whinny of a Pegasus foal.

Where the tree line met the valley floor, and the rock walls were at their lowest height, a light gray Pegasus stallion lay dead on his side. My gaze raked over his dead body, peppered with three crossbow bolts. The young male had not been experienced enough to avoid the trap of the cliff faces and had unwittingly led his family into capture. His body was laced with cuts that seeped blood. He had put up a mighty fight, but a bolt to his heart had ended his life.

I inhaled deeply, and the smell of crevasse and stag moss flitted faintly past me, filtering down from the wagon. There were no Pegasus mares in sight, just the dead stallion and the sound and scent of Pegasi young and what other ice-like creature they had locked away with them in the wagon.

Several officers patrolled the camp, their tame horses stood picketed at the open end of the valley and their hunting dogs barked and prowled around the edges. The soldiers were uniformed but bore no banners to show where their allegiance lay. I inhaled again, filtering through the hundreds of scents that passed by me. Colladonian, Petish, and Aarinian men I knew, but this lot wasn't from any of those places. They smelt of a distant sea.

Men hadn't tried to capture Aarinian Pegasi since the black mare, Harper, years ago, and she had been deemed a failed experiment.

Silently, I circled the camp to its southeastern edge, staying downwind of the hunting dogs. I had kept Orrin some distance behind me, the wild ward magic keeping him mute and still. Settling into the white-dusted brush, I brought up my crossbow and scanned the northern edge of the camp, where the forest met the cliff face.

Three animals waited in the darkness beyond the fires. Two stags, brothers in arms that were still loyal to the forest spirit, and Gracien.

They topped a piece of forested high ground and halted. The muted light turned them into creatures of silver and darkness. As silent as wraiths, they stalked toward the camp.

My heart was a steady war drum in my chest.

A shout rang out over the camp, and a man's cry echoed through the trees.

An ear-splitting roar came from the sky, and it thundered across the campsite. The higher-pitched cries of Pegasus mares joined the bellow of a stallion, a chorus of anger and hatred.

Like three arrows loosed from a bow, the stags and Gracien bounded from the rise and galloped straight for the heart of the camp. The wild ward had sneered at what Gracien was about to do, at his inherent kindness and compassion for other equines.

The soldiers were in chaos, their sea air scent coated with confusion and fear. Men ran for their weapons and their horses screamed in terror as the Pegasi swooped low over the tents and lone wagon. The cavalry mounts strained and snapped at their tethers, bolting into the woods, fleeing the thundering bellows of the Pegasi.

Gracien weaved around the tents and fire pits; the stags close on his heels. Adrenaline licked my veins, but I kept a tight leash on it, wielding it at will. The stags bucked, cavorted, and reared amongst the scrambling men, adding their own furious cries into the mix. The sight of my crossbow tracked Gracien as he turned for the wagon.

The wheeled monstrosity sat like a slumbering giant through the chaos. The King of the Forest skidded to a halt before it, the wooden and metal walls towering over him.

Four soldiers circled him, spears pointed low in their hands. He was trapped with no way to reach the bolts of the wagon door. I snarled, unable to get a clear shot past the soldiers.

Gracien snaked his head low and snapped his teeth, daring the soldiers to come forward. Although pale with shock, one barged closer. The Mountie spun away on his forehooves and double-barreled the soldier who snuck up behind him. Whinnying in defiance, nostrils flaring, Gracien reared.

A red-tainted shadow dropped from the sky and landed with a sickening thud behind the nearest soldier. My breath hitched as I took her in. She would be a mighty prize. A blood bay Pegasus mare.

She lunged, grasped the soldier's navy shirt, and flung him aside. Gracien leapt for the opening she created. The red mare flattened the two remaining soldiers, then propelled herself back into the smoke-washed air.

It amazed me how agile the females were on the wing. The wild ward had warned me that some Pegasi had overcome the killing instinct and had sided with Gracien, but to see it in the flesh was insanity.

Four men bolted from the largest tent. They looked about hastily, weapons in hand. Then their gazes fell to the wagon, and Gracien's earth and gold frame beside it.

His time had run out.

He reared, his yellowed teeth grasping the freezing iron of the wagon door bolt.

The eldest man of the group, a weathered and grayed forty-year-old, wrenched up his recurve bow, knocked an arrow, and loosed. Smooth and efficient, but not deadly.

The bolt on the door sprang free with an unearthly groan as if it were awakening from hibernation, and Gracien scrambled backward as the arrow struck the wooden side of the wagon, where his skull had just been.

The panel slammed into the earth, creating a ramp.

The red Pegasus mare was at Gracien's side in an instant. *"I'll take care of the young ones."*

Gracien nodded and bared his teeth at anyone who dared approach as the lead mare ushered three foals from the wagon and into the chaos. The formidable mare checked each one, ensuring they were whole and well. They were small and terrified, but they clung to the red mare's flanks as she led them away from the wagon and then up, up into the sky.

A sergeant beside the elder yanked up his crossbow and aimed at the mare.

Gracien roared a warning.

The elder loosed another arrow in his direction, and the stallion dove to his knees as the arrow skimmed the top of his mane, skidding to the earth behind him. The red mare banked harshly, the other Pegasi mares joining her, shielding the foals from sight.

The Sergeant aimed once more at the mares.

Gracien flung himself into a gallop, his hooves eating up the ground as he ran straight for the Sergeant and the elder. Men yelled back and forth all around him, and they created a deafening holler that mixed eerily with the whinnies of the Pegasi that darted like meteors across the night sky.

The Mountie snorted, his entire body trembling now as he dodged another arrow and hurtled for the assembled group of four men. Swinging his head low, Gracien jumped, forelimbs snapping to his chest as he soared through the air, as if he, too, had wings.

A Trinitor reborn.

The elder gaped as Gracien lunged for him. I could see every detail on his face. He was handsome for a human. Hands clenching, he flung up his bow.

My breath was cool and calm as I readjusted my aim. I wondered if the King of the Forest knew he was going to die tonight. Gracien appeared suspended in time, the night air freezing us all, slowing the stallion's flight as his powerful body cut through the dark.

A wave of power, spirit magic, ancient and raw, refracted over the campsite and swept over me as my finger pressed the trigger. The crossbow bolt speared into the night. Time seemed to regain itself, as Gracien's forelimbs buckled beneath him as he reconnected with the ground. His brown and gold body crumpled to the snow-dusted earth.

The elder stared aghast, toward the fringes of the trees beyond the camp to where I knelt, shrouded in gloom.

Silence washed over the campsite.

Gracien tried to swallow, but he struggled to even breathe. His limbs twitched as he fought to regain his footing. He whickered and looked about wildly, his eyes rolling.

Darkness coiled around my shoulders, sending a shudder down my spine. Yet I felt no remorse, no guilt, as I shouldered my crossbow and shifted in my hiding place. The forest seemed to pulse around me, recoiling at what had been done. My nostrils flared and the muscle in my jaw ticked, as Gracien nickered softly once more, then lay still.

Gracien's death washed over the encampment like a tidal wave. The dramatic thud of his brown and gold body hitting the earth had brought the commotion of the raid to a standstill. A sudden breeze shifted through the trees, and it chilled me. In the heart of the camp, some of the soldiers were doubling over to vomit on the ground. Others stood frozen, as the Pegasi fled into the night.

I had brought the King of the Forest to his knees, just like the wild ward had envisioned. Pride and bloodlust swelled my chest as I looked down at the carnage from my vantage point of frosted undergrowth.

The elder stared and stared at my hiding place.

I stiffened.

He had tracked where my crossbow bolt had originated and was staring at the snow-topped ferns. The soldier turned and made a step toward me. The Sergeant noted where the elder was looking and pivoted to see for himself.

I melted into stillness and held my breath.

The wild ward's magic in my bones trembled with anticipation. Oh, how I would delight in taking the soldiers down too.

"*No,*" her voice resonated in my skull. "*I have a need for the soldiers. You are to leave them alive.*"

I hissed at her command.

The Sergeant clenched his crossbow. He swept the sight along the border of vegetation that shielded me from view.

"Retreat, my hunter. Your work here is done for now."

"The Pegasi," I seethed quietly as I watched the rest of the herd fly from the encampment, led by a midnight black Pegasus stallion. I remembered that stallion, I knew it. Yet as much as I stared up at his flying frame, I couldn't place him. "You promised me more blood."

"Which shall be spilt in time. Return to my home. I have someone I want you to meet."

I slunk backward deeper and deeper into the depths of the trees until the Sergeant was aiming at mere shadows. Once out of range from his crossbow, I turned and reached out for my mental grip on Orrin.

Only to find it incinerated to dust.

I snarled.

The young stallion was nowhere to be found.

I cut through the darkness on foot, cursing the young Mountie with every step I took. I could feel the wild ward seething within her cave, a prowling ceaseless predator. With his death, Gracien had set his son and only heir free with one final pulse of spirit magic. Magic so strong and ancient, a power that had originated before wild wards walked the mountains, it had snapped through her stranglehold on Orrin. A knife severing a rope with one lethal strike. Why the great stallion hadn't severed it when I had in my crossbow sights in the glade, I wasn't sure. But then he must have known about the Pegasus raid and wanted to intervene.

And his compassion had gotten him killed.

The wild ward still held power over the creatures that resided within Glentay, but the forest itself remained free of her clutches.

I had to admire Gracien's sacrifice as much as I admired my shot that had slain him. The kick I had gotten from firing the bolt had set my nerve endings ablaze. I wanted to feel that again, and soon. I was hungry for it, more death, more blood. The miles between the encampment and the wild ward's lair diminished until I spied the faint, fire-lit glow of the entrance within the weather-damaged rock faces.

I was about to walk out from the trees and into the open when I sensed she wasn't alone. Retreating deeper into the undergrowth, I inhaled sharply, taking in the scent of wood smoke, blood, and something totally unfamiliar, yet it tugged on my survival instinct.

Danger waited in that cave. Danger and death.

It was an earthy scent, coated with musk and a sweet acrid note.

Stalking the tree line, I edged closer to the cave's mouth. I wanted a good look inside before I stepped foot within it. Notching a bolt into the crossbow, I knelt amongst the tree trunks and ferns.

Two tall, horse-like figures stood just beyond the jagged cave mouth. I saw the wild ward's cloaked silhouette beside them.

They were winged, but they weren't Pegasi.

My finger on the trigger twitched as something ancient and powerful awoke in my veins at the sight of the two predators. My mortal blood, despite the magic that flowed with it, told me to run and keep running. Their kind had slaughtered hundreds.

Nijinxes.

The smaller of the pair turned its head from the wild ward to stare … but it couldn't stare. Where eyes should have been situated in its skull, there were just empty, black silken hollows. Yet it seemed to gaze right at me. The leathery wings on its back twitched as it issued a series of soft clicks.

Within the cave, the wild ward turned to look at the forest. "She knows where you are hiding, Asher. There is no point in concealing yourself from her."

I rose slowly from my crouch and cut through the ferns toward the trio. The wild ward smiled as I approached, her face still shrouded by her cloak hood.

The female Nijinx cocked her head as I neared. Silvery fangs glinted at her mouth, and those pits in her skull made even my hardened stomach turn. The huge male at her side took a step back, yet lingered close to the female's flank.

"Asher, meet the Queen of the Nijinxes." The wild ward waved a casual hand at the female. "Vesperum, meet Asher. And this is her mate, Pherox."

CHAPTER
THIRTEEN

ORRIN

I t was too much information.

I was blinded by it. Choked by it.

In several quickened heartbeats, I knew every tree's name, their sons and daughters. I could recall every mammal that had ever resided within the forest and who their great-grandchildren were. Time halted and spun, retracted, and lanced through me.

Too much.

This was all too much. My father was dead. A gold and bronze corpse atop the snow.

I was the last one. The last Mountain Horse to walk the earth. Tellervo, the forest spirit, ran a calming hand down my neck and back.

"*Easy, Orrin,*" he whispered. I flinched at his feather light touch, the otherworldliness of it. He was neither human nor beast. No fur, scales, or feathers decorated his skin. The spirit was ethereal, yet so solidly *there*, it was like he was galloping alongside me, stride for stride.

"*The forest is yours. Listen. Understand.*" Tellervo harnessed my grief, my anger, and confusion and settled it, channeling it into one bearable mass that wouldn't break my mind with its magnitude.

The trees spoke in ageless whispers all around me. Their roughened, ice-tinged words licked down my spine as I galloped past them.

King. Ruler.

Long live the King.

The forest spirit lives within him.

War is coming.

Long live the King.

Asher had fired the lethal bolt. He had killed my father. My gallop grew faster, faster. The swiftest Mountain Horse ever born. All around me, the caverns, rocks, rivers, and trees, such unending trees, watched as I tore past. Tellervo pulsed alongside me and within my bones, the spirit my father had borne all these years.

King of Glentay. King of the Forest.

Justice ... the forest murmured quietly as my mind focused on the hunter, on what he had done. *I would kill him for this.* Limbs churning the snow-covered ground, I galloped past the Breccan River, putting as much distance between myself and the wild ward's seat of power, her lair and the stone monolith just beyond it.

"*We must break the wild ward,*" warned Tellervo, his voice echoing and deep, worn yet timeless. "*Yet we can't do it alone. Ilmari, Perama, and I, we are not enough, nowhere near enough, to defeat her. The other great spirits are trapped. The mountains, Serebo, Ghel, and Bronzo, the wild ward locked them away first, knowing in a united front, we could overthrow and destroy her. Only the Night Pegasus can free the mountain sisters, but his Koskivarri is imprisoned in the southern lands.*"

My gallops slowed as I passed my father's old glade. Grief ravaged me. He had freed not only me, but the small Pegasus family, too, his final moments spent trying to unify Pegasi and Mountie.

I thought of another who had desperately tried to do the same. *Ebrel.* I cast the thought out to the forest and was met by a timeworn silence as Glentay processed the request. Like melting ice, the forest slowly began to reply. Its thoughts clouded my mind, almost broke it apart; there was so much. I was overrun with information.

Grounded. Wounded. Sighed Glentay in unison.*Blood mount. The yellow city. South.* It paused, as if taking a laboring breath. *Our King is needed beyond the moorlands.*

I needed no further instruction than that. She was *alive.* And I wasn't about to abandon her to a fate worse than death, to be handled by man.

"Find the Koskivarri, too, Orrin, if you head south. Find her and bring her north. Bring her home, *"* whispered a softer, more female voice in my mind. Ilmari.

The lakes and firs, cliffs and pines, even Mount Serebo herself, the Queen of Mountains, watched on with her imperishable, ice and magic-trapped gaze as I galloped from the Anduns.

To Ebrel.

CHAPTER
FOURTEEN

DESTRY

They kept me under guard at the Adacus Residence the evening after I had taken my vow, and they would return me to the Ilrair cavalry fortress the next morning. I had been herded away from the royal square with its limestone-tiered seating into the cavernous royal household itself. The gleaming yellow building was a testament to all things limestone, with sweeping atriums, vast hallways and ballrooms, and lofty mezzanines. Light poured in through the countless windows I had spied on my flight here, yet it did little to warm the place. The Residence felt cold, formal, certainly not a place where one could find a sunny corner and relax, and certainly not for a woman like me.

My vow felt like an iron chain around my throat as I was escorted through the main body of the castle to the ancient and central heart of it. Here the limestone was grayed, worn away from hundreds of years of torch smoke and human breath. This core piece of the palace was the original building the first king of Ilrair had built, and his predecessors had constructed around and around it. A simple arched doorway waited up ahead, flickering torches on either side and worn steps dipped into the darkness beyond the opening.

I felt my steps faltering, but the guards on either side of me, the same ones from this morning, their firm hands on my elbows, pushed me toward the doorway and halted.

"Go, *winny*," said the one on my right, his words dripping with distaste. "She waits for you."

"And be quick about it," snarled the other guard. "Linger too long here and I'll shove you down those steps myself."

I bared my teeth in warning and yanked my arms free from their grasp. Tentatively, I took a cautious step onto those descending steps. Only darkness awaited me, yet the air that filtered upward from below was warm, humid, and scented with ylang-ylang.

Swallowing harshly, my right hand braced on the rough-hewn curving wall. I felt my way down the steps, dropping deeper into the archaic seat of the Residence. Around me, the air grew hotter and more humid, so much so I began to sweat beneath my rider's uniform. Finally, a faint glow appeared, showing the end of the stairwell and smooth flagstones beyond it. I paused on the last step, the heavy air coating my damp skin. Was this a trap? A final prison for Jaryn to cage me in? I surely had to be below ground level now.

My gaze adjusted from the gloom of the stairs to the vast chamber that lay in front of me. A huge rectangular pool glistened beneath sconces held high on carved limestone pillars. Steam curled from the water's rippling surface. Along the long sides of the pool, half hidden by gauzy curtains, were plush daybeds tucked into dark alcoves. The low ceiling made the space feel like a womb, a sanctuary. My flicker of unease lifted slightly.

A hot spring. No wonder the first king had built his castle here. My gaze trailed over to the far end of the pool to where a lone woman sat. She had braced her right hand on the pool's lip while her legs slowly swirled the water. Fat, guttering candlelight flickered off her dark brown skin. The silvery gown was gone, replaced by a simple cream shift that draped over her sensuous curves and floated around her legs. Her hair was swept off her face into a beautiful navy and gold turban that matched the tawny flecks in her eyes perfectly. Tendrils of steam curled around her silhouette. Amadea.

I froze as my body registered who she was, my light flickering in response. Her beautiful face lifted, and that golden gaze pinned on me. She was only a few years older than me, but those eyes, wisdom, and grace lay in her gaze.

A queen who could wield water. I glanced down at the pool, hoping it wasn't about to become my watery grave.

"Come, Destry." She patted the bare flagstones on her right. Her voice was rich, alluring, tinted with the accent of her native homeland. "Sit with me."

I sensed no malice in her words, but she was the only other person down here. No ladies-in-waiting, no courtiers, no guards. Maybe she didn't want any witnesses to my death. I stepped down onto the main floor around the pool, the muffled echo of my walking resounding faintly through the thick air. Only my breathing, Amadea's swirling legs, and the dripping of water could be heard.

Cautiously, I shucked the wool-lined leather coat from my shoulders, and I felt instant relief as my body cooled. Taking inspiration from the southern Queen, I removed my boots and socks and rolled my loose breeches to my knees. Slowly, aware of my every movement was being noted by her, I lowered myself into a seated position that mirrored hers, albeit a healthy distance away from her. My hands curled in my lap, and I held in my sigh as the perfectly warm water wrapped around my lower legs. It felt heavenly and soothed the cut from the arrow on my calf.

"Relaxing, isn't it?" Amadea gave me a small half-smile. "It was one of the conditions of the marriage that I be allowed down here, alone. I needed a space that was just for me. I was surprised when Jaryn kept his word."

She shifted, leaning forward to brace her honed forearms onto her thighs. Her words sounded like a peace offering, an armistice. Yet I couldn't trust her, not yet.

"It's a beautiful space," I murmured, my body still tense, wary, and so, so tired.

Her gaze took in the calm surface of the water. Sadness lingered on her beautiful face. "The heat, the humidity … it reminds me of home."

"Omivarra?" I guessed, naming the larger of the two twin islands beyond the Alsida Archipelago.

It was her turn to sigh now, an exhaled breath filled with longing, and I realized that she surely missed her homeland as much as I missed mine. I half turned to face her, patiently waiting for her to fill the calm, almost serene silence between us.

"Yes, Omivarra. My home is on the northeastern coast amongst jungle waterfalls. My family elders assumed it was the reason I had my gift; I had absorbed it from the cascades that roared all around our home. There's been a few of us water wielders scattered throughout my bloodline, male and female … but I'm the first one to leave." Her shoulders tensed and then went loose. She curled a stray brown hair that had escaped her turban behind her ear.

"Did you have a choice?" Had she been torn away from her home like I had?

The shake of her head was answer enough.

Her right palm uptilted and … and that was indeed droplets of water dancing over her fingertips. "Jaryn had men scouring the jungles for years, looking for someone like me. He had heard the rumors of water wielders and wanted one for his own forces. The money he had offered my father had been obscene, irrefutable. In the month that followed … I was made Queen of Ilrair." She levitated the droplets before us, each one twinkling like stars. "The court welcomed me publicly, but I know ... I know I'm not wanted here, by his people."

"That makes two of us." I offered her a small, warm smile.

She smiled faintly in return, a faint glow of warmth lighting her features. "I'm going to be used militarily. The title of queen is just an honor, nothing real. I've sat in on every military council since we were wed, and I know Jaryn wants me to train you too."

Not *my husband*, or *my love*, just his name. Indeed, I wondered if Amadea held any affection for that cruel snake whatsoever.

My fingers knotted together in my lap. "And will you?"

Her smile turned cunning, the white of teeth flashing in the soft light. "I have said that I will, down here, away from prying eyes ... but I have a feeling there's only one who can teach you. I know you Northerners call him the Night Pegasus. His sister flies over our deep southern skies; we call her *chorapesi*, Painter of Light."

My skin flushed as I thought of him, heat licking up my spine.

Amadea assessed me closely. "He has visited you. Here?"

That flash of heat was doused as quickly as it had flared. She could feed all of this back to Jaryn to use as fuel against me. She was cunning, yes, and all of this could have been a ploy for me to open up to her.

She must have seen the look of concern on my face, as her elegant right hand reached across, simple golden rings flashing on her long fingers, and clasped mine, her body turning to face me. "I know it goes against all your instincts, but you can trust me."

Could she be ... an ally? Spirits ... even a *friend?* I wanted to hope, to believe it. By the look on her face, I wondered if that was what she desperately wanted too. I had so many enemies in this yellow palace. I would take the risk if it meant I could form one relationship that wouldn't end in my death.

I took a steady breath. "Only once, and only briefly. Without lambent stones to amplify his power and mine, he can't stay here for long; I'm too far south."

She squeezed my hand tighter in acknowledgment. Sharing those words could cost me everything. "Jaryn will be expecting some progress from you before he shifts us up north to Saltfen again. I'll try and get a lambent stone for you. Discreetly, of course. We'll both end up in trouble if he discovers I'm *not* the one training you."

"What will we do with our time down here?" I squeezed her hand back in return, and instantly, the air felt lighter, less strained, as if an invisible pact had been formed between us, bonding us. A part of me was terrified, but part of me wanted to weep with gratitude for what she had offered.

She released my hands, placed her palms behind her, and gazed up at the low, shadowed ceiling. Her grin was conspiratorial. "We shall do what women do; we will plan and take those bastards down."

When I ascended the steps from the pool almost two hours later, my guards looked even less pleased than they had beforehand. Their silence was mutinous as they escorted me to a guest suite not far from the hot spring within the boundaries of the original castle. After they had locked the door behind me, I took in the dusk sun that streamed through the carved duplex windows. The room was like the one I had stayed in at the Roost last night, outfitted with plush cream bedding, gilded mirrors, and potted ferns. A plate of cold meats, cheese, and bread had been set on the pale wood dresser alongside a pitcher of lemon-infused water. On the huge wooden bed, a different set of night clothes was laid out for me, the gauzy dress gone. In its place was a navy silk buttoned shirt, the sleeves cut to the elbow and matching long, loose-fitting pants. Omivarra fashion, I realized, smiling to myself. I rubbed the fabric between my fingers. I had never owned anything so luxurious before. Stripping out of my rider's uniform, I donned the night clothes and sat on the bed, watching the city beyond fade into darkness as night enveloped it.

I knew deep in my bones that he wouldn't visit tonight, sensing that seeing him the night prior had drained his power somewhat. Longing burned under my skin. I yearned for his touch again, his presence, his power that felt all-consuming, daunting, and thrilling all at once.

If I were to survive in this pit of vipers, I would have to learn to control this light that he had gifted to me. To coax it out of the shadows of my heart and bend to my will. In the oncoming dark, I felt for where it hid in my body, flickering faintly, nothing like the roaring torrent I had experienced that night in Aarine.

I lay back on the plush bed, my bare feet dangling off the edge to the floor. A deep wanting thrummed in my blood, but as the darkness deepened and washed over everything in the room, he did not visit. Grief, loneliness, and tiredness sang me a haunting lullaby until I was swept away into a fitful sleep.

PART TWO

THE WINGED

CHAPTER FIFTEEN

ASHER

Defend and death.

That is the way of the Nijinxes. Defend the females and dole out death.

They had been the first words that Pherox, Vesperum's consort, had snarled in my mind that night in the wild ward's cave. He was not the largest male in the Queen's kin swarm, but that was not why Vesperum chose him to be at her side. No, she chose Pherox because he was the most lethal Nijinx to have ever lived. He was a few years older than I was, and when Vesperum had refused a rider as part of the wild ward's pact with them, her willingness to obey the witch only extending so far, Pherox had stepped forward instead. No man would tarnish his mate's ebony skin as long as he drew breath. The wild ward held enough respect to honor the demand, and so, the privilege to be a rider had fallen to me and to Pherox.

His voice had been deep and velvety as he had flashed those silver primary fangs at me in the cave. *"We shall be one cohesive unit, you and I. One being."*

I don't know what had made me do it, but I had found myself bowing to the huge, muscled male, a hand braced over my heart. *"Defend and death, King Consort."*

The Nijinx couldn't smile, but I swear I felt a ripple of approval against my mind as he sensed the bloodlust that hounded me day and night.

Vesperum's kin swarm, her brothers, sisters, cousins, and most devoted followers would fly with her to their deaths if she asked them to. Such utter devotion to their Queen had played right into the hands of the wild ward. Control the Queen of the Nijinxes and you have command of an elite force of killing machines.

Over a meal of roasted venison and parsnips that night, the wild ward regaled me with the tale of how the Nijinxes followed her command. I had been surprised that she ate mortal food at all, that her otherworldly magic could snare hundreds of beings, but not sustain her. Sitting opposite from her near the fire, I leant into her words.

When the Trinitors had been cursed eight hundred years ago, the Ilrairian mage that had doled out the magic had originally cleaved them into three separate beings, to diminish their power: Unicorns, Mounties and Pegasi. Yet there had been a fourth being, the deepest and darkest shreds of the species, that was trapped away under the earth, left to fester and roil. The Nijinxes.

The wild ward had discovered them not long after harnessing her magic from the land and made a deal with them. She would set them free from the earth's underground caves and caverns if they followed her command. Vesperum had agreed, and her kin swarm had feasted that night, and for many nights after, as the Nijinxes swept south over Petowin.

The country's name had rung like a bell in my head but was swept away a moment later by a whisper of magic. I relaxed at the touch of it but didn't miss the wild ward's smirk. A sliver of unease ran down my spine as darkness pulsed through my bones.

The next morning, it dawned overcast and carried the threat of more snow. Pherox landed just outside the cave, having flown in from wherever he and the kin swarm were roosting currently. His ebony coat shimmered over his taut, muscled frame and he turned to face me with that hollowed face, the two primary fangs flashing. I don't know why I had even bothered with Orrin; *this* was a creature made for me.

Pherox stood square and tall before me, neck arched. He had no mane or forelock, but he did have a long, lustrous tail that fell in shallow waves of ink to the snow. I had noted it the night before, but to see them in the daylight gave me a sense of glee. All four of his long, iron-strong legs ended in webbed and taloned feet. Talons that matched the silvery fangs glinting at his mouth. Atop the apex of each immense leathery wing, another talon shone.

The male must have sensed my appreciation. He clicked twice and extended those wings so that the meek light glowed through the dark brown membranes, highlighting nicks and silver scars from the countless battles he had fought and won for the right to be Vesperum's mate.

He clicked once more as he held those mighty wings aloft. *"Shall we see how good a rider you are, huntsman?"*

Adrenaline pounded through me as I approached him. I barely came up to his shoulder. Pherox shifted in anticipation, but his right wing swept forward, allowing me to stand beside his huge chest. His head turned as if he watched me beside him, but he couldn't *see*. Normal horse-sized ears graced his equine-like head, but they twitched delicately.

"My clicks echo back to me, painting a picture as if I could see just like you do. I can sense every bone in your body, the pounding of your heart, that alien magic in your blood, and the darkness that rests beneath it."

I placed my hands on his jutting wither and crouched, my blood a heady song in my veins. In one swift motion, I hurled my legs upward and over, and then I was astride him. Pherox flexed his wings, adjusting himself to the odd weight on his back. Only for his mate would he do this, not for the wild ward, not for me, but for Vesperum.

A whip of energy against my mind was my only warning as Pherox bolted into the gray-washed sky. Every muscle in my body tensed as I sunk down into my seat bones and pressed with my thighs, just like I had done when ... when ...

The memory was there, faint, tainted by mist, and the passing of my early childhood, yet the vision of me astride a bucking little pony was real, it pulsed for but a moment, then filtered away, the magic sweeping it under its surface like a wave.

Again, that feeling of unease ran over me.

I hunkered low behind Pherox's powerful neck as the male breached the tree canopy and flew in low over it. His wings a steady, controlled beat against the snow that began to fall, leaving it flurrying in our wake.

The cold breeze lashed against the exposed skin of my face and hands, but I felt utterly in control of my body as Pherox banked westward. The male didn't speak, but I felt another flicker of approval against my mind. I couldn't help but smile. This was insane. Beautiful, but insane. Pherox's body was like a honed blade cutting through the snowfall and with every one of his wing beats, I felt that darkness that lined my bones get stronger, subtly growing against the magic in my body.

And as the great male banked again, curving toward the cave within the forest, I realized I could quite happily spend an eternity up here. Two hunters working together. Where I had daggers, Pherox had his talons. The Nijinx male clicked beneath me, and I smiled again. He agreed.

CHAPTER SIXTEEN

DESTRY

C oen waited at my door the next morning after breakfast, arms crossed over his chest, sword at his side. Farrow stood behind his Commander, and he gave me a small polite nod. Like me, they had forgone the leather coats due to the heat that even the solid limestone blocks of the castle couldn't keep out.

"We're heading back to the Roost?" I asked as I finished knotting my near-black hair at the base of my neck.

The Commander shook his head, his ear-length blond curls swaying. He didn't wear his tri-corn hat today. As always, when I was in his presence, he didn't look pleased. The strong planes of his face set into grim lines, those green eyes cold as I looked up at him. "At the Queen's request, you are to stay here at the Residence so it will be easier for her to train you in magic. So, you are to conduct your military aspect of your training here in the courtyard upstairs."

I blinked, the only surprise I dared show. Amadea had suggested it last night before we parted ways, but I didn't think she would get her request granted so quickly.

Coen stepped back into the wide, paved corridor, his cream shirt sleeves rolled to the elbow, revealing his strong, suntanned forearms. His gaze took in my uniform that matched theirs, then he elegantly gestured with a large hand. "After you, winny."

I stepped into the corridor, thinking that, even though I wasn't armed with weapons, I had nails, and teeth, and my brain, if he so much as tried to hurt me ... "I have a name, you know."

A name that isn't technically mine, but better than whatever insults you can come up with.

Farrow was a quiet, lethal shadow at our backs, a hand on his short sword, as we treaded up the hallway to where sun filtered through at the far end beyond a short set of yellow stone steps.

Coen arched an eyebrow at me. "Oh, I know. I'll use it when you deserve it. And since I can hardly bandy around your surname here unless you *want* to be killed in your sleep, then *winny* it will be."

I threw him a glare as we walked side by side.

"I didn't realize you needed a bodyguard." I gazed over my shoulder at Farrow, who rolled his eyes and sighed.

A muscle in Coen's jaw twitched. "*He's* going to be the one training you. I'm only here because His Majesty requested to see me after I escort you to the courtyard."

"Two elite Ilrair cavalrymen for one defenseless Petish woman? That's a bit extreme," I chided, unable to hide my smirk.

His hand snaked out to catch my elbow, halting us just before we entered the bright morning sun of the courtyard. His voice lower than I had ever heard it, he whispered, "You and I both know that you're not some defenseless damsel. I know you took out Narve, his medic, *and* Lonan, so enough of the mouthing off and get in that courtyard. I'll be back in an hour."

I snatched my arm away from him, albeit his grip hadn't been as hostile as the first time he'd grabbed me at Saltfen. Nonetheless, I glared at his retreating back, as Farrow stepped past me and into the glorious winter sun. His grin was wide, three days' worth of stubble gracing his jaw, and he gave a shallow, mocking bow.

Trying to gather my wits, I followed him up the steps and into the limestone-paved courtyard. A beautiful square surrounded by ancient archways sat before me with potted olive trees on either end, and a small fountain of the Lady of the Cape, trickling water in the center. Despite the Residence's formality, this space, you could very well sun yourself out here. But there was no idyllic outdoor seating, just a rack of wooden training swords and shields braced against one of the archways. A small white-iron table sported sparring pads and hand bindings. Farrow walked over to the training equipment, not bothering to check if I followed him. Efficiently, he unstrapped his sword and shucked off his vest.

I stood awkwardly in the courtyard and faced him.

Farrow rubbed his palms together and smiled at me. "Coen mentioned you had some hand-to-hand combat training. Care to show me?"

My hands clenched into fists at my sides. "No."

He stopped smiling and he straightened. "We need to train you; His Majesty won't let you return north until you're proficient in the basics, at the very least."

Fine. I felt my body settle over my legs, bracing myself, digging the soles of my boots into the flagstones. Farrow gave me the tiniest of smiles. He knew what I was doing, saving energy by letting him come to me.

He strode forward, his arms loose at his sides, until he was within striking distance.

His voice dropped an octave. "Hit me."

I didn't wait for him to think twice about what he just said. My rage spiked at being knocked unconscious by him, for being dragged and kept here. My fist flew for that stupidly perfect jaw, but his right hand swung up and caught it. He barely drew a breath as he wrenched me around and pinned my back against his hard chest. I hissed, and I could hear his low chuckle as he released me.

"Sloppy, try again. Try refining that rage and make it useful."

Letting my grief roll over me, I whirled, coming from below with an uppercut, but he caught that, too, and twisted my arm. Pain shot up my right shoulder as he locked my arm, driving me downward until I was on my knees.

"Better, but not good enough. Weaponize your rage." He let go and stepped backward, dipping into a half crouch, readying himself.

Pins and needles replaced the pain in my arm as I shakily got to my feet. Shame and rage made my cheeks flush, and I felt that faint flicker of light in my chest. *Yes.* In my mind, I grabbed that light with both hands and desperately coaxed it to burn brighter.

I glowered at him, fists clenching and braced myself. He flew at me with a warrior's speed, a punch raining down. I ducked both of his fists, driving my own hand toward the side of his head. Farrow twirled, shoving me. My feet stumbled, but I twisted, quickly regaining my balance, and kicked out. He easily sidestepped, like he predicted my every move and came at me again. I blocked him, taking the blow with my shoulder, and pain bloomed across my back.

Wincing, I flattened my palm and struck toward his throat. The move surprised him, but he blocked it without a second thought.

Anger beat steadily alongside my own heart, and I moved quickly, edging round him to land a kick to his right knee. I stalled for a breath, amazed that I'd landed a blow on him, and he used that pause to sweep my legs out from under me.

Air smacked from my lungs as my back connected to the flagstones and I gasped. Chuckling, Farrow knelt on one knee beside me, forearms crossed over his thigh. "So, you do know some moves."

Air trickled back into my lungs, sweat streaming beneath my shirt as I panted harshly. His copper gaze met mine, and I didn't let him guess my movements before I shoved my right hand toward his stubbled jaw. Pale green light shot from my hand as I grappled almost blindly with my power.

Farrow cursed and leapt to his feet, shielding his eyes, but it was too late. I'd blinded him, albeit momentarily. That flash of light in my palm snuffed out, and I propped myself on my elbows as Farrow blinked and muttered to himself a step away from me.

He shook his head and blinked again, his sight returning, then he turned his head to look at me. A look of amazement flashed across his face, then it was gone. "This hour is for hand-to-hand training, *not* magic."

Walking over, he held out his right palm. I grasped it with mine and he hauled me to my feet. Guilt racked through me, despite my small dose of pride that I'd managed to muster some power after that night in Aarine. "I'm sorry."

He quirked a smile at me. "Just don't blind me again, okay? And probably best you don't show Coen that little magic trick. He'll be pissed."

I let out a huff of a laugh. "Isn't he pissed off at me all the time anyway?"

Farrow shrugged, as if to say, *fair point.* "Still, no magic here. Just combat. Understand?" I nodded. I was in desperate need of a drink. Farrow walked over to the sparring pads. "Then let's get started."

By the time my hour was up, my knees were trembling, and I had drained a whole jug of cool water. My arms felt like lead as I set down my glass. The midmorning sun shone down on us, adding to the sheen of sweat that coated me. I was drenched. Farrow, curse him, looked like he had been out for a pleasant jog and was barely winded. My lungs, on the other hand, felt like they were on fire. We had gone through basic punching drills and footwork, reinforcing the bare basics I had learnt in Aarine. I would wake up tomorrow morning with sore muscles that I didn't even know I possessed.

That spark of light I had used was gone now, huddled back in my chest, spent. It had taken all my mental strength just to gather up that one small dose of it, and I inwardly cringed about trying to harness more of it.

I prayed the Night Pegasus would visit me tonight and give me some guidance in whatever way he could. I leant into my longing to see him, as it was better than feeling the loneliness and grief that ravaged me instead.

"Same time tomorrow," said Farrow, draping his vest over his arm and turning to face me.

I nodded in agreement, straightening as Coen appeared in the archway we had come through earlier. His gaze raked over my sweat-soaked body and rumpled hair, and I didn't balk from him. I simply lifted my chin in a silent challenge. He stepped out into the sun, almost having to duck under the archway, the sun bleaching his dark blond hair.

He finally tore his gaze from me to look at Farrow. "Well?"

"She did fine. I'd put her on a level with our newer recruits for hand-to-hand combat least. The footwork needs sorting out, but we'll get there."

If Coen was surprised at that, he didn't show it. "Good. Time to take you back, winny. The guards will collect you later when Her Majesty is ready for you. I've had some books on our history taken to your room, for you to read in the meantime. Just standard issue books that all our recruits cover."

I dipped my chin and headed out of the courtyard. "Thank you."

His full lips quirked into a half-smile, the first one he'd ever given me. I blinked in surprise, as those handsome features softened just a fraction. He overtook me easily, his long stride eating up the ground, Farrow falling into place behind us again. The short walk back to my quarters was silence-filled, rippling tension suspended between the Commander and me. This morning was the most mannerly he had ever been with me, probably because he was under orders from Jaryn to not kill me.

If he did shove that beautiful, curved blade that hung from his hip between my ribs, he would be put under military trial for murdering a fellow soldier now, not just some last of the line Kivisto.

He reached for a pocket in his vest, brought out a long iron key and unlocked my door. I blanched. He had a *key* to my room. I just thought it was the guards who had access. Certainly not him. He must have sensed my worry, as he looked across at me as he swung the door open wide. "Don't worry, winny. I won't be one of those people that kills you in your sleep, despite knowing what your last name is."

Fear was a heavy knot in my stomach. I stalked into my room and slammed the door in his face.

I had shoved my dresser and the matching chair for it against my door that night, content that if Coen did try and murder me in my sleep, then the furniture would slow him down, and I could try and find something to defend myself with. A heavy brass candlestick would be my first choice, and jagged pieces of terracotta from a pot I'd smashed would be next. I discreetly hid the pieces under my mattress, the edges sharp enough to draw blood. A long, thin sliver of pottery I had tucked into the inner pocket of my vest, just in case.

My mind was foggy from the reading I had done over the afternoon, although one chapter had stood out to me. It categorized some of Il-rair's older enemies, and my gaze had lingered on one small paragraph.

Mark my words, the Petish on the back of Trinitors were the fiercest fighters this scholar has ever researched. The few who encountered them rarely lived to tell the tale, hence, so little information is recorded here. Blood Riders make for a formidable enemy. Their military prowess on the back of a winged horse is unmatched.

And yet, the Trinitors were no more, and Petowin had fallen into ruin, leaving Ilrair to rise as conqueror. A small part of me couldn't let go of the notion, though, that my ancestors had formed an alliance with the greatest magical creatures to have ever existed.

My discussions with Amadea beside the pool had taken up most of my evening. We shared a platter of seeded bread, cheese, and balsamic vinegar oil as we talked about our previous homes. Our feet dipped into the luscious warm water. I'd been tempted to plunge my whole body in, my body aching from the training, but I still didn't trust Amadea, not quite yet.

Although I could feel my guard dropping slightly as she told me of her younger sisters and cousins who remained on Omivarra, her favorite cascade pools to visit, and how she had hand raised a rainforest toucan once.

In turn, I had gone over my engagement to Narve and my capture by the Bromtide Platoon. I wondered what the Heir Lord of Moray would be planning and what side of the war he would bend his knee to.

Having changed into my sleeping clothes, I sat on the bed ... waiting. The waning moon arose, but he did not come.

He didn't visit the next night or the night after that. My training with Farrow and talks with Amadea filled my days ... but my nights ... that loneliness in me grew, nullifying my hope in me. I tried to bolster myself at each dusk, telling myself that I didn't need him, that I could survive this. Yet as each night passed alone, my resolve began to waver.

I craved to be held, taking my time in the bath of an evening just to feel some sense of warmth over my body.

I ached for connection, and although my alliance with Amadea looked promising, I needed more, both my mind and my body needed more. I'd had a few dalliances with the odd male at the castle in Aarine, but they had always been rushed and ended with me leaving unfulfilled and feeling more isolated than before the encounters even took place.

Three more nights passed and still, he did not visit.

CHAPTER
SEVENTEEN

ORRIN

When Tellervo's power began to wane, the further I galloped south, Ilmari whispered into his place. The air spirit admitted she felt strange to use a Mountain Horse as her scion, having used Pegasi since the curse, yet she would not fail in her promise to my father. The two spirits would watch over me as I hurtled closer to the moorlands.

Harracombe was a snow-covered, rolling expanse of land in the distance. It was ancient, that place, untouched by man. It felt wilder than even Glentay. The wind tossed heather and irregular tors of gray, ice-cracked rock rose above the horizon, as the need to get south barreled through my core.

There was a moor spirit, Ilmari told me. It resided within the rock spires and cared little for the lone travelers that passed through the land. It did, however, raise its otherworldly head in interest as it detected Ilmari dancing over the snow-topped bracken as I paused on its northerly fringes.

The spirits acknowledged one another, yet let each other be. Although conflict was rare between them, Ilmari was not taking any chances. Battles would see territories and landscapes torn apart. There was little in the way of hierarchy between the custodians of the land, yet Ilmari was seen as a queen of sorts. She could not be harmed. Not in ways the forests could be torn up, or rivers dammed. You couldn't grasp air; you couldn't control it. She was untouchable, yet she could devastate in turn. A mighty hurricane or a raging tornado, Ilmari could tear a vista apart.

Yet her power and that of her fellow spirits was waning. Only a few humans left little offerings now, only a few respected the terrain and sky in which the spirits resided and called home. The more power the wild ward rendered and wielded, the weaker the spirits became.

The Koskivarri.

It all depended on her.

I could gallop no further today. Mud and slush lay splattered against my body, and even with the power now thrumming through my blood, I could only push it so far. My veins snaked and span across my heaving pelt as I gulped down breath after breath of cold midnight air.

Sheltering under a towering rock spire on the very edge of Glentay, I sank to my knees on the small, dry patch of dead grass I had found. Snow clouds tumbled and raced across the sky above, casting the moorland ahead into an endless gloom.

I assumed it would be several days to get to the next human dwelling, where Ebrel was rumored to be held. Slowly, my breath began to ease, and my quivering lessened until I finally relaxed against the frigid ground beneath my limbs and stomach.

Images of my father in his last final moments haunted me. He had looked like some form of god, arching through the air on invisible wings, blond mane billowing over his neck. I had never felt so much pride as I had in that moment. That had been my father. My loss yawned in my soul like a shifting void, one that I teetered on the very edge of. I would never get to know him and learn all his life's lessons. Now he was just fleeting images that the forest brushed against my mind when I had raced past.

As my eyes began to stutter and close, relieved at a moment's rest, I jerked awake.

Ilmari and I were alert in an instant, our gaze cast skyward toward the roiling snow clouds.

"Pegasus. A lone one," she murmured.

I lurched to my feet, exhausted. My skin tingled with apprehension as I sensed, rather than saw, what was tearing through the low-lying cloud. Then I scented her.

A newly mature Pegasus mare, a mother and a leader, sweat-soaked yet determined to reach us.

The blood bay Pegasus dropped like a stone from the cloud cover and cut across the night sky toward the rock spire. Her breath was heaving, her wings beating the air with all her remaining strength.

She circled above us and landed heavily on the snow. Her knees quaking, her muzzle grazed the ground as she struggled to remain upright. I approached her with severe caution, yet I recognized her with her pelt the color of dried blood and her black wings. She had been at the encampment, herding the young ones away, working with my father to save them from the huge wagon.

Hesitantly, I whickered.

Her head hung low, yet she gazed up at me with tawny-colored eyes. The muscles in her wing joints twitched with exhaustion as her massive black wings draped across the snow.

"Orrin?" she panted.

"Yes?" I replied, stepping closer with concern. *"Who are you? Why have you come here?"*

"My name is Murrkill." The mare's legs quaked where she stood. *"Nijinxes are coming. They are roosted on the northern fringes of Glentay, in a disused mine in Bronzo's foothills."*

I froze at her words. Ilmari curled inward in fear.

"I came to warn you, to fight with you. We owe Gracien everything, and with his passing, that debt falls to you."

"What of your foal?"

"She is safe with my herd. My second and Carter, your half brother, are caring for her in my absence."

I backed up a step. I had a half brother? Had his mother abandoned him as she did with me? Shaking my head, I focused on the Pegasus. I would worry about my one remaining family member later. *"Come, shelter here; you need to rest."*

Shivering with every step, her energy utterly consumed by the speed at which she flew, Murrkill walked over to the shelter and lay down in the darkness.

"One of the Nijinxes had a rider, an unfathomable thought. He was armed to the teeth, just like his mount." Murrkill took a shuddering breath. *"It's the wild ward, isn't it?*

I stood over her, my skin quivering once more. I knew exactly who that rider was and what he could do. *"Yes."*

The Pegasus mare shuddered. *"Myself and all the Pegasi can feel her pull on us, the temptation. Some have already fallen to her command, like Spearian and his band. Yet others, like my herd, remain steadfast. I will not kneel before her. She is not my Queen."* Murrkill scented the air, and her feathers bristled. *"The air spirit is here. I can feel her against my skin. She is who I bow to, not some invading witch. We need—"*

Ilmari brushed her invisible fingers over the mare's feather, and Murrkill sighed in comfort. Inwardly, I frowned. Ilmari had never extended that comfort to Ebrel.

"You need to rest; we'll travel at dawn," I said gently. *"I seek a branded loner. Spearian nearly killed her. She saved my life and I want*

to get her back. There's a human woman also that could free us of the wild ward. I hope to bring them back north together."

But it wouldn't just be the wild ward we were fighting. Now there would be Nijinxes under her control. Elite killing machines that had already devastated an entire country with their hunger. A massacre of that scale had not occurred since Petowin, but I guessed that the wild ward had been readying her strength, preparing the Nijinxes for the next battle against us and the spirits themselves.

Murrkill gazed up at me, her tawny eyes filled with anger. *"They say that when Colbass, King of the Trinitors, was cleaved into three, a fragment of him, the most dangerous portion, was siphoned off by the mage that doled out the curse. The magic was locked away, deep down within the earth. That slice of soul was left to merge and form into another, a fourth creature."*

"The Nijinxes," I breathed.

"My granddam, Row, was from Petowin. She was there that day when Nijinxes broke free from the earth and began to raid the villages. Row said that the explosion had been caused by a burst of brindled light. Wild ward magic. How she knew where to find the swarms, or even how to control them, I have no idea."

Neither did Ilmari it seemed. I felt the air spirit curl inward once more and glance to the dark skies around her.

The Nijinxes were free of their subterranean prison. Petowin had already felt their wrath, and now we were next.

CHAPTER
EIGHTEEN

ASHER

E very morning at dawn, Pherox and I trained together, hunting little creatures, and trying out more and more daring flight maneuvers. By the end of our fifth day together, I could leap upon him from a run, reload and fire my crossbow, and jump down from his back as he swept in low over the ground but didn't land.

The heady feeling of flying was a rush that I clung to with all my power. It gave me a sense of self beyond the wild ward magic that pulsed in my body. At night, I slept but I did not dream. There was just darkness, deep, unending archaic darkness. I ignored the wild ward's advances toward me. I knew she wanted me, had sensed her gazing at me across her cave, and her touches were becoming more daring. Only last night, she had run her hands over my shoulders and chest, lingering there, and it would have taken one word from me, and she would have been on her back, baring herself. Yet I had refused her, taking to my bedroll, entwining myself with the shadows instead, welcoming them.

On our sixth morning of training, Pherox flew west, past the mine where the kin swarm was roosting, leaving Bronzo's foothills altogether. I didn't ask where we were traveling, or why. I was just content to feel the biting cold on my face. My reindeer hide and leathers keeping the rest of me warm.

The mountain plains and forest swept beneath us, and finally, Pherox began to descend. This was the furthest I had ever been away from the wild ward, and the magic between was pulled taut, yet it did not bend or break.

The Nijinx's wings plumed snow all around us as he deftly landed amongst craggy granite cliffs.

"Why are we here?" I asked, as I swung a leg over his neck and dismounted, taking in the eerily quiet valley. The cliff faces loomed darkly on either side of us, capped with fog.

Still, the male did not speak. He simply walked forward, the snow barely hindering him, toward the far end of the tight valley.

Frowning, I followed the path that he had tracked, inwardly cursing that I hadn't brought my snowshoes. Pherox halted and turned that wise yet fearsome head to face me, fangs glinting. *"Do you remember, hunter?"*

I stepped around him, the snow coming up to my knees, then froze entirely and not from the cold. Two makeshift wooden crosses, the thin planks lashed together with strips of leather, protruded at uneven angles from the snow.

My ears started to ring and that magical anchor in my chest pulled hard, fighting to cleave its way deeper. I could barely feel the wild ward at the other end of it. I inhaled sharply and instantly felt nauseous.

"I made those crosses."

Why? Why had I made them?

Panic leached over my body, as my memory and that darkness battled to resurface. Only fleeting images broke through. That same singed hand and a glowing white feather. But there was more. I knew there was more, shoved under layers and layers of brindled, abhorrent magic.

"Do. You. Remember?" Pherox snarled in my head.

"I can't," I gasped, my hands clenching and unclenching in desperation. What had she done? What had that witch *done* to me?

Pherox gnashed his fangs. *"You must."*

I closed my eyes and ground down on those faint images. The faces of two older men flashed behind my eyes and I flinched. Two faces for the two crosses before me.

"It's all there, huntsman. You just have to reach for it. Want it."

"How did you know this was here?" I croaked, feeling chilled to my bones. I reached out with a mittened hand and braced it against his muscle-covered shoulder.

"I can smell you all over this valley, can still smell the pyre you had built to burn them."

Not graves, but ... memorials. For two men who had meant something to me. My vision blurred as the magic in me yanked downward, ordering me back.

"Fight it, huntsman, as we all do. Fight it, for there will come a time when that witch is dead, and we will be free again."

CHAPTER NINETEEN

DESTRY

My training with Farrow progressed to basic footwork twinned with preliminary attacking and blocking with daggers. He was like a ray of sunshine compared to Coen's roiling storm cloud; I wondered if the Bromtide Platoon had been named after the Commander's personality. He always escorted me to the courtyard and back, and we barely spoke a word to one another, but the air between us felt taut whenever we walked side by side, and I wondered if it was because he was plotting my demise, or something else.

I had been in an Orman for just over a week, and I had not progressed at all with my magic. Without the Night Pegasus to guide me, and Amadea having no clue how my light worked, I was literally left in the dark. As each fruitless dawn arose, I felt a small piece of me crumble, just like the ancient walls of this limestone castle. I desperately wanted to talk to Damara, to hug her, to beg her for her counsel. *What should I do?*

On the tenth morning of my training, my body aching from the days before, I walked over to the iron table where the wooden daggers lay, only to have a prickling sensation crawl down my back. My shoulders tensed, and I turned to where Farrow stood. Coen was still beside him, taking off his rider's vest. He must have caught my wide-eyed stare as the Commander looked at me and smirked. *Shit.* It wouldn't just be Farrow training me today.

Coen rolled up his shirt sleeves and stood facing me, feet spread apart in a fighting stance that his warrior's body seemed to settle into on instinct. My back went ramrod straight as I snatched a dagger off the table and stalked to where they stood.

Farrow glanced warily between us. "Commander, I don't think—"

Coen wholly ignored him. "Time to see what you've learned so far, winny."

"It's been ten days," I countered, clutching my useless wooden dagger like it was a life raft.

Those piercing green eyes didn't leave mine. "So, you have ten days' worth of training to show me. It won't be Farrow you'll be fighting on the battlefield, will it? It will do you good to go against different opponents."

He walked into the middle of the courtyard, next to the trickling fountain and lifted his right hand. Slowly, he curled his pointer finger at me. "Come play, *winny.*"

Rage flared in my veins, just like it had on that first day with Farrow. Coen seemed to register something on my face as he braced himself, anchoring his feet into the flagstones. "War doesn't wait for you, winny. Let's see what you can do with that dagger."

The sun glanced off his broad shoulders, and he gave me a mocking, taunting grin. I saw red, ignoring how his smile made my body flush. Screw him, this man who had done nothing but insult me since I had met him. My body launched forward, and I'm sure I saw Farrow flinch at my form, or lack of it. But I didn't care; if this was my one chance to pummel Coen, I'd take it.

I flipped the dagger in my hand and broke into a run. I made to stab toward the right side of his abdomen but feinted just as he swept down to block it, sending my left fist into his side instead. Farrow's training settled over me. *Weaponize your rage.* My heart pounded in my chest as my fist brushed the soft cotton of Coen's shirt, but then his tanned fingers were there, grabbing my offending hand. He twirled me as if this was some lethal, chaotic dance, and my boots spun on the limestone.

Using all my upper body strength, I wrenched our twinned hands down just as my knee rose to his groin. His low laugh skittered over my bones as he barely sidestepped in time, hauling me forward and nearly yanking me off my feet altogether. He let me go, sending me hurling into the fountain's stone lip. My left arm scraped against it, and I hissed, swiping with the wooden dagger as he dodged to my right side. Of course, I missed his iron-strong thigh.

Their fighting styles were so different. Farrow was graceful and a touch slower than his Commander. Whereas Coen ... Coen was just brutal, deadly efficiency. He circled me, pacing around to my unprotected back. I staggered to my feet, panting, and pushed off the pool's stone edge. I charged at him, again and again, but he blocked me at every turn, his body a solid wall of muscle that countered every rage-filled maneuver I hurled at him.

My light flickered over my heart, my lungs, but I leashed it, terrified of revealing it here, as much as I wanted to hurl it into that aggravatingly handsome face. Coen must have sensed my inner turmoil as he went from blocking to attacking.

He moved to the offensive so quickly, I barely had time to dodge the fists he threw my way, yet even then, I knew he wasn't using his whole strength behind them. *Fuck*, if this was just a fraction of his hitting power, then ... I launched myself backward, spinning and blocking with every frantic beat of my heart. Coen kept coming at me, his face set with steely determination. It wasn't until the solid stone of a courtyard archway slammed into my back that I realized he had been herding to this exact spot.

My rage flared and I went to shove myself off the stone, but then he was suddenly *there*, his toned forearm jutting upward to ram my chest back into the stone. His left hand snaked out to where I held the dagger, pinning it to my hip. *Prick.*

He pressed closer, our bodies nearly flush and his heat swept over me, my panting breath filling the small space between us. Coen was hardly winded. That cutting green gaze met mine, then his eyes flared wide with surprise as my free left hand jabbed the thin, cutting sliver of terracotta against his unprotected lower ribs.

Those full lips of his parted in shock as something akin to delight swept over his face. I'd pushed the sliver in just hard enough to nick his skin, but his upper abdominal muscles felt like solid rock beneath it.

My heart pounded, loud enough for us to both hear it, the adrenaline leaving a heady feeling in its wake. Yes, I probably would be dead if that had been a real fight, but for this, it was worth it. The muscles of his thighs shifted against mine, and my own eyes widened at the electric current that caressed my skin. I didn't realize just how much taller he was. He swallowed, the muscle in his jaw ticked, and the pressure of his forearm against my collarbone softened. His gaze dipped from my eyes to my mouth.

We both tensed, however, as slow, leisurely clapping sounded to my left.

My bones felt brittle as Coen instantly stepped away from me and bowed. Cold air brushed against me, and I fought my nausea as I bowed too.

Jaryn stepped away from where he had been leaning against a sun-drenched archway and strolled over to where we stood, hands gracefully tucked into his vest pockets. How much of my training had he seen? Quickly, my hands partially hidden just behind me, I deftly prodded the slice of pottery up my shirt sleeve. I hadn't seen Jaryn since my vow and was glad for every day that had passed without being in his presence. Even just the sight of him made my knees start to quake.

I locked my spine as I straightened from my bow, not even daring to look across at Coen. Farrow remained by the table, watching the three of us intently.

"I'm glad to see you're taking her training so seriously, Commander." Jaryn glanced between us, his tone cold.

I barely held back my flinch in time. Jaryn didn't wear his crown today, just his usual boots, breeches, and pristine cream shirt, but wrapped around his torso was an exquisite navy and gold silk half cloak. Amadea's family colors, I realized. His gaze lingered on me, and I looked down at the cracked and sun-bleached flagstones, my mouth paper dry. My light that had sputtered to life during my dual with Coen, banked to darkness.

I sensed Coen straighten. He crossed his arms over his chest and looked over at me. My scalp prickled under his gaze, and I looked up at him. I couldn't even begin to understand the expression on his face, but the delight that had been there a moment ago had utterly vanished.

"You have to take her north, my king. Her power is useless here." His eyes burned with loathing then, as he looked me over from head to toe. "Just like the rest of her."

I recoiled like he'd struck me, and I couldn't hide the hurt on my face. He hadn't even seen my powers, and I could have easily stabbed him just then. Had Amadea betrayed the fact that I had barely any control over directing my light and how much I could muster? I kept my hands clasped behind my back to hide their shaking, and my jaw ached as I clenched my teeth together. I had been foolish to hope that he could see something else in me other than a supposed murderer's daughter.

Yet being taken back north would increase any power that I had and bring me closer to the Night Pegasus. I blinked, my mind whirling. Did Coen really mean that insult? The look on his face gave me little confidence.

Jaryn stepped closer, and I instantly backed up from the pair of them. The King's lips set into a thin, grim line. "I'll be the one to determine whether or not she is ready, Coen."

I openly glared at Jaryn. "The Night Pegasus does not fly this far south. He's at his full strength in the north, and so am I. The wise thing to do is to take me back to the barracks at Saltfen. You're wasting time by keeping me here."

"You seem to forget who gives the orders around here, soldier," said Jaryn, his features darkening. "You're staying in my palace until I say otherwise."

No. I was going to break under the relentless loneliness that crushed me with each passing day. The rage that I felt from day to day was the only emotion I could cling to. And maybe ... maybe that was Jaryn's plan all along. Imprison me here until I was just a broken, spiritless doll under his crushing palm. No. No. No. *No.*

I bared my teeth at the King, letting him see the wildness in my blood, the untamed feral creature I really was. One quick flick of my wrist would see that piece of terracotta embedded in the King's throat.

Jaryn glowered at me, his fists clenching. "Take her back to her room. She isn't to see Amadea tonight."

You fucking snake, taking away the one social interaction I had started looking forward to.

Coen bowed again. "As you wish, Your Majesty."

I practically thrummed with hate, and I snatched my arm away from Coen as he slowly reached out to clasp my elbow. "Don't you dare touch me."

Turning on my heel, I strode from the pair of them, Jaryn hissing at my impunity as I turned my back on him. Farrow hastily fell into place behind me as I stalked past him to my room. Coen walked steadily behind us. I wholly ignored the Commander as he overtook me, unlocked my door, and gently pushed it aside.

His eyes were shadowed as I walked past him into my room. I went to slam the door again, but then his boot was there, jamming it to a stop. My gaze wrenched from his foot to his face and the words that began to form on his lips.

But then he shook his head, and whatever he was about to say died in his chest. He threw me one last worried glance, then softly closed the door behind me. The clank of the lock echoed in my ears.

I breathed deeply through my nose, my body quaking, and went to sit on the edge of the bed. My palms were clammy as I placed my forehead into them, and I gazed down at the pale tiled floor.

The midmorning sun danced through the eastern-facing window, streaming beams of light across the dresser and the headboard.

Something flashed sage green and white on my right.

I blinked, slowly lifting my head to stare and gape. A small teardrop-shaped piece of lambent stone, a loop of waxed thread strung through it, hung from a carved wooden post on the headboard.

I picked it up delicately, worried it would vanish into thin air if I handled it too roughly. My fingers tingled at the contact with the stone, a sensation that traveled all the way up my arm. It was a small, polished fragment, barely a quarter of the size of the one I had taken from Narve in Aarine, but I could still feel it amplifying what light I had in my body.

With great care, I draped the thread over my head and around my neck, so the lambent stone lay tucked under my uniform, beneath my collarbone. It flared against my skin, sending a ripple of power down my torso. *Sweet heaven*, Amadea had done it. She must have snuck it in here whilst Jaryn had been in the courtyard. I sent a prayer out to her and clasped a hand over my chest, right over that flicker of power.

"Thank you," I whispered to her, to the spirits. My light roiled in my chest, curling over and over itself. Then I sent up another prayer. *Don't let me be alone tonight.*

I lay face down on the mattress, the thin sheets wrung around my body as I tried and failed to find sleep. My arms were tucked protectively around my head, and I failed to get a handle on my breathing. The lambent stone was a delicate weight against the hollow of my throat. Hope was a fragile entity I clung to.

The candle on the dressing table guttered, then winked out.

I stiffened, blinking, my eyes adjusting to the hushed darkness.

That guttural voice, one I dreamed of hearing again, whispered against my upturned ear. "You found a lambent stone in this pretty prison; what a clever creature you are."

Stronger, his voice was so much stronger now, more corporeal. Stunned, I half-turned onto my side and looked up. Banners of white and sage green light flickered across the room, matching the iridescence that sparked in the lambent stone. My own light danced across my vision to mirror his, barely sparks compared to what it had been, but it was there.

Cautiously, afraid this was all just some desperate dream, I raised my right hand, expecting my fingers to trail through and scintillate his light, but they didn't. The striations pulsed against my touch, supple and unyielding.

His voice breathed down my bare neck and I trembled. "Your loneliness brands me, wild one."

A filament of glowing silver traced a sensual path down my bare, uplifted arm, then it curled over my shoulder, my neck. His touch, I had never felt anything like it, never imagined I *would* feel anything like it. The crushing solitude in my soul lifted a fraction. I couldn't remember the last time anyone had touched me with kindness.

I propped myself up to turn onto my side, facing the edge of the bed. His light lowered, quivering, hesitating over me. Then it spiraled gently beside the bed, molding around the broad, sculpted shape of a man. The strong planes of his face warring between shadow and sage green light. I wondered how many mortals had seen this version of him.

His eyes, amber rimmed with the darkest ochre, met mine. I could barely move, barely breathe, as he knelt before the bed and reached forward, interlacing his left hand with mine. With the other, he reached up and swept a tendril of hair off my face. His touch was cool, like a fine mist, nothing like the heat of Coen that had swept over me earlier. Yet the gesture, the small act of kindness ... tears I'd fought all day to contain, spilled over.

He gently swept them away with a brush of his fingers. "What is it you need, my darling light?"

I ran a thumb over his knuckles, amazed at how ... human he felt. Yet the power that pulsed from him, the otherworldliness of it all, I knew he was anything but mortal. "I need to not be alone."

His right hand swept down my bare arm, and I felt that power of his press in closer around me, caressing my every sense. I sucked down a breath in response, the lambent stone flaring.

He shifted into a crouch so that his face was just above mine. His right hand brushed back up my arm to cup my face, my skin stippling in his wake. "Shall we torch this loneliness together?"

My heart rate racketed, and I gazed up at those golden eyes. "How?"

"Can I hold you?" his gravelly voice whispered over the shell of my ear, and I swallowed.

"Yes," I breathed, and he gently released his hand from mine. His body swirled into a cloud of darkness and light, and then a solid weight shifted on the mattress behind me. The exposed skin of my arms and lower legs prickled against the charged air as he tenderly nestled his body behind mine. A strong, shadowed arm looped around my waist to clasp my hand again, while his other forearm tucked under the small open space between my neck and the pillow.

A small sigh escaped my lips as his fingers traced the line of my throat and collarbone. His chest did not rise and fall behind me, and no heartbeat pulsed, but tonight he was a man, and the safety and security I felt in his arms in that moment had me tipping my head back to rest it on his muscled shoulder. Every worry, every anxious thought in my mind, lifted for a moment, and I reveled in that sense of relief. I knew it wouldn't last forever, that his actions tonight would drain him, even with the lambent stone, but I cherished every second of it.

"If you find a mortal man worthy of loving you, then you won't need me for this anymore," he murmured onto my skin. His arms tightened around me, and my body sang with the sensation of it. "But until that day comes, I don't share what is mine." He pressed a tender kiss onto the soft skin below my ear. "Sleep, my darling light, for you are safe tonight."

CHAPTER TWENTY

ASHER

It was the first clear night in two weeks, and the Night Pegasus raced across the massive expanse of star-speckled heavens. His fire feathers scorched the air, turning it green, purple, and pink with every brush of his blackened pinions. The light danced, arcing and swirling in iridescent bands that contorted above our heads.

The kin swarm of forty Nijinxes flew not as one large group but with a half-mile spread between each beast. Twenty females flew at a higher altitude, whilst the accompanying twenty males flew below them, their bulk and muscle-tacked bodies preventing them from climbing as high as their mates.

Vesperum led the way. Her sleek body was a black canvas up above, as the fire feathers glimmered across her flesh, turning her into a vision of emerald, then a creature of amethyst. She was engineered for the night, her leathery wings cutting apart the frigid air like a honed blade.

A series of soft clicks rang out from above.

Pherox clicked in return, his chest rumbling with the sound that carried through my body. Despite the extra weight of me and all my weapons, he did not falter or slow in his flying. Steadily, we lowered in altitude and continued south.

We had left the disused mine near Bronzo at dusk. The wild ward had promised to meet us at our destination and had bid us farewell. Yet none of us escaped the cold, magic-riddled talons she had caressed down our minds. We had better meet her there, or we'd be slaughtered. The entire kin swarm and I had flinched, even Pherox. Yet the huge male had snarled at the threat, tucking Vesperum closer to him.

Even now, as we flew through the icy sky, I could sense him keeping a close watch on his beautiful mate high above us. I placed a mittened hand on his muscled neck and he clicked softly in response. Where would I be if I had not met this creature who was crafted for death by sharpened talons? The wild ward may have ripped my very self away from me, my very soul, but I had been gifted with ... an alliance. A partnership even. Pherox knew the wild ward kept me under a tighter grasp than she did with the Njinxes, and we had been taking off for longer and longer flights. Yet we had not returned to the valley that was coated in the scent of death and fire.

The faces of those two men haunted my every waking moment. Even my darkness-filled sleep had rippled around those two men and the crosses I had built to memorialize them. I knew those memories still existed somewhere beneath her magic. I just had no idea how to cleave through it and touch them.

Vesperum gave a short, trilling whistle, and the swarm banked as one. We spread out even further, as far as their clicks and whistles could travel across the night air. Turning once more, we descended upon the northernmost fringes of Ilrair, where the southern King's lands brushed up against the ancient and rugged moorlands.

I huddled down against Pherox's back, my core tightening in anticipation. I loved this part. Pherox was the first to dive, a song of clicks and whistles streaming past me on the frigid wind. The land below bounced back to him, and he dived fast, wings tucked in tight. I hunkered over him, adrenaline bursting in my veins as the air ravaged us.

High above, the Night Pegasus convulsed as if trying to warn the creatures below who descended upon them. I spotted it then, the huge cavern carved deep into the earth. Vesperum and the kin swarm were an undulating shadow at our backs.

Pherox swept down to the land, his wings flaring wide at the last possible moment, the air turning even colder as we plunged into the cave's entrance. Darkness consumed us, and the male's clicks echoed off the solid rock walls we flew through. We had entered another abandoned mine. The sound of leathery wings and whistles bounced all around us, the din growing louder as we made the final turns into the main excavation cave. The magic in my blood morphed my eyes to widen, to see as the Nijinxes do, painting the world in silvery gray shadows.

The squeals, clicks, and whistles of forty Nijinxes grew louder and louder. As their Queen rounded the final corner, the swarm erupted into a cacophony of sound to welcome her to her new home. Wings flapping with excitement, the creatures clung deftly to the slick rock of the mine, their eyeless heads tracking every move of their Queen.

Vesperum landed first on a central, rearing piece of rock, her razor-sharp talons finding easy purchase on the chiseled granite. Pherox was beside her in an instant, yet I remained on the male's back. He breathed steadily beneath me, the sweat on his flanks and shoulders already drying in the damp and cool air of the mine. The smell of musk and acidity filled my nose, but the scent of the Nijinxes no longer bothered me. If anything, I smelled more and more like them with every passing day, and I was content with that.

Pherox's fangs flashed as I saw what he and Vesperum stared at, at the far end of the landing platform. A column of brindled stone contorted upward, nearly brushing the roof of the cave.

Vesperum hissed at it, as did the kin swarm in turn. Power, raw and undiluted, pulsed from the monolith until it coated my tongue and teeth. I snarled and dismounted, stepping around Pherox's leathery wing.

The stone seemed to know it was being observed as a low rumble rolled through the cave. I stepped toward it, a dagger in my hand. Pherox's click of warning brushed the nape of my neck. The stone rumbled again, sending tiny specks of granite skittering past my worn boots.

"She's coming," whispered Vesperum.

I glanced at the Nijinx Queen, then back at the monolith. *This* was how the wild ward traveled? The column was not of the same stone as the cave, like it had been placed here specifically for the wild ward's purposes. It felt abhorrent, just like the magic she wielded. The golden veining that ran through it started to glow. I crouched, flipping the blade in my hand.

The Nijinxes shrieked then as the soft glow flared brightly until it was nearly white. I threw up my arm to shield my eyes, unable to adjust quickly enough to the sudden source of light that blasted through the cave.

A clawed hand gripped my soul and squeezed. Snarling, I sheathed my dagger and backed away until Pherox's body heat warmed me. Blinking, the glow burned onto my retinas. I couldn't help the feeling of loathing sweep over me as the wild ward stepped away from her monolith and onto the stone parapet. Her gaze fixed on me, her red lips sneering in distaste as if she had known I could have used the dagger on her. Not *could* have but would have.

The lone woman was surrounded by the most vicious predators the Boreals had ever seen, myself included, yet she didn't even flinch. She merely lifted her chin and graced us all with a slow, cunning smile. "Welcome to Ilrair, Vesperum kin swarm."

With Pherox and Vesperum safely ensconced within the main cavern, I strode toward my new accommodation. The old miners' quarters were dusty, rickety, and smelt of mold. Water trickled down the walls, and it had ridiculously low ceilings, yet it held enough space for my bedroll, pack and weapons.

I sat heavily upon my bed, my body still singing from the flight and from the bloodlust of having my dagger in my hand. Flexing and curling my fists, I tried to cool that scorching fire in my blood, the need to put the wild ward down swiftly and brutally. I knew Pherox felt the same.

I looked more closely at my weather-worn hands. They were flecked with my own blood from where my nails had cut in and smeared with Pherox's sweat. If I looked closely enough, the specks of blood created whorls and galaxies across my skin, another world where the stars shone maroon and promised only death.

When the wild ward's voice flickered in my veins, I knew she spoke solely to me. I tensed.

"These men you keep seeing, they are nothing to you."

Her magic pulsed, reaffirming her words. I could feel my soul swiping and clawing back at her. My spine stiffened at the memories and some internal defense finally snapped. It was like a floodgate had opened. Memories, from old to new, rushed through my mind, and the wild ward hissed at the onslaught of emotion.

"Aye, Edgar, the boy can ride. Did you see that pony he sat on? Bucked with all his worth but the boy didn't budge."

"He clearly inherited your riding skills, Oban."

They kept coming.

"This time next week, you'll be a Pegasus hunter, and there will not be a father prouder than me, your uncle too."

I could feel myself choking.

"Asher! Asher! Stop them! Son!" My father's screams harried me, turning my blood to ice.

A palomino Pegasus, blood upon the snow, eyes the color swirling amber, a deafening roar. Splintered and burnt wood, an equine body dead upon the snow.

I could feel the wild ward hauling her power into her grip on me, trying to stem the flood. My soul snapped at the fluttering tendrils, snarling in reproach to her touch as I clung fiercely to those memories.

My father.

My father.

The wild ward was reaching, cleaving deeper than before to the fighting core of my very self. I hissed, frozen where I sat, as her magical hands curled around it, and finger by finger, she *crushed*. Each memory winked out like the throes of a dying star until all that remained was unending blackness. No light could survive that darkness, it would be hunted down and devoured. I drifted within it until the wild ward's magic latched onto my mind, anchoring it one last time to her power with ropes cored with steel.

CHAPTER
TWENTY-ONE

ORRIN

W hat was once a small human settlement consisting of farm-houses and a tiny tavern, had grown significantly into an Il-rair cavalry outpost. Thick, wooden palisades ringed the now bustling town, and besides the rows of huge canvas tents were simple wooden command buildings. A watch tower was under construction at the northernmost edge, beside granite foundations of a fortress wall. Soldiers alternated their patrols, both on foot and in the air on the backs of their southern Pegasi.

Murrkill had rumbled deep in her chest at the sight of the finely built creatures, their pelts gleaming, and bodies well fed with grain and hay. Her nostrils had flared, and so had mine at the scent of them. The Trinitor curse had been executed from within the palace of Ilirair, and every Trinitor within the country had felt its wrath the hardest. These southern-winged creatures were amenable, tame, compared to their ruthless northern relatives, where the curse had to fight harder to find purchase on the Trinitors it found.

The blood bay mare and I had moved across the moorlands slowly and at night, Murrkill keeping to the ground with me. Progress was painful as we stuck to the divots and channels that had been carved out over millennia across the land between the gorse and gray stone. Murrkill had shown me how to bite through the spikey, plentiful shrubs and thistles, making a meal of them, which meant we didn't have to keep digging for grass under the snow.

I sensed the moorland spirit watching us with silent curiosity as we crossed its ancient expanse. It rolled on and on, a never-ending ocean of hills and stone. After a week of cautious walking, we had breached the final flat-topped hill, hidden by the rocky outcrops, and stared down at Saltfen.

Ilrair flags snapped in the westerly wind that blew across the rugged winter land, and below it, smaller banners bearing a golden crown on a red background fluttered. I inhaled deeply yet caught no scent of Ebrel. But she had to be here.

Four days ago, we had come across a patch of blood-soaked snow, frozen against the ground. Ebrel's blood. But she was nowhere to be found. She had crashed into the earth a crumpled heap, but she hadn't died there. Hoof and boot prints had been dotted all around the spot with the faint scent of Ilrair men and steel still hanging in the air. They had taken her, and they must have moved her here.

To this wooden prison.

I bared my teeth, restraining the part of me that wanted to tear into the town, breaking men's backs until I found her.

"If fog settles over the town tonight, I'll fly around and see if I can scent her," assessed Murrkill, Ebrel's scent firmly embedded in her memory from the blood she had seen in the days before.

I nodded in agreement, knowing not to get in the way of the mare and a plan she had conjured. Murrkill was phenomenal, her body practically thrumming with strength and the song of the winter wind.

"You said she loved your older brother and was branded for it?" asked the mare as she rested a back hoof.

"Yes, and Spearian killed him."

"We won't condemn her to a fate ruled by man," Murrkill's voice promised violence.

I felt Ilmari brush along my neck, and I turned my head as if I would be able to see her fluttering there, but I could see only ice-covered heather.

"You never answered any of her prayers, Ilamri," I spoke softly to the air spirit.

The spirit of the air sighed, and it was a sound filled with unending sadness. *"There are some fates, King of the Forest, that not even I can tamper with."*

"But you couldn't offer her any source of comfort after the pain she endured?"

"There are spirits stronger than I am, Orrin, and even though Pegasi act as my scions, I cannot lay claim to all of them. I did not get to Ebrel in time before that stronger spirit claimed her for his own," Ilmari's voice was dangerously quiet.

I tilted my head. *"Who?"*

"I won't speak his name here." She quivered. *"His father watches over us during the day."*

I felt her unearthly gaze shift skyward to the winter sun that battled to break through the snow clouds. I snarled up at the heavens. *"Then he is the one that truly abandoned her."*

Ilamri quaked. *"Do not provoke him. He is trying to break the wild ward just as much as we are."*

A rumble echoed deep in my chest, and I turned to look back down at Saltfen. I had an inkling as to who Ilmari was talking about, and I cursed the fact that I didn't have wings, so that I could take to the skies and demand why the Night Pegaus had left Ebrel to fight all those terrors on her own.

It was the coldest, clearest night in days, but a thick fog had settled over the town, cloaking it from view as I stood atop a rocky plinth. Murrkill gave no word or warning beside me as she launched her body skyward, her huge wings beating the air until she gained enough altitude to bank east and head over the town.

We had waited until the last cavalry patrol had returned to their posts before trying to find Ebrel. The torchlight and flickering furnaces of the town were barely visible through the thick fog. I watched on, as Murrkill swept in low, her hooves curling the cloud below her. She began an analytical glide over the town, switching back and forth to ensure she didn't miss a spare inch of it.

She was halfway through when I felt the ground beneath my hooves shift. It was barely perceptible, but maybe it was Tellervo's magic in my veins that made me sensitive to it. Ice cracked over a frozen puddle on my right.

I sensed Ilmari a moment later, tearing across the moorland, kicking up heather and small boulders in her wake. Her fear drenched the night air. Turning in place, I looked skyward. What started as a faint green glow to the northern horizon, grew stronger until it bannered fully over my head, shrouding the stars from view. It jack-knifed and contorted, shifting to purple, then white, flickering in an elegant dance.

The Night Pegasus had come. I pinned my ears as I stared up at him, but it wasn't he that Ilmari was so scared of. A flutter of bright white spiraled toward the northwest, showing the threat that flew toward us.

I had never seen them before, but I knew in my bones what they were, knew that I should run and keep running until my heart nearly gave out. Murrkill was still flying over Saltfen, unaware of the Nijinxes that were heading our way in a military style formation.

Inhaling deeply, I unleashed a roar of warning that echoed over the frozen night air. Murrkill caught it instantly. She paused mid-flight, her great wings pummeled the fog as she twisted to look north.

The Nijinxes dropped lower in the sky, their formation shifting into that of an arrowhead. Murrkill raced for me, swifter than death itself, and I dived off the granite plinth, tucking myself beside it. The blood bay mare was beside me a heartbeat later, her nostrils flaring for breath.

In awe and horror, we watched on, as the swarm lifted upward, then dove straight for the moorland. The ground shook once more, violently this time, as the Nijinxes disappeared from view as if the earth had swallowed them whole.

From the settlement, a hollering whinny echoed into the cold air. *Ebrel.*

CHAPTER
TWENTY-TWO

DESTRY

I didn't speak a word to Coen the next morning, and he was inclined to return the favor. He merely watched me cautiously as I strode for the courtyard, my steps measured and steady, head held high. The lambent stone was a small reassuring weight against my chest, and I reveled in the sense of calm it gave me as if the Night Pegasus still held me, guided me.

He had spent the entire night holding me, and I had fallen into a deep, dreamless sleep. Part of me felt shame that I had needed him to feel myself again, but I tried to brush the thought aside. My entire world had been flipped on its head, and with each night of crushing loneliness, I could feel my sense of self slipping away as hard as I tried to claw and dig to hold it together. The woman who had been my mother in every way, bar blood, was gone. The only home I had ever known was stripped from me, and my true homeland sat in ruins under the talons and fangs of Nijinxes.

My rage was still there, but the Night Pegasus had tempered it, honed it, with his cool, mist-like touch. The reassurance that he was simply *there*, had cradled me in my darkest hours, was enough.

I plucked a longer wooden dagger from the table and twirled it. Both cavalrymen silently assessed me, Coen's face awash with a question I knew he wouldn't ask. I crossed my arms and turned to face them.

Farrow peeled away from the wall and walked over slowly. He paused in front of me, hands tucked into the pockets of his training leathers. "You seem different today. More grounded."

Coen's gaze lingered on my chest as if he could see through my shirt and to the lambent stone that hid beneath it.

"Let's just say I no longer want to be *useless.*" I threw a glare at Coen.

The Commander crossed his arms over his chest and said nothing. *Fine.* But his eyes met mine and fire burned in his gaze. My resolve held, and I stared right back, flipping the dagger in my hand. He was the first to break off, turning on his heel and disappearing into the castle. My shoulders sagged slightly, the air rushing from my lungs.

Farrow smirked. "Well, let's get to your training then, shall we? Remind me not to cross ... what did you say your surname was again?"

I tensed and quirked a brow. "I thought you knew my surname?"

The Sergeant shrugged and plucked the wooden dagger from my hand, replacing it with a wooden short sword. "Petish surnames are confusing as hell, no offense."

I offered him a small smile. Really, besides Amadea, Farrow had been the only pleasant person I had dealt with, despite shooting me in the leg. "Kivisto."

He winked at me. "Ah, that's it. I knew it was 'Kiv' something. Now come on, show me what you can do with that knife."

Mullin and Karlos, the guards who escorted me to the hot spring each evening, waited for me at dusk, and I tried not to race ahead as we walked toward it. When I saw Amadea that night, I threw my arms around her and hugged her tightly. She chuckled at me and hugged me back. "Oof, what was that for?"

"The lambent stone." I stepped back and smiled at her.

The Queen had brought down a bottle of dark red wine and another platter of beautiful looking food. I sat on the slick tiles and looked up at her.

There was only confusion on her face. "What lambent stone?"

Despite the humid, warm air down here, my blood turned to ice. "The ... the lambent stone necklace you left in my room?"

She crouched next to me and clasped my hand tightly. "Destry, I didn't leave a lambent stone in your room. I've been trying to source one for days now, but I can't find *any* within the palace." Gracefully, she sat next to me. "I was worried sick last night when you didn't arrive. Jaryn hadn't told me a word about why you might not visit. I thought the worst. He didn't visit my rooms; I only saw him again at breakfast this morning, and he looked murderous." Her elegant hand squeezed mine. "Do you have any idea who might have gifted it to you?"

Confusion washed over me. "I have no idea. Everyone here, apart from you, despises me. They see me as an imposter, a murderer's daughter. *Useless.*"

Amadea sighed and cast her gaze about the beautiful, torchlit room. She lingered on the veiled day beds that were cast into shadow, then she squeezed my hand again.

"Humor me," said Amadea. She slipped into the chest-deep water, her navy gown floating around her. She held out her right hand. "Pass a memory to me. I want to see if I can prove something."

"A what?"

"A memory, think of one, envelope it in that light of yours, then pass the light to me."

I straightened and glanced down at her upturned palm. She waited patiently and nodded in encouragement. Taking a deep breath, I closed my eyes and reached out for my earliest memory, one of blood-drenched snow and screaming. Delicately, I wrapped my light around it, carefully covering it and willed the image to flare in my palm. Amadea's eyes widened in awe as my hand glowed with a small band of sage green light. It all felt so much easier with the lambent stone like I wasn't wading through mud.

Gently, she placed her wet hand over mine and closed her eyes. My light flared under her fingers, and I felt a small pulse of power from her as she swept that small portion of me into the water around her.

Her eyes opened, and I stared at her and the silver glow of her irises. A water wielder. The Queen turned to face the rippling blue pool. Her palms caressed the water, and a pulse of her power sent a small wave skittering over the surface.

I held my breath, waiting, as Amadea uptilted her palms and raised her bare arms.

All the air was sucked from my lungs as the water moved with her.

Her wrists twisted, and the water rose into a huge inland wave, suspended in time before it came crashing down on our heads. I launched to my bare feet as the pristine clear water morphed into a scene from my memory.

The water sparkled and hissed as it shifted into the shape of a huge Nijinx, its maw open in a silent scream of flashing fangs. Beneath it, a meter from where Amadea stood calmly in the water, two men appeared.

I stumbled backward. One man roared before the Nijinx, his raised arms holding a shimmering broadsword. Amadea's hands clenched, and the water molded over the reindeer antler crown he wore.

My gaze ripped from the Petish warrior to the man that lay on the ground behind him. I heard Amadea's shocked intake of breath. The man who lay on what would have been snow-covered earth was an Ilrairian soldier. And the Petish warrior was defending him from the winged death that swept toward them.

I fell to my knees.

Amadea cried out and the sheer volume of water she had carved bucked under her control. She arced her right arm, and the pool's water crashed back down, sloshing and cresting over the stone lip and into the walls.

The Queen whipped her head to face me and hauled herself out of the water. She was beside me a moment later, wrapping her drenched body around me, as if she could absorb my sobbing. My father, that had been my father wearing that antler crown and wielding a phenomenal blade, had died trying to protect an Ilrairian. I was devastated that I hadn't been able to see his face.

"Lake Wylda," she whispered, her own voice hoarse.

"I knew it," I panted through my tears. "It had been the Nijinxes all this time. I knew it."

"The Kivistos died trying to protect the Ilrair soldiers who had been sent as aid," Amadea murmured. She pulled back and clasped my face between her palms. "You are not the daughter of a murderer, Destry Kivisto."

"Coen seems to think so."

She glared at the room around us. "He's a fool. Raised to believe in the lies his forefathers told him."

The Queen stood and pulled me up with her. We were both soaked. Lucky it was so warm down here. She gave my hand a final squeeze before reaching down for the bottle of wine. "I think this momentous occasion deserves a drink."

"How did you do it? That's more than water magic, surely?"

She uncorked the bottle, took a deep drink, then passed it to me. "Not really. I merely carved the image that you gave me. Now you have someone else in the world that knows the truth. You would have been too young to comprehend what you really saw at the time. I assume Damara rescued you the next day?"

I swallowed the wine, the flavor heady and strong, and it left a stain on my lips. The alcohol eased the pangs of grief in my chest. "She told me the story often over the years. The detachment from Aarine arrived the next day. What Petish survivors there were had long since fled."

"I imagine it was sheer fearmongering by Jaryn's father that started the rumor of the Kivistos murdering Ilrairians. A rumor that was solidified into an altered reality of what happened," Amadea mused quietly.

"Thank you for letting me share that memory with you."

She gave me a warm smile. "Thank *you* for taking a chance on me. I know it's hard, but you *can* trust me, you know."

I gave her a smile in return, and I knew in my heart that I could.

The dark wine we had drunk sung in my veins, and I traced my hand back up the curving stone staircase. The cotton of my shirt hung damp over my skin as I pondered who the hell had gifted me the lambent stone. It hadn't been Amadea. Coen had a key to my room, but he was the last person who wanted me to use my powers.

And that memory Amadea had carved, the Petish warrior I had seen. My father. It felt like tiny slivers of ice were making my heart crack apart. I wished I could have seen his face. My steps were a touch unsteady as I walked out into the dimly lit corridor above. Against my chest, I felt the lambent stone pulse a wave of power over my skin.

I frowned. Where were the guards?

Pain burst through my skull as something long and heavy struck the back of my head. I fell to my knees, my hands snatching out and bracing me against the floor. Dark spots dotted my vision and I blinked, trying to gather my senses as to what the hell just—

That weapon struck again, into my right ribs this time, tossing me onto my back. I cried out, clutching my chest and looked up.

The shorter, red-haired guard, Mullin, held a long, iron bar in his hands, the end tapered like a wrench. He sneered at me and raised the weapon.

The lambent stone flared, and I rolled away as the bar came crashing down with a loud crack against the flagstones, right where my head had been.

I scrambled to my feet and faced him, fists raised. My heart galloped in my chest, in my throat, and I fought to rein in my shock.

Mullin laughed and twirled the bar in his hands. "Told you she would put up a fight."

"Looks like I owe you a pint," snarled the other guard from behind me. Karlos.

I whirled and ducked as Karlos swung his sword at my neck. Not giving him a second to re-aim, I tackled him, hurling my body against his and ramming him into the floor. My right boot slammed down onto his sword arm as my left knee ground down into his chest.

Adrenaline rocketed in my blood as my heart pounded against my injured ribs. Fisting the guard's shirt in my hand, I punched that hateful face. Pain cracked over my knuckles.

He swore, spitting blood.

We were alone down here, and although I was quick, they had brawn and weight on their side.

The air behind me shifted as Mullin barreled toward us. I twisted, reaching for my light. The lambent stone answered my call, and I speared a torrent at him. The deep purple banner jackknifed from me then flared to a brilliant white as it struck Mullin across the face.

He yelled, stumbling backward and flailing, but he kept a hold of the wrench.

Karlos shifted beneath my knee, and I whipped my face back around, yet I was too slow, thanks to the wine, just as he leant forward and smacked his forehead against mine.

I saw stars and felt blood trickle down my scalp as Mullin shoved me off him. *The sword, the sword, the sword.* I kicked out blindly, my boot connecting with his left wrist, knocking the hilt of his sword free, sending it clattering to the floor.

"You fucking Kivisto bitch," yelled Karlos.

Shit. That's what this was about.

He shoved me off him, wrenching my loose hair into his hand. Pain ripped over my scalp as he half-turned on the floor, yanking my head down next to him. I lashed out, my nails slashing at his bloodied face and neck. He hissed and kicked, his heavy leather boot connecting with my abdomen. I doubled over, whimpering, panic rising in my blood as Karlos braced himself on his forearms and heaved himself upward, my hair still clenched in his fist.

I didn't hesitate. He was at the perfect height as I punched him in the groin. His yowl echoed off the hallway walls, and he released my hair. I scrambled to my feet, stumbling from the pain that lanced down my head and back, and leapt for the discarded sword. It was heavy in my two-handed grip, but I whirled it with all my might as Mullin came crashing down the hallway, swiping blindly with the wrench. It smacked down onto the blade and the force of it whipped up my arms and shoulders.

I staggered but did not yield. Swords were mostly foreign to me, but I sure as hell wasn't giving this one up without a fight. Hauling my weight behind the blade, I swiped at Mullin's unprotected thighs. Slivers of blood bloomed along his breeches, and he snarled at me, reassessing. Karlos was up, and he charged forward, a dagger in hand. I brought the sword down toward him, but Mullin roared and slammed the wrench into my exposed left side. Karlos laughed darkly as he feinted away.

Releasing the hilt into my right hand, I threw up my left to catch the cold bar of metal as it crashed down against my neck. The power of his assault knocked me into the wall, and Mullin pounced, jamming the wrench against my throat and punching me in the gut.

The air in my lungs ripped from me.

My light sputtered with the pain as Mullin stepped back and let me collapse to the floor. Distantly, I could hear footsteps running to us. Mullin moved aside and let a limping Karlos edge forward. Savagely, he wrenched his sword from my hand and raised it in a two-hand grip high above his head.

I was going to die a crumpled mess on the floor. I sensed Damara near me, welcoming me with open arms, and I held back my sob. Wading through the pain in my skull, I mustered one final tendril of light and aimed it, whipping it into the world with my last scraps of thought, but Karlos was ready, and the sword came down.

A golden warrior skidded on a knee toward us, curved sword in his outstretched hand. The two blades clashed together in a duet of fury just above my head as that plume of light flashed in the small space.

I gazed up and almost passed out. The warrior lowered his other forearm that he had used to shield his face from the light blast.

Coen.

"Destry," he whispered, taking in the scene in the span of a heartbeat. Anguish flitted across his face, then it was gone, replaced with an icy rage.

He shoved upward, knocking Karlos and his sword aside as if he was no more than a sack of grain. One second a dagger was in Coen's spare hand, the next it was lodged expertly in Karlos' right wrist. The guard screamed, dropping his sword. I used the last of my energy to roll out of the way as Karlos collapsed to his knees, clutching his mutilated arm.

Darkness swirled and my vision ebbed, my head radiating with pain. Mullin froze mid-swing with his wrench, his face paling as he took in the Commander.

Coen's curved sword sang as he twirled it in his grip. "I'm going to fucking kill you both."

I rolled onto my side, my bloodied and bruised back braced against the rough wall and watched through blurry eyes as Coen advanced. There was no mercy on his face.

"Commander, she's ... she's a—" whimpered Karlos, blood pouring from his arm.

"I know exactly what she is." His blade was a flash of silver, expertly dispatching Karlos' head from his neck. Blood gushed from the guard's body as his head rolled away from me. Horror gouged my mind, the blood ... there was so much blood.

Mullin screamed then, dropping his wrench. He backed away, trembling hands raised. "Her people murdered ours; we can't let that go unpunished. She must pay."

Coen treaded past me, his voice deathly low, "Her people are innocent."

The shock of what he had said snapped at my consciousness, forcing me to stare wide-eyed up at him. He knew.

Mullin's scream was cut short. Not by Coen, but by the water that was shoved down his throat, by Amadea standing behind him, her chest heaving as if she had just pelted up the stairwell. Her tawny eyes glowed silver with her power.

Mullin gurgled, his skin turning gray and bloated, then Amadea lifted her palms from his throat, and he collapsed to the floor, drowned and dead.

Coen re-sheathed his sword and gave the Queen a small nod, hardly disturbed at the carnage and blood at his feet. And Amadea, her features were cold, distant, like she had seen scenes like this a hundred times before and Mullin was just another corpse at her bare feet.

Then Coen was at my side, cradling my head and neck. The warmth of him radiated into me as he hauled my battered body against his. I ... I was in his arms. I expected panic and fear to overwhelm me, but his touch was gentle, caring, and instead, a wave of relief washed over my skin, nearly taking my consciousness with it.

"Stay with me, Destry."

My eyelids flickered at the sheer command in his voice, but my head was in agony, my throat ravaged. "How ... how did you ... get here ... so fast?"

"I've been staying here at the Residence." *What?* "Destry, who did you tell your surname?"

My vision fogged, my head cracking with its own pounding beat.

Amadea dropped to her knees on my other side, running an assessing gaze from my bleeding head to my panting chest.

Coen lifted a bloodied hand and swept a tendril of hair off my face. "Destry, *who knows your surname?*"

I met his gaze, and a cold, murderous understanding lay there. His arms tensed around me as if he fought the urge to go right there and then, to do to Farrow what he had just done to Karlos.

Amadea saw it too. "We keep this contained, Commander. Take Destry back to her quarters, and I'll have your most trusted officers bring Farrow down here. We'll bring him before Jaryn in the morning."

"I'll kill him; I fucking knew it. He's probably long gone by now." Coen's voice was a deadly snarl that reverberated in my chest. "He didn't have the guts to try and do it himself, the fucking coward."

Amadea's face was grave. "Regardless, get Destry out of here. I'll send for a medic once I've spoken to Jaryn."

Coen scooped me up into his arms and stood as if I weighed nothing. I'd be impressed, awed even, if my head didn't feel like it was about to split in two. "We have to go north; I can't get through to him, De. You have to try to convince him."

The Queen reached forward and squeezed the Commander's arm. "I'll try. Now go, I'll get this mess cleaned up."

Coen looked down in disgust at the bodies at their feet. I gazed up at him over my blood-matted hair. This man, who had done nothing but loathe me since meeting him, had even threatened to leave me for dead ... had saved me from exactly that. My confusion made my head pound even harder, and I moaned.

He didn't hesitate, as he swept me down the hallway toward my room, somehow keeping a hold of me whilst simultaneously unlocking the door. *Spirits.* His breathing hitched as he set me down on the bed with surprising gentleness.

I leant back against the headboard, my limbs shaking as the adrenaline slowly receded from my body, and my mind tried to grasp the fact two men had attempted to murder me over my last name. I swallowed harshly as bile rose in my throat.

Coen unstrapped his sword belt and set it down on the dresser. Then he walked into the bathing room, and I could hear water running. He returned a moment later with a small bronze bowl and a large, cold, damp cloth. Setting the full bowl down on the bedside table, he passed me the cloth, our fingers brushing, and I placed it over the throbbing pain at the back of my head. I ignored the jolt of electricity that tingled up my arm as our hands brushed against each other and instead focused on not vomiting all over the bed.

Coen moved slowly, as if trying not to startle me, and sat on the very edge of the bed. The room felt insanely smaller with him in it, like the very air, the torchlight, my breath, were drawn to him.

We gazed at each other, and silence hung between us, taut and fragile. Tucking my throbbing knees to my chest, I wrapped my quivering left arm around my legs and looked across at him. My voice was hoarse, like I had been screaming. Maybe I had been. "You didn't let them kill me."

His stubbled jaw clenched, and his long fingers curled into fists. The deep tenor of his voice rolled over my skin. "No, I didn't."

"Why?" I breathed, my gaze not leaving his face.

He looked down at his hands, then back up at me. I could barely begin to decipher the look on his face. Why the sudden change in attitude? Why was my life suddenly something that warranted saving?

His throat bobbed as he swallowed. The torchlight flickered over his dark blond hair, turning it golden. "I ... I was there tonight. When Amadea carved your memory from the water."

What? My eyes widened, causing me to wince and hiss. Amadea had known he was there from the glares she had been throwing around the room. "You've been spying on me? That's why you've been staying here and not the Roost."

A small, barely perceptible nod of his head.

I lowered the cloth, trying to ignore how blood-stained it was. My voice was dangerously quiet as I said, "If you *hadn't* seen that memory, would you have let them kill me?"

He shifted on the bed, coming to sit beside me and gently took the cloth from my stiff fingers. My heart hammered in my chest, and my breath caught in my throat at the closeness of him. He doused the compress in clean water, wrung it, and softly pressed it against the base of my skull.

My spine locked at the contact as his scent washed over me, cedarwood and amber, and heat flushed across my core. The intimacy of this moment completely contradicted the violence he had displayed not half an hour ago. I scrambled at my torn wits to remember that this man had just killed someone, the blood of whom was still smeared on the curve of his sword.

"I would have still saved you. Everything I thought about you ..." he trailed off, and I thought he was finished, but then, "the look on your face when Jaryn made his offer, the fear but also the wildness that lay there. I knew you would fight it, fight him. Yet I know all too well that loneliness is a curse, that it can break the strongest of souls if wielded just right."

He dipped the cloth again, and this time, wiped the blood away from my cheek and lip. I didn't dare move an inch, it was difficult to even breathe, even with the pain against my ribs. Our breath intermingled and his shoulders were tense with his effort of concentration on my face.

"I also suspected Farrow, which is why I stepped into your training. I wanted to see for myself if he was setting you up for failure. But I also wanted to let you feel an emotion that wasn't just grief and sadness, even if it meant coaxing out your rage."

And he had certainly done just that. I blinked, my body glowing with the heat that pulsed from him. The lambent stone against my chest sent out a small pulse of power. I ignored it, enraptured by him, but ...

"You were right. I'm useless. I couldn't defend myself tonight."

His gaze darkened, knowing that his words yesterday had struck deep. "You're anything *but useless*, Destry."

My name on his lips. Spirits above. "Then why say it? In front of *Jaryn?*"

"I know and so does Amadea, that the longer Jaryn keeps you here, that power in your body will wane. It was my shitty way of trying to convince him to send you north."

He withdrew his hand and put the cloth in the bowl. Slowly, he stood, and I stared up at him. His head turned to look at me over a muscled shoulder. "I ... I blamed you for something your family hadn't even *done*. You, who would have been a child at the time, helpless. I blamed you for it all." He dragged a hand through his tousled hair, then down his face. "And for that ... I'll understand if you never forgive me."

With that, he picked up his sword and gave me one last heated glance. His full lips parted as if he would say more, but then his chin dipped and he stalked from my room, taking all his heat with him, leaving me feeling cold, confused, and reeling.

CHAPTER
TWENTY-THREE

ORRIN

Murrkill and I stood beside the rocky plinth beyond the town, huddled together for warmth. The Night Pegasus had flown away, taking his fire feathers with him, leaving only sparkling stars and a solemn half-moon in its wake.

The blood bay mare flinched as she shifted her weight over her hooves, and once more, I worried after her. Exhaustion from our days of travel had left her body stiff and sore, just like mine. We eyed the fogged town below with unease as we sensed the people below milling about despite the late hour. My distrust for the soldiers and settlers yawned like a bottomless pit. Despite the wide expanse of sky above us, I was beginning to feel trapped, with humans to the south and Nijinxes and the wild ward to the north. I knew it wasn't just from the cold that Murrkill shivered.

Yet we couldn't leave, not without freeing Ebrel first. Her whinny had cut through the night air like a knife and still reverberated in my bones. She was down there, encased in stone and wood. I would not abandon her to a life that I had suffered for years.

Ilmari rippled around us, alert to all those who moved within the town. The air spirit had tried to take on the Nijinxes, yet the wild ward's magic had knocked her back and spiraling away. She couldn't get near them to rip the wind out from under their wings.

I froze.

Murrkill tensed in turn as our mutual gazes locked onto the dove-gray mare Pegasus that burst upward from the fog and flew steadily over the town. She wore no tack, but her build and condition gave her away as a Southerner. Banking east, she nosed the air keenly, and Murrkill stilled in response as she slowly flew toward us.

I walked a step forward, muzzle low to the ground, nostrils flaring, a warning squeal rumbling in my chest and throat. Murrkill spread her wings to their full length and bared her teeth to the oncomer.

The stranger landed sedately, calmly, and she approached not head-on, but from the side, so that we would see her coming clearly from yards away. Her gaze was downcast, her head low, and she licked her lips and chewed as she treaded through the snow.

I am not a threat, her body language whispered. *I am submissive. You are in charge. I am not a threat, not a threat.*

The gray mare smelled like dew after a spring dawn. She was only six years old, a year older than Ebrel. Clinging to her dappled pelt was the scent of a soldier, ingrained so deeply with the mare's I could easily pick up the leather, bergamot, and earthy notes of him. Twenty paces out to our left, she halted and continued to lick and chew.

Murrkill half folded her wings, though she trembled.

Cautiously, I took another step forward, then another, angling myself in front of Murrkill. The stranger barely breathed. I sensed Murrkill tuck her wings beside her body and follow me across the snow-topped grass.

"I mean you no harm, King of the Forest." The soldier's mount nodded to me, then Murrkill. *"Or you, wing sister."* The gray's voice was lyrical, beautiful even. It brought to mind endless winter skies. Ilmari leapt across the snow, ruffling the southern mare's mane.

"How does a southern Pegasus know of me?" I questioned.

Murrkill pressed her warmth against my flank, ready to fight if need be. The difference between the two mares was stark. The Northerner was lean from the harsh winter, honed and rugged, whereas this stranger gleamed with care, her muscles rippling under her pelt.

"I know more about the spirits than you probably do, no offense." She cocked her head at Murrkill's whine of warning. *"Is it the roan one you seek? Ebrel?"*

I bared my teeth. *"You imprisoned her?"*

Her ears flattened at my tone. *"We are healing her. She was left for dead at the edge of the north moorlands. Her wing was damaged, but she will fly again soon."*

"Your master must trust you greatly to extend that leash of yours to here," hissed Murrkill.

"My rider *is the only one I trust, and he trusts me in return."*

"Because he knows you'll return for food, warmth, and safety," Murkill's voice dripped with disgust.

The stranger raised her head higher than the blood bay's, pride shining in her dark brown eyes. *"There is no shame for wanting and needing such things."*

I took a step forward past Murrkill, whose gaze promised a slow death, in the hope of preventing the two from fighting. The stranger yielded to me, and her head dipped again. *"We mean Ebrel no harm. I believe we were meant to find her that night and seeing you both here ... there's hope yet."*

Murrkill snarled. *"Hope for what, tame one?"*

"To free the spirits and defeat the evil at work here."

"Aren't your masters the evil ones?" I countered.

"Not mine. I was gifted the kindest of men as my rider. Others are not so fortunate." Her voice was clear, calm, and filled with conviction. This mare believed every word she said, despite the ludicrousness of

it. To be so bonded to a human made me feel sick, I felt ... sorry for her. I had only eaten their hay and grain out of pure need, starvation being my only other choice, but to willingly want it, to love this tame life, the notion was utterly foreign to me. *"If you mean Ebrel no harm, then free her."*

"I ... I can't do that." For a moment, her resolve seemed to waver.

"Because your master says otherwise?" Murrkill beat her wings angrily.

She stamped a forehoof in frustration. *"My rider, not my master. And no, not because he wills it, but because he does."* The gray mare looked skyward to the now starry night sky, but I knew exactly who she was referring to, the spirit who had laid claim to Ebrel before Ilmari had gotten a chance. I glared upward, inwardly cursing the spirit's name, despite whatever good intentions he might have.

Ilmari pulsed around us and ran a calming hand down my neck. *"The southern mare speaks true. It seems the Night Pegasus has a plan at work here, and we would be utter fools to intervene."*

I snapped my teeth in frustration. *"I am not abandoning Ebrel."*

"Then stay here. Our platoon ..." she trailed off and gazed down at the town below. *"There will be little warning of our departure, but you're welcome to join us, help us even, in defeating the wild ward. We know you can't do it alone. My rider awaits the arrival of the Koski-varri. Once she's here, our plans will be put into action."* She pinned me with a pleading gaze. *"There is a chance your forest can be saved if we work together."*

"I will not have a man on my back," I snarled, and she flinched.

"And nor will you. You will both remain free."

Murrkill rolled her eyes and snapped her teeth. *"Are we really meant to believe the words of a creature bound so closely to a human, that she shares his scent?"*

"Watch your words, wing sister. My tolerance for your insults is wearing thin. You judge something that you know nothing about."

Even Murrkill blinked at the dominant tone in the stranger's voice, and surprise rocked through me when the blood bay didn't snarl a retort.

I tossed my brown head, and my decision was made. Despite the call of the forest in my veins, a beautiful siren's song that lured me home, I would not leave Ebrel now, not after I had given her hope in our presence. *"Tell Ebrel we are here, and we will remain here until we are assured she will come to no harm from your humans. Nijinxes are roosted north of here. You should warn the others. This town is no longer safe."*

The dove-gray mare extended her gleaming wings and prepared to take flight. *"It was a pleasure to meet you, King of the Forest. My name is Kalana, and only by working together can we survive this."*

CHAPTER TWENTY-FOUR

DESTRY

I dreamt of Damara that night. I felt the wool of her dress as I hugged her and took in her parchment and pear scent. We sat beside a roaring fire in the library of Reckforton Castle, towers of books lying scattered around us. Her face was cast in shadow, but I nestled into her warmth.

There was a time when all I ever wanted in life was endless books and the time to enjoy them, but as sweet childhood filtered away and expectation lay heavily on me, those dreams changed. I prayed to find a man who would share my dreams in going to Petowin, not to rule it, but to restore it to its former glory. That hope had grown when I initially met Narve, then it had been killed as quickly as a fresh spring blossom in a vicious frost.

The dream filtered away, despite how hard I clung to Damara, until I awoke in the chilled pre-dawn air of my room. I half turned on the bed, wincing as my ribs protested the movement. Amadea sat curled up on the fabric armchair tucked into the corner of the room, a woolen blanket draped over her body. She had arrived not long after Coen had left me, telling me the unnerving news that Farrow had deserted, a notice was out to hunt him, but no one had seen him since that morning after training.

Groggily, my head feeling marginally better, I shifted from the bed and padded silently across to the bathing room. Bracing my hands on the marble sink, I steeled myself and looked at my face in the large oval mirror. Biting back my sharp inhale, I took note of the damage. A long bruise flowed over my neck to my collarbone. The blood had dried, but a jagged cut ran down my right temple, and my lower lip was scabbed over at the corner of my mouth. My knuckles ached from how tightly I gripped the marble, and I looked down, taking in the bruising and cuts over my fingers.

Coen had been right in one regard. I *was* useless. I had been utterly inept at defending myself last night. If it hadn't been for the Commander and the Queen, I would be as dead as Damara right now. The dark curtain of my hair hung knotted and limp over my shoulders as I swallowed back my tears. My hand-to-hand combat, my light wielding, my sword fighting, all of it, useless. The Night Pegasus hadn't visited me, and I loathed myself for relying on him, for needing that unearthly touch to help hold myself together.

I met my brown gaze in the mirror. Spirits, I was a mess. A weak, useless mess. It was a good thing Jaryn took *Kathkar* from me, because I would never be able to wield such a mighty blade as that. Like my father had done before the Nijinx.

Amadea appeared behind me and leant next to the bathing room doorway. Her gaze was solemn, sympathetic even, as she hugged her elbows.

"You've seen death before," I whispered to the mirror, my voice hoarse.

She swallowed, her shoulders tensing beneath her long-sleeved navy gown. "I have ... many times, and I'm afraid last night won't be the last. It never gets easier for me. Whenever I must take a life, I will carry every death with me until my own claims me."

I turned to face her, bracing my lower back against the sink. Sorrowful silence pulsed between us. "You killed a man for me."

Amadea stepped forward and gripped my hand in hers. "And I will again if I need to. They were going to murder you, Destry, and I don't let people murder my friends."

I blinked across at her, shock tingling my skin. This Queen considered me her friend? I looked to the floor, swallowing harshly, feeling utterly undeserving of it. Gently, her brown calloused fingers lifted my chin, and I felt stupidly vulnerable and exposed in front of her. Yet Amadea didn't shy away.

"What you see in that mirror is not what I see, Destry Kivisto. You carry an inner strength that cannot be tempered or crushed. Petowin blood runs in your veins, and the song of the wilderness echoes in your heart. You are as untamable as the northern sky."

Her left hand slowly lowered while her right squeezed my fingers.

"I can't even wield a sword, Amadea. Coen was right, I'm—"

The Queen's face darkened. "I would not trust the Commander as far as I could *throw* him. I consider him an ally, yes, yet in this nest of vipers, he is still a snake. You have the strength and the courage to learn sword fighting and more. When we get to Saltfen ... there's someone there that I trust. Completely. I'll have him train you."

Her voice was filled with such longing, such utter sadness, that I tilted my head in intrigue. "We're going north?"

"Jaryn gave the order last night before I came to see you. We will fly there this afternoon."

We dressed efficiently, wrapping up warm in layers of leather and wool. Amadea had passed me fleece-lined gloves and a matching headband that covered my ears to keep out the chill of the winter wind we'd be heading into. Slowly, my fingers sore, I braided my hair and followed the Queen out of my room.

As we rounded a corner of the ancient palace, headed toward the landing station outside the Residence, I noted a carved doorway. I slowed, drawn to the power that emanated from it. The wood was darker than what was typically used throughout the palace and carved on it was a Trinitor. Spanning the entire height of the door was a rearing Trinitor stallion, his forehooves tucked to his chest, a dark mane flowing over a curved spine, and a magical horn adorned his handsome, baroque head. The wings on his back were half-arched. Yet it was the painted silver collar around his upper neck that defined the Trinitor for what he was. Colbass, King of the Cursed. The creature that had doomed his entire species with one murderous act.

Amadea stopped when she noticed I wasn't following her. I stared up at the door, at that now dull silver collar. The Queen stepped up beside me, her voice a whisper, "The old throne room lies beyond. Jaryn's ancestor had it sealed off after the curse was doled out and Colbass was dead." Her fingers rose to hesitantly rest on the carved tail of the old Trinitor king. "To fracture an entire species apart ... such power is ... unfathomable."

I ran a fingertip over an intricately detailed feather on his wing. Power, ancient and freezing, licked at my skin, and I yanked my hand away. Indeed, the edges of the door were rimmed with lead, letting no one in and no one out. The history and magic behind the door were imprisoned for an eternity.

"This way," murmured Amadea, and I trailed after her toward the landing station, casting the door one final look over my shoulder.

Bromtide Platoon waited outside in neat rows of ten, their Pegasi saddled and ready to fly. Jaryn, his inner court, and guards stood off to the side, their mounts pawing at the sand impatiently. Coen stood dead center beside his gleaming palomino stallion, the Commander deep in conversation with the King, who tightly held the reins of his own iron-gray mount.

Farrow was nowhere to be seen.

Jaryn looked over Coen's shoulder, and the Commander turned to watch us walk closer. He gave me a small, warm smile as I approached and held out a gloved hand to me.

"You're flying with me."

I was still in shock to see him smiling at *me*, but I placed my hand in his, and he drew me beside him and his beautiful Pegasus. Jaryn wholly ignored me, his gaze steely as he helped Amadea onto her light gray gelding that had been led over.

Awed, I placed a hand on the palomino's muscled neck. The stallion exhaled, and he nosed my coat with his gray muzzle, his white wings blinding in the sunlight.

Coen gave his mount a gentle pat. "This is Hestian."

The Commander's face glowed with pride as he ran his gaze over the palomino, and I could understand why. The Pegasus was a perfect example of just how beautiful the species could be: noble, refined, strong, and just downright humbling. They were so different from their northern cousins, and I think I knew deep down which version I preferred. The version that was as untamable as me.

Coen mounted up gracefully and didn't give me a chance to think as he gripped my hand and hoisted me behind his saddle, where an extra saddle pad had been attached to the high-backed cantle. My ribs twinged in protest, but I smothered my hiss of pain. Hestian nestled his huge wings on either side of us as Coen wrapped my arm around his waist and kept a hold of my hand against his stomach. I tried to remember to breathe as the front of my body sat flushed against his iron-strong back.

Gently, almost absentmindedly, he ran his thumb over my knuckles.

Jaryn mounted up last, his body utterly attuned to being on horse-back. The King's gaze fixed on me for a scathing moment, then carried over the platoon. "We fly for Saltfen."

"What got him to change his mind?" I whispered over Coen's shoulder.

He turned his head, and I leant backward as his lips came dangerously close to mine. "Amadea, but from a military viewpoint only. Aarine is readying its forces, forcing Jaryn's hand."

My arms tightened around Coen as he clucked with his tongue, and Hestian launched us into the fresh winter sky in response. The wind cut across my bare face as the rest of the platoon and the royals followed suit, the sun lancing off countless fluttering Pegasi feathers.

We flew throughout the day, only stopping to water, feed, and rest the Pegasi. I tried to ignore the fact that Coen never let me out of his sight during those brief stops, and that I didn't want to move far from him anyway, hovering close to him like a planet in orbit. I knew deep in my bones that it wasn't just because he saved my life last night.

Saltfen was still a few miles away when the sun began to dip below the horizon, the temperature plummeting with it. I was grateful for Coen's warmth as the freezing wind tugged at us. Snow clouds gathered in the north, dousing the land below in darkness. As one, the platoon lowered in altitude, the faint flat-topped hills of Saltfen just dark specks in the distance.

My entire body froze as my light suddenly roared through my veins and speckled my vision. Coen squeezed my hand in response. I wrenched my chin up and looked over his muscled shoulder to what was coming for us through those roiling snow clouds.

Green light flashed across the sections of clear sky, illuminating the rolling, snow-covered land below. Light that did not come from me.

I couldn't hear the Night Pegasus or sense him close to me, but I did feel his warning on the air. *Danger, wild one.*

A prime evil keening echoed through the air.

I knew that sound; it haunted my nightmares night after night. Deadly shadows flitted across the dusk sky straight toward the platoon.

"Nijinxes!" I yelled.

Two short horn blasts echoed over the sky, and Coen nudged Hestian with his heels. The golden Pegasus curled into a dive, his white wings folding to plummet us toward the snow-carpeted ground and a tiny village below us. Shouts whipped up all around us, as half of the platoon landed swiftly beside Hestian, whilst the other half picked up speed, heading directly toward the oncoming threat.

High above, the light flames of the Night Pegasus lashed across the night sky, coaxing the power in my veins to a ferocity I had never felt before, stronger than the night in Aarine. It took all my strength to rein it back and not unleash it all. Aware, alert, and trembling, my power bared its teeth and *snarled*. Yet it wasn't just Nijinxes. I could sense something was coated over them, tainting them.

A foreign, repulsive feeling licked through my veins, *wild ward magic*, it warned.

I leapt down from Hestian's back, but Coen grabbed my hand and spun me round to face him. He leant forward in his saddle and cupped my bruised cheek with a broad hand. His gaze was earnest and filled with worry. I raised my right hand and placed my palm over his.

"Find somewhere to hide, and do not come out until we give you the all clear," he ordered, the dominance in his voice gentle but unyielding.

"I will," I murmured in return, my heart clattering in my chest.

Coen pulled back and urged his stallion back into the sky as the Nijinxes raced toward the small cluster of buildings I found myself beside.

Guards rushed to rally around Jaryn and Amadea, leaving me alone in a stone-cobbled farmyard.

Then I spied the first Nijinx, a large male.

Ochre black, he dived down from the green-lanced sky, undercutting the cavalry above and swept in low over the motionless, frozen lake beside the village. His huge wings lofted him with deadly grace through the air, directly toward the village. In the orange gleam of the torchlight, I saw those baneful silver fangs snap. My gaze roved higher over his bulk to the *rider* on his back, armed with a crossbow. Horror gripped my bones. They had riders?

I dove to tuck beside the wooden and brick wall of a barn. The huge male Nijinx reached the first tiny, whitewashed cottage. Landing awkwardly on the thatched roof, his webbed and clawed feet scrambled on the neatly laid straw. Swinging a leg over the male's neck, the rider dismounted, unsheathed steel glinting at both hips.

The rider knelt into a predatory crouch, crossbow in hand. Light curled over my fingers in response, the lambent stone pulsing against my chilled chest. Villagers screamed and hid in their homes as more Nijinxes landed, riderless this time. I glanced upward to where Bromtide Platoon battled with the airborne killers, easily spotting Hestian in the gathering dark. Evading every killing blow, the Nijinxes taunted the platoon.

The Nijinx rider wrenched open the cottage's door and shot dead its occupants with two bolts at point-blank range. He whooped with joy as his mount tore apart the dairy cow in the lean-to.

I trembled as his brown-eyed gaze swept across the thatched houses, then finally, he rested on me. My light sparked at my fingertips.

He ... he looked Petish with dark brown hair and tan skin. I blinked, shocked. What in spirit's name had happened to him to become a Nijinx rider? To ride the beasts that had slaughtered his kin?

His leathers, reindeer hide, and the way he moved marked him as a hunter. His gaze locked with mine, and he smiled. It was a grotesque gesture, filled with a crazed bloodlust. The same killing frenzy that had swept fear throughout all the Boreals, as the people of Petowin had fled south. The hunter stalked forward as he brought up his crossbow and aimed it at my chest. Still, he smiled.

I yanked blindly on my power, roughly pooling it into my open, gloved palm and whipped it straight at him, just like I had with the guards the night before. Sage green light arced over the open space and flared. The hunter threw up a hand to shield his face, and I dove for the snow-topped ground. A muted *thud* sounded next to where my head had been. An embedded crossbow bolt shook within the wooden support beam of the barn wall. Holy shit.

People began to scream as more Nijinxes dropped down from the burning night sky. Crouching on the snow, I willed more flickering light into my hand. The hunter shook his head, hissing in rage and lifted his crossbow once more, a fresh bolt loaded and primed. He took in the fresh, sparking light over my fingers and a frown flickered across his rugged features. Gold flickering light glowed faintly over his chest, and the crossbow lowered barely an inch. It had to be the wild ward controlling him. Surely, he wouldn't be flying with Nijinxes otherwise.

I sent another plume of light toward him, softly this time, and let it wreath around his shoulders and neck. *I am Petowin,* I mentally whispered to him as my light brushed his cheek. I was clutching at straws, desperate to rid him of the wild ward magic that ensnared him, but having no idea how. *I am the Koskivarri. The wild ward has claimed you, huntsman.*

The crossbow moved an inch lower.

Lower.

The wild ward magic around his chest retreated, dimming to a subtle flicker within his ribcage. The Night Pegasus changed to curtains of white light in the sky above, burning the night with his wings of fire. Thundering hooves and horn blasts echoed around the small village as cavalry members landed and took flight.

I threw myself to the ground and rolled as the wild ward's magic burst through the hunter's chest in a billow of power. He gasped, a choking sound resounding in his throat. His gaze was wild, frenzied, as he tried to track me once more.

The ground rumbled as I rose on one knee, arm drawn back, ready to wield my light at him, but his Nijinx mount had landed again. The huge male grasped the hunter by his shirt collar and dragged him onto his back. The hunter barely had time to hold on before the male launched himself into the night sky that now flared with undulating strips of purple and the flashes of steel swords.

Then I was running, drawing strength from the fire that danced across the sky as the swarm of Nijinxes took on the Bromtide Platoon. I made it to the village square and dived behind an overturned cart for cover. Illuminated by arcs of green and ladders of purple, Pegasi and their riders battled with the leather-winged predators. Screams and yells washed over the buildings as the villagers cowered in their homes. It was a scene so hauntingly familiar; it made my blood turn icy within my veins.

I would *not* be frightened. Frightened meant I was too far gone to be of use. I could be scared. Scared meant you still had common sense. Fright was what got you killed.

A Nijinx swooped low over the square and landed heavily on the muddied snow. A young female, she scented the smoke-ridden air keenly with her slitted nose. Wiry, yet riddled and torqued with muscle, the predator ran her hollow gaze over the shuttered and squat buildings. A series of clicks echoed from her fanged mouth, and her ears twitched this way and that to catch the returning sounds.

Her eyeless head locked onto the overturned cart and my huddled body behind it. Fingers shaking, I held my breath and aimed my light silently at her ebony skull. Then I noticed the magic that danced over her empty eye sockets. The female lowered her head, nostrils flaring wide, and delicately stepped toward me like a ballerina of death.

Glinting gold, brindled with navy, magic danced where the Nijinx should have had eyes. The clicking from her mouth intensified, and she altered her course toward the rear cartwheel embedded in the snow.

My hiding place.

Her bobbing skull danced in my sight as she ambled closer, closer.

Five meters.

Three.

Shadows cast by torches danced across her black, silken pelt.

She was eerily mesmerizing. A creature so ensconced with the night, she seemed to be carved from darkness, a consumer of stars and light. A spectral beauty. I wondered if she could look at humans and Pegasi, as I looked at her.

Two meters.

Her quivering lips peeled backward, revealing the full length of her primary fangs. The gold-brindled magic flowed downward from her sockets to dance and ebb around her maw.

I shuddered behind the cartwheel, my instincts screaming at me to run. This was no ordinary Nijinx female.

"Greetings, Koskivarri." The Nijinx flicked an ear as her voice resonated smoothly in my mind. *"Come out of your hiding place, human. Let me see you."*

Webbed feet shifting, the female backed up a pace, leaving me enough room to stand. My knees shook as I rose, yet I stood defiantly before her. "You can talk?"

"Our wild ward is the most powerful to have ever existed, human. How you have changed, Destry Kivisto. No longer a cowering child amidst the windblown snows. You look nothing like your father, well, from what my sire told me anyway."

My muscles went rigid with rage. "You were there that night by the lake?"

With lethal grace, the female cocked her head. *"Oh, I was just a yearling, but the tale of my sire taking on Chief Lochlan is so well known now amongst my kind, it's practically legend. We feasted for weeks after that night."* The Nijinx locked her gaze on mine. Had she been human, she would have revealed a savage smile. *"We are due another feast like that."*

I tried to block out my family's ghostly screams. "Who are you?"

She chuckled. *"We are alike in most ways. Queens of our clans, doing whatever it takes to ensure we survive. I have to admire you, really I do, for fighting for so long. Yet the stronger creature always comes out victorious in the end. Some animals should accept their fate. Petowin belongs to the Nijinxes now and so will the rest of the Boreals. Just like the Mountain Horses, you are a dying creature doomed for extinction. With any luck, the rest of your human friends will follow you."*

The Nijinx paused and lifted her head skyward.

I followed her line of sight and gasped.

The large male Nijinx from before, the hunter astride him, barreled through the air, and slammed into Hestian and Coen, casting the pair spinning wildly out of control in the night sky. The palomino tried desperately to right himself, yet man and Pegasus tumbled toward the frozen lake beyond.

A scream tore from my throat as they plummeted into the ice. The excruciating sound of the ice cleaving into two, then fracturing apart, echoed around the village.

"He is a swift giver of death, my beloved," said the Nijinx with a voice laced with devotion to the male Nijinx that flipped and turned on his wings in the night sky. *"Yet males can be slow. We females are quicker, more efficient."*

The Nijinx female lunged.

I hurled myself backward as she leapt, fangs glinting.

"My name is Vesperum," she crooned as her fanged mouth swung to grasp a handful of my coat. She tossed me to the ground as if I were no more than a ragdoll filled with smoke.

The air was smacked clean from my lungs as I landed on my back in the slush. Blood roared in my veins as I tried desperately to suck down a breath. I hurled my light at her, and it washed over her like a waterfall, utterly useless.

The Queen of the Nijinxes was on me in an instant, pinning my chest to the earth with a daggered and webbed foot. I could feel those lethal blades cutting through the leather and fabric like a knife through butter. A shift in her weight and she would rip my heaving chest open. Her breath was hot on my trembling skin as she lowered her muzzle to my jaw, my neck.

In a voice that was a gentle whisper in the biting night air, she said, *"Good night, Destry Kivisto."*

Her head retracted like a viper readying to strike, and her mouth was a yawning hole of darkness as she inhaled. Primary fangs glinting, she clicked with the contentment of an easy kill.

Yet a blow did not come, and death did not greet me. Instead, that brindled magic began to seep from her jaw and creep toward my own panting lips. My power pulsed and thrashed, yet it was useless against a creature of darkness and sound. My nails began to bleed as I raked the frozen earth at my fingertips. I thrashed my head back and forth, lips peeled back in a defiant snarl.

Vesperum clucked softly. *"So savage, you Petish beasts. Fear not, Destry, the wild ward will capture us all in the end."*

The brindled light fluttered around my mouth, pulsing against my tongue. It burned with every touch against my skin. I began to scream.

The earth beneath me rumbled, and the tiny puddle of melted snow beside my torso trembled as a roan Pegasus mare tore around the cart and smashed into the side of the Nijinx Queen.

The Nijinx keened in pain. Her clicks and whistles that followed were the most high-pitched I had ever heard, laced with rage and bloodlust. Righting herself upon the trodden snow, Vesperum wheeled her ebony body around to face the roan Pegasus mare who stood protectively over me.

I shoved myself up onto my elbows and stared up at the heaving chest of the northern Pegasus. *By the spirits, what the hell was happening?* The two equine females eyeballed each other, power and animosity thrumming from their bodies.

Vesperum arched her wings. She was a slimmer beast compared to the roan, but she did not lack any muscle or strength.

"I look forward to slitting your throat, you winged heathen," spat the Nijinx.

The roan snapped her teeth at the predator. Without the wild ward magic marring her body, I couldn't hear her like I could the Nijinx Queen. Vesperum snaked her head, then whipped it to the right. Across the square, a stallion's war cry ripped through the night air.

The roan whinnied in a mighty greeting to the third equine that entered the fray. A young Mountain Horse stallion stepped confidently toward us. Head low to the ground, brown ears snapped back to his skull, his billowing blond mane and tail gleamed in the torchlight. A warning squeal rumbled in his huge chest as he drew closer, closer.

Vesperum bared her teeth at his approach.

The stallion reacted in kind, followed by a harsh snap as he brought them together again.

The Nijinx tucked her wings in tight. *"Would you look at that,"* she breathed. *"A Pegasus and a Mountie working together. I never thought I would see the day. I was intrigued to see who would appear when Destry's life was on the line. Now we know,"* murmured Vesperum. *"The wild ward* will *have your soul, Destry Kivisto. One way or another."* Brindled magic trembled across her sockets and mouth.

I gazed in shock, as it twisted into a glinting and shimmering bridle upon the Nijinx. Vesperum hissed at the magic and tossed her head viciously, then she was flying, her black wings beating wildly, as she rose higher and higher into the night sky. Her mate, the huge male who had knocked Hestian clean out of the sky, joined her, the hunter still on his back.

A piercing horn blew through the village. Somewhere in the wilds of Harracombe, another platoon was approaching.

The roan gripped the back of my shirt and hauled me to my feet. She let me go, and I whipped my body around to look at her in awe. Her gaze met mine. As I looked into the roan's eyes, thoughts of Petowin flooded my mind. The scent of the glens after a downpour, fires burning and crackling, the warmth of a cloak against the chill of the night.

I blinked.

Our eyes were the same color.

I could see her heart pounding against her chest wall as she dragged in a heavy breath. Utterly spellbound, I held out my hand to her, but didn't approach. The mare lowered her brown-flecked head, and she nosed my gloved hand warily. She snorted and inhaled again, taking in my scent. I didn't think I was breathing, my bruised chest clenched in pain. She stepped back and raised her head, as she ran a critical gaze over my mud-covered uniform.

"Thank you," I whispered, and instinct had me dipping my head in gratitude to the young mare that had saved my life. I hoped I would have time to find her later and thank her all over again. I glanced up at the night sky that still thrashed white and green and wondered if the Night Pegasus had intervened through this lovely mare.

The mare whickered a low, gentle sound. I stepped back, my gaze turning toward the lake's now pulsing waters. Beyond the fragmented ice, I could just make out the thrashing of Hestian as he struggled to keep himself and his rider afloat in the pitch-black water. Some onlookers crowded on the lake's surface, yet none dared to enter the freezing water.

Coen.

Spurring my legs into action, I ran. Skidding to a halt on the ice-encrusted perimeter, I yanked off my boots and rider's coat. I turned and spied Kramer landing on the shoreline. Her mount, a light brown gelding, gleamed with sweat and was breathing hard. I just prayed he wasn't too tired. Kramer dismounted, and I took my chance.

I ran and leapt atop the gelding. The officer lunged for the reins, screeching, but the brown gelding gave his rider little choice in the matter.

He yanked the reins from Kramer's hands, and he took off across the snow-coated sand and flew like a bronze dagger, as silent as an owl through the air. I quickly settled into the saddle and gathered up the reins. Turning with ease, the brown gelding's hooves sliced the water's trembling surface.

I heaved my weight forward and, with zero grace, tucked my feet up so that I was standing on the saddle. The gelding dropped low, angling himself above the water. In the maze of ice, I caught sight of the fallen pair, their breaths ragged and frozen as they struggled.

I dropped the reins, swung my arms over my head and dived.

Blackness swallowed me whole and an icy cold punctured through my body, stealing away every thought and breath. I had never felt so cold, my mind battling to send messages to my limbs to *move, get out of this fucking water, now!* I kicked and kicked, striving for the jigsaw-like surface that was licked with gold from the torchlight.

I broke through the water with a heaving gasp. I had minutes now, scraps of time to get them to safety before my body, and theirs, seized up with the cold.

Hestian was struggling. His huge white wings were his downfall in the water. He flapped and heaved, nostrils flaring to keep his head above the water.

Coen, a dead weight over the palomino's saddle, wasn't helping.

I swam for them, kicking hard as the ice-cold water tightened its grip on my body. Blistering pain swept over my extremities as the cold leached under my skin.

The Commander was unconscious, and his lips were a dangerous shade of pale pink bordering into blue. I heaved him off the leather saddle and gently turned him onto his back in the water.

"Go, Hestian," I croaked, patting the stallion's neck.

With the extra weight of his rider relieved, the Pegasus began to swim for the shoreline. Soldiers and their mounts landed on the snow-covered sand as villagers heaved more wood onto a growing fire, the Nijinxes now gone.

I turned my back to the village, looped my left arm around Coen's solid chest and began to tow him to shore. His head rested limply against my soaked neck, and his breaths were faint, barely there.

Hestian made it to the lake's edge. Soldiers grabbed handfuls of his mane and his saddle and hurled him onto the snow. The stallion collapsed.

Other Pegasi dropped to their knees beside him, offering their body heat to warm him as soldiers began vigorously drying him down with straw and blankets.

The muscles in my arms and legs were screaming, and they trembled with fatigue. Coen was a muscle-hewn, dead weight in my grip. I wouldn't let him down, not now.

We were ten meters out when my body started to betray me.

My chest grew tighter and tighter, the icy water constricting around my torso like a snake. With the reduced oxygen, my limbs began to fail until it was all I could do to keep our heads above the water.

The roan mare who saved me bellowed a whinny over the ice from the southern side of the lake.

I was too cold to reply.

So cold now, colder than I had ever been. Even when I had been bundled into a snowdrift as a child, I had never been as frozen as this.

I kicked, losing all sensation south of my hips. My foot connected with the murky sludge at the bottom of the lake, and I tripped, nearly throwing myself underwater but, I was so close now.

Nearly there, *nearly there.*

As soon as my bare feet touched the snow-covered sand, I hauled Coen up, *up*, out of the water and onto my abandoned coat. He was so fucking heavy in my exhausted arms. I got him as close to the fire as

I dared, then I knelt in the snow and began to strip him. I had lived in the north long enough to know what to do with an ice water casualty.

Working frantically, I tore away his coat, vest, shirt, and breeches and tossed the soaking garments aside. His muscle-hewn body was ghostly pale. Using the last of my strength, I heaved him onto a dry blanket and covered him head to toe with more warming layers.

Flight medics ran toward us.

I could hear Amadea shouting. "Let me through, *let me through*. I can help!"

"Your Majesty, please, we can't risk—"

The roan mare cantered up behind me and nudged my shoulder, a worried whicker in her throat. I would wonder about the amazement of that later, my very mind feeling like glass cracking apart.

I could do this.

I could save him. I wouldn't be useless tonight.

Terra yelled in the distance. "Keep Her Majesty back. I do *not* want them jeopardized."

"Go to hell," screamed Amadea. "You know I can help!"

I tore my gaze from Coen's muscled torso, lanced with scars, to the tattoo on his right bicep and the corded leather necklace he wore around his neck. All things he had kept hidden under his uniform.

"Get me a bucket of warm water!" I screamed.

His breaths were shallow, mere sips for air.

A soldier ran forward and placed a bucket at my side. Shock at my orders being listened to was barely registered. I plunged cloths into the warm water, rung them, then covered his bare temple, stomach, chest, and groin. His body was shivering hard, battling to rewarm itself.

I didn't realize that I, too, was shivering so hard my bones felt brittle.

The medics reached us, yelling orders to one another. In the faint winter wind, I could hear the residents of the village wailing, crying over their dead. The Nijinxes had fully retreated. Another blaring sound of a horn blasted through. A second platoon had landed.

Coen blinked.

I froze, clutching a fresh, damp compress, although my hand trembled with the effort.

The roan nosed my shoulder gently, her sweet, warm breath trickling down the back of my frigid neck.

Coen blinked again, his gaze quickly searching, assessing. He looked down at his shuddering body wrapped in blankets, then up at me, taking in my still soaked and freezing frame, the cloth in my hands. Something akin to realization seemed to dawn upon him, and then I saw it, a sheer, warm glance of respect and awe.

His throat bobbed as he swallowed. "Destry ..."

We ... we were even now. He had saved my life, and I had saved his. My trembling hand rested over his chilled fingers, and I squeezed gently.

Silvano, I wanted to say, but I couldn't reply as much as I tried to.

Amadea skidded to her knees by my side, sand and snow spraying, as my heart thundered in my too tight chest. Only then, as I snapped out of my feverish focus of tending Coen, ensuring he survived, did I falter upon the snow, my body slumping at the roan's hooves.

The Queen gathered me up in her arms, and I could feel the lake shift beside me.

"Don't you *dare* use your magic here," hissed Terra.

"I am your Queen, and I will warmher," snapped Amadea, as lukewarm water enveloped me.

In a hissing whisper that only Amadea and I could hear, Terra replied, "You are no queen of mine."

Yet the flight medic dived out of the way, as a near snow-white Pegasus mare slammed to the snow and bared her teeth at Terra. Her bearded rider, two short swords strapped to his back, leapt from the saddle and ran for us.

CHAPTER
TWENTY-FIVE

ASHER

I stood on the water-slicked parapet, hands braced behind my back. Vesperum and Pherox flanked me on either side, our apprehension intermingling as we appraised the new human in our midst. We had just made it back from our raid to try and take the *Koskivarri*, and this man had followed us back. He had come alone, fully trusting his ability to defend himself against me and the Nijinxes. Either that, or he was an outright lunatic to face us on his own.

My eyesight still sparked from where the young woman had lashed me with her ethereal light, and I blinked in the darkness. It had been an effort to not kill her, but at least I'd managed to scare her witless instead and show her the power of the wild ward and me. The wild ward had wanted her alive, but the villagers ... their deaths and the bloodlust had left my body reeling, craving *more, more, more*.

Pherox huffed a deep breath from the darkness, the meek light bringing a glinting sheen to his bared fangs. Vesperum stood silently, assessing the human's every move. Soft clicks echoed throughout the mine as the Nijinxes communed with one another, questioning the identity of the man before us. Only the wild ward, it seemed, was utterly unfazed by him. She stepped down from the parapet to stand level with the tanned stranger.

His head was utterly devoid of hair, yet slight stubble peppered his jaw.

He did not bow before her, and I bared my teeth at the disrespect. Cutting green eyes flicked to me as I stood wreathed in shadow.

"There was no need to *visit*, Jaryn," said the wild ward darkly.

Jaryn. Fucking *King* Jaryn Adacus of Ilrair. I blinked in surprise on two counts. The first being that I knew what his name meant; the wild ward must have slipped her leash a little to let me know that snippet of information. And the second being that he really had come alone.

From the darkness, a low rumble resonated in Pherox's huge chest.

The King stalked forward, grabbed a fistful of the wild ward's hair, and shoved her to the ground in one effortless motion.

I snarled and launched toward them, daggers drawn. The wild ward threw out a hand and the magic in my body yanked me to a halt. Sweat broke over my brow as I strained at the command, but the order held.

Kneeling on one knee beside her head, Jaryn lowered his mouth to her upturned ear. "You tried to claim my *Koskivarri*. That was not part of the plan, *Meredith.*"

The shock of her true name being spoken struck through the kin swarm and I like lightning. I gazed down at her, eyes wide, the daggers still held in my fists. Such ... such a mortal, human name for a creature who wielded magic. Jaryn had spoken it with such familiarity like he had known her for years.

She hissed in response. "I have received no word for months and you expect me to do *nothing?*" She made to rise, but the King shoved her down again, pressing her cheek into the cold, damp stone. "So, I took matters into my own hands."

The King bared his teeth. "You only react to the orders *I* give you. My spies got wind of you relocating, which forced me to come up here too early." He shoved himself away from her, standing to his full height and he cast his gaze over the shifting shadows that surrounded him. "They will obey my orders?"

The wild ward, fucking *Meredith*, stood slowly on shaky legs, but quickly gathered her composure, despite the blood and dirt that marred her ethereal face. We all felt it then, that sudden clenching of the magic that wreathed in our chests as she reminded us just how much control she wielded. Her voice was cold and otherworldly. "They are yours, sire."

Pherox and Vesperum loosed outraged snarls of anger, their fangs flashing like quicksilver. This ... this wasn't part of the agreement between beast and wild ward.

Jaryn frowned. "I don't believe you, Meredith."

"The males worry after their mates, is all, sire."

"Tell them that if they don't follow orders, they will be put down. My forebearer brought them into this world, and I will just as easily take them out of it."

Jaryn's forebearer. The ancient king who had ordered the curse upon the Trinitors. A wave of silence swept over the mine as every Nijinx went utterly motionless. No one had threatened the kin swarm since they had broken free of the earth. Like morphing sections of night sky, the Nijinx males shifted themselves in front of the females. As one, they all inched closer, hovering inwards toward their Queen.

Vesperum clicked softly and stepped forward.

Jaryn raised a brow.

"Get back into your place, Vesperum," whispered the wild ward, who half turned to face the Nijinx Queen.

Vesperum's hiss of outrage was answer enough for the wild ward.

Meredith clicked her fingers, the sound echoing all around us.

Toward the rear of the mine came a harrowing screech of pain. Gold and navy magic flared from the wild ward's hand and fired toward the poor creature she had targeted. Wings bound to its side, the Nijinx was hauled to the parapet with flickering cords of light. Whistling and clicking in fury and fright, the kin swarm watched on as a young Nijinx female was pinned down before the King.

As quietly and quickly as I could, I slunk back toward Pherox until my outstretched palm reached his red-hot pelt. Murderous thoughts rampaged through the male's head.

"Hold it together, Pherox."

His string of clicks pounded through my skull, but I didn't break contact with him. Instead, I pressed my fingers into the tight muscle of his shoulder and steeled myself as Jaryn stepped toward the struggling youngling.

"Tell your Nijinx Queen, that if she or any of her kin swarm step out of line, this will be the consequence." Slowly, he drew a fine blade that had been sheathed at his hip.

The female strained with all her might against the magic. Her fangs snapped and flashed as she fought to get close enough to the King's flesh. Her bonds would not yield. The wild ward looked away, her hands trembling, yet I stared on, my hand clenched against Pherox, struggling with the effort to hold him back.

Vesperum was distraught. Her velvet ears flicked back and forth, and her body shook as the King struck the blade against the female's throat.

She kicked once, twice, then lay still upon the cold ground. And despite her magic in our veins, despite the control she doled out, Pherox and I both looked to Jaryn with the same hunter's intent.

The wild ward we couldn't yet touch. But Jaryn ... every muscle in Pherox's body shuddered with the need to strike. The male twisted his neck to look at me, and I simply nodded.

To murder a member of the kin swarm was to sign a death warrant.

We had a new creature to take down.

I sought out Pherox again that night, giving up on sleep altogether, my dreams contorted with shadows and green light. It was the animal that now solely resided in me, a beast that wanted to seek the Nijinx out, hunter to hunter, killer to killer.

The royal male scented me as he clung to his roost within the mine. His knife-like talons retracted, and he unfurled from the slick rock to land with surprising softness before me. The huge Nijinx exhaled warily, taking in the scent of the wild ward's magic, magic that now so thoroughly coated my veins. I couldn't distinguish it from myself because that humane self no longer existed.

My chest glowed more brightly because of it as the magic pulsed with every beat of my human heart. The same magic danced over Pherox's eye sockets.

We were her puppets, her givers of death.

In near-total darkness, I raised my upturned palm, and Pherox placed his slick muzzle upon it, those lethal primary fangs resting on either side of my tanned fingers.

"If we do this for her, we shall be free and the night skies will be ours for all eternity," murmured Pherox, his gravely tones rumbling through my mind. *"We know our fate beyond this human war, hunter. Yet your future ... I do not know what lies ahead for you."*

"Neither do I, Pherox, and that is what worries me."

"Defend and death. That is the male Nijinx life, his sole purpose. I forever align my life with Vesperum's, to protect her, to kill all those who threaten her. I have known this since the day I was brought to being. Yet you … hunter, the human you once were, it has been devoured like a dying star. What lies ahead for you now, only the spirits know."

The cave echoed with faint, hissing breaths of the swarm and the glossy, soft sound of leathery membranes brushing against one another.

My breath hitched. *"You believe in the spirits?"*

"The ones that matter to us. The ones that rule the night sky and regulate the stars, spirits that snuff out light and carve the shapes of the waxing and waning moon. Spirits that the humans naturally fear, that make them quake when they find themselves lost in a forest, or in the heart of a blackened cave. The Pegasi kneel to the air, the Unicorns kneel to the ice, and the Mounties to the forest. It was how the wild ward first lured us. She proclaimed she was the scion of Iltavorn, the spirit of darkness to whom we kneel before. If I had known, then …" Pherox's lips brushed my thumb as he raised his head and a barely audible clicking resounded from his mouth. *"We were the darkest shreds of Colbass. Many believed we were left to fester, to sour and decay. Yet in the total darkness, as Iltavorn whispered over us, we thrived. The slaughter on Petowin was a feast for our kind; we hadn't fed for eight hundred years. The other factions of Colbass would have never endured for so long. The creatures of the sun have had their time. The wild ward promises us freedom, and I will make sure she keeps that promise. I will see my beloved fly beneath the stars; her kin swarm behind her, with no magic marring her beautiful body. Maybe, my brother of death,"*—Pherox pressed his muzzle to my glowing chest—*"the wild ward will relinquish you, too, and I will land upon the earth to visit you, and we will hunt the little creatures once more."*

If I could only have one future now, I would accept the one offered to me by this mighty predator. I rested my forehead against his and huffed a soft breath, which Pherox returned in kind.

"Defend and death," I whispered.

"Defend and death, hunter."

CHAPTER TWENTY-SIX

ORRIN

E brel was distraught. She paced on the hillside opposite the medic tent in Saltfen, snow clouding around her limbs as she pawed at the powder.

Destry lay within that tent. Sweat began to coat Ebrel's strawberry roan pelt.

I watched the roan Pegasus, bewildered and trying desperately to understand. I was relieved to see her, as was Murrkill, but the mare was changed. We had received no warning, not even from Kalana, as dusk had gathered and Ebrel had broken free of the barn within the cavalry camp. Not a moment later, the Night Pegasus had raced across the sky, followed hauntingly by the Nijinx swarm. I held no doubt that it was the Night Pegasus who had warned Ebrel and helped her break free, but I still had no clue as to *why*, considering Ebrel was now acting as if her first foal had been ripped from her side.

Murrkill and I had raced after her into the oncoming dark, but Ebrel's wing had held strong as she took flight over the moorlands and to the small village south of Saltfen. The human woman Ebrel had saved had been the *Koskivarri*, and I wondered if the Night Pegasus had claimed the roan for surely that one purpose, to save her from death by a Nijinx. If it was, I wanted to tear into the spirit with teeth and hooves for torturing the mare for nearly all her life, just for one small fraction in time.

Yet something else ate away at Ebrel that caused her to pace back and forth in the snow. I'd never seen an equine react like this to a human. Not even the tame horses I came across whilst I was in captivity. Her anxiety distressed me; to feel like that over a human so suddenly … it was like she had been compelled.

"She needs me," whispered the young mare, and she began to pace once more.

I stepped forward and pressed my muzzle to her withers, her neck, her cheek. *"Hush, Ebrel, hush. She will be alright, your human woman. She seems valuable, too valuable for them to hurt."*

The notion that Ebrel even *had* a human woman was worrying. Ebrel was no southern Pegasus who had grown up amongst mankind since she could walk. She was as wild as the northern sky, totally untouched by man. What had the Night Pegasus said to her?

Ebrel's reddish-brown ears flicked with unease, and her brown eyes glared at the medic tent. She bared her teeth at the fluttering canvas. Murrkill was a silent sentinel behind me, watching Ebrel warily.

"Why do you worry after her so? She may be the scion to the Night Pegasus, but … she's a human*, Ebrel,"* I whispered. Despite Ilmari's instructions to bring the *koskivarri* home, seeing Ebrel react in this way made me resent my orders. No equine should be beholden like this.

The roan tossed her head. *"I barely understand it myself, but the Night Pegasus, he said that she was a loner … like me … and that he had saved me from near death in the moorlands so that I could save her in return."* Ebrel blinked and sighed heavily, turning her pretty head to look straight at me. *"I judged Kalana so hatefully for what she has with her rider, but now … I think I'm only just starting to understand."*

Ebrel grew quiet, despite Murrkill's whicker of disapproval at her words. Our attention focused on Kalana and her rider as they landed in a field opposite the medic tent. Her rider dismounted, untacked the gray mare, and turned on his heel, walking steadily over to where Destry was recovering.

I watched on, the pull to return to Glentay an ever-present feeling in my chest, yet I wondered if Ebrel would want to go with me.

CHAPTER
TWENTY-SEVEN

DESTRY

"They are more agile than I believed possible, far quicker and more athletic than our Pegasi. Even the most well-trained and fit Pegasus would struggle to out maneuver them on the wing. We match them for speed, yet we fail miserably compared to their agility."

Coen.

The Commander was talking softly on my right, and almost fainted again with relief. Another male voice on my left, Jaryn, answered, "They proved themselves tonight. They may be useful. We had no military casualties, only villagers."

"You can't be *serious*, Jaryn. You can't just *recruit* them. *They killed your subjects.*"

"I've already decided."

"*What?*" I had never heard Coen so distraught and angry. Jaryn had recruited the Nijinxes into his war, after they had attacked *us?* My head pounded in response.

I was lying on an army pallet between these two men. Coen was *alive.* Where the hell was I? How the spirits did I end up here? Fear lanced down my spine. I fought to move my limbs, but they were sluggish to respond. Panic creeped into my veins. I had to move, had to get away ...

Jaryn utterly ignored his Commander's complaint. "We go on the defensive, for now. The outlying settlements, Bantam, Tregothnan, and Gerron become aerial combat support stations for Piper, Knock, and Murmur Platoons. Keep Thorra's Royant Platoon settled here in Saltfen. Have the other Wings on standby, but only pull East Wing out of training as a last resort. I don't want new recruits and their mounts slaughtered when we move to take Aarine."

"Fucking *hell*, Jaryn," hissed Coen.

My eyelids finally ripped open, and my gaze fell first on Coen. The Platoon Commander shifted his gaze from the King to me, a flash of something warm and desperate washed over his face, then it was gone. He looked pale, but a good deal better from when I had pulled him out of the water. He was alive, thanks to me, and a small amount of pride glowed in my chest.

My gaze shifted to Jaryn, and nausea filled me at having him so close, almost leering over me. Heart hammering, I glanced down at my prone body. I lay in the medical tent, swathed in a heap of blankets, my uniform hung up to dry beside a brazier. Freezing fingers twitching, I patted my body under the blankets. Someone had stripped me of my uniform and put me into a plain woolen shift, leggings, and socks. Who had changed me? There were certainly no medics around. I could only remember being beside the frozen lake, no more than that. Amadea, I hoped.

I hated the feeling of Jaryn being above me, over me, so I heaved myself up into a sitting position, my abdominal muscles quivering with the effort.

"Welcome back, Destry," murmured Jaryn, yet there was no warmth in his voice.

Before I could muster a reply, the tent's entrance was swept aside in a loud crinkling of canvas and a gust of cold wind billowed into the relative warmth of where I lay.

Jaryn and Coen fell silent, and the air was stolen from my lungs as I looked up at the man who stood in the entrance.

"Figured I'd find you three in here, sire." There was a rustle of soft fabric as the newcomer bowed to Jaryn. "Good to see you're looking less like a corpse now, Destry. Won't be taking winter swimming up as a hobby, I take it?" His throaty yet appealing voice took a hesitant pause, and he kicked the snow from his boots. "I'm glad you pulled through."

"We're all *glad*," muttered Jaryn.

I blinked, my thoughts scattered on that frigid wind and looked upon the stranger who had entered the tent. He filled the height of the doorway, another uniformed commander like Coen, yet he stood at least two inches taller and was broader compared to the silent, brooding man sitting next to me. The hilts of two dark, short swords poked over both of his muscled shoulders.

I peered more intently from where I lay.

Those were not green eyes that looked down at me with a warm smile. They were dark bronze. His trimmed beard and mustache were the darkest I had ever seen on an Ilrairian, and his brown hair was raked back into a knot. Even his skin was a duskier shade, more akin to my own flesh than to that of Southerners. The row of buttons of his rider's coat and tailored vest lay undone down his chest and abdomen, and the loose wool material fluttered in the night air, revealing a bare section of skin at the top of his muscled chest. He was devastating to look at.

His smile grew feline as his eyes met mine, pinning me to the spot. I blinked again, the intensity of his gaze spearing straight into my soul. Common sense grappled with my mind, reminding me that the last man who had smiled at me like that tried to have me murdered.

"If you were trying to celebrate Volaarite, then I'm afraid you're a little late to that party," said the stranger, as he stooped to sit down beside Coen, his movements displaying restrained wildness and strength, as if the winter storm outside whirled within him. The entire tent seemed to shrink with him in it. Only his voice was like the men who sat around him: smooth, educated. Sitting side by side with Coen, I noted little age difference between them.

My gaze tracked his every move, highly suspicious.

Coen's jaw clenched, and he frowned at his fellow officer. "Destry, this is Aalto Thorra, Commander of Royant Platoon. Thorra, Destry."

"Lovely to meet you," said Thorra, with another easy smile and a genuine glint in his gaze.

I blinked; he ... *meant* it? He didn't shy away from what I was and where I had come from. I cocked my head with intrigue, the muscles in my neck twinging in protest at the movement.

"In answer to your question, I won't be taking up winter swimming as a hobby, as you can see." I gestured to the blankets swathing me. "I'm not very good at it."

Thorra chuckled, the sound warm and alluring. Coen glanced between the two of us, his brows furrowing before settling on me. "It was Thorra's Royant Platoon that flew into the village tonight and helped us get back to Saltfen."

I swallowed, my throat scratching like sand. I couldn't hold Coen's worry-filled gaze. "I heard the horn blows."

Thorra swiveled in his seat, unclipped a leather water skin from his belt and handed it to me. "Here."

"Thank you." I tried, yet failed to keep the surprise out of my voice. The water was heavenly and cool, soothing my ravaged throat, and I refused to acknowledge the warmth of his hand on mine as I passed it back to him.

Coen looked across to his King, then back to me. "One of the Nijinxes had a rider. Some of the riders noticed you had an interaction with him."

Tensing on the army pallet, I suddenly realized what this was and hurt settled in my chest. They weren't here to ask how I was faring, or for Coen to give thanks to me for saving him. All three of the men were armed. I was not. No. This was an inquisition. After I had nearly died trying to save one of their own.

"How is Hestian?" I asked, my skin bristling from their silent assessment.

"He is fine." Jaryn gazed down at me. "Healing well."

No praise, no thanks. I knew I shouldn't be surprised, but after my discussion with Coen and the truth he now knew, I had expected something different between us. How wrong I was.

"Who was he, Destry?" asked Jaryn, as his green gaze searched my face.

"Damned if I know. As you have clearly pointed out before, Your *Majesty*, I have no friends." I took a breath, steeling myself. I considered Amadea a friend now, but I wasn't about to tell Jaryn that. Thorra's gaze burned with an intensity I had never experienced before, so my gaze drifted toward the rippling canvas ceiling above our heads. "He is of Petowin, but the wild ward had control of him, and he tried to kill me. Seems to be a fucking theme around here." I looked back down and leveled a glare at Jaryn, ignoring Coen's flinch beside me. Thorra threw me a questioning look. The King stood slowly. "You're going to take control of the Nijinxes?"

Thorra straightened in his seat, his rugged features darkening as he cut an assessing glance to Jaryn. "Is this true, sire?"

Jaryn didn't back down from my glare. Instead, he gave the smallest of smirks that made my stomach twist with unease. "I already have taken control. The attack on us this evening was a mistake and will not happen again."

"They killed villagers," I protested. "Was the fall of Petowin not warning enough to stay the hell away from them?"

The King of Ilrair stared me down, unflinching and unfeeling. "You do not give the orders around here, Destry. You may rule over Petowin one day, but you have *no* jurisdiction here. My word is final."

"You made a bargain with the wild ward?" asked Coen, his voice cutting and low. Lethal, like it had been last night with Karlos and Mullin.

Jaryn glared at his Commander with leashed rage. Coen, to his credit, didn't back down from it. "I have the military aspects of which will be discussed at a later point, certainly not here."

Jaryn stalked out of the tent. I stared at the space where he had once been. The Platoon Commanders sat silently beside me, tension rippling between them. The King had lost his spirit's damned mind. Recruiting Nijinxes? Working *with* the wild ward? The same wild ward that had tried to claim me with her darkness and magic?

Thorra cleared his throat. "He's losing it, Coen."

Coen stood and raked a hand through his dark blond curls. "Well-the-fuck-aware, Thorra."

I gazed up at them both as they eyeballed each other. A current of hostility wrapped around them, and I sat a little straighter. My voice was surprisingly steady as I said, "He must have something considerable over the wild ward to get her to make a bargain."

Coen's features hardened, then his shoulders slumped, and his hand reached across to run a thumb over my shoulder. I couldn't hide my sharp intake of breath at the contact. He shook his head, his dark curls swaying. "You were … you should rest. I'll try and talk some sense into Jaryn."

"Amadea?" Thorra gazed up at Coen, his jaw clenched tight.

Coen stilled, his features warring between empathy and frustration.

Thorra's gaze flicked to me, then back up at his fellow Commander. "Just tell me, Silvano."

"She's unhurt." He cut a scathing glare at Thorra, who looked calmly up at him. If the Royant Platoon Commander felt any relief at Coen's words, he didn't show it. "You should let Destry rest."

Thorra stretched out his long legs and crossed his ankles. Lazily, his lips twisted in a small, barely there smile; he glanced between Coen and me. Those bronze eyes noted how Coen hovered beside me, and how I naturally leant toward him. "I will, in just a moment. Don't worry, she's in safe hands, Silvano."

"*She* is sitting right here." I rolled my eyes at the pair of them.

Clearly riled, Coen walked stiffly from the tent. My exhausted gaze followed his tension-riddled body as he left, leaving me with just Thorra.

The Commander tilted his head in question, worry dancing in his bronze-colored eyes. I met Thorra's questioning gaze, and I felt utterly bare before him. Alone with Coen, I felt unprepared and always questioning his feelings. Yet with this Platoon Commander, I felt … reassured somehow. I was still wary of the newcomer. He could be just like Farrow for all I knew, yet I suspected that Petowin lay within him and surely … that meant he was an ally?

Hesitantly, I whispered, "What is Volaarite?"

His lips parted in a crooked grin. "I hoped you would pick up on that. It's a Petowin holiday, one of only five in the recognized calendar." His features softened, and he ran a large hand over his trimmed beard. "It's customary to undertake a lake swim, although there is usually a hot, alcoholic drink waiting for you at the other side, not a medic tent." Thorra chuckled, and I found myself smiling weakly in return. "You'd need alcohol to get me *in* the water, let alone out of it."

He knew about Petish holidays, and he was an Ilrairian officer? It didn't make sense. "What does it celebrate?"

"The first day of winter and the creation of Petowin itself." He paused and chewed his full lower lip. "Destry, I hate to ask this, but being a winny, and a Kivisto at that, why don't you know this already?"

He knew my surname or suspected it. *Shit.* "What makes you think I'm a Kivisto?"

I sure as hell wasn't going to confirm it for him. I just hoped he believed the bravado in my voice.

One of those perfect eyebrows arched. "Let's just say I'm very well connected. Every platoon has its own spies and if something is happening that involves Petowin, I'm going to know about it."

Heat colored my cheeks. How much did he truly know, or was he just hedging his bets? "I was never taught all the Petish culture at the Reck. I learnt Petowin fighting styles, most prominent battles, exports, and fashion as a matter of course, but never things like holidays. I hate it ... not knowing." I looked at my now dry uniform hanging on the stand. I couldn't fully understand why I was opening up to this man. He was heavily armed.

Yet as Thorra followed my gaze to the limp rider's uniform, I saw an understanding flash in those bronze eyes.

Thorra leant back in the small folding chair. "There is so much to know, so much of Petowin that is not general knowledge. As I'm sure you understand, the written word is rarely used. Most young men and women, when they are of an age to leave home and fend for themselves, travel around Petowin to stay with other clans and families, to act as a *paija*, a helper of all trades, herding, cooking, fishing, etc. That is usually when most people learn about the deeper aspects of the culture of being Petish. The whole history is passed down via tales. So, Destry, let me tell you the story of Volaarite."

I smiled at him and found myself relaxing a fraction against the blankets.

"Comfy?" he asked, his voice velveteen in the cool air.

"As comfy as one can be on an army issue pallet."

"Not very much then?" He shook his head at my hoarse bark of laughter. When ... when had I last laughed? I couldn't remember, and my ribs ached from the sound. "You try sleeping on a scree-sided mountain, it'll feel like a feather bed after that. Now, where was I? Volaarite. It all began with the earth spirit, Perama. Daring and bold, the spirit decided to swim through the freezing Nitarn Sea. The water spirit, Merivis, was enraged at the encroachment onto her territory, and she hunted him down. In Perama's haste to flee her water, he leapt from the sea and dragged the northern continent out with him.

"Merivis was so angry at him, no one had dared enter her realm before. She flattened most of the land he had created, swiping chunks off the tops of the mountains with tsunamis, creating the fells and pummeling the land with rain, creating the lakes. Sad at seeing his brother's lands so barren and broken, the forest spirit, Tellervo, grew tree after tree for his brother. He created huge forests larger than even his own Glentay. Merivis saw the green land flourish beside her northern sea waters, and she admired the country Perama and Tellervo had created. Two spirits working together was something she had never seen before, yet she felt sad, too, she would never be able to create something so beautiful from the earth, all her beauty lay beneath the waves.

"In apology to the destruction she had caused Perama, she sent thousands of snowflakes down on Petowin. A frozen kiss for every tree, white being one of the few, yet the purest color she could create. For three months, Merivis bestowed the land with kiss after kiss. Perama found that he loved the snow and abounded about the land. Each day, he traveled to the ocean's edge, and thanked her for her gift. Yet, eventually, the sun grew stronger, and the snowflakes melted and returned to the sea, back to Merivis. In thanks to her gift, Perama built the mighty waterfalls for her, so that she could create rainbows in the water's falling spray and play in any color that she could dream of."

"That was ... beautiful," I murmured, lost in the story he had told me.

He nodded, a small, playful smile on his full lips. "That concludes Thorra's storytelling for now. You should rest."

"Thank you, Platoon Commander Thorra ... for telling me about Volaarite."

The Commander rose and snuffed out the two oil lamps beside him, pitching the tent into darkness. Adrenaline surged through me, and my light flickered at my fingertips in response. I felt Aalto shift toward the entrance.

"Good night, Destry Kivisto *Koskivarri.*" He peeled back the canvas flap, and I saw faint starlight beyond, framing his warrior physique. I watched him closely as he paused, his gloved hand braced against the support pole. A gray Pegasus mare strode up to him and gently jabbed her nose against his shoulder. "I am a man of mixed blood and heritage, so believe me when I say, I know exactly how you are feeling right now. It's the Petowin in us that makes us gravitate to others of our kin. Do not let them pummel out that wildness, Destry. You hold onto it with both hands and wear it like armor. When the wilderness sings in your veins, you can't ignore her."

The draught of empty air hit me after he left, sweeping his scent to where I lay. I inhaled deeply.

The Petowin in us.

CHAPTER
TWENTY-EIGHT

ORRIN

The camp was quiet, and all three of us watched the fluttering tents and torches intently from where we stood in the paddock. We knew Kalana and her rider were nearby, their plan waiting to form into action.

As silent as the spirits themselves, the men and women of Royant Platoon stalked around the camp, silencing those of Bromtide Platoon who were still awake, albeit not indefinitely. They weren't as soulless as to murder their fellow soldiers. The world was about to be blown to hell, and I would need to run for my life. I could feel it in my bones and Ilmari pulsed in the night air.

Ebrel exhaled warily, then set off silently across the paddock, stretching her wings, testing them. Content, she headed for the medic tent. Murrkill and I waited for her signal, tense and ready.

CHAPTER TWENTY-NINE

DESTRY

I was in a deep, exhausted sleep when something covered my mouth. My eyes shot open, and I tried to suck down a panicked breath. Hands grappling and tearing blindly, my fingers found the strong column of a male throat, and my nails dug into the skin and wool. Whoever it was pushed into my grasp, barely deterred by my attempt of a chokehold. A soft breath curled into my ear, and a dominant whisper rolled over my skin. "Easy, winny, easy. It's me, Aalto. If you could stop trying to strangle me, that would be great."

Slowly, my fingers stiffened with shock. I retracted my hands as Thorra removed his gloved palm from my mouth. In the pitch darkness, the Commander rocked back onto his heels and stood. I bolted to my feet, staggering in the gloom of the tent.

"What are you *doing?*" I hissed on a silent, deadly breath, my body braced for a fight. The faint trust I had attempted to build earlier shattered between us.

"Getting you out of here."

"*What?*" Finally, my sight adjusted, and I blinked as I appraised him, and the twin swords strapped to his back. Then my gaze snapped to the prized weapon in his grasp.

Without a word, he passed it to me. Deftly, I took the dark sword from him and braced it before me. *Kathkar.* The dark blade was sheathed in a new, simple leather scabbard, but the obsidian stones in the hilt gleamed up at me. How the *hell* did he find it?

"I need to leave? With *you,* of all people?" I whispered harshly.

"You're in danger here. For all our sakes, and if we are to stand a hope in hell against the wild ward, then we need to leave. *Now.*" His tone was soft yet forceful.

I swallowed. "My vow—"

"Is about to go up in smoke, along with mine and my Platoon's, but it's the only chance we have."

"We'll be wanted for treason," I hissed.

"A price I'm willing to bear, trust me."

The faintest flicker of light wreathed my fingertips, but there was no hint of the Night Pegasus to guide me now, as if everything had led me here, to this moment, to this decision. "Jaryn will kill us all."

"He can die trying," snarled Thorra. "You and I both know Jaryn's descending into madness. Coen knows it and yet doesn't have the balls to do anything about it."

The Commander stepped closer, and I backed away into the shadows. This was insane; we'd be hunted down and killed. Yes, we'd be free, but we would be wanted for life and was I really going to align myself to a man I had just met? And I would have to leave Amadea behind. My heart splintered at the thought.

And Coen ... a fragment of me yanked at my mind, to pause, to *think*.

Coen.

Thorra's voice was lethally quiet as it cut through the dark, his presence capturing and holding my every sense. "If it helps your decision, then know this." He stepped closer again, and I held my ground, readying for a fight, as his right hand rose and brushed against the lambent stone that lay hidden against my chest. His touch had my skin stippling in its wake. "I'm the one that gifted that lambent stone to you. I had it smuggled into the Residence for you."

"It was *you?*" I whispered, not believing his words.

His hand fell away slowly, yet his gaze held mine, fierce and determined. "Come with me now and fight for your freedom or stay here and remain prisoner to that monster."

The lambent stone flared a pulse of power over my chilled skin, as if in confirmation. I sidestepped Thorra and set *Kathkar* down on the pallet. In a whirl of motion, I hurriedly dressed in my rider's uniform, Thorra having the decency to look away after a tense moment of silence. I strapped *Kathkar* down my spine, reassured by the weight of it, despite not having the skill to wield it yet.

Standing to my full height, I turned and faced the Commander in the darkness, that feeling of leashed violence and strength pulsed from him again, radiating over me. I looked up at him and lifted my chin. He silently assessed me, his gaze raking over my long, loose hair, still damp from the lake.

"Betray me or try to kill me, Thorra, and I'll shove this sword through your throat."

His eyes narrowed in silent amusement, and his voice dropped an octave. "Is that a promise, Destry?"

I stepped closer to him, and he held his ground, a smug, satisfied smirk on his lips. "Then let's get out of here."

He placed a large palm over my right hand and squeezed it gently. "Follow me."

Thorra's gray Pegasus mare awaited us in the moon and torch lit the darkness of the camp, beside the wild roan Pegasus from the village. Slowly, I walked over to her and paused beside her shoulder but didn't touch her. The mare turned her head to appraise me, wings lowered, yet her pelt twitched with anxiety.

"We found the roan near death on the edge of the moorlands weeks ago. Her wing has healed well, and she is fit to fly. She's not let anyone near her since, though, not even me," explained Thorra, mounting up on his gray mare like the dignified horseman he clearly was. "You have two choices: attempt to ride her now or fly with Kalana and me."

The lambent stone pulsed gently against me, and I brushed a gloved hand over it.

The roan must have sensed my uncertainty, as her muscled neck turned, and she reached over her huge wingspan to pluck a single, long feather free. Gracefully, she looked back to me and pressed the feather to my chest with her soft, gray muzzle.

I could feel Thorra's gaze burning into us as I removed my glove and reached up to clasp the pink and brown speckled feather in my hand. The light in my body thrummed. My vision became speckled with gold, and for a moment, Saltfen spun around me, blurring into darkness.

Then, in a voice that was hauntingly beautiful, ancient, and musical, I heard the mare's name.

E-brel.

My light curled around the knowledge, settling it deep within my core.

The world stopped spinning. I don't think Thorra or I were breathing.

"My name is Destry," I whispered softly.

Her brown, sentient gaze locked onto mine, and I could sense her comprehending me, all of me. Who I was, where I had been, what I possessed. She could understand every word I uttered to her, and although she could not reply in kind, I could read and sense how she felt, receiving an inkling to what she thought in a far deeper connection than any mere horse and rider.

I felt her very soul, and she, mine.

Two loners who were not alone anymore. The lambent stone flickered again, and another sense of confirmation echoed in my mind. The Night Pegasus had orchestrated this, or maybe my ancestors had. Whoever it was, I was so utterly grateful to them.

Ebrel. I reached up around her neck and hugged her, fighting back tears. Just like me, she had been chased out, abandoned and left feeling desolate. Two loners.

Her head lowered, her muzzle pressing down against my shoulder. She inhaled deeply, taking in my scent that was no doubt awash with awe and lanced with grief.

She lowered her wings further, and slowly, she knelt, not in submission, never that from this beautiful, wild beast, but as an act of partnership. We had to flee and to do so, we had to fly, together as one.

I leapt upon Ebrel's back, gently clasping my calves to her sides. I felt her settle herself, grow accustomed to this strange, foreign weight on her. This was a creature that I imagined would refuse to wear a saddle or a bridle.

"I've never seen that before," breathed Thorra.

Instinct told the young mare that any weight on her back was a predator that wanted to kill her. Her ears flicked back and forth, and she snorted warily, wings half spread.

"I won't hurt you, sweetheart," I whispered so only she could hear me.

Ebrel turned her head to half gaze at me, those brown eyes appraising my body above her, the oddity of it all. The bond we shared did little for quashing those flight instincts that pulsed through her bones.

It was Thorra's moon-gray mount, wings folded delicately over her strong back, that walked steadily over to Ebrel and nosed her cheek.

It's alright, the mare seemed to say. *It's alright, you'll see.*

I brushed a gloved hand through her brown, tousled mane, then tucked her feather safely within my coat pocket. Ebrel pulsed her wings, once, twice, the muscles now sure and strong.

Thorra turned Kalana and prepared to take flight. The town was eerily quiet, too quiet, just as a horn call blasted through the camp.

A familiar blond-headed soldier bolted from his tent and froze when he spotted us. Ebrel pinned her ears at him, her nostrils flaring in a silent challenge. My gaze flicked upward to meet his, and I shivered at the white-hot fury that burned on his face. Yet that anger wasn't directed at me. No, the Bromtide Platoon Commander was snarling at Aalto.

"You fucking traitor," he seethed. Aalto just smirked at him like he already won this war. Coen turned to me, his gaze desperate. "Destry, please, don't do this. Don't trust him. He's—"

"I think she's heard enough from you and Jaryn, Silvano," growled Thorra.

My lips parted, teeth bared.

Slowly, Coen withdrew his curved blade and pointed it at Thorra. "I'll hunt you down," he snarled. *"I'll hunt you fucking down.* Please, don't do this, Destry."

And my heart, for fuck's sake, my wounded heart, which was already crumbled beyond repair, fractured just a little more. That fragment in me, that wanted him, that had wanted him to stay last night after he saved me, begged me to *stay* here with *him.*

But he was chained to Jaryn. He would always be chained to Jaryn, and that would cost me my freedom.

"Shit," breathed Thorra as he looked south, wholly ignoring Coen.

In the western paddock, thirty Pegasi and their riders bounded into the sky and sped north, Royant Platoon. Yet Thorra didn't look at them; he fixed his gaze southward, to the three large, oncoming triangular flying formations as they crested the horizon.

"Piper Platoon," whispered Thorra, as his mare shifted beneath him, her gray wings arching.

Another horn call sounded, and Bromtide soldiers started to run for us, weapons in hand. Jaryn stormed from his tent, half-dressed and bellowing orders. I looked back to Coen, my heart in my throat, the beat pounding through my skull. He had saved my life. I had saved his. The debt between us had been settled, and I would never, *ever*, be useless again.

Ignoring that shuddering part of my heart, I lashed out with my power. Green light snapped through the air, cloaking us from view. Jaryn hurled orders as more soldiers came running from every direction.

Thorra threw one last glance at the royal tent, his face filled with longing.

I gripped Ebrel's sides with my calves and twined my fingers through her mane, the only thing I could hold onto, as the Pegasus mare turned on her haunches and galloped across the snow, Thorra right behind us.

I hunkered low over Ebrel's back, trying not to grip with my knees and using all my strength to not impact her stride.

Up ahead, the Mountain Horse from the village was already running, a breathtaking creature of brown and gold. He cleared the paddock fence in one swift leap, and tore north across the moorland, a blood bay Pegasus flying above him.

Thorra galloped past and his mare spread her wings and took flight.

"Follow us!" yelled the Commander.

Snorting with effort, Ebrel propelled all her power and momentum into one huge surge, her pink-dusted wings arching and swooping downward, swirling fresh snow behind her, as she bounded into the now clouding pre-dawn sky.

My stomach lurched into my throat, yet my blood sang in my veins as Ebrel rose, higher and higher after Aalto and his mare. Ebrel's mane whipped and danced across her neck as she tested the strength in her wing. Clouds misted beneath us, and I could just make out the Mountie keeping pace on the ground below.

I tucked myself low over Ebrel's neck, the wind tearing at me as her wings lofted us through the air, faster, faster. No wonder it was the female's role, for both Nijinxes and Pegasi, to be the attackers. They were swift, lethal, upon the air, elite aerial warriors.

Something sailed past my right ear, arched, then plummeted. An arrow.

Followed by another, then another.

I urged my light to dance behind us, shielding us from view from the archers, yet it took all my concentration to both wield and stay mounted on Ebrel. I was no natural-born rider like Thorra, and every muscle in my body screamed as I clung on to Ebrel.

Casting my gaze behind me, Piper Platoon was giving chase, its female commander at the helm.

Ebrel swung evasively from one side, then to the other, as she tried to avoid the arrows that were fired blindly now.

A bloodred form hurtled past us, flying in the opposite direction and rose higher, disappearing into the clouds.

Ebrel released a whinny of pure glee.

The tight formations that they flew in, although impressive, made the platoon too big a target.

The wild Pegasi fought in single, lone units.

The blood bay, an apparent friend of Ebrel's, appeared within the whirling clouds, wings glinting as if she were a burning dwarf star. Then her body tilted downward, pinning her forelimbs to her chest, she dived.

There wasn't a thrum of fear for her in my body as she hurtled toward the assembled soldiers flying below.

Only a peregrine was faster.

Ebrel banked to the west, staying close on Thorra's tail, her wing holding for now.

The blood bay dropped from the cloud cover and flipped once, twice, three times on the wing, just as I had seen the royal male Nijinx fly.

She dodged the arrows with ease. Using the power of her dive, she broke her flightpath by banking sharply, then righting herself on the turn. The red mare was an aerial acrobat. She doubled back and rose once more, displaying a wide variety of twists and turns. Her climbs through the air were swift and efficient, garnering her the power she needed to accomplish the evasive and attacking flying skills.

Ebrel and I both huffed with appreciation.

The red mare swooped down, forcing the soldiers of Piper to haul their mounts to a pounding hover and nearly knocking the riders clean out of their saddles. Some gaped at the spectacle. If Ebrel were human, she would have worn a smirk on her beautiful face.

The distraction afforded us a lead, and we sped north through the clouds, Thorra's platoon clearing the way ahead of us.

Free, breathed the wild light in my blood. *Free.*

Let us go home.

Yet we couldn't go home, not yet. Not when the wild ward still prowled the lands and held nature within her deathly grasp.

Ebrel was tiring. Our hard and swift flight out of Saltfen and the evasive flying we had undertaken afterward, flitting from cloud to cloud, had left the mare with just her quivering energy reserves.

We were barely withstanding the wind currents, and we would have to land soon, before Ebrel lost total use of her wing again. We had stayed above the cloud cover, roughly following the rugged north-western coastline northward, yet I didn't recognize the mist-covered peninsula below us. It wasn't recorded on any maps that I knew of.

The sun was descending, the light leaching away from the sky. Sleet battered us from the west as we lowered in altitude, finally breaking through the cloud cover to fly above the sea-carved and stark landscape below us. Rolling, snow-topped hills and forests abruptly gave way to the gray and frothing Nitarn Sea, the waves of which battered the cutting, blade-like cliffs with a pummeling ferocity. Oh, Merivis was in a foul, frustrated mood today.

I couldn't feel my hands, face, or feet, all numb with cold and exhaustion.

Kalana and Thorra altered their flight path and dropped toward a tiny clearing in the heart of a woodland several meters back from the peninsula's tip. Royant Platoon had already landed.

Battling the piercing wind, we descended into the circular section of white amidst the towering pines and firs and landed.

Blowing hard, all three Pegasi, the blood bay, Ebrel, and Kalana had their noses to the ground, nostrils flaring for breath, steam rising from their sweating pelts.

A thundering gallop echoed through the trees, and I gazed in amazement as the Mountie stallion slid to a halt upon the snow. Every inch of him quivered in exhaustion as he rested his neck beside Ebrel's.

Hating it, yet knowing I had to, I slid to the ground from Ebrel's back, my numb feet smacking into the earth as pain ripped up my shins and thighs. I hissed, my fingers still tangled in Ebrel's mane, too cold and stiff to move yet.

Barely looking affected by the flight or the cold, Royant Platoon was already falling into their set routines. Some peeled away to gather supplies, whilst the rest led their own sweating and shivering mounts to the warm shelter of a cave that lay beyond the trees.

I looked over at Thorra, my eyes widening in surprise, as the sleek form of a male hen harrier swooped up to his outstretched, gloved hand. I blinked, unable to breathe for a moment, as Thorra ran a long finger down the bird of prey's chest. The Commander glanced at me, and a knowing smile played on his full lips. He whispered something to the harrier, and the bird launched from his hand, and up, up, up, into the cloud-washed sky.

Thorra walked over. "Come, this way. We need to cool the mounts down."

I nodded, and we led the Pegasi and Mountie into the trees. Here the wind lessened, and gray-washed light enveloped us. Trembling with every step, I almost sighed with joy as the cave revealed itself fully.

Hidden amongst the copious trees, the gigantic mound of rock had been carved out into room upon room, stable upon stable. Ebrel balked at the stone, yet followed nonetheless as we slipped through its jagged entrance, a pair of guardsmen standing on either side, recurve bows in hand.

In the warm stables, soldiers worked furiously to tend to their mounts, steam rising from every winged mass we passed. Yet still the Royants nodded as Thorra passed, and he acknowledged each one of them in turn.

Finally reaching an empty stall, I led Ebrel inside and began rubbing her down with straw. A pail of warmed water was set down for her, and I allowed her to have small, controlled sips. Glancing over the wooden partition, I could see Thorra doing the same for Kalana. The Mountie and the blood bay, however, weren't letting anyone near them.

Ebrel nudged my hand away with my fussing.

I gathered fresh supplies to tend to the blood bay. Her ears snapped back at my approach, and I moved slowly, yet deftly, around to her side. Picking up a handful of straw, I gently laid it on her steaming hot skin. Her pelt twitched at the contact, and her eyes were wide as she appraised me, yet she did not kick or squeal as I proceeded to rub her down.

Eventually, she relaxed into the massaging motion, her breathing becoming slower. With fresh water, hay, and warmed bran mashes for every animal, Thorra issued orders to set up camp and rotate the guards.

As darkness finally fell over the peninsula, I staggered away from the Mountie, exhaustion singing in my bones. Ebrel must have conversed with him in their own way to allow me to tend to him. He had stubbornly let me rub him down but had given me a snap of his teeth to tell me to go away when I was finished.

Kathkar was still a reassuring weight on my back, but I flinched at every strange sound that echoed through this massive cave. Faint white light tinged my fingertips as my control lapsed with my tiredness. My power felt stronger so far north like a stream had been undammed. Content that Ebrel was settled and cared for, awe still washing over me that the mare had claimed me for herself, Thorra caught my gaze and led me dutifully from the stables. We treaded deeper into the cave. Voices, male and female, echoed softly off the rock as we entered the main excavation hall.

Two large oil lamps illuminated the space as the platoon set up pallets and set out meals of bread, cold meats, and cheese. Two large fires burned in the center of the space; the smoke cleverly filtered out through the ceiling. Many of the soldiers were undressing and heading down a carved set of stone steps that disappeared into gloom.

I inched closer to Thorra's elbow, my gaze taking in every soldier, every weapon and escape route.

A Sergeant strode up to us, his wild blond locks thoroughly wind-shocked beneath his hat. His uniform was soaked, and grime coated his skin. I tensed at the sword on his hip.

"I'm quite liking treason, sir," he said with that wolfish grin, as he removed his hat and shook the water droplets from it, before settling it back atop his curls. *Sherwood* was stitched on the name tag on his chest. "Nice food, a warm bath beckoning and I'm sure it's a nice view outside when the weather's pleasant."

Thorra smiled and clasped his hands in front of him. "I'm glad to see you're treating it as a holiday, Sherwood. All settled?"

The Sergeant looked at the rest of the platoon, readying their new quarters. "We're pretty much there. All the mounts are abed. Grier and Nion landed not five minutes ago, and we have the first guard watch out in the lookouts. I'll have them rotate every two hours. Grier will have her report ready for you as soon as she is able. Marte awaits you on the mezzanine."

Thorra nodded. "Sherwood, this is Destry. Destry, meet my second in command, Shep Sherwood."

Shep bowed at the waist. "It is an honor."

I smiled weakly; his manner seemed genuine. "Honor is all mine, Sherwood."

"Shep, why don't you go get a bath? By the spirits, you need one," ordered Thorra with a laugh.

Sherwood rolled his eyes and clapped his hand on his Commander's shoulder. "You can talk, sir; I don't think I've seen that handsome face quite so disheveled before."

Sherwood had a point. Thorra did look utterly windswept, and it did nothing but improve how he looked. It suited him.

Then, with a merry wave, Sherwood strode to the stone steps, passing jokes to the other soldiers as he went. With their returning smiles, my unease lifted slightly. I blinked, returning to the cave, and I ignored the questioning glances from the soldiers that were thrown my way.

Thorra turned to me, his voice soft, "Come with me. There is someone you need to meet."

We left the main hall and delved deeper into the gray rock. The cave held more rooms than I could count, holding vast supplies, hot springs, and endless tunnels. I could hear the sea pounding the shore in some parts. In others, just a faint trickling of water down slick stone.

Guided by small oil lamps set on the ground, I followed Thorra out onto a carved mezzanine that overlooked a calm and serene hot spring. Steam rose from the surface and dampened the jagged rocks above our heads. The calm water reminded me of Amadea, and pain coiled in my chest. I had abandoned her with no explanation and no goodbye, and I felt like an utter wretch because of it. Flickering candlelight cast dancing shadows across the water's surface, and I was nearly transported back to the Adacus Residence. My stomach roiled. I was free, hunted but free, and she remained trapped.

As I stepped up onto the mezzanine, a hand on the carved balustrade, I vowed to go back for her. Come hell or high winds, I wasn't going to leave her there with *him*. She could shelter in Petowin, or find refuge in her home country, a land of lush rainforests and mist-shrouded mountains.

Thorra stepped to one side and revealed an aged female copy of himself. At least sixty years old, the woman had the same bronze hair and eyes. She was as tall as I was, yet Thorra towered over her.

Then it was her dress that snagged my attention. A teal green traditional Petowin dress, high-necked, long-sleeved, made of warm Norwickan wool. Around her trim waist, she wore a braided belt, its center knot intricate and braided with gold. Thorra's mother swept into a deep bow, emulating a natural grace and poise that I could never master, no matter how hard I tried.

"Destry," she murmured as she returned to her full height and smoothed down the panels of her skirt. Her gaze was warm, approving even, as she appraised me. "It is a joy to finally meet you."

Her voice was beautiful, a traditional Petish accent that filled my dreams and chased away my nightmares, mixed with a minimal southern Ilrair tone.

I bowed in return and approached her, my hands tightly clasped.

"This is my mother, Heara Marte Thorra, widow of the Petish ambassador to Ilrair," said Thorra with heart-wrenching devotion. Well, that explained how much he knew about Petowin and how he looked.

Marte was a lady of Petowin nobility, to be given the title of heara. Yet, once more, I was knocked by how little I knew of my homeland, its ways, customs, and families. Oh, Damara had tried. She had gotten every resource she could lay her hands on without raising suspicion within the Reck, and I thanked her with every breath for that. Yet my unknown knowledge was like a yawning hole that grew by the hour.

I stepped forward, shadows dancing across my vision. "It's lovely to meet you."

Marte grinned and gently gripped my elbow. "Come sit. I brought up fresh food. You must be famished, and I know you are exhausted, but there is much to discuss."

The heara led Thorra and me to a small, stone-carved table that boasted three chairs and a spread of bread, cold meats, cheese, and steaming cups of warmed blueberry juice.

Stiffly, Thorra and I sat, the Platoon Commander emptying his drinking cup in seconds, before reaching for the pitcher. I ignored the working of the strong column of his throat as he swallowed more.

Marte allowed us to eat several hurried mouthfuls of food, before clasping her hands on her lap and meeting my gaze with her worried, bronze eyes. "Jaryn works with the wild ward and her animals to take Aarine and, eventually, the entirety of the Boreals."

Thorra leant forward and braced his muscled forearms on the table. "It's the main reason for our treason. We refuse to work for a man that utilizes such abhorrent power."

The food turned to lead in my stomach. Mother and son shared a knowing glance and Thorra swirled the contents of his wooden cup.

"If we are to stop Jaryn, then we need to destroy the wild ward and her control over not just the Nijinxes, but the spirits too," explained Marte softly. "We believe the wild ward seeks to kill or control the scions of the spirits, weakening them even further. There ... there is a mirror. The Kottin Mirror. Do you know of it?"

I shook my head, glancing between them, shame coloring my cheeks.

"It was a gift made by an ancient race, the Lowlanders, to the people of Petowin. They knew they could not be saved from another wild ward that plagued them, and that the mirror was their final defense against them and the evil magic. They gifted it to us due to our twin beliefs in the spirits, and that the Anduns should not be occupied by humans."

"What was it built for?" I asked.

Marte sucked down a heavy breath. "To destroy the wild wards' power. It can fracture apart their magic systems."

I leant forward, my body chilled under my damp uniform. "How does it work?"

"That we do not know. The Lowland people did not have enough time to grant us such information before they were wiped out. All we know is that the current wild ward tried to destroy it when the Nijinxes raided Petowin, yet she failed. We've heard rumors that she locked it away within Serebo. Many have tried to reclaim it, yet they have all perished," murmured Marte.

"Serebo is the most logical place. No man has crested that summit. They die of oxygen starvation before they can get anywhere near her. The air is too thin to fly to the top, so we can only reach the northern col. I'd take the entire platoon with me if I could, but it would attract too much attention." Thorra ran a frustrated hand through his hair, which he had tied up with a leather strap. "So, we go together. You and I, the roan and Kalana."

Just me ... and *him?* A man I had met not even twenty-four hours ago? "I—I don't even *know* you, and we're going to climb a *mountain* together?"

He *winked* at me, and I scowled in return, distrust twisting my stomach. Spirits above. "It'll be a great chance to get to know each other then, won't it? Someone's got to stop you from diving headfirst into frozen lakes."

"If we are to defeat this wild ward, we need that mirror. The spirits don't stand a chance in defeating her unless the strongest ones are freed." Marte reached across the table and gripped my hand, and I was amazed by the coarseness and strength of it.

I looked into those brown eyes and saw the fierce determination there. "The strongest?"

"Serebo, Ghel, Bronzo ..." said Thorra softly. "The mountain spirits, the wild ward imprisoned them before they had any chance to retaliate. As for the person who could wield the mirror, the wild ward couldn't find them and eliminate the threat."

Thorra looked at me pointedly, and it was Marte who explained, her lilting accent sounding like music. "She couldn't find it, because it had been hidden in the snows from her and hidden once more in the disguise of an Aarine noblewoman."

I blinked. The pieces slowly, slowly, coming together.

"Many spirits choose a scion to help them. Tellervo has the Mountain Horses, Ilmari has the Pegasi, Merivis often uses the Orca, yet the Night Pegasus chose a place, and a specific female family line to aid him."

"The Kivisto women," I whispered in the candlelight, steam licking at my cool skin. The lambent stone flared in response.

"Yes," murmured Marte. "And now you are free from the box Jaryn tried to trap you in. Now you can help the others who are still caged."

I glanced across to Thorra, who met my gaze with a shrewd smile. "Where do we start?"

Marte's breath caught. "We need to find the mirror."

CHAPTER THIRTY

ASHER

I stalked around the parapet, filtering through dank shadows.

The Nijinxes were abed. They had clustered closely around Vesperum for comfort and reassurance. Wings tucked tightly around one another, they created a near-impenetrable shield of leathery wings and glossy fangs. Males tucked their mates close to them. All their senses straining for any sign of Jaryn arriving at the mine.

The slain Nijinx's body had been moved to a different part of the mine. Yet the echo of what happened here tarnished the very air that I breathed.

Meredith had knelt upon the slick rock, her bare body bathed in a singular shaft of sunlight that had broken through the curved roof above. The moss upon the magic wielder's joints glowed in the dim light, and the tattoos on her flesh seemed to simmer. Tilting her head back, arms held loosely by her sides, Meredith emitted a sigh.

I flinched.

The brindled flicker of her magic glowed in her chest and began to curl and twist in the huge open space before us. It started to convex up and up, spiraling around itself until it created a glittering pillar that connected the wild ward to that lone light and the entrance from which it shone.

My chest constricted, and my heart pounded as if the magic before us was bearing down on not just me, but everything living, everything wild.

The magic pulsed. All around us, the mined rock began to groan. The creatures of Glentay and the Nijinxes were already Meredith's servants. Yet she wanted more. Jaryn *needed* more. A mere forest's population, even a forest as great as Glentay, would not satisfy them. Raising her arms above her head, Meredith slammed her palms together.

The resounding boom that followed made me drop to my knees and cover my head with my arms as shards of rock dislodged from the ceiling and skittered across the floor. I glanced up, up at Meredith's glorious and lustful smile. Her magic quivered in response and lashed upward, darting for freedom.

The wild creatures of the Boreals would not stand a chance against her. I almost felt sympathetic.

CHAPTER
THIRTY-ONE

ORRIN

The spirits had helped craft the Kottin Mirror and had shown the Lowlanders' visions on how to assemble it. Merevis had directed them to one of her finest and purest of lakes in the dead of winter. A northern swan had led the way, showing the chieftain a large and irregular, yet utterly glass-like section of ice that had been cleaved from the very center. Ice that did not melt in the dead of summer. No cracks marred it. In the sunlight, it shone like an ancient jewel.

Tellervo revealed to Ilmari his finest standing of birch trees from which she had blown down the smoothest and glossiest of branches. One of Glentay's wolf packs had carried them deftly to the edge of the Lowlanders' caves and laid them in the shape of the ice.

Using the hide of a reindeer, cut into supple strips, the chieftain had built the birch frame. The Kottin Mirror was born and hung, for a time, within Spell, a gigantic ice cave near the base of Mount Serebo.

For twenty days, a small party of the finest trackers treaded north to Petowin. They entrusted it into Chieftess Kivisto's care. Yet it was too late, too damn late for the Lowlanders. An ancient male wild ward sprung forth and set out to seek and destroy the mirror, yet he had failed and destroyed an entire race in retribution.

And now, this current and powerful wild ward had found the mirror and had swiftly and brutally trapped Ghel and Bronzo, encasing them within their ice-hewn palaces with a blanket of curses.

With the two peaks caged, she had trained her focus on Serebo, yet the mountain spirit had not gone down without a mighty fight.

Yet her ibex, varki stags, snow sirens, and Unicorns were no match for the wild ward, who locked up Serebo with a haunting laugh that shook the Boreals.

Only the Kottin Mirror could break Serebo and her sister peaks free of their curses.

And only Destry could wield it.

Watching the Royant Platoon train was eerie. Using the packed, level earth beneath a huge rocky overhang that jutted out of the cave, the platoon was as silent as the dead. In two lines, they performed push-up after push-up. Waves crashed onto the cliffs below, and rain still pummeled beyond the shelter of the overhang.

No one spoke as they transitioned into balance exercises, the Platoon Commander leading them through the motions, his breath even, steady, and utterly controlled.

Each soldier kept their eyes trained on Thorra.

The Platoon Commander balanced his body weight over his bent arms, his legs and back as straight as an arrow as he slowly lowered his head to just above the floor. His entire body quivered with the effort, but he stayed statutory as the other soldiers followed suit with varying degrees of success.

Destry, the young Petish woman, walked up beside me, yet stayed a healthy distance away. According to Ebrel, the woman had been advised to take a morning's rest, yet she had awoken at the crack of dawn like everyone else. She had braided Ebrel's feather tightly into her hair, and it fluttered in the wind.

Ilmari wove between Destry and me, sifting through her long, near-black hair. Destry sighed and tilted her chin upward. Whether she sensed the spirit's presence or not, I could see the tension in her shoulders ease with Ilmari's unseen caress.

Boots scuffed the sand as the platoon began to stretch out after their training, talking quietly amongst one another.

My breath exhaled upon the air, creating a billow of cloud that was snuck away by the westerly, rain-lashed wind. Turning on my haunches, not balking at the low ceilings this time, I headed into the cave network to seek out Ebrel and Murrkill.

The two young mares stood laterally from one another, just within the main entrance. Tails flicking lazily, they mutually groomed each other, their teeth gently scuffing over their withers. Their wings drooped with the joy of it.

Ebrel's brand was barely visible in the faint light. To watch her kneel before a human had made rage flicker through me, and another emotion I couldn't place. Ebrel had willingly allowed Destry to climb up onto her back, giving the human the honor that no other had been granted in centuries. Whereas I had never been granted an option like that, my free will ripped from me every damn time.

I paused several meters away and drank the scene in. Ebrel was practically ecstatic, and I wondered when she would have been that close to another of her kind. Spearian's lot would have paid her no heed.

Fintan perhaps?

Grief gripped me fiercely for a moment. Father, brother, all gone. I sucked down a rasping breath. Yet somewhere out there, I had a half brother, a beast I shared blood with.

I longed to meet him, just as I yearned for my forest home.

Wings rustled softly, and I turned my neck away from the grooming mares. Kalana breezed to a halt beside me. She looked like a ghost in the shadowed light. The Royant Pegasi were allowed to roam a large, flat portion of the stone cabin with hay and water at hand.

"King of the Forest," whispered the mare. *"How are you feeling?"*

"A little sore, as I'm sure you are too."

She huffed a soft equine laugh. *"We'll rest up for today. My rider will pack supplies tonight and we set out tomorrow. We don't have long."*

"Serebo will take no prisoners. Do you think they can do it?" My gaze drifted to Destry and the Platoon Commander, who spoke quietly behind us.

"They will. We have no other options. We need Serebo and her sister peaks, and Aalto needs that time with Destry."

"I will go north with you, as far as I can. The more eyes we have, the more luck we will have in tracking down a Unicorn and the mirror." If there were any left to find.

Even if we did find one, by some sheer stroke of luck, it would need to be one with enough magic stores to work in conjunction with Destry and take on the wild ward.

It sounded like utter folly, yet it was the only plan we had.

I fell quiet as the Commander and Destry walked side by side past us toward the roaring heat of the underground smithy. They moved with an ease around one another, and I knew that Kalana felt it too. The Pegasus mare met my gaze, and we watched on as the pair stepped down into the darkness to prepare for a mission that was also a death sentence.

CHAPTER
THIRTY-TWO

DESTRY

As I followed Aalto into the depths of the rock, toward the smithy, I was still in awe from watching them train. Both the men and women were strong and flexible. They were barely panting through their training regimes.

Spirits, they could all do handstands on *one hand*. Just the mere thought of trying to achieve that set my palms sweating. And Thorra, holding his entire body weight with perfect posture with his bent forearms over the packed earth floor ... the man had a warrior's physique.

I would insist on training as well. I didn't want to get left behind or compensated for.

We walked deeper, down into the stone cave, until we reached the smithy. The Royant Platoon's swordsmith, Elmar Hild, was a soldier of mixed Ilrairian and Colladonian blood. His tanned face, streaked with black smut marks, loomed over his anvil, and the sound of metal clashing against metal filled the huge room.

It was boiling in here.

Sweat trickled down the warrior smith's neck and back, yet he smiled broadly when he saw us enter his sacred space. After washing and drying his hands on a cotton cloth, he saluted to his Commander and bowed gracefully to me. Having everyone bow to me was just bizarre.

He was a sheer powerhouse of a man, a few years older than Thorra, yet he was double the brawn. Ilrairian military tattoos curled around his powerful forearms; he clearly did not hold much esteem for his Colladonian heritage, bar his love affair with the country's famed steel.

"How can I be a service, Commander?" The smith's green eyes flashed in the semi-gloom.

"Destry has a request, if you are able, Elmar?" asked Thorra, turning to look at me.

With a small smile, I withdrew *Kathkar* from its plain leather scabbard and laid it warily on the smith's pocked and scratched workbench. The Colladonian steel gleamed in the flickering light, and the onyx stones glinted faintly.

Elmar, his hands clasped behind his back, peered expertly down at the sword. "It's a fine Colladon blade, Destry. I don't see any imperfections. What would you have me do?"

I met the smith's gaze, those emerald eyes unnerving me. Coen and Jaryn flashed through my mind. I washed the memories of them away with a cooling breath. "It is my belief that every sword has a soul and this sword ... well ... let's just say I'm not the original owner and it has a ... dark past ... a dark soul ... if you will."

"Ah," said Elmar knowingly. "You're not the first person I have met who believes that." The smith picked up the sword and tested its weight and balance.

"The onyx stones in the pommel ... they remind me of the eyes of a spider ... the eyes of its original master," I whispered.

Beside me, Thorra crossed his arms over his chest, his body tense.

Flipping the sword in his grasp, Elmar ran a roughened thumb over the embedded stones. "You are its master now, Destry, and I think I have the solution you are looking for. A sword's soul can be changed for the better, just like a human's can."

Returning the sword to the bench, the smith strode to a huge wooden draw case. He rifled through several compartments before returning with a brown paper packet. Grinning at me, he emptied the contents onto his huge, calloused palm. There, flashing white and green in the low light, were four oval cut, polished lambent stones.

Thorra smiled.

"I've seen the Night Pegasus, Your Majesty, and I have heard rumors of your light wielding. I think these stones will be a worthy replacement for your sword. Legend claims that these are formed when the Night Pegasus flies through storms, that they are hewn from ice, light, and fire. Another Petish legend, and my personal favorite, said that the night spirit, Iltavorn, trapped the Night Pegasus into the cliffs beside the northern Nitarn Sea, in a fit of jealous rage. An ancient Kivisto Chieftess set off to save him. She saw his green light glinting within the rocks, struck her spear into the cliff, and cleaved it wide open. The Night Pegasus was freed, and as thanks, he left behind the lambent stones whenever he graced the earth's surface."

"They are sacred in Petowin culture," murmured Thorra, his voice caressing my skin. "That legend is entwined with your family, Destry. It is understood that your great ancestor was the Chieftess who freed him, and why the Night Pegasus favors the female line so greatly, why he blessed you with his light."

"I bought this cluster from a northern Colladon farmer, who claimed to find them in the snows of Petowin itself, during the winter before the Nijinxes came. I have carried them with me ever since, never really finding the right piece to pair them with. I'm glad I waited."

I picked up the largest one, and it pulsed against my skin. The light and power in my veins sent my nerve endings ablaze as the lambent rested in my hand. Tilting it in my grasp, green and white danced across its face in a feat of iridescence. A perfect miniature replica of a night sky.

"I shall remove the onyx and set these into the hilt for you. Leave the sword with me for today. I shall return it to you in the morning."

"I cannot thank you enough. How will I pay you?" I asked Elmar.

"Don't worry about that for now. Think of it as a gift for the pair of you." The smith smiled warmly, his gaze bouncing between Thorra and me. "I'll see if I can source more for you. If you think they will be beneficial?"

The pair of us? I quirked a brow and clutched the lambent stone in my hand for a few more seconds, marveling at the delicious and powerful feeling it gave me. It was like being held by the Night Pegasus again. "The more the better."

"I'll ask my mother regarding sources, Elmar. She will know," said Thorra, the smithy fire gilding his face and neck.

I quickly averted my gaze from the Commander. Thanking the sword smith once more, leaving *Kathkar* in his experienced hands, Thorra and I retraced our steps to his private quarters, a stone's throw from the main hall. Despite being kitted out with a bed, the Commander preferred to sleep in the hall with the rest of his platoon on a pallet. Yet he still used the quarters to store weapons and hold meetings.

He deftly lit the oil lamp beside the lone bed, while I hesitated on the threshold of the tiny room that boasted a rustic table with chairs, a leather trunk and weapon cupboard that took up a whole wall.

"I have some things for you." Thorra knelt beside the trunk.

I took a wary step into the tiny room. This was a very small space for just him and me.

I was not afraid of him. He had only ever shown me respect and friendliness. Yet, like that first night with Coen in Saltfen, I would go down fighting if he so much as laid a hand on me the wrong way.

Coen ... I shook the thought of him away.

No, it was another emotion entirely that had me pausing away at the doorway.

Something that I had not felt in a long, long time.

"Oh really?"

He smiled up at me as he flicked open the latches. I gazed quizzically down at him, the sight of him kneeling leaving me a little breathless.

"I had Nion, my wisp spy, track this down for you. She found it amongst Jaryn's military uniforms."

I blanched. I had been too wired to sleep the night before, too full of adrenaline to join the others in the series of heated pools deep below the main hall. Seeking out Ebrel and her warmth and bulk, I had slept in her stable, curled under her strawberry roan neck. If Thorra thought I looked a state, he was polite enough not to say or show it.

I probably still had straw in my hair.

The Commander stood slowly and took a step toward me, a familiar dusky blue bundle in his arms. I breathed in sharply as my hands fumbled forward, clasping the soft wool with shaking fingers.

The Kivisto cloak.

Furiously blinking back tears, I shook out the wool until the whole glorious garment tumbled down in a wave. It smelt faintly of lavender and wood smoke, as if someone had gently washed it and dried it over a crackling fire.

Thorra crossed his arms over his chest, his gaze warm. "My mother took it under her wing. She laundered and repaired it. She hoped you wouldn't mind, but she added some traditional embroidery to the hemline."

I glanced down, and there twinkling in the soft light, were silver Petish symbols of reindeer, trees, lakes, spears, Pegasi, stone cabins, and mountains. Either side of the clasp, she had stitched two curving river fish.

"Thank you. Thank you so much. I'll wear it with pride."

He bowed his head with a sincere smile. "You're most welcome. It feels good to reunite it with its rightful owner."

I folded the cloak back into my arms, lovingly clutching it to my chest. "Thank you, Commander Thorra."

The chuckle he uttered was low, lovely, and charming. "Please, call me Aalto," he countered.

Our gazes met, and my breathing hitched.

"Okay, Aalto," I said softly.

"I have two more items for you. It's Petowin tradition to carry them, and I gift them as a pair to anyone who joins my platoon."

He twisted toward a short, wooden dresser by his left hip, pulled a draw open, and delved inside. Large, calloused hands grasping, he turned back and proffered the items to me.

"I've seen these before, in a book Damara found." I ran a thumb over the object in his right hand, a supple leather drawstring pouch, its clasp made of glinting whorled silver.

"This is a *merradan*. Clans people usually attach them to their belts, but smaller ones can be worn like a necklace. They're primarily used for keeping flint, tinder, knives, and money, but many of my soldiers use them to carry keepsakes and good luck charms, such as braids of their mount's tail hair, and molted feathers. And this"—he held up a hand-carved, wooden drinking cup before me—"is a *koukka*."

He rolled the word on his tongue, drawing out the *O* with ease; he was clearly no stranger to the Petish language. Whereas I tripped and stumbled over it like a newly-born fawn.

"Thank you, Aalto. I'll treasure them." I smiled up at him, my arms now filled with precious heritage.

His gaze turned soft. "We should go up to the main hall, breakfast will be getting made. After that, we'll pack and have a meeting with Shep and my mother. We'll have the equines present too. The rest of the afternoon is yours to do with what you will. I only ask that you don't leave the stone cabin. We've yet to secure the outer perimeter of these lands. I want them fully locked down before we let people out to wander. I know the stables are comfy." He winked. "But Shep has made up a pallet for you in the main hall. You'll find fresh clothing, weapons, and travel bags waiting for you. I highly recommend trying the hot pools before we leave. They are heavenly. I doubt we'll get to experience anything like it for a while."

"Are you saying that a hot pool is better than sleeping on a scree-sided mountain, Platoon Commander?"

Aalto laughed. "Much better, trust me."

Another question formed on my lips, but I hesitated.

"What do you need, Destry?" He stepped closer, the essence of him pressing all around me.

I looked down at the cloak in my arms. "Do you have a spirit altar here?"

"We do," his voice dropped to a gentle murmur. "Come find me after you've eaten and bathed. I'll show you how to find it."

Gingerly, doubting myself and hoping I wasn't putting my trust in the wrong person, I reached out and squeezed his calloused hand. "Thank you."

Aalto reached up with his free hand and pulled a small strand of straw from my hair, his touch sending an electric current from my head to my toes. I swallowed. His fingers ran over Ebrel's feather knotted in my hair, tucking it behind my ear. His voice was throaty and low. "You're welcome."

I backed away from his hand, turned on my heel, and left the little room, feeling Aalto's gaze burn into my retreating back.

Coen's warning burned in the back of my mind.

"Don't trust him."

I found my pallet in the main hall half an hour later, after a breakfast of warmed blueberry juice, toasted bread, ham, and cheese. Despite being underground, this place felt far warmer and more welcoming than Ilrair. Sitting on the pallet, my entire body aching from yesterday's flight, I looked down at what clothing Marte had laid out for me, and it certainly wasn't an Ilrairian soldier's uniform. Working clothes for a Petish woman, ideally suited to the winter climate. Fur lined, knee-high boots made of reindeer leather, thick brown woolen leggings, a teal green traditional Petowin riding and fighting skirt, also known as a *holtka* tucked into which was a thick, high-necked dark gray jumper over a soft cream shirt.

I rubbed the gloriously soft fabrics between my fingers, amazed at how close my culture was now to hand. I could reach out and touch my ancestors by wearing this clothing alone and be one with my people for the first time in forever.

Gathering my things, I turned on my heel and headed for the bathing pool.

Mercifully, the hot spring was empty. Like the pool beneath the mezzanine yesterday, this one was serene and calm, lit by flickering and guttering beeswax candles on various stone cutouts.

I couldn't strip my body of its clothing quickly enough.

The feeling of the warm water lapping against my skin was practically euphoric as I lowered myself into the pool and swam deftly to the far end, where the pool curved out of sight from the entrance. At the very back of the cave, a small, trickling waterfall cascaded down the jagged rock walls.

I rested my arms on the stony rim, letting my bruised legs float up to the surface. Tilting my head back, I gazed up at the candlelit ceiling. The tension eased from my aching body, and I sighed, my breath mingling with the steam that curled from the water.

I had just finished scrubbing my skin of grime, using the jasmine-scented oil that sat in copper tubs on the pool's rim, when footsteps sounded down the small and narrow stairwell. Stilling, I sunk up to my neck beneath the shimmering, dark water. Thankfully, the water was near opaque from the shadows beneath.

Aalto rounded the corner. He didn't realize I was there; the curve of the pool concealed me. Deftly, he began to undress. *I should leave.* My hand reached for a cotton towel I had set on the side, but I rested my palm upon it, hesitating.

I could pretend I hadn't seen him. I should call out that I was here to save myself any embarrassment. I barely knew the man.

He removed the twin blades and their scabbards that were crossed over his back, resting them gently against the stone. Then he shrugged off his woven leather armor, laying it down on a flat outcropping beside him. Followed by his shirt, his fingers freeing the buttons one-handedly in quick succession as his other hand undid the leather tie binding his chin-length hair.

I swallowed. I really should tell him that—

Aalto's hand reached for the hem of his shirt, and he shucked it off his shoulders. He turned as he knelt to untie the laces of his boots, giving me full view of his glorious back.

Spirits.

His tan skin, scarred in too many places, shifted over corded and toned muscles, the furrow of his spine arching in a sinuous curve, where it narrowed at his waist. He removed his boots and rose again, hands reaching for his belt.

Too far, I had let this go too far. I cleared my throat just as he undid his leather belt. Aalto's gaze snapped to the waterfall, his shoulders tensing.

I peeked around the stone, shoulder-deep in water. He smirked, his thumbs looping through his belt. He shook his head. "Forgive me, Destry. I didn't see you there. I'll come back later."

My cheeks flamed. "I ... it doesn't bother me. Your platoon all shares this space anyway. Don't make exceptions for me." I paused, treading the water, as my heart hammered. "I'll close my eyes."

He huffed a laugh and removed his breeches, revealing sculpted calf muscles and strong thighs and—

I squeezed my eyes shut.

Lowering himself into the water, he sighed with contentment.

Feeling braver, I opened one eye then the other to see Aalto dunk beneath the water, then pop back up, his now dark hair swept off his face. He rested his back against the pool's rim. The water rippled up to his pectoral muscles, and steam slicked along the corded strength of his chest, arms, and shoulders. His bearded jaw lowered, and he looked across at me, his gaze piercing.

I could feel him assessing my face, noting every scratch and scar and the now yellow and purple bruise that lanced my neck from the wrench. Yet his gaze lingered the longest on my mouth.

My toes clenched, and I gasped, hissing in pain as a cramp tore across my right foot and spread up my calf. Grasping the slick rock, I reached down through the water to grip the contorting toes.

"Are you okay?" asked Aalto as he swam closer. "Are you hurt? The rock can be sharp under the water."

"Cramp," I hissed, my lips pressed together in a grim line. "Foot."

Aalto swam closer, then stood, this end of the pool seeming far shallower than I first thought, the water now at his upper abdomen. I tried not to think of the fact that we were both naked in the water, and he was within touching distance now.

With an arched eyebrow, he asked, "You don't ride often, do you?"

I shook my head as pain ripped through my leg once more.

"I can help, may I?" He proffered his right hand, water dripping from his golden skin.

I nodded, teeth gritting.

Aalto reached out and gently took the afflicted foot from my grasp and held it deftly under the water. The first touch of his hands on my skin had me stilling again, my chest clawing for breath in the water. Holding onto the rock for balance, I watched on in amazement and shock as the Platoon Commander gently manipulated my toes, gradually easing the pain out of them. A small moan escaped my lips as he expertly massaged my foot.

He shook his head, not looking at me. "As an apprentice, I used to get the worst foot cramps. In your first week, you have ride tutoring three times every damned day. By the end of the first week, you can barely walk straight, and for a mountain river lad who had barely sat on a horse before training, I was hardly a natural at it." He ran his thumbs down the arch of my foot, and I couldn't hold back another moan of appreciation. His eyes lifted to meet mine. "Keep moaning like that, winny, and it won't be just your foot getting all of my attention," he murmured, his bronze gaze dark under his thick lashes.

My heart raced as I looked across at him, as a heightened energy skittered over my skin. I swallowed, my hands clenching against the rim of the pool. He caressed the arch again, and I leashed my groan as my head tilted back.

"The pain will fade in a minute or two." His hands swept upward, skimming over my calf in the water.

A man hadn't touched me like this ... no, a man had *never* touched me like this. The rest of the world and its worries melted away as I looked down again, panting. Aalto smirked at me and gazed down at the water, at a foot he couldn't see, only feel, his face filled with concentration. The intimacy of the moment banished my loneliness into the shadows beyond the candlelight. Steadily, the pain retreated.

I took a nervous breath, and with more bravado than I felt, I said, "I want you to ... train me."

He arched a brow, lips pursing. "Is that so?"

My heart rate racketed. "Yes. I don't want to be useless."

"Destry Kovisto Koskivarri, you are not useless and never will be." His right hand ran up my calf again to cup the back of my knee. My jaw clenched as desire rippled over me and pooled in my core. That was the emotion I couldn't place before. Spirits above, my own body was betraying me. As his thumb grazed over the outside of my knee, he murmured, "I won't go easy on you, Destry."

"Is that a promise?" I met his gaze in a silent challenge, and my breathing hitched again as his hand pushed higher and caressed my thigh.

"Of course." Aalto's smile was one of pure cunning. He gave my toes a final, playful squeeze, then set my foot back down into the water.

"Thank you," I said faintly, breathily, letting go of the rock as I struggled to think straight. *Get a fucking grip, Destry.*

Aalto pushed back into the water, creating a wide space between us, giving me a chance to breathe. Yet his gaze was heated, not leaving my face. "You're welcome."

I swam to the water's edge, and Aalto turned his back to me as I hoisted myself out of the water, deftly wrapping the large cotton towel around me.

"I'll come find you once I'm done here, and I'll show you the altar room." Aalto gazed up at me from the center of the pool.

Gathering my things, I turned to face him. Our eyes met again, something silent and urgent pulsing between us. Then I padded barefoot from the cavern, my heart hammering in my chest.

CHAPTER
THIRTY-THREE

DESTRY

I t was an effort to concentrate.

Spirits, it took sheer will to *not* think of Aalto in that pool with his hands on me.

Now was not the damned time or place to think of that. I didn't know him or trust him. I could appreciate that he was beautiful, but he was still a stranger.

I stood before a solid oak door. Aalto knocked once, then pushed the heavy thing open to enter the sacred room. The altar was carved into the rock itself, adorned with only four candles on the long upper mantle shelf. It was the only thing in the small room. The earth before it polished to a sheen from the many knees that had graced it.

Hanging above the altar, embroidered with silver and gold thread, was a dark blue tapestry of the spirit's symbol, known simply as the oval star. Aalto had the same symbol tattooed on his left bicep.

Dotted on the oval's compass points were four circles, representing the four sister moons upon which the whole spirit family was founded upon. In the north, Ullko, the North Star. To the east, the sun, Aurin who took on the mighty fire spirit, Tavaris, his flames forever claiming her. In the south, our home, Earth, and finally in the west, Amahri, the moon. Crisscrossing over the face of the oval was an eight-pointed star. The four lines that did not touch a sister moon represented the elemental spirits; Ilmari, Merevis, Perama, and Tavaris. Where the lines connected at the center in a solid dot, the other spirits were held, such as Tellervo and his kin.

The altar was simple, as were most Petish altars. The religion of the spirits was not one for extravagance. It was felt out in nature, in a summer storm or upon a still fen. Yet the altar boasted the basic requirements for such a thing. A posy of winter flowers had been placed in a little clay pot. Nitaria bells, named after their white, bell-shaped blooms on long, curving stems, interspersed with sprigs of winter birch and wafers of bark. Dotted along the shelf were small offerings to appease most of the spirits. A speckled feather, a piece of knotted driftwood, a moss-covered branch, and a lit, tapering white candle.

Aalto stepped to the side, allowing me to draw level with him, and I felt myself relax in this cool, dark place. It felt right to be down here. It was instinct that had me sinking to my knees upon the worn floor, my whole body sagging.

Bowing my head to the altar, I sensed Aalto backing out of the room and gently closing the door behind him. I waited until his steps were out of earshot before I began to cry. The sound was entrenched in grief and loss. Soul-wrenching sounds. Like a doe caught in a vise, gasping for air. I had needed to feel this alone, in my own space, with only the spirits to console me.

I prayed that Damara and my true family were proud of me, despite feeling like a pawn that belonged to too many players wielded by everyone apart from myself. Hands shaking, I reached up and clutched the lambent stone necklace in my cool fingers. The stone glowed in response, my light feeling so at hand here. It didn't feel like I was wading through mud to wield it anymore. If anything, I was struggling to contain the vastness of it. Every mile I had traveled north had unleashed a small fragment of it.

I heard his voice a moment later.

"Welcome home, wild one," breathed the Night Pegasus, his voice solid and velveteen against my ear. He didn't materialize like he had in Ilrair. Only his voice and power wrapped around me in a sheen of sage green light.

"We're going to Serebo," I whispered, my voice hoarse from my tears. Yet, I felt lighter, clearheaded. My grief no longer a gargantuan mass in my mind, but something more bearable. It would always remain there, I realized, but I felt like I could carry it with less of a strain against my crushed heart.

His light brushed my cheek. "I know, and I shall meet you there when the time comes, once you have the mirror."

"You haven't visited me since Ilrair." I closed my eyes, and I felt his power press in closer.

"No, I haven't, my darling light, but you have everything you need now, even a mortal man worthy of loving you."

"*What?*" My voice was a gasp in the cold air, but the Night Pegasus was gone.

I knew he could hear my footsteps approaching in the snow. Keeping my eyes fixed ahead, I listened out carefully as I wove through the trees to where he lay. Darkness had long since fallen, yet I could sense him beyond the gloom of the tree line.

Aalto was a mere shadow upon the ground to me.

My voice whispered over the fresh snow, soft yet sure, "I came to find you; Sherwood told me you would be out here."

His hands remained behind his head, and his legs were stretched out on the thick reindeer hide and furs he laid upon. "I don't get the time to enjoy this often, so I take the chance when I can."

With us moving out at dawn, I doubted we would get such a luxury as this again.

"I'm sorry. I shouldn't have disturbed you." I turned to leave.

He propped himself up on an elbow, his gaze cutting through the dark to see me standing there, shrouded in my family's cloak. "You didn't disturb me at all. Come and join me if you like."

Silence beat between us as I weighed his offer. Then, I ventured forward into the clearing, my heart a steady pounding beat in my chest, lying down beside him on the reindeer hide, yet keeping a healthy distance away. Aalto gazed down at me for a moment, then laid down and gazed up.

Our breathing was the only sound, clouding and intermingling on the night air above us. The high trees created a circle of boughs; the artwork framed a sky full of shimmering stars with no moon to take away their light. The more we gazed, the more stars seemed to appear, flickering to life in a silent greeting, assessing us as much as we assessed them. This ... this feeling of smallness and weightlessness was what I had ventured out into the night to find.

"Aalto?" My voice was deathly quiet.

He seemed alert to my every word. He turned his head to look at me, hands clasped on his abdomen. "Yes, Destry?"

Ripping my gaze from the stars, I propped myself onto one elbow and looked down at him, half of his face was cast in darkness. What little light there was shone on his inky hair. My light did not wreath my fingertips. No, it has hidden deep within me tonight, safely ensconced within my body. "Why did you do it, Aalto? Why did you and your platoon go against your vows?"

He squeezed his eyes shut, letting the direct question run over him. When he opened them again, the stars seemed more vibrant, and the trees were absolutely still around us, pausing, listening. "It had been in the works for a while, the ... dissension. I think for me it was a kernel that had always been there, even before I was an apprentice, before the Petish embassy was ransacked when I was a young boy. As I was promoted through the ranks and put through the bonding process with Kally, that really settled it for me."

I tensed. "What happens in the bonding process?"

"No one will tell you the answer to that, no one in my platoon anyway. Not enough time has passed. The horrors of it ... some of them still have nightmares about it, their mounts too. I was extremely lucky to be paired with Kalana. Since that bonding, I strove to fight for her, to make the world a better place for her and when I was given a platoon, I wanted to make it a better world for them too. You may have noticed, but there are only a few pure-blooded Ilrairians in my platoon, and those that are, have witnessed exactly what their fellow soldiers and countrymen are like. Platoons are deeply competitive against one another. Old scores run deep." He took a deep breath.

"When I took over Royant, I promoted Shep and Grier to help me make the platoon what it is; fair, loyal to each other, hard-working, and above all else, to strive to make the world a better place. We were welcomed with open arms after a few years to most of the country. We all sensed it. Jaryn's longing for more power, more territory. He wants Aarine, the Anduns, Colladon, Petowin, the distant North. He wants what his ancestors never achieved, total control over the Boreals. He tried to garner it by marrying you, but Cormac denied him. He won the southern lands beyond the Cape of Kitrinos by eventually marrying Amadea ... then we discovered she had the water powers. He's been expanding his naval fleet ever since.

"Grier heard rumors of the wild ward alliance, and she had noted the spies and elite soldiers sent into the Anduns. Jaryn must have gotten wind that we had seen it and had us ship out to the eastern coast in the middle of spirits damned nowhere. Then we all saw the Night Pegasus light dance across the night sky, the farthest south he has ever been seen, and we knew then ... our time had come. When

Jaryn discovered what you were, he sent Coen to catch you before Cormac and Narve could." His voice was laced with anger, and he clenched and unfurled his fists. "Coen and Jaryn ... the pair have always been close; their families are deeply connected within the court. They trained together, Jaryn using Bromtide as his own personal task force whenever he saw fit."

Aalto turned onto his side, propping himself on his elbow and resting his bearded chin in his hand. My breath caught in my chest as he gazed down at me, the muscle in his jaw clenching. "I had my hen harrier, Haral, and Nion, another one of my spies, track you and try to keep you safe, but Bromtide was quicker."

I shifted on the hide and sat up, bracing my weight on my right palm as I gazed across at him. The folds of my skirt and cloak keeping me warm in the chilled air.

"It was then that Shep and I decided what had to be done. The entire platoon conceded with us. Anyone who wanted out, would never be shamed for it. We flew to Saltfen that night. Not long after that, we found Ebrel on the edge of the moorland, and it felt like another puzzle piece was put in place. All that was missing was you." His hand reached across and swept a dark tendril of hair off my face. I kept utterly still. "You know there were no military casualties the night of the Nijinx attack? Just civilians?"

I nodded, my fingers curling into fists with rage. Innocent people, *Jaryn's* people, had died under his orders. "Once we free the spirits and defeat the wild ward, what then? Jaryn won't stop."

His jaw clenched, and the intensity of his gaze left me reeling. I blinked, focusing on my breathing; the words of the Night Pegasus tumbling through my mind.

"I hope to convince Colladon to strengthen their borders and send reinforcements to Aarine. My spies are already trying to turn the senate against Jaryn and have him ousted from power."

I tensed, a feeling of unease trickling down my spine, and I gazed right back at him. "And Petowin?"

Aalto ran a hand through his dark hair. "I hope to rally my countrymen and rid it of the Nijinxes."

"Have you heard of a warlord, Rekorius Neimi? Doesn't he have the same goal? Jaryn mentioned he's gathered quite a following in Colladon; maybe you could join forces?"

With Aalto's spies, he would have surely heard of him. I was worried Jaryn would get to him first and kill him before he had a chance to bring Petowin to its former glory.

"I know who he is," said Aalto. His hand rose to cup my cheek, his thumb grazing my flushed skin. "And I hope to find him soon."

Every thought in my head eddied out as my eyes widened. Energy, dark and full of need, refracted between us. Aalto's lips pressed together, and his hand slowly fell away. Common sense rattled through my brain, and I shifted back an inch.

I wrapped my arms around my knees. "How are you so different? To Jaryn? To Narve?"

He moved into a seated position, legs crossed in front of me. "I did not want to turn into that kind of man, the kind who wakes up at dawn and does not see the beauty in it."

I held his gaze, appraising and processing his words. I blinked and glanced down, my gloved hands laced together in my lap.

Aalto watched me closely, giving me the space I needed.

"I should go. It's late." I stood, shaking the snow from my cloak. "Good night, Aalto."

Dawn brought drifts of fresh snowfall, painting the land outside the stone cave into a crisp, frozen new world. A good omen for us, still permissible weather to fly in, whilst shielding us from view as we flew east toward Serebo's foothills.

Kalana, the Mountie, and the blood bay Pegasus stood ready beyond the stone entrance, their breaths clouding in the bleak morning air, huddling close for warmth.

Ebrel and I stood just within the cave's mouth, my gloved hand gently stroking the mare's gray, velveteen nose. Aalto had paused further within the cave as if he was taking in the scene in front of him.

I was dressed in the clothes that his mother had selected for me. The Kivisto cloak wrapped over my left shoulder and under my right, leaving my sword arm free to move effortlessly. With Elmar's work complete, that once dark blade, the lambent stones flashing green in the low light was strapped securely down my spine over the cloak. The swordsmith had also bestowed another gift upon me. A newly crafted black leather scabbard, silver thread work of moons and ice adorning the length of it. Elmar had instructed me to baptize *Kathkar* in Serebo's ice, effectively ridding the blade of its previous sins and making it belong wholly to me.

Over my woolen layers, I wore a woven leather breastplate that matched Aalto's, the fit snug over my torso. Tilting my face toward the Commander, I gave a half-smile that did little to hide my nerves. Cool apprehension was already coursing through my blood, the anticipation of the work to come a steady thrum in my body. I took a deep breath, accepting the challenge but willing that adrenaline to go, to cool and settle myself. I had to stay alert, wary and focused, and above all else, grounded. I couldn't let my flight instinct hold sway over me. And the thought of doing it all with Aalto at my side ... spirits above.

Aalto strode for me, his legs eating up the shadowed earth between us. Like me, he wore traditional Petish clothing under his leather armor, warm yet loose trousers, tucked into battle worn calf-high boots. A tunic of thick Norwickan fleece over his upper layers would keep him warm as we flew, and he, too, wore a cloak. Dark, earth green, braided and clasped in silver, tucked under the twin sword scabbards strapped to his back.

"Ready?" I murmured, giving Ebrel a gentle pat on the neck.

"I was born ready, sweetheart." He winked, and my nervousness abated for a moment as I mentally whirled at his endearment. I couldn't hide the flush of my cheeks, but I could blame it on the cold, at least.

"It's okay to be afraid," he murmured. "Spirits, I'd be worried if you weren't."

A ghost of a smile played on my lips. "Are you afraid?"

"Of course. For Kally, for you, for me, for all of us. Come now, let's get mounted up. I assume the Mountie will follow as much as he is able?"

We walked outside, and I hopped onto Ebrel's back with only little help from her this time. Aalto stroked Kally's nose, the mare huffing warm air into his gloved palms as he gathered up the reins and mounted up.

The Mountie gazed at me, a vision of brown and gold, those huge, doe-like eyes missing nothing. The young stallion snorted, the powerful muscles along his neck and back quivering in anticipation. You could practically feel it, the need for him to run like the wind, and keep on running, limbs flying across the ground.

"Good luck out there. I'll send out Haral on the next dawn to find you." Shep leant against the entrance, his usually jovial face grim. Grier was a solemn shadow behind him.

"See you soon, sir," the spy called out.

"Come hell or high winds," Aalto called to them, gathering up Kally's reins.

The mare pawed at the snow, eager to take flight.

"Come hell or high winds," said the pair in unison.

Aalto signaled for me to follow, and we took to the skies, the Mountie whispering into the trees, all of us hoping and praying that we would find what we so desperately sought.

CHAPTER
THIRTY-FOUR

ASHER

Pherox's wings beat the night air without effort. The huge male held himself suspended in darkness, Vesperum a lithe shadow high above our heads. The soft sigh of air over leathery beating wings was the only sound. The kin swarm was ready. They had little choice but to be anything but.

Snow fell silently around us, falling upon the outlying farms of Aarine far below. Smoke wafted up to us, bringing with it the scents of the city: meat, sweat, mud, and feces.

Pherox's slitted nostrils wrinkled in distaste.

In a few hours, Aarine would fall to Jaryn's rule. All we needed was the signal to begin. On the city's northern border, Glentay at their backs, an Ilrair aerial cavalry platoon waited. There, so far below, it was but a pinprick of light, fire. First at the eastern gates, then it spread south, engulfing the defensive stone and wood walls, until the entire city was encircled in flame. It only took a few minutes for the screaming to reach us. The city and its soldiers had received no warning to prepare for this onslaught. An attack of fangs, feathers, talons, and claws.

Then, finally, two short horn blows from the north.

It was all we needed. Ice-cold air bit savagely at my face, as we descended through the sky, the kin swarm keening at our backs. Vesperum led the way, snow instantly melting upon her hot skin as she flew, wings slicing through the air as we swooped as one. We swept over the city from the south.

I gazed down, hardly believing my eyes as bears, wolves, stags, eagles, and mountain lions rampaged through the streets, taking on everyone, sparing no one with Meredith's magic lashing through their veins. Far beyond the city's outer reaches, Jaryn stood safe with his water-wielding Queen, watching the night-washed bloodbath from his hilltop stronghold.

Just the mere thought of the King had the bloodlust creeping through me. Pherox, too, had the same thought. The male Nijinx unleashed a mighty roar so deafening, it made those still alive down below wail in fear. The kin swarm landed in the thick of the fighting, amongst a district filled with shops and large, stately townhouses. I felt nothing as I cut down citizen after citizen. Felt nothing as blood dripped from my daggers onto the soot-covered streets. Felt nothing as I stalked the cobblestones, Pherox watching my back and Vesperum's.

A mountain lion leapt past me, paying me no heed as it pounced onto a fleeing middle-aged man dressed only in a sleeping gown. I rounded a corner onto a vast stone esplanade and halted. Across the wide-open space stood a row of storefronts. I knew that two-tiered shop with its currently shuttered windows and trade sign hanging over the wooden double doors.

Pherox snarled at my lack of movement. *"Defend and death, hunter."*

My boots made no sound as I treaded across the fresh snow and pools of blood.

Faded memories fluttered in my mind. Memories of freezing cold nights and blistering summer days, my hands folding pelts, sharpening knives, notching arrows.

Fields and Son's Hunting Co.

The shield-shaped sign did not move in the night air as I stared up at it, wild ward magic snapping down my nerves, slicing away those memories that tried in vain to resurface. I sensed, rather than saw, Vesperum land in the square behind me. She killed one, two, three people and then strode for me, her strong legs finding little trouble on the frozen ground. Her soft maw gripped my muscle-hewn shoulder, and she wrenched me around to face her.

I glanced at that ebony face, freckled with blood like some foreign constellation in a galaxy far more savage than ours, eyes as dark as mine, harrowed and ringed with killing magic.

Pherox keened softly to his mate, blood dripping from his fangs.

"This is your father's shop no longer," she said, her voice laced in warning and anger.

The wild ward magic thrummed in my bones, reasserting Vesperum's words as she stepped away.

Your father's.

I knew his name, but could not recall it, could not grasp it with my mind. It slipped away from me like a river fish.

"Leave it be, Asher," murmured the Nijinx Queen. *"She's watching our every move tonight."*

"My mate speaks the truth." Pherox prowled to my side.

I could barely feel my own legs, as I turned my back on what would have been my livelihood and future, and mounted Pherox once more.

"We are your future now," he said.

I ran my thumb down his neck, knowing within my soul that the male was right.

The kin swarm reformed over Aarine, climbing higher and higher into the night sky, as Ilrair Pegasi and their riders completed the battle below.

Civilians lay dead or dying in the streets. Grief did not pummel me. Sorrow and guilt were all but shadows, meaningless, and not worth the effort of feeling them. My future was night-lanced with the flashing of fangs and the beating of leathery wings. It did not alarm me that the wild ward's magic was not a part of what I envisioned. I would complete this task for her, then I wanted rid of it, this prowling beast in my veins.

The magic had broken and crafted me, created a dark and blood-lustful creature, one that I was at peace with, and could live with now without the magic's help.

I knew Pherox felt the same.

We descended into Glentay, landing within Meredith's stronghold of the standing stones. Even this far away, we could hear the wailing of the dying and the crackling of the fire siege. Meredith would debrief with Jaryn after the battle, so we had a moment's peace without her direct control.

The kin swarm huddled close, soothing one another after the at-tack, males ensuring their females were whole and well. We had lost no one during the battle. The province of Colladon had been so utterly unprepared for our arrival that not even a catapult had been erected in time or archers assembled.

I dismounted Pherox, letting him have a moment alone with his Queen. The male extended a leathery wing and tucked Vesperum close to his side. They nuzzled one another in the darkness.

Shadows enveloped me, and I welcomed them, allowed myself to be wreathed by them. This felt like a different sort of magic, something ancient, a force that had existed before the earth knew light. The forest was silent around me as I kept my breathing to that of a hushed whisper. I put more distance between the standing stones and myself.

The bloodlust in my body receding to a slow, pounding beat in my torso.

The darkness of the forest pressed in closer, and I halted, palms uptilted. I felt at peace out here, bathed in shadow, until it felt like I had no beginning or ending, that my entire being *was* darkness itself. A shrouded power that had lived alongside the wild ward magic, claiming me, branding me with its ancient touch. I gazed down at my palm, the shadow that curled and wreathed there, belonging not to the forest.

But to me.

CHAPTER
THIRTY-FIVE

ORRIN

We had reached Serebo's foothills by the following dusk, skirting north around the end of Jacob's Pass and into the vast, open plains beside the Arenne River. A small copse of wind-haggard birch trees provided our only shelter, while the soldier and Destry set about creating the small campfire and a snow cave. The soldier then set about showing her how to use the dark blade strapped to her spine, going over simple blocking and attacking. The approaching night was still, calm, yet snow continued to fall, shrouding the mighty mountain and her sister peaks from view.

Kalana, Murrkill, Ebrel, and I dug for grass under the snow, the motion keeping us warm at least after our long trek. Aalto warmed ice for us to drink and set out bran mashes for us to eat, before settling down to cook a meal for Destry and himself. The two humans naturally huddled close together for warmth, and we were all thankful for the lack of windchill that night. The land around us was eerily quiet. I had least expected to hear a wolf howl or ptarmigan call by now.

Yet there was nothing, just the hush of snowfall and the snap of the fire.

Ilmari confirmed my suspicion just as night fell.

"*The wild ward called them away. There isn't another being for miles around,*" I said.

"I'll go see what I can find. If the land has been cleared even this far north, then I may have to leave. My foal may be in danger," said Murrkill.

Her foal that she had left in Carter's care, deep within Glentay. I had received no warning of danger from Tellervo, yet I was probably too far out of range to hear from the forest spirit.

"You're right," said Ilmari, her presence lingering as still as a doe in the dark. *"Yet even I cannot reach Tellervo. The wild ward has called every creature away to Aarine,"* Ilmari paused, her voice too faint and weak. *"The wild ward is garnering more and more power. Orrin, you must return to Glentay. If she takes the forest, there will be no stopping her."*

The Pegasus mares stilled, not hearing the spirit's words, but sensing that she was there. Kalana snorted softly, unsure what to make of the astral being in their midst. Aalto, noting the uneasy way in which his mount cast her gaze about, stood and walked over to her.

Ebrel strode over to me as I turned to her. *"Murrkill and I must leave. The wild ward has forced every Glentay animal south to Aarine."*

"Aarine has fallen to the southern king," Ilmari whispered through my mane. *"Nijinxes and Pegasi fight with him."*

I translated for the other equines, who shifted their weight over their hooves in unease.

Destry joined the fray. "Something's happened; the animals can sense it."

"I know," murmured Aalto. "This land is far too quiet."

"I must go." I pressed my muzzle to Ebrel's cheek.

The young mare whickered in return and inhaled my scent. *"Be careful."*

"You too. Watch each other's backs. The humans too."

Murrkill backed up, wings arching as she prepared to take flight.

Aalto missed none of it. "Kally, is there something wrong?"

The snow-gray mare bobbed her head. She extended her right wing and swept it back.

"There's trouble in the south," said Aalto to Destry, as she laid a palm on Ebrel's quivering neck. Kalana reared and bared her teeth, ears flat to her skull. "Fighting. Is it Aarine?"

Bobbing her head once more, Kalana lowered a foreleg and bowed wings drooping at her side.

Aalto cursed. "Aarine's fallen to Jaryn."

Destry blinked. "How—"

"We set up a ... language, many years ago, for situations such as this. The Mountie and the blood bay must leave?" Kalana conveyed her knowledge to her rider, relaying my information with precision in her strange motion language she held with Aalto.

The soldier bowed his head to Kalana and turned to Destry. "The blood bay and the Mountie are leaving. She has a foal to look after, and he has to ... care for the forest? No, be *King* of the Forest. Ebrel and Kally will stay to help us."

Destry, looking weary and exhausted, gave Ebrel's neck a final pat. "Very well. The spirits are guiding them, it seems. We'll manage on our own."

I gave Ebrel and Kalana a farewell whicker and loped into the darkness beyond the campfire, Murrkill a night-slicked shadow in the skies above.

We were ten miles north of Glentay, in the snow-filled plateaus under Bronzo's watchful gaze, when we encountered our first signs of animal life. A day of galloping behind me, my energy was metered out, and I sucked down deep lungfuls of frigid air. My knees quivered ever so slightly as I waded through the snowdrifts.

Dusk was all but a few hours away.

Murrkill landed behind me and together we walked closer and closer toward that distant tree line.

Home.

My soul almost sighed with relief at the sheer sight of those ancient and gigantic trees. The boulder field before it was nearly swallowed up with snow, yet the taller rocks jutted out in the blazing orange light. The snow had long since stopped, yet a string of clouds cloaked the skies to the east. I reached out once more to seek Tellervo, yet it yielded no response from the spirit of trees and forests. Worry slicked down my spine. Not a dove called nor a deer tread. A ghost land filled with snow, forest, and rock. Not a living thing to be found.

Maybe it was the eight-hundred-year-long feud between us that made my skin tense and ears prick, as I sensed him before even Murrkill did.

Or maybe it was the fact that he murdered most of my family.

Spearian.

I froze upon the snow and cast my gaze toward the oncoming dark.

Murrkill rumbled a warning squeal and inched closer to my side.

His coloring matched that of the distant cloud cover perfectly. The roar he unleashed ripped over the land in a blaze of anger and glory. We were sitting ducks out here with miles between us and the cover of Glentay. A second silver shadow appeared behind Spearian. It had to be his lead mare, Hex. No wild ward magic marred their skin, yet here they were, when there was no other creature to be found.

"Murrkill, get to the skies, now!"

"I'm not leaving you down here."

My ears flicked back. *"I need you to lead Hex away. Distract her whilst I deal with Spearian."*

The blood bay Pegasus glanced between the oncoming duo and the faraway trees.

"Orrin, the forest ... you might not make it."

"I can make it. Now go! Don't come back to help me. Just keep flying, find your foal."

The mare brandished her wings and screamed at Hex, who swept in nearer. Murrkill nosed my cheek. *"I'll see you again, King of the Forest. This won't be our last goodbye."*

We exchanged hurried breaths, and then she was gone in a great downdraft of freezing air and snow. The mare clawed her way into the sky, a dark, furious star, and then she turned on the wing, black pinions beating swiftly, and she belted for Glentay. Ilmari whispered under the mare's body, garnering her more speed.

I hurled myself after her.

Spearian raced against the darkening sky. His lead mare drew level with him for several meters, then soared upward in altitude to chase Murrkill down. I leapt through the snow, faster than the wind, faster than any stag or Mountie before me. Clouds of snow billowed behind me as I sprinted. The trees beckoned me closer. Winter-laden boughs susurrant against one another. I was too far off to hear their ice-coated voices.

"I cannot rip the air out from under him," sobbed Ilmari. *"He is one of my own. I cannot harm him. I can't."*

I had no words to offer her. No notes of comfort or advice. What mattered was the oxygen coursing through my throat, and the blood pounding in my limbs as I galloped faster than ever before, even as my body trembled with exhaustion. *Stop,* it pleaded. *You cannot run forever.*

Spearian was a dark gray nimbus in my right hind field of vision. His wings pounded the sky as swiftly as my limbs galloped across the ground.

The trees were close, but Murrkill was right.

Not close enough.

The mighty Pegasus stallion, who would never be crowned King of Pegasi whilst Rosken took breath, unleashed a barrage of sound from his lungs and swooped.

I would never make the trees.

I hurled my body to a standstill, hind limbs skidding on the frozen ground as Spearian rocketed overhead. We snarled at one another. Spearian doubled back, flying more slowly this time as if he had all the time in the world now. He had me trapped upon the snow. His muscled, battle-scarred body standing between me and my rightful kingdom.

The Pegasus stallion landed with ease. Snow clouded around his hooves.

We glared at each other. Here was a creature that had killed my mother and brother and had done so gladly. He had allowed the wild ward access to Ebrel, to brand her, then he had chased the mare away, sending her plummeting from the skies to her death.

"Orrin." The great stallion exhaled and arched his neck. *"You are the spit of your father. I wonder if you will die like he did? With a mare's name on your spirits forsaken mouth?"*

I pawed at the snow, teeth bared. *"Get out of my way, Spearian."*

"I will have your dead body beneath my hooves before the sun has set."

We walked parallel with one another for a meter or so, sizing each other up. I matched him for height, yet he had far more muscle and brawn than I did. He would yield brute strength, and I would match him with speed.

I exhaled a huge breath. Then I lunged.

Spearian threw up his head and rocked back on his hind limbs in alarm. Yet the battle-worn stallion was far too experienced for my bite to find its mark. My teeth missed his throat as he darted to the side, wings brandished to keep his balance upon the slick ground. I withdrew as quickly as I had attacked.

Spearian took his chance. He bounded forward, throwing all his weight into the charge, his wings blocking any escape. Ears flattened to my skull, I pin wheeled to the side, hind hooves aimed at his chest. We danced and darted, roaring all the while. My golden mane blending with his silver, earth clashing against the sky. Soon, I was hoof raked and teeth marked.

Yet, so was Spearian.

Our breathing turned ragged.

I was beyond exhaustion. It took all of me to guess every move of the Pegasus. Rearing, my teeth found Spearian's withers, and I bit down hard. The stallion roared in defiance and twisted his neck around, clamping down hard on the muscle above my right knee. I couldn't stop the squeal of pain from my throat, and I backed up, snaking my head from left to right. Pain ripped up my right leg. Lameness was a death sentence out here.

Spearian laughed on a panting breath. *"The wild ward will have Glentay, Orrin. I will ensure it."*

"And what about Ilmari, the spirit that chose your kind? Who championed you after the Trinitors were ripped apart?"

"The wild wards are the way forward." Spearian folded his huge wings along his sides. *"I chose what was best for my herd, for our future."*

I scoffed. *"What's best for your herd? The balance of nature will be gone if the wild wards take over. Spring grass will not grow when it should, and you will starve. The thermals you use to fly will be gone. The mighty and little creatures will no longer live in equilibrium, but will be used and conquered, just like she is using them now."* I looked Spearian square in the eye. *"The spirits are the rightful custodians of this land, not the wild wards, not the humans. They have cursed, captured, and tamed anything that they deem fit for purpose. The spirits were here long before the wild wards were. Trinitors roamed the land before humans even set foot upon the Boreals. If she takes control, we all lose."*

Spearian snarled. *"The witch promised me protection for me and my herd."*

"Of course she did. Yet listen, Spearian, what other creatures do you hear? It is just you and me out here. She has called every other animal south to fight in the southern king's war, to be used as voiceless pawns."

"The southern king?" Spearian tossed his scarred head. *"She is working with him?"*

"Working for *him, Spearian. She follows his orders."*

He bared his teeth. *"You speak lies, half-blood colt. I killed your mother, brother, and joy ran through my veins when I heard that bastard Gracien had been put down. You will be the last Mountain Horse."*

Spearian charged, teeth aimed for my wounded knee that now dripped blood. I barely shifted back in time, unable to get weight onto my right leg.

A scream erupted from above the trees.

Spearian tossed up his head, and we both paused to look.

Murrkill. The mare was harrying Hex, unleashing blow after blow on the gray Pegasus. Hex was no match for the blood bay. She began to lose control of her flight and started to fall. Spearian cried out and did not even glance back at me, as he leapt into the sky toward his lead mare. Murrkill did not stop her attack, as Spearian flew in, desperate to save his mate as she plummeted toward those distant trees.

Hex tumbled through the sky, her hooves and wings flailing to right herself. She was half a mile above the trees, and Murrkill continued to drive her down, down, toward the pikes of fir.

"Spearian!" Hex's voice screamed out over the frozen tundra.

Murrkill banked sharply away toward me just as Spearian drew level with his mate, mirroring her dive. He tried everything to right her. Biting, pushing, using his own wings to up-tilt her. Yet it was of no use. Together, they plummeted down. Spearian hurled himself away from Hex, then doubled back in a mighty swoop underneath her. Using all his brute strength, he shoved himself and Hex upward, wings fighting furiously against the tightening pull of gravity.

Murrkill swept in low over the snow and landed at my side, breathing hard, yet she was unharmed. Standing close to my side, we watched the Pegasi. Spearian fought harder and harder, wings flapping endlessly, yet to push both himself and Hex upward was impossible.

The gray stallion gave one final surge upward, and Hex righted herself, banking deftly off her mate's back. He was a handful of meters above the trees. Spearian unleashed a glory-filled whinny, and he followed Hex above the trees, wing beats slowing into a cruise. Together, they doubled back, exchanging a quick nuzzle upon the air.

Neither I, nor Spearian, could have predicted what broke free of the forest below and launched upward. A Pegasus as black as a shadow of death. He was an ancient line of Pegasi, had a horn graced his head. He would have passed for Colbass himself, the Trinitor that had ripped a species apart.

Spearian turned sharply away as the beast of wings and hooves jettisoned toward him, a primal scream on its lips.

"*Carter,*" breathed Murrkill.

Neck and maw outstretched, the black Pegasus grabbed hold of Spearian's left hind limb and cleaved him from the sky.

Hex dove for her mate. Yet she was too slow.

Spearian raked the air with his hooves, yet it did little to help him.

Carter, flying above Spearian now, hurtled in close and drove his hind hooves into the gray stallion's rib cage in a deadly rear kick.

The black stallion, in the prime of his life, hovered above, wings brandishing the dusk air, while Spearian was enveloped and caged within the trees. Branches snapped and groaned as Glentay ensnared *the Bringer of Storms* deep within its core, snuffing out the gray stallion's life instantly.

Hex's harrowing whinny echoed over the frozen land. Carter roared in return, and the gray mare scrambled through the sky, back to her own territory, land that sat ripe for the taking now that its dominant stallion lay dead amongst the ferns and spruce.

A chilling breeze hushed over the snow-topped boulders.

Carter turned with ease and flew down to us.

My half brother. We shared the same mother. I stared at the winged entity as he landed with utter grace upon the snow. Here was a king of the sky. A Pegasus stallion who could even bring Rosken to his knees. His night-kissed skin rippled over cords of muscle as he strode toward us, neck arched proudly, his nostrils flaring at my scent.

Murrkill stepped forward to meet him, and they nuzzled each other gently, their breaths intermingling in the darkening air. Carter nosed the blood bay mare's cheek and throat, a soft huffing sound emitting from his mouth as if he were reassuring himself that the mare was indeed unharmed.

Then he stepped back and fully appraised me.

It did not come. That ripple of hostility that flowed between Mounties and Pegasi, even though I had braced myself for it, my body tense with apprehension. Yet Carter simply bowed his head, black ears pricked with intrigue and wariness.

"Brother of the forest," he said, in a voice that invoked twilight-tinged skies and fog-shrouded peaks.

Had I been human, I would have smiled. *"Brother of the skies."*

Carter lowered his head, and I mirrored him until our foreheads rested against one another. We inhaled and exhaled softly, memorizing each other's scent, as our ears relaxed to splay outward.

"How are you here? The wild ward's magic?" I asked.

"We retreated to the heart of Glentay, to Gracien's old home in the glade; her magic couldn't touch us there. We felt its pull, but it couldn't penetrate through the trees, as if it were guarded somehow. The herd is still there. I heard the bellows of you and Spearian fighting and came to investigate, then I saw Murrkill fly overhead and decided to intervene. That bastard needed to die."

Carter pulled away to stand close to Murrkill.

Indeed, the gray Pegasus had slaughtered our mother and older brother and had nearly slaughtered me too. I glanced down to the seeping wound on my foreleg.

Carter followed my gaze. *"You won't run for a while, Orrin. That leg needs resting. Come with me to Gracien's meadow, you'll be safe with us."*

I shook my head. *"I cannot stay. I left friends in the north that have set out to defeat the wild ward's magic once and for all. I need to help them."*

"Not with an injured leg, you won't." Carter huffed, authority seeping from his every pore. *"Rest tonight and we will reassess in the morning."*

My head lowered, yielding defeat. He was right. I would cause more harm than good if I tried to return north tonight, and Glentay still needed me. With Carter on one side and Murrkill on the other, the pair bolstered me between them, and we slowly treaded toward my home.

CHAPTER THIRTY-SIX

DESTRY

With the blood bay Pegasus and the Mountie gone, it was just the four of us that made our way toward Serebo's foothills the next morning. We landed on the southern bank of the Arenne River. Formed by meltwater from Serebo's eastern face icefall, the river swept under a crust of ice and snow, carving her way across the landscape. Her path cut through the valley, curling westward, before jackknifing to the east and the lands beyond.

"How did expeditioners cross?" My gaze took in the pure vastness of the ice-covered river, and I listened to the water gushing beneath it.

Aalto followed my gaze, his face grave. "They usually tracked east for a week, where she becomes less vast. They even took a temporary bridge for one year. Had a whole team of horses haul it up there."

"Poor beasts," I whispered and shook my head, a wave of dizziness washing over me.

Simply being this close to Serebo made me feel strange. As if I knew, deep down in my bones, that we shouldn't tread here.

This was a land for beasts, spirits, and ancient rock, not humans.

With a rare winter sun blazing above our heads, the ice gleamed frozen blue before us. The Pegasi tossed their heads at the river, the sight making them uneasy. Ebrel huffed at it, surely thinking of the frozen lake at Saltfen. Pegasus feathers were waterproof, hence why they couldn't fly silently and were in such high demand by clothiers, yet being submerged in icy water? Even a Pegasus couldn't withstand that for too long.

My mind raced back to Hestian and his rider. My heart squeezed tight, and I released a long breath, unable to ignore the look on Coen's face the night I had pulled him from the water.

The high mountain air was like knives in my lungs and our breath clouded before us.

Serebo sat in the far distance. Her jagged peak pierced the cloak of blue that shrouded her. An imperial, ice-crowned queen that took no prisoners, even while she was caged under the wild ward's curse.

Aalto fetched water, raising it to body temperature before offering it to the Pegasi and to us, whilst I stared up at that kingdom in the sky. Our goal for today was to seek out Spell, the giant ice cave that was somewhere near Serebo's base. It had once been a resting place for the Kottin Mirror and worth exploring in case it had been hidden there once more.

Refreshed, we mounted up and took flight, a snow-filled landscape flitting beneath us. Ebrel and Kalana took to the mountain thermals with ease, using little energy to soar through the winter-wrapped valleys. The sun slid past its midday peak when we passed into true Serebo territory.

It was like flying through a gossamer shroud.

A sighing hiss echoed over us, thrumming over our skin and rustling Ebrel and Kalana's feathers. The Pegasi did not sense it until it was too late. My light pulsed in my veins, cracking like fire under my skin. A warning. *Get back! Go back!*

The two mares slammed to a halt in midair. They snorted warily, eyes rolling in their sockets.

"We tripped a magic ward," I yelled to Aalto, my fingers gripping Ebrel's mane with all my strength.

We tried to turn back. My light screamed at me to turn around. We were so high up, the Arenne River was a silver strand far below.

"By the spirits," Aalto whispered. "Easy, Kally, easy."

The snow-pale mare did not listen to Aalto. She wrenched the reins from his hands, tucked her head between her knees, and bucked savagely. It was years spent on horseback that kept Aalto within the saddle, his legs gripping around Kalana's girth.

Ebrel whinnied to her wing sister and trembled hard as if she was fighting off whatever was having such a strong effect on Kalana.

Then I saw it, a muted flicker of brindled light, wrapping and twisting itself around Kalana's bridle. She bucked and bucked in the air, and Aalto held on with all his might as the mare fought to unseat him. Her wings lashed out, sweeping this way and that to swipe her rider to the valley floor far below. Sweat dripped down Aalto's skin.

"We need to get to the ground, Ebrel, help them!"

The strawberry roan darted forward, teeth bared at the wild ward magic that was trying and succeeding to possess Kalana. Using her entire body mass, Ebrel forced Kalana lower and lower, distracting the mare long enough to shift her focus from bucking off Aalto to fighting Ebrel.

"Hold on, Aalto!" I yelled.

Roaring at one another, the mares struck out with teeth and hooves, and we lowered in the sky, the ground rising closer and closer to meet us.

Ten meters from the valley floor, Kally wrenched free of Ebrel's grip on her neck and twisted away. Squealing, the mare bucked once. Twice. Then shot skyward. Aalto, who had kept leaning back in the saddle to counter the bucking, flipped back and out of the saddle.

As straight as an arrow, Kalana climbed.

Ebrel and I launched after them. A scream lodged in my throat as Kalana, magic blazing around her head, jackknifed to the right, completely unseating Aalto.

"Go, go, *go!*" I sobbed.

I tracked his fall in a frenzy, his clothes fluttering around him like useless, broken sails. He flailed midair, grasping and gripping at nothing. Ebrel's wings pummeled the frozen air, shooting toward him to meet his fall. Arms outstretched, I reached out to catch him. His frantic yell was ripped away by the wind.

Closer and closer, he fell. Ebrel swooped up to meet him. My gloved hands brushed past his legs and waist, desperately grappling to find purchase and wrench him toward me.

Iron strength gripped my forearm like a vise, and I wrapped my other hand around his torso as he crashed into us. Ebrel fought to stay airborne, the weight of him tipping us all sideways for a heart-stopping moment. Muscles burning with effort, I heaved him aboard, pushing my weight back to level out Ebrel's. Aalto's breath was ravaged against my cheek, and his chest slumped along my back.

"We've got you." I clutched his forearm to me. "We've got you."

Yet he replied with only one, heartbreakingly distraught word. *"Kally."*

Ebrel, not waiting for or needing any direction from me, landed swiftly and brutally atop the valley floor. She nosed my leg impatiently, then looked back up the valley, watching Kalana grow smaller and smaller in the midday sun.

I dismounted, dragging Aalto off with me.

Ebrel huffed into my hair and looked up at Kalana once more.

"Go, follow her, keep her safe. We'll take it from here." I ran my hand down her forehead, and she pressed into the touch.

Then she was gone. Her pink and brown-dusted form chasing Kalana down. Aalto watched them go until the pair disappeared.

Slowly, I sat down next to him and clasped his shoulder tightly, forcing him to look at me. "Ebrel will watch over her."

Aalto shook his head and shuddered. He ran a hand over his face. "I have never seen anything like it, even during the bonding process, Kally was never, *ever* like that."

My gaze searched his. "That was not Kalana, that was pure wild ward magic. It was the same with that hunter and the Nijinxes. It possesses them wholly to the wild ward's will. We'll free them of it, Aalto. We have to."

"We go on foot from here." Aalto cleared his throat.

That quickly, his training and warrior instinct took over. I could still sense his grief and shock. I had never seen such a broken man before. Yet it was like he had tucked it away for review later. Tucked it somewhere so dark and deep, probably in the same shadowed place he kept the bonding process in and would reach for it only when he could. His fingers shaking only slightly now, Aalto withdrew his map from his inner tunic pocket and spread it out on his lap.

Sat in a pool of brittle sunlight, we poured over it together, matching our surroundings to the undulating, striated lines on the thick paper before us. Spell was not officially marked on the map, yet Marte had drawn three logical positions for it with blue ink.

Aalto tapped the closest blue circle. "We should make it here just before sundown. Let's get going."

I helped him to his feet, and we dusted ourselves free of snow. To be without our mounts left not only a physical sense of loss, but a monolithic emotional one as well. I wondered when Aalto and Kalana were last separated and then swiftly pushed the thought aside. His mere defeated posture alone told me enough. Walking up beside him, I gripped his gloved hand in mine and squeezed tightly.

It felt totally natural when he did not let go and we walked that way, hand in hand, deeper into Serebo's queendom.

Drinking little and often, sharing scraps of food when we dared to, we climbed along to the next valley, sweat trickling down our bodies.

"A rare day," said Aalto ahead of me, twin blades peeking over his shoulders, "for it to be sunny this high up."

We traversed a deer trail notched into the snow-covered mountainside, too narrow for us to walk side by side now. To our left, the rock jutted away and up, an impregnable wall of snow, and to our right, the land dipped down to a circular frozen lake with a tiny stone island piercing it. Reflecting the clear sky, it blazed white and blue like a snow-trapped sapphire.

All I could hear was the steady breath of Aalto and I, and the repetitive crunch of our boots passing over the snow.

Aalto stepped around a boulder. "So ... tell me, do you remember anything about your family?"

A distraction, surely, from the significant loss we both felt.

"I know I had a mother, father, and an older sister. I have only been told that my father's name was Lochlan."

This lack of knowledge haunted me day and night. To know someone's name was such a basic piece of information. It gave someone or something an identity, an idea of their personality and inkling to their forefathers for choosing it.

To not know my mother's and sister's names ... I was like a planet out of orbit with nothing to latch on to.

"I don't remember their faces. When I look back." I paused momentarily on the trail, gaze fixed on the lake. A lake not unlike the one my family was slaughtered beside. "I remember warm, elegant hands and laughter. That was my mother, I think."

Aalto stopped and walked back beside me. Tentatively, he brushed my hair off my cheek. His voice was feather soft when he spoke, "Your mother's name was Ariadne, formerly of clan Rovesi. She was the Chieftess' second youngest daughter, and she married your father to form a stronger alliance between the two clans. That, and the two were madly in love with each other if tales are to be believed." He chuckled, a sound that I longed to hear again. "It's said that your father took a sleigh full of lambent stones into her village to try and woo her. She told him to exchange the stones for arrows for her and her sister's bows if he were to stand a chance. He happily obliged, and she kept the most beautiful of lambent stones for her engagement ring."

Air-ee-ad-nee. It was a beautiful name, fitting of a famed Chieftess, and the sound rang in my ears as if the very breeze whispered it to me.

I gripped his hand. "Thank you."

He smiled. "You are most welcome. As for your sister—"

"Shhhh."

"Don't you want—"

"No, wait a minute." I cocked my head and slowly turned in place. *"Listen."*

Aalto realized it at the same moment that I did, and we both turned toward the sound.

To the left of us, pummeling toward our trail at a sickening speed, in a plume of powder and roaring all the while, was an avalanche.

My entire body locked up. "The sun ..."

Fools, what fools we were to not think and worry about it. How the sun would weaken any snow shelves above our heads. That the very valley in which we stood, now that I recognized it, had been forged by countless avalanches, the trail as clear as day as I pieced it together.

"This way." I grabbed Aalto's arm, turned us to face the distant lake and together we ran at an angle down the slope.

A crashing winter chariot, the avalanche consumed all in its path as it thundered down the mountainside, spitting up stag lichen, boulders, and ice. As it came down, the more power and size it gathered. Like a hurricane out at sea, it would only grow more powerful the further it crashed downhill.

Arms cartwheeling to stay upright, we pelted away from its path, praying we could run far and wide enough in time. The lake glittered in the distance, a shining beacon of refuge. Yet danger lurked beneath the snow. At any moment, one of us could catch an ankle, or a shin on some unseen obstacle, and bones would break on impact.

Dread drenched me. Keeping my gaze locked on Aalto, I didn't dare glance behind me. The avalanche crashed and powder clouded around me. My lungs burned from the freezing air. I kept pace with Aalto as we ran for our lives.

Gaining more speed as it tumbled down the slopes, the avalanche plumed meters into the air as it swept toward us.

I gasped for breath, my arms, torso, and legs adrenaline-fueled and sweat-soaked.

Aalto looked back once, blanched, then dived toward me, tackling me to the ground and rolled us away. Down and down we tumbled. The world became tubular, spinning out of control, until I couldn't differentiate between snow and sky. Eyes clenched shut, I barely registered the fact that we had stopped rolling, or that the deafening roar had reduced to a rumbling groan.

Weight pressed down against my entire length, and I sucked down a panicked breath. I was buried, buried alive. I needed air, and my hands clawed at the weight that pushed down against me.

Yet wool and leather met my touch, not snow.

I looked up, blinking in disbelief at Aalto lying on top of me, his arms braced either side of my head. His breathing was jagged. His whole body shaking, and he looked down at me. His hair, which had been tied back off his face, now hung down to his bearded jaw and was filled with snow clumps and a sprig of stag lichen.

He looked so ridiculous that I couldn't help but release an adrenaline-fueled, shaky laugh. The sensation was so foreign that I kept laughing, reveling in a sound that I couldn't remember when I last made it.

Aalto cocked his head and raised an eyebrow, a bemused grin on his face. My laughter shook the pair of us, and it wasn't long before he joined in, dazed and relieved. We sighed, shocked at the fact that the avalanche had gone into run out and had finally come to rest several meters from our heads. Heat of a different kind flickered through my body as the glorious weight of him pressed against me.

He stilled above me as I reached up with a gloved hand and pulled the sprig of lichen free from his hair. Slowly, our breaths intermingling, he pressed his forehead to mine, burning me like a brand. Then he shifted his weight from me and slumped onto his back. "That was a close call and not one I want to repeat in a hurry."

"A natural event, or another wild ward device?" I panted, both from the adrenaline and the desire that coursed through me.

"It's hard to say. Either way, I'd be happy if I never experienced that again."

"Me too." I rose slowly, muscles aching and helped Aalto to his feet.

We shook our cloaks free of snow and checked our packs and contents were undamaged. The food looked a little worse for wear, but our weapons remained sheathed and intact, thankfully.

I looked over to our main goal and dusk settled heavily over the base of Mount Serebo. I tried not to blanch as I gazed upward to those ridges and peaks that stretched up and up, lacquered in snow and deadly ice.

Aalto smiled softly. "We'll make it, one way or another."

"Yes, we will."

He took a step away toward the lake. And the ground swallowed him whole. "Aalto!" I screamed.

I dove after him. The ground had yawned open into an underground cave, sucking down a ton of snow and Aalto with it.

Terror gripped my bones. He was buried alive down there. I skidded down the newly formed snowbank and scrambled over the bottom, my hands frantically feeling for any sign of him. It was so dark down here, and so, so cold. Colder than any winter night I experienced so far.

My light sparked from my skin, illuminating the small space. *Where are you, where are you? Where are you?*

Being buried alive under snow was my absolute chronic fear. Freezing around you so quickly that your limbs were held tightly in place, caging any oxygen with you. Air that quickly vanished and you would gasp and gasp, yet there was nothing to fill your lungs, only panic and dark and cold ...

"Aalto," I cried, sweat dripping from my temple as I desperately dug for him.

He'd be running out of time and air.

I lost all sense of feeling in my hands. A minute ticked by. Two. Then, *there*, buried several inches away from me ... the tip of one of his twin blades. I tore through the snow, gouging through it till I felt his muscled shoulder, then his neck.

Deeper down into the snow.

Air, he needed air.

I clawed and raked. Down, down into the tomb of snow. Finally, his face, then his mouth, his lips woefully pale. A beatific gasp sounded from him, and his whole body juddered. A drowned man. Wrenching off my mitten, I dusted the remaining snow from his face, then I got to work on his chest.

Aalto sucked down deep, gasping breaths, color slowly creeping back into his face. He gazed around frantically, dazed and confused.

"You're alright," I said, more to myself than to him.

My palms wrenched away handfuls of snow.

"What happened?" he croaked.

"You've fallen into a cave." I reached up and gripped his face between my frozen hands. His eyes burned bronze, rimmed with gold, and his pupils were constricted. "Aalto, is anything broken? Can you feel your arms? Your legs?"

He blinked. Blinked again. Shock gripped him tightly and unforgivingly. Finally, he says, "I can feel everything." He glanced down at his body, wincing as he still lay waist-deep in snow. "Nothing's broken."

Sweat drenched through my many layers of clothing and chilled my skin. I shrugged off *Kathkar*, then my cloak and wrapped it around Aalto tightly, making sure to cover his head to retain his body heat.

With my muscles exhausted, I slowly worked his arms free, then his legs and feet.

Rising onto my knees, I wrapped my reindeer hide that had been rolled up on my lower back, around his abdomen and legs, until he was completely covered. Then I sagged against the snow and stared at him.

Slowly, my adrenaline receded. My voice was hoarse. "At least there's no wind chill down here."

My light danced around us, revealing more of our small cave, which sat half-filled with snow. At the very back, opposite to where we sat, was a tunnel, which cut deep under the earth and into oblivion. My green light hesitated at the entrance, then curled back to me. It was not keen to probe further unless I was closer.

Dusk was swiftly approaching, and I didn't want to move Aalto at this time of day. The temperature would only drop further, especially with such a clear sky overhead. Using the last of my energy, I heaved Aalto to the very back of the cave, yet still a healthy, watchful distance from the tunnel, and set up the camp and dug a latrine away from the cave.

Once our small fire had taken, I warmed water and broth for us both and tucked into a small meal of dried and salted reindeer meat, fleshy blueberries, and a hunk of cheese. Aalto ate slowly, as emotionally and physically wracked as I was. I tried not to dwell on the fact that he had nearly died three times today. Tried not to dwell on his oxygen-deprived, fear-swept face when I had dug him free.

I never wanted to see that face again.

There were no trees this high up. Yet there was something else that burned just as well, and it grew so well here, it practically ruled the landscape. I reached into my leather pack and withdrew a small handful of stag lichen. Pale green with silver highlights, the antler-shaped, low-growing shrub carpeted the mountainsides and tundra all year long, and Aalto and I had been harvesting it as we passed through the valleys. Mixed with our small cache of dried ferns and birch bark, it afforded us a small fire each night.

Aalto, it appeared, practically worshiped the plant. Keen to move on from the events of the day, he nudged closer to me, still wrapped in our hides and cloaks. "Stories say that Serebo grew stag lichen so that it would beckon varki deer, reindeer, and ibex to her and her sister peaks so that they could watch the animals pass through." We sat huddled close together, sharing each other's body heat and the heat of the crackling fire. I was more than glad to nestle in closer, pitifully grateful for the reassurance of having Aalto living and *breathing* next to me. "The varki and ibex, in particular, were grateful that some went on to serve Serebo as her own personal guards and lookouts."

"Have you ever seen a varki?" I tucked my hands under my arms, gaze captured by the fire. I had always felt it to be cleansing, watching fire, the flames licking and soothing away your troubles and worries. Maybe it was my light that was drawn to it, one familiar to another.

Aalto shook his head. "My mother did see a doe and fawn once when she was a young woman traveling from her clan to a neighboring one. She said they were the most beautiful creatures she had ever seen. Pelts as pale as a full moon with antlers sculpted from silver."

I looked across at him. "They sound beautiful."

Resting my head in my hands, I watched the flames, daunted and exhausted. I clung to three things. Ebrel was unpossessed, for now. Aalto was alive and now I knew.

I whispered it to myself, too low for Aalto to hear. I repeated it as if it were a verbal talisman, a prayer, a protection spell. My mind clung to it, that spark of knowledge, grasped it so tightly as if it were a life raft in a bitter sea. Within the flames, I saw her hands. In my mind,

I heard her laugh, and I repeated it, again and again. Her name, over and over, a tumble of sighing sound, so magical and alluring, it could be disguised as a spell chanted by some ancient Lowlander mage.

Ariadne.

Air-ee-ad-nee.

Another name joined the chant.

Damara.

Dah-mar-ra.

And then finally, one last name to complete the trio.

Ebrel.

Ee-brell.

CHAPTER
THIRTY-SEVEN

DESTRY

I awoke before dawn, the Kivisto cloak tucked snugly around my broad shoulders. A solid, warm weight flexed against my back as I stirred, and a strong arm banded around my waist, a hand splayed protectively against my lower abdomen. Another arm was tucked under my neck, the hand resting against the hollow of my throat. I released a soft, low hum of contentment. *Coen.*

Blinking the last remnants of sleep away, my whole body stilled as realization struck me. Our scents intermingled in the cold air: wool, bergamot, leather, and something that was purely Aalto. By his steady, even breath against the nape of my neck, I could tell he was still asleep. I, on the other hand, became fully aware, each one of my senses attuned to him as he held me against his muscled body.

I swallowed, trying to keep my breathing quiet and even as I glanced down at the broad, tan hand that rested against the top of my skirt. *Holy shit.* I had thought this was Coen, had wanted it to be Coen, holding me here, safe in his arms. *Spirits above.*

Aalto was still a stranger to me despite having saved his life on several occasions, and it did not entitle him to hold me like this.

Aalto shifted behind me, the muscles in his arms flexing against me, and his hand on my stomach pressed me closer to him. *Sweet spirits above.* This man. His breath caught in his throat as he fully awoke. I felt him prop up onto his forearm, his hand leaving my throat, and he gazed down at me fully against him, noting his hand on my skirt.

"Destry ..." his voice was coarse, rough from sleep, and it did little to douse the fire under my skin. He withdrew his hand, and I swallowed.

I turned my head and looked up at him. His gaze burned into mine, the gold flecks in his eyes glinting in the low light. He lowered his head, and his nose nuzzled the curve of my ear, his breath skittering over my skin. My toes curled in response, thankfully with no cramp this time. A fire erupted under my skin, but I doused it, not yielding to the desire that suddenly coursed through my blood.

He withdrew slightly, his sensuous mouth hovering over mine. My panting breath intermingled with his; controlled, restrained. My heart raced as it racketed between confusion and need.

"The things I would do with you, Destry Kivisto, and this alluring body of yours." His hand lifted to gently cup my cheek, and my breath froze in my throat. Those long fingers swept down to caress the line of my throat, hovering over the long bruise there. "When our lives aren't on the line, I'll have all the time in the world to worship you and chase your nightmares away."

My throat bobbed as I swallowed, and my voice was barely a whisper. "Is that so?"

I wanted all those things, but not with *him*.

His jaw clenched, the muscle in his jaw feathering and he shifted, the motion lithe and confident, to place a tender kiss over the throbbing pulse in my neck. "The things I could show you," he murmured against my skin.

I went utterly still at the promise, the innate sensuality, in his words. Then he was withdrawing, standing fluidly, and stretching his arms over his head, revealing a sliver of tanned, muscled abdomen.

I ripped my gaze from him and looked up at the icy ceiling, willing my body to be as cold as its surface, yet my hormones refused to obey, and I continued to burn for him.

Dawn brought fog. It carpeted the nearby lake, the valley, and Serebo, blocking it all from view. Unease washed over me. I hated fog; it blanketed every sense. No sounds penetrated it and the air smelt only of earth and frigid snow. Even my footsteps sounded muted, unearthly, as if I was trapped under a smoky glass orb. I eased myself back down the snow ramp and into the cave to find Aalto armed and ready.

I smiled cunningly. "I'm bruised all over from yesterday. I blame your tackling skills."

"Not the avalanche? Or the mountain trek?" He smirked.

Donning my sword, I turned my back on him and gathered my pack. "Definitely the tackling."

"Noted." He came to stand beside me and leant in close. "It'll be better next time."

We stood at the mouth of the tunnel, having swept the snowbank clean of our footsteps and smothering the small fire with a mound of more snow. We hesitated before the oblivion.

"It's worth a look," I breathed.

Uplifting my palm, my light crept forward, slowly at first, then expanded, a flickering white and green curtain that painted the walls of the tunnel. It extended for several meters before arching downward, deep into the earth.

In the direction of the lake.

I stepped forward, hand outstretched before me. Aalto brought up the rear. It was damn freezing down here. The air was still, permeated with age and echoes of times long passed. Ancient hands and tools had carved out this place. The walls were gouged with pock marks that showed the direction in which it had been dug out. Hard, laborious work that would have taken years to complete.

We delved deeper into the rock, and still the green and white light twined ahead of us, pulling us onward. We must have covered a mile and a half of ground when I finally slowed. The tunnel made an abrupt right-hand turn up ahead, a vulnerable place to explore.

Aalto placed a hand onto my shoulder and gently stepped past me, his boots silent on the ground. He withdrew his twin blades, the Colladonian steel reflecting flashes of white light, the battle worn hilts solid in his grasp. The move was crazily attractive.

Mirroring him, I unsheathed *Kathkar*, and the lambent stones on the hilt flickered to life. Our backs to the wall, we crept closer to the turn, as silent as ghosts. Signaling for me to hold my position, Aalto balanced his weight over his knees and slid around the corner, blades twirling.

He froze. His swords stayed lofted in front of him, and the expression on his face turned to one of awe. My gaze burned into him, not wanting to speak out in case someone or something might be listening. Slowly, he lowered his swords. I rounded the corner and stepped to his side. My jaw slackened.

The lake we had seen was not a lake.

It was *Spell*.

In unison, as if we could sense our Petowin ancestors whispering to us to pay homage, Aalto and I dropped to our knees on the ice-covered rock. Our gazes tilted upward in an effort to take it all in. A curved chapel of ice so pure and old, it flashed clear and blue before us. Water dripped from inverted crystalline spires and towers to create a small reflection pool, mirroring the ice-carved ceiling above. Around the pool, gently set there by countless people thousands of years ago, were little mounds of cairns, frozen solid in place so that time could not alter them.

My light pulsed forth, refracting against every surface until the place glittered like the night sky. The island we had spied yesterday was, in fact, a gigantic pinnacle of rock that cleaved through Spell's center, an obsidian column that glittered under a cloak of ice. Inscribed at its center, the largest depiction of it I had ever seen, was the oval star. And below that, was an ancient rune of the spirit of ice and snow, Varranar, son of Merivis.

Spell was not just an ice cave; it was a place of worship.

Where the rock met the stony cave floor, a hollow had been carved out and there, as transparent and flawless as the finest glass, bound neatly within its curving birch frame, was the Kottin Mirror. It was fixed firmly in place within the hollow, a sheet of ice trapping and suspending it.

I rose slowly, instinct guiding me and wreathed in my light. I stepped toward it. *Kathkar* in my right hand, pulsing light in my left, my boots moved as silently as a doe around the shallow pool.

Aalto stepped after me, continually shifting his gaze around the cave. Did the wild ward leave any surprises in store for us?

The air around us crackled and pulsed as we approached. The ice felt aware, watchful. Its mystical gaze noting every breath we took, every shard of rock we stepped upon.

I paused, fingers tightening around my sword as I faced the hollow. Apprehension coated my skin, and I readied myself for what might come. Good or bad, friend or foe. Dropping to one knee, the Kivisto cloak billowing out around me. I reached outward.

I sensed Aalto step toward me.

Removing my mitten, my hand splayed out, and I pressed my trembling fingers onto that pane of flawless ice. The first touch of it sent biting tendrils of cold against my skin, ice so cold it burned, but I did not falter. My body braced itself and yet my voice was surprisingly strong, steady, like I knew in my bones that I was born for this. A moment suspended in time. "I am the light that burns the darkness. I am the glens under snow and ice-covered lakes. I am sky and wind and hope and grief. I am Destry Kivisto Koskivarri, and I am here for you."

Spell groaned like a beast waking from hibernation. I cast my gaze around, assessing, yet the cave did not quake or splinter. The ice held steady, flickering from dusk blue to emerald. My lips set into a determined line, and I applied more pressure onto the mirror, fingers arching before it. The gift of my light flowed from my skin, brushing against the ice that held the frame firmly in place within the hollow, sweeping and twining against it like a cat.

A primitive murmuring echoed around us in a language far too intricate for us mortals to comprehend or understand. It clicked, sighed, and cracked, sending pulses of light fluttering away where it spoke from the walls. Not removing my contact with the mirror, the ice around it retracting millimeter by millimeter, I whispered, "What is that sound?"

Aalto swallowed behind me, his voice breathless. "The ice spirit, Varranar."

At the mention of its human-given name, the reflection pool quivered, remaining in a liquid state despite the freezing temperature here.

"We freed it?" I panted.

Aalto looked up to the spired ceiling that glittered like a thousand distant stars. "It would seem so."

A brief smile lit up my face, and my light brushed deeper into the hollow, its warmth melting away the ice that held the mirror secure. And then finally, with a puff of steam, the Kottin Mirror began to slide free. Quickly setting aside *Kathkar*, I scooped it up into a tight grasp, my quivering hands clasping either side of the birch frame. I had done it. Blinking in bewilderment, I studied the mirror.

"It's so *light*," I breathed as I gazed into it, my eyes wide with sheer wonder. "And so *clear*."

Cautiously, Aalto gazed over my right shoulder. About the size of a standard piece of parchment and several inches thick, the ice was pure perfection.

"It's less like a mirror ..." he offered.

I lofted it before us. "And more like ... a *window*."

"A window to where?" He gazed quizzically at it. "There's nothing to say how to wield it?"

We glanced back into the hollow. Yet it boasted only an empty space where the mirror had once been, nothing more.

"We take it to Serebo," I said, pride blooming in my chest. Delicately, I passed the mirror to Aalto, who received it like a precious newborn, then I turned to pick up *Kathkar*.

Fingers carefully wrapping around the bare blade and hilt, I lowered the longsword into the shimmering pool. Ice-cold water burned my fingertips, just like it had at the lake near Saltfen. I fought back my hiss at the frozen temperature of the water and held the sword steady. It felt right to do this, to burn away the blade's dark history not with fire, but with water from Serebo. Water that was cold, ancient, and pure.

My light arced over me, twining down my arms and over the water's stippling surface.

A second later, a hissing breath curled over my mind, so similar to the Night Pegasus. Yet this voice was older, harsher, tainted by frigid darkness and endless patience. Varranar. The spirit of ice.

"You bring a dark blade here, wild one," he murmured in our mortal tongue. *"And a man of clever, dark ways."*

My entire spine went rigid, and I held back my flinch. I could feel Aalto watching me closely. I cast a thought back to Varranar, *Kathkar* trembling in my hands. *"Aalto has been nothing but kind to me."*

"You and I both know, Koskivarri, that you don't believe the pretty little words he whispers to you." His glacial voice wrapped around my entire being, numbing my very core.

The image of Coen, distraught beside his tent, flashed before my eyes.

"Are you alright?" Aalto stepped closer.

"I'm fine," I breathed back to him, a little too quickly. "I want to make sure I do this right."

I could no longer feel my hands or my wrists. Varranar's power slicked over my shoulders in an invisible, chilled caress. *"Ice and fire hold the power of truth. They burn away the lies. You freed me, wild one, so let me give you this."*

Kathkar began to glow a deep vibrant blue, the blue of the heart of a glacier. Aalto whistled a low note behind me in appreciation.

"Keep the sword close," warned Varranar.

I swallowed and began to pull *Kathkar* from the water, bright blue droplets dripping from the hilt. *"I will."*

I rose slowly, Aalto's arm brushing mine. I felt a final pulse of cold magic against my back as I sheathed my sword and blew warm air into my numb hands. Spell groaned once more and the pool trembled, sending out ripples to lap at the cairns that ringed it.

Shifting my cloak from my shoulder, I wrapped it neatly around the mirror. Content it was safe, I secured against my lower back.

I turned to face Aalto, and his smile was radiant. I made myself smile meekly back at him.

"Well done," he murmured, his gaze searching my face.

"Thank you," I breathed, restraining myself from stepping closer to him. "It's so beautiful here. Beats any other place of worship I've ever been in."

We tilted our heads upward, our gazes drinking in the sight of Spell one last time.

CHAPTER
THIRTY-EIGHT

ASHER

There were soldiers in the forest. A lone cavalry platoon, stationed within the trees north of Aarine. A platoon that had left the province in ruins. Its citizens lay dead or dying. Any survivors had fled into the wilderness, seeking out coastal routes where they could. No one dared venture south to Ilrair or seek shelter in Glentay.

We ruled the forest now.

Yet I could still feel the trees watching, listening, and resisting as we brushed past their snow-laden limbs.

Pherox and I walked side by side through the forest, which was thick with fog. We couldn't see the platoon camp until we stepped past its sentry line. A burgundy flag hung limply atop its post, the storm cloud embroidered upon it glinting silver. A row of tents stretched away from us and into dark gray gloom. We could both scent the Pegasi ahead. Yet there was another, different scent clinging to the air. One I vaguely remembered.

Pherox uttered a series of silken clicks.

The camp fell quiet as we stalked toward the large command tent. Two soldier guards stood at the canvas entrance, blades at their sides. They blanched as we approached, faces gaunt under their hats, and their fingers flinched upon their sword hilts. Pherox and I paid them little heed. We could rip their throats out in the blink of an eye.

The canvas was swept aside, and as one, we entered the lamp-lit space. Pherox's clicks intensified as he mapped the room with sound and echo, his velveteen ears twitching this way and that. Firelight danced on his glinting fangs.

Palms gripping my daggers, I assessed the people present just as quickly as Pherox did, cataloging their scents and what weapons they bore. Shadows lined the edge of my vision, and I urged them back. *Not yet.*

A huge table dominated the vast majority of the space, Jaryn at its head, a gloved hand braced upon a map of the Boreals.

Murderer.

Meredith stood wreathed in candlelight on the King's right, her eyes bright beneath her hood. A male stood in agitated silence at the opposite end of the table, his features brooding beneath his tricorn hat. A storm cloud was stitched on the chest of his uniform. Our gazes slid to one another and locked.

I sniffed delicately. We had crossed paths before, in Saltfen, on that night when civilian blood had been spilled. The officer folded his arms across his broad chest, his eyes like chips of frozen emerald. I shifted my gaze to Jaryn, ignoring the officer wholly. Yet Pherox kept his head pointed toward the soldier, his ears sliding back flat against his skull.

We did not use it, that inner channel between our minds, not with Meredith present. We had discussed it late into the night before this meeting. At such close range to the wild ward, the Nijinx and I had decided to let our mental communication go dark, lest the wild ward heard us.

Instead, we relied on that killer instinct that thrummed between us, two predators. That sought revenge for the life taken from the kin swarm. Pherox had killed her mate that dusk, at the broken male's request, his grief too much to bear. At least the pair were together now, roaming Iltavorn's realm as free swathes of darkness, never to be harmed again.

"The hunter and his mount," said Jaryn, raising to his full height.

He wore no crown today, just a General's Ilrair uniform and a navy and gold cloak draped over his left shoulder.

"He can understand every word you utter, King. He is not my mount ... rather my ... partner."

Pherox clicked his approval.

The officer opposite Jaryn stiffened. "You will address the King as Your Majesty."

My gaze flicked to him once more. My heart was cold, still, like a frozen ancient lake. "I do not take orders from *you*."

I felt it then, Meredith's wild ward magic pulse around us. Yet I bore down on it, latching against it with my own will. I didn't object to it, not like previous occasions, yet I didn't submit to it either. All of one second glance to Meredith confirmed that she did not suspect that I was parrying her with my own darkened, shadowed soul. I was still the image of a willing, doting servant. Her huntsman.

"Coen, meet Asher. Asher, this is Bromtide Platoon Commander, Silvano Coen," said the King.

I ignored the officer and jutted my chin at the map. "Aarine is yours now. What's left of it. No doubt your actions will have already been reported to Colladon's king."

"Indeed, it is mine." Jaryn rested his fingertips on the map, which was scattered with wooden carvings. The positions of his other platoons, I realized. "Colladon is readying its armies, yet they won't move across the Anduns, not in the dead of winter. Their small navy is hemmed in with ice. We wipe Aarine clean and build a fortress to act as our northern stronghold."

Which would take months. Only some of the sturdier stone buildings had survived the onslaught, the castle, and a few larger townhouses. The cities' fortifications had been reduced to cinders and ash.

"And in the meantime?" I tested.

A crooked grin from Jaryn. "We rid the Boreals of the spirits. Meredith is close to gaining their power, and thus, she will have elemental control over the land, sea, and air. And as you saw at the attack, the wild creatures too."

My gaze flicked to the wild ward. "Close? What's stopping you?"

"When the Trinitor was cleaved apart." Her teeth flashed in the darkness. "The spirits latched onto the creatures that followed, using them as scions to help them from dying out so quickly. Ilmari chose the Pegasi, Serebo the Unicorns, Tellervo the Mounties, and Iltavorn ... the Nijinxes. As the spirits wane, they cling onto their scions as a final anchor to their power."

Pherox subtly shifted closer to me, muscles tensing under his dark hide.

"You need to kill off the scions?" My voice was guttural. If they so much as touched Pherox or Vesperum.

It didn't surprise me. The need to protect them.

Meredith stepped closer to the table. "Not all of them. A sacrifice for each creature. With a Nijinx already slain, it leaves three creatures remaining."

A Nijinx that had been killed by Jaryn. Yet that would have meant the spirit of darkness would have been slain also. Shadows curled in my mind, and realization struck me like lightning. Spirits could choose more than one scion.

"I doubt one of your soldiers will hand over their Pegasus." My gaze cut to the Commander.

"They most certainly will not." Coen's voice was low. Lethal.

"I have an equine in mind." Meredith trailed a pale finger over the map. "A wild loner that I branded several years ago."

Branded. She had *branded* it. I could almost smell the singing, burnt flesh of the creature. Coen stiffened, and I noted the quick look of alarm on his face. My gaze rested on the hand-drawn image of Glentay. "There is only one Mountain Horse left."

"Indeed, there is." Meredith looked up at me.

I looked at all three of them. Realization settling into my gut. "You want me to hunt them down ... bring them to you?"

Jaryn's voice was a pure command. "Yes. Hunt them down, disable them, and bring them back to us alive."

"Disable them *how?*" I ground out.

"I have two spelled daggers. A cut from the blade will render them unconscious, long enough for them to be transported here by Bromtide." Meredith tucked her hands back within the folds of her feathered cloak.

"Only two daggers?"

Jaryn and Meredith displayed a grin laced with greed and malice. Snakes, the pair of them. Coen just looked mutinous.

"Follow me." Jaryn strode out of the tent and led our party back through the fog to a rough sawn wooden structure at the heart of the camp. Four guards surrounded it, one for each wall. I recognized that structure from the Pegasus raid when I had slain Gracien.

The strange scent we had discovered earlier ... it intensified as we drew closer. The shelter was sealed shut to the outside and no light gleamed from within.

Pherox snarled softly, and a shiver went down his leathery wings.

Jaryn halted at the only door and patted it. "It took my spies two months to find it. We had to blindfold it so that it wouldn't know where to direct its remaining power."

Coen unsheathed his curved sword as Jaryn heaved the door open. The wood had to be at least ten inches thick. A container, for *what?*

I felt Pherox's hot breath on my cheek as I peered inside. Dark, just endless dark, then there, a rope secured to each leg and brutal cross ties at its head ...

Pherox snarled again, louder this time, the thrum of it echoing out over the camp.

The bound beast snarled a challenge in response. A phantasmal creature of crystalline white and storm gray. Pherox's complete opposite. Its moon-pale pelt seemed to glow as if it were Amahri, the moon, reborn. Yet despite the hessian bag over its head, I could still make out that unmissable, twisting horn on its forehead and the gleam of eyes the color of ice. She smelled of glacier, freezing sky, and primitive power. She was motionless within her binds, despite her warning squeal, as if she were saving her strength and biding her time. A creature that had mastered patience and stillness, like the mountain land she had once called home had flowed into her veins and settled there.

Meredith breezed to my side, her features proud. "Her name is Olwen."

I stepped back, having seen my fill, Pherox shadowing me.

"Say I bring you the Mountie and the loner. What of the *Koskivarri* I saw at Saltfen? What are you going to do about *her?*"

Coen stilled, and I noted it with a hint of surprise. Jaryn surveyed me closely. Meredith ground down on me once again with her power, and I bowed my head to her.

It was Coen who answered, Jaryn simply nodding in agreement. "We'll capture them, soon enough, the dissenters too."

I didn't believe the bravado, the lie in his voice, but his King did.

Jaryn gave me a wide, smug smile. "I've sent my newest dog, the Heir Lord of Moray after them, we'll have them in chains sooner rather than later."

Coen went utterly motionless then, a killer about to strike. He stood just behind his King, and Jaryn missed the white-hot fury that washed over the Commander's face. I subtly inhaled, taking in Coen's scent. Only ... it wasn't just his. Interwoven amongst it all were subtle notes of alpine flowers and the earth after rain. The fucking *Koskivarri*. The light wielder.

Beside me, Pherox cocked his head as he registered it too.

"And Petowin?" I asked, the air rushing from my lungs.

"It's mine," snarled Jaryn.

CHAPTER
THIRTY-NINE

ORRIN

The small family group of Pegasi appeared like spectral beings through the fog as Carter, Murrkill, and I stepped into my father's ice-crowned glade.

Tellervo, far fainter than before, barely a wisp of energy, whispered to me, *"Orrin."*

"I'm here. I'm home. I've come to help." I felt the spirit almost sigh with relief, and I felt that power clinging to me with all that it had left. The trees whispered together. *Our King is home.*

"She is so powerful now," murmured Tellervo from far, far away.

"Save your strength, Tellervo," replied Ilmari.

My ears flicked nervously. Yet still the forest was aware and unbending before the wild ward magic. Its creatures had succumbed, yet the forest had not. Not yet. The five mares within the glade, foals tucked close under their wings, nickered softly as we approached. Murrkill broke into a high-stepping trot, and she floated across the snowy ground to her own offspring, a black filly. The pair nosed each other gleefully, the foal quick to nuzzle and suckle.

Carter and I paused a healthy distance away from them. It wrenched my heart. That picture of a little family, the iron-strong bond between dam and foal.

"Nessa, our mother, loved us," said Carter softly. *"She died protecting you from Spearian. He would have killed you, too, had she not led him away and disguised your scent."*

"I'm sorry." Guilt racked me.

"Whatever for? You were born from love, wholly and utterly. Gracien and Nessa adored one another. It was Spearian that killed Nessa, not you, never you."

"Gracien ..."

"Was a father to me. It was hard for us ... to go against that killing instinct, especially when I matured. Yet it was his love for my mother that made me respect him, and what he did for Ebrel that ensured I would never, ever, harm him. It is I who is sorry that you will never know him as your father. He was the finest of stallions, brave, loyal, and utterly devoted to this forest." Carter cast his gaze over the fog-covered trees.

Trees that stared silently back, ancient and snow-laden.

"This is your herd now?" I asked softly. The mares huddled around one another, the foals in the center and they dug for grass under the snow.

"If Murrkill will have me. Their old band stallion is dead, and the other bachelor herds have fled north. It's Pegasus culture for the lead mare to decide if a stallion is worthy of the herd. The previous lead mare had been shot and acted as a lure for the old band stallion, leaving Murrkill in charge." Carter watched the blood bay closely, his winter pelt quivering. *"I hope she says yes."*

They would make a mighty pair. *"I'm sure she will."*

The stallion's lips quirked. *"We shall see."*

After a night's rest and hours spent grazing in the meek dawn light, the pain in my injured leg reduced to a faint, dull ache. The wound had clotted; the skin blackened beside the red crust, yet it would be a long while before I could run like I had yesterday. The six foals with their fluffy winter coats huddled together beside a trio of silver birch trees. Murrkill's filly, the only black foal amongst them, stood with her muzzle resting atop the back of a smaller, dun-colored filly. Watching the little group closely, the dams grouped together beside Carter and me, keen to discuss the next step.

"We are safe here with our little ones. We should hold fast and defend it," said the dun foal's mother.

"I know, Bracken, but trouble will only head north. We should move out and seek refuge elsewhere." Murrkill looked at each of the mares in turn. *"I think we should—"*

"Do you hear that?" I asked, twisting my head toward the boulder field Murrkill and I had crossed yesterday.

Carted snorted. *"Yes, I do, Orrin. You're with me. Murrkill, stay here and defend the glade."*

Slowly, we trotted from the wintery sanctuary to yesterday's battleground.

Two forms raced across the sky, and I recognized them instantly. The brown and pink flecked body making my heart leap with joy, but it was on Kalana that my gaze rested upon. On the gold, brindled bridle over her head.

They bore no riders. No, the soldier and Petish woman were gone. Ebrel was harrying Kalana, forcing the mare lower and lower toward Glentay, their bodies streaked with sweat, and foam came flying from their mouths.

Carter leapt into the sky, a behemoth of dark feathers and pure power. Working with Ebrel, the pair drove Kalana toward the tree line and down, down onto the snow-topped ground. We formed a wall of equine bodies around the gray mare. Kalana screamed in rage, neck and wings extended, a distant creature to the docile, lovely being whom I had come to know. Her gray tail lashed her haunches, and she turned about, glaring at each of us.

Then her white-ringed gaze turned on me.

The bridle glowed brighter, a burning aura around the mare's head. Kalana squealed in pain. Ebrel stood rock still.

My voice was soothing yet crisp, like an autumn dawn. *"Easy, Kalana. We're not going to hurt you."*

The mare stamped a forehoof and squared up before me, neck arched.

My forest magic, what little Tellervo had left and had gifted to me, probed forward and examined the bridle around the mare's head. A vicious, horrible thing, crafted from a power that the wild ward had tricked and manipulated to her whim, so similar to what I had been cursed with. *"I'm going to try and free you, Kally."*

Kalana stilled momentarily as if my words had pierced through the blinding panic the bridle gave her. She trembled where she stood, her saddle torn and slipping around her barrel.

My father had freed me from the wild ward's grasp, and I hoped that with her so far to the south, I would have enough power to cleave through that wretched bridle. I looked inward into that well of power that had been bestowed to me when I became the King of the Forest.

Yet an awareness, a *tug*, pulled on my mind, and I *felt* them creeping around the western flanks of Glentay, moving quickly and silently.

A streamed clogged with storm-damaged trees whispered their numbers. Numbers that far outweighed the equines before me.

I blinked, my gaze wrenching to Carter and Ebrel. *"Nijinxes are coming, a human with them. You both have to leave now."*

"Nijinxes?" Carter cursed, and he seemed to grow taller and broader.

"They're headed here, for us."

"The herd," whispered Carter.

Mares, little ones, they were in danger. *"Go to them. We'll hold them off."*

The black stallion wasted no time and galloped into the trees.

Kalana tried to dart for the opening he created, yet I leapt to the space, blocking her off. She bared her teeth at me, and I clacked mine in return. *"Hold still."*

The mare arched her wings, and I faced her head-on. I dived into that well, scrambling for the scraps of power that remained there, waiting, and heaved it upward with all the strength I had left in me. I roared a great stallion scream that shook the snow from trees behind me. The sound blasted forward at Kally and the monstrous bit of magic. The power left my body in a surge of moss green light, whipping my mane like a typhoon as it speared for Kalana's head. Ebrel hemmed her closer, her wings stretched as far as they would go.

The magic fractured apart, bleating as it went, and Kalana dropped to her knees on the snow, her chest gasping and heaving as the spell was ripped from her.

I felt empty, utterly empty.

Ebrel snarled, her neck turned away from Kally. Toward the four Nijinxes stepping through the curtain of fog.

Asher sat astride the largest Nijinx, a huge male of midnight black, its wings folded neatly along its back. Four sets of fangs flashed as they surrounded us. Kalana, now free of the wild ward magic, arched her wings and backed up to Ebrel and me, creating a three-pointed star of pissed-off equines.

My gaze locked onto Asher.

The hunter smiled and slipped from his mount's back.

"Orrin," he said, by way of greeting. He stepped forward, hands on daggers that were strapped to either hip. The blades of which shone strangely in the faint light. "You've made some friends, I see."

His gaze roved over Kalana's back, resting on the twisted saddle. "You'll be coming with us. You and the branded one. The little snowy mare we'll shoot and feed to the Nijinxes as a message to her treasonous rider."

Kally rumbled in reply to the threat.

Asher simply smiled once more, his eyes dark with wild ward magic. His whole body pulsed with it, the Nijinxes too.

"You'll never catch Aalto." I barely recognized Kally's voice, it was savage and guttural.

The hunter shrugged. "You're right, I won't. But the Heir Lord of Moray and his dog most certainly will. A dissenter and a *Koskivarri*, what a hunting prize they will be."

Ebrel and Kalana froze behind me.

I had never wanted a rider, a burden along my spine. Yet the two Pegasus mares, they were bound so tightly to their humans, of their own free will, that if any harm should come to them ...

I subtly nudged Kalana with a hind hoof. A silent, urgent command. Ebrel locked her gaze on me, and understanding washed over that beautiful, flecked face. She gave the tiniest of nods, her breath tight.

I lowered my head, practically beckoning Asher forward.

The hunter gripped the hilts of the daggers, sliding them free from his belt and the blades, I realized with a sliver of horror, were coated in a spell so powerful, it made my nostrils flare. My entire body tensed. I felt Kalana's hocks lower ever so slightly.

"Go to hell," I hissed.

"I'm already there," Asher snarled in reply.

I lunged. Ebrel leapt forward, teeth bared and screaming at the nearest Nijinx. Kalana took to the skies in a thunderous, powerful wingbeat.

Asher moved like a night-kissed wind, his movements edged and powerful, dagger in each hand, he backstepped. The huge Nijinx male moved as quickly as the hunter did, dance partners to some brutal, hellish rhythm. The Nijinx barreled into my chest and knocked me clean off my hooves, smacking me into the snow with such force that the air whooshed from my lungs. I gasped, straining to get back up, but a taloned foot rested powerfully on my quivering flank and the Nijinx snarled by my face, his fangs like razor blades.

"Be still, Mountie, or I will slit your throat," said the male.

I strained my neck to look at Ebrel, who fought with the remaining Nijinxes, bucking and squealing as another one tackled her to the ground, pinning her neck with fangs spread wide.

I whinnied to her and struggled again.

The Nijinx male before me flinched and snarled viciously once more. *"Be still."*

"Why not slaughter us both?" I panted, my own amber gaze taking in the Nijinx's empty eye sockets.

"Not here," he murmured, his voice midnight soft. *"Not yet."*

Ebrel whinnied back to me, her legs kicking out as Asher bound her wings with straps of leather. Satisfied, the hunter strode forward and, with a swift downward strike, swept the edge of the blade straight down my head, between my eyes.

I screamed against it. The pain that ripped outward over my body as the wild ward magic aimed not to possess, but simply to render me motionless, took effect. My cries joined Ebrel's, and the last thing I saw were the four dark Nijinxes hovering over us, and far in the distance, in a break in the fog ... Kalana, flying at breakneck speed away from us.

CHAPTER FORTY

DESTRY

With the mirror a light, yet solid presence on my back and *Kathkar* now hanging from my belt, Aalto and I plotted our way through the fog. We climbed up, through the spectral, dim light, our arms and legs burning with effort. Aalto led the way, his breathing even and controlled.

I admired him. He was in far better shape than I was. I had upper body strength, hence my broad shoulders that apparently never went well with fancy ball gowns, according to snickering courtiers back at the Reck. I would never pass for a willowy damsel. Too tall, too manly. One peacocking courtier even described me as a gentle giant at one royal event simply because I matched him for height. It had taken all my strength not to pour my mulled wine over his head, and I had made sure to stand on his toes as often as possible when we danced.

I peered up at Aalto's back, my attention snagging on his twin blades. "Do they have names, your swords?"

Aalto paused on a snow-covered stone shelf. "You're one of the few to ever ask that."

I climbed up alongside him, my heart a pounding rhythm in my chest. The air was so thin up here. My head spun slightly as I leant against the rock.

"*Vorna*," he patted the right sword hilt over his shoulder, then the left. "And *Vayla.*"

"Night and day," I murmured. "Very poetic."

His cheeks flushed as he grinned down at me. "They act as a reminder that life is all about balance. Light and dark, death and life. You can't have one without the other. Without one of the blades, I become unbalanced, but using them together ... well, I'll show you sometime."

"I'll hold you to that."

"I could teach you. How to wield two blades?"

I shook my head. "At my age? I'd never grasp it."

"Nonsense." Aalto commanded my gaze until I couldn't tear away from him. "You can do whatever you set your heart upon. I won't deny that it will be harder, your body more likely to frustrate you, but it's certainly not impossible, Destry." He glanced down at *Kathkar*. "We could have another blade made for you, one to balance out your current sword. Due to the length of *Kathkar,* you'd need something shorter, otherwise, you'd be poking my eyes out." Gently, he reached toward me and gripped my left wrist. "You could wield a parrying dagger. With a lot of practice, something the length of your forearm would be sufficient and wouldn't get in your way."

He stepped back, smiling, and toed my boot with his own. "Let's start with this: when you set off walking, use your left foot first, rather than your right. Get your body used to being used equally."

He set off again, and I went to follow, yet I stopped and looked down and for the first time in forever, I had to *think* about walking.

"It'll get easier," called Aalto over his shoulder.

I rolled my eyes at him, and with aching limbs, we climbed ever upward.

We climbed all day through the fog, coming to rest in a tiny valley cupped between two smaller peaks. Hastily, as the temperature dropped, we dug out a snow cave and set up camp for the night.

A headache pulsed in the back of my head, and I longed for a hot cup of tea. My back braced against the wall of the snow cave, *Kathkar* tucked close beside me. I beheld the Kottin Mirror in my lap.

"I'm just going to collect more stag lichen," said Aalto.

I smiled weakly as he left the cave, then looked down once more. In the dim light from our small fire, my face barely reflected at me in the ice. I could just make out my straight nose and jawline.

It really was more like a window.

Hesitantly, I released a tiny flicker of light from my fingertips and swept it out over the pane of ice. The green and white light seeped over the entirety of it, like a rush of water and ... nothing. Not a thrum of power or energy. Frowning, I lifted it away from my knees and suspended it before me. Keeping the light where it was, pooling over the surface closest to me, I twisted my neck and peered behind the mirror.

My eyes widened.

The light, which was lucid and flowing on my side of the mirror, became column-like, spearing from the back of the mirror in a beam of green light as straight as a blade. The beam crackled and stretched for no more than a meter or so, but then again, I was barely releasing but a whisper of the light inside of me. If I could give it more then—

From outside the cave, a yell was whipped away by the brisk winter wind.

I was on my feet in an instant, *Kathkar* in my hand the next. I tucked the mirror under my cloak on the floor and banked the fire, then I strode for the cave entrance.

A night-washed valley greeted me, the fog finally leeching away from the landscape. It was deathly quiet. I stepped out, *Kathkar* in a steady two-handed grip before me. I had received a handful of lessons covering the basics of sword fighting from Aalto, barely scraping the surface on using the weapon efficiently. Yet the hilt felt solid in my grasp and the sword thrummed against my fingers, the lambent stones flashing in the pommel.

Aalto hadn't been wearing his swords when he left. They sat freshly honed within the cave. Something snagged my attention on a nearby jagged rock. It fluttered delicately in the breeze. I stared and stared at the long, gray primary feather with the leather cord looped around the quill.

Aalto wore it around his neck, never taking it off.

Someone or something ... Aalto.

Releasing a cool breath, I stalked toward the boulder to where the valley curved into the next. The dark blue of twilight embraced me. I treaded silently through the snow. The lambent stones flickered again, answering to the anger in my blood.

I sensed the tall, hulking form moving through the remaining fog before I saw him. A breath of silence fell over the valley. From his sheer height alone, I recognized him even before he stepped into my field of vision and threw back his hood, revealing his clean-shaven head and stubble-covered jaw.

Lonan Donahue.

I swallowed harshly and joined him on the valley floor. He tracked my every move as I halted away from him, the tip of *Kathkar* reflecting the shadowed snow at my feet.

"There she is."

Throwing back my shoulders, I gazed up at him. "Where is he?"

Lonan smiled. "Lost someone, have we, my sweetness?"

I remained silent, my entire body quivering in anticipation. I could just make out the hilt of his new sword peeking out from the edge of his cloak.

The guardsman folded his arms across his massive chest. "Are you looking for the man who is wanted for treason? Who King Jaryn Adacus is offering a mighty reward to be captured alive?" He gestured to the valley behind him. "Oh, he's just up there."

A misdirection, more likely than not. My lips set into a grim line.

Lonan stepped forward. "You're the most wanted people in the Boreals, and my lord is quite keen on getting *you* back." He proffered a gloved hand. "Come with me, and you and your soldier won't be harmed."

"I'm sure I've heard you say that before, Lonan. Look how well that turned out for you last time."

His expression darkened, and his hand casually lowered to grip his sword. "My lord has requested you unharmed."

I arched an eyebrow. "Your memory must be very poor indeed, Lonan. You do remember the night when I knocked you the fuck out?"

"Watch your mouth."

"Or what, Lonan?"

"Or I'll—" He stopped dead, gaze dropping to finally assess his sword in my grasp.

Not his anymore.

Mine.

"You bitch," he spat. His new sword sang as he unsheathed it. The longsword gobbled up any light there was, the steel darker than *Kathkar.* Then he let out a bark of a laugh. "Although it is rather poetic that you wield the blade that once belonged to your family. I see you've replaced the obsidian with lambent stones again."

I blinked and glanced down at my sword; it glowed a faint blue in the darkness.

"*Soul Guardian* is what *Kathkar* translates to. I thought that half-Petish bastard would have told you that?"

I had no time to wrap my mind around the knowledge. Lonan lunged, and I countered him, my light flashing before his eyes.

Blind him, I seethed.

Yet Lonan simply laughed as he twirled away. By whatever magic or spell gifted to him, my light did not affect him. My courage faltered and panic gripped my bones. Hastily, I coiled the light back to my body, and I braced myself for the onslaught.

We clashed again, swords resounding off one another as the blades flashed in the growing twilight. I had forgotten how strong Lonan was. He was pure muscle beneath the plain, black uniform and an utter god-like creature when a sword was placed in his hand.

He twirled, again and again, strike after strike, forcing me to yield *Kathkar* up to him like some sacrificial gift. The force of the impact against my sword was enough to make my bones jar in their sockets. Green light sparked and puttered at my fingertips, yet it would be no use here, not anymore.

I rammed upward, pushing every ounce of strength I had to force Lonan back, pressing the cool surface of his sword against his skin in a steel-covered kiss. Metal scraped against metal and my body trembled with the effort to hold him off. Sweat ran in rivulets down my spine.

"I like wildness in a woman," Lonan grinned savagely. He shoved me backward, sweeping his sword back and up to cut at me again. "It makes taming her all the more enjoyable."

My breath came in hurried pants as I leapt to the side to miss a swing to my thigh. "You obviously never courted a Petish woman. We can't be tamed."

Lonan bent low over his knees and stalked forward. "I like a challenge too. I see your Platoon Commander has taught you some of his sword skills. I could teach you so much more."

I twirled the sword in my grip and bared my teeth.

He was like a never-ending wave, and despite how much I countered and parried him, he was getting the upper hand. He knew I was tiring. Lonan swept into a broad swing, and I dove away from it, only to connect with his booted foot. He kicked hard, sending me flying and tumbling back over the snow. Blood sprayed. I could taste it in my mouth. *Kathkar* lay forlorn atop the snow, the lambent stones gleaming.

I panted for breath and heaved myself upright. Lonan ripped off his right glove and drove his fist into my face.

I regained consciousness just as Lonan topped a rocky rise and into a stone cave lit by two large fires, guards flanking them. He carried me over his shoulder like a dead doe, and pain pulsed through my skull. Lonan walked to the back of the cave, threw *Kathkar* to the dirt-trodden floor, then my body after it. Something cracked in my chest as I hit the stone surface, and my lungs struggled to draw breath.

I rose on one elbow, my gaze wild as I looked ...

Aalto strained against his bonds, hissing and swearing over his gag, fighting with all his might at the rope that cut into his wrists. I looked across at him from where I lay, panting and broken, on the cave floor.

His bronze eyes were frantic, yet brimming with glacial-cold rage. Sweat coated his brow and bruises marred that handsome face.

Tall shadows moved and tapered along the stone walls, then paused. I craned my neck, stars dancing across my vision as pain lanced up my spine with the movement. My rib cage shuddered as a breath choked from my lungs.

"Hello, Destry, my love."

Aalto snarled at the endearment.

Flanked by Lonan and two other guardsmen in plain black livery, Narve smiled fondly down at me. His face was tender, yet blood tainted his hands. *Aalto's* blood coated those perfectly rounded, short nails and grazed knuckles. The Heir Lord of Moray stepped forward and knelt fluidly beside me. He flicked the tails of his long coat behind him, then reached forward to stroke a bloodied strand of hair from my face.

Bile rose in my throat at the touch, his skin hot against mine. I mentally screamed at my limbs to move, to rake and claw and punch the fucker into the next century. Yet only pain answered my silent plea, blistering pain that sent burning tendrils down to my fingers and toes.

"Having trouble moving, my dearest? Pity ..." His grin showed that this was anything but a delight to him. Reaching into an inner coat pocket, he withdrew a small, brown glass vial. "You remember my friend, Medic Wylmar? His profession was poisons." He popped the cork top and smeared a fingertip along the vial's rim. "This is a fine concoction of his. One of my favorites."

Narve set the vial down and withdrew a small glass syringe. Quicker than a dune snake, he snatched my wrist into his grasp and tucked my knuckles to his lips.

Aalto swore and thrashed, yet Narve's attention remained wholly fixed on the bare skin of my forearm.

"A strange mixture, in that when it touches unbroken skin, it is harmless. No more than a spatter of warm rain on a summer night." Holding me firmly, Narve filled the syringe and placed a single droplet on the hand which he had just placed a tender kiss.

Panic overwhelmed me.

Pain was coming, more than I could bear.

Narve's grip tightened even further. "Yet if the skin is cut open, say, by a sword," Narve deftly tapped the torn and bloodied flesh of my left bicep, and I couldn't hold back my cry. "Then it can enter the bloodstream. Where it causes great pain, immobility, and *sometimes* even rendering the wounded unconscious."

Aalto spat and snarled against his bonds behind me, more feral than an enraged wolf. I met Narve's gaze with a cutting look that promised I would never forget this moment, and would gladly, happily pay him and his men back in kind. He merely smiled gently once more as he placed the first one, then two drops into my wound.

I don't know how long I screamed and wreathed for before sweet darkness took me under its wing and swept me away.

CHAPTER
FORTY-ONE

AALTO

I wouldn't beg, yet I found myself on my knees, sweat coating my back and chest as fury coated every sense I possessed. The muscles in my abdomen, arms, and legs quaked with the strain I was placing upon them. My anger battled between ice and fire, sparking and tensing every soldier's instinct in my body. Silence now held court over the cave. Destry's screams now no more than faint echoes on the winter breeze beyond the cave's mouth. The fires spat and crackled.

Guilt ravaged my soul. Destry was just another woman I had let down, had left unguarded to be beaten and brutalized.

A guard walked up to Narve, his face ashen, and whispered, "The Bromtide Commander has ordered that we cease and desist, that if we hurt her, he'll—"

Narve simply waved a hand. "Too fucking late for that. *She's mine.*"

The three guardsmen turned on their heels, leaving just Narve, Destry, and me.

I was a wolf, snared and bound, yet I could still kill him. I just had to get close enough to rip his throat out. The need to end him, the Petowin bloodlust, pounded in my veins and pulsed with every beat of my heart.

After removing my gag, Narve stayed close to Destry, his gaze hovering over her limp body as if he were guarding a treasured prize. Her bloodied face was downcast, facing away from him. The wounded arm lying prone on the ground, her fingertips barely grazing the bastard's knees. Blood matted the crown of her head.

"I like to think, Thorra, that I know what makes people tick." The Heir Lord rocked back onto his heels, his green eyes flicking upward to gaze at me.

"You sure like to hear the sound of your own voice, don't you?" I wouldn't use blades or arrows to end him. I'd use my bare hands to crush his windpipe. The primitive, Petish way of killing.

Again, that lopsided smile of his. "Knowing what inspires people, what motivates them, is the key to their undoing." Narve chuckled.

Spirits if he killed her, if we lost her ... the Petowin bloodlust roared in my head. Weeks ago, I would have let him kill her, but now ... I checked Destry, assured myself that she was still breathing, still holding on, the power in her veins clutching onto whatever was keeping her here. How long would the poison claim her for?

Fuck, if my people discovered that I hadn't protected her ... she had saved my life three fucking times, and I could barely return the favor.

Just like you did with—

I shook that memory free as the scent of ylang-ylang burned the back of my throat.

Fuck.

"It may not be very original, Thorra, but it's true. Take Destry as a lovely example. I'm sure she does more than just make you *tick*." Reaching over with an elegant hand, he grasped Destry's chin and turned her to face him, exposing the tan and smooth plane of her neck. The Heir Lord eased back into a predatory crouch, his weight braced upon all fours. "I'm sure she makes your heart pound when you look at her."

The fury in my blood sparked into a primal, shuddering rage as Narve held my gaze, then, slowly, lowered his head closer and closer to Destry's. Lips parting, he hovered millimeters from her mouth.

I hadn't been there when the woman I had loved, *still* loved, was assaulted, hadn't been there to guard her from harm. The memories of her battered face haunted every moment of my day.

Yet now, being here as a trapped spectator, this was a new level of hell. I didn't love Destry, would never love her, if I was being honest with myself, but this was still horrifying.

I barely recognized my own voice as I hissed, "I'm going to slaughter you all."

Narve grinned. His gaze never leaving mine, a leopard facing down a wolf. He lowered himself even closer, their breaths intermingling in the cold air. Panting where I knelt on the frigid stone, I could only watch helplessly as Narve pressed his lips to Destry's in a soft, lingering kiss.

And he was right. The bastard was right. I was utterly undone. My plans had all gone to utter shit. Destry had been distant with me since Spell, and now this bastard was ruining things even further. Narve withdrew and rocked back onto his heels, his gloved hands dangling between his knees.

A dramatic sigh escaped his mouth. "It's no fun when there is no fight in them."

Blood dripped from my wrists. "Poisoning will do that to a person."

The Heir Lord chuckled. "I like you, Thorra. It's a shame you picked the wrong person to try and defend. I guess it's too late to ask you to join my men. Being a treasonous bastard and all."

Like I would ever go with monsters such as him and Lonan.

"Will you tell her, I wonder, that I kissed her? If she pulls through? The poison can have varying effects on the inflicted. Some never rise from it." Again, that drama-laden sigh. "She has such beautiful lips, doesn't she? Full, sensuous. The Petish nose I could live without. It's rather a *strong* look for a woman, and I'd rather not sleep with a woman of her height ... but ... she's a treasure all the same."

He trailed his pointer finger from her lower lip and down her neck and chest. Reaching her abdomen, his palm flattened out and rested there. "Once Jaryn has had his use of her—" I was going to burst out of my skin. "Then she'll be mine, and you'll be hanged for treason. You and your sorry platoon. Your mounts will be shot and turned into ornaments, maybe even ripped apart by my hounds. I may even have one stuffed and prancing in my townhouse. It's a snow-gray mare you have, is it not? That is a color that's coming into fashion. I could even turn her into a cloak." A sly grin parted Narve's lips. His hand pushed torturously slowly back up Destry's torso, cupping her left breast, then he retracted it. With the grace of a wild cat, he rose and stared me down. "We leave for Aarine at dawn. Sleep well, traitor."

"What does the Colladon king think of your betrayal, I wonder?" I seethed. "What will Rekorious Niemi think when he discovers that you assaulted his betrothed?"

Narve straightened. "I have been guaranteed protection by King Jaryn. He has assured me that my lands will remain mine. And as for Rekorious," the Heir Lord said while spitting at the ground. "She's *my* betrothed. Not his. He never came to claim her. The warlord is a king of nothing and no one, *especially* if he doesn't have *her.*" He gestured casually to Destry's barely breathing body.

"I wouldn't be too sure about that. Everything Jaryn gives you comes at a hefty price. And the warlord will *fucking kill you* for what you've done tonight."

The Heir Lord clasped his hands behind his back and cocked his head. Silently, he studied me, hissing and snarling before him. "I wouldn't trouble yourself, traitor. By this time tomorrow, you will be dead."

"You expect to walk to Aarine in the space of a day?"

"The King has loaned us some of his Pegasi to transport us."

My body froze. *"Loaned?"*

"Indeed, the King even said I could take my pick of the finest as my own mount. As old as they are, they still look rather grand."

I wasn't quite sure I was breathing. "He has loaned you the Pegasi of dead soldiers?"

"Dead or alive soldiers, I don't care. They're mine now."

It was tradition to place the Pegasi of fallen cavalrymen into lifelong retirement so that they would carry no other man or woman into battle and live out their days in peace. To haul them back into a life of service for men who had not undertaken the bonding process was abhorrent.

If we got through this, I'd set them free.

Narve reached down and plucked *Kathkar* from the ground. He dusted off the blade, then tucked the sword through his belt. The lambent stones flashed three times in the low light, like some ancient scrying stones. Narve swept out of the cave, no doubt to another one further along, to debrief with Lonan. Four guards took up their positions just within the mouth of our cave and tended the great fire next to them.

My gaze slipped to Destry, who lay broken and bleeding and out of reach. Her chest barely rose, and her light didn't flicker at her fingertips. Not even the faintest of glows could be seen.

Come on, Destry. I silently implored her.

Pull through this. Hold on, hold on, hold on.

CHAPTER FORTY-TWO

FIRE PRINCE

The stars crackled, burned, and with every flicker of light in the night sky, they whispered.

Night Pegasus.

From far, far below, spearing up into the night-laden sky, came three brilliant sparks of his own gifted light. A silent cry, a plea, a call for aid from the stones that contained his own life's blood. Yet not just from any stones. But from lambents that belonged to that female bloodline that had saved his soul so long ago. The light called to his own and his feathers tingled as he recognized it.

The *Koskivarri* was in danger.

A mountain that no human had yet discovered, its peak higher than even Serebo, in a place so far north, it sat in near total darkness year-round, beckoned. Pausing in his flight, the Night Pegasus peered down to where the precipice pierced the blackened sky.

Mount Nychta.

The mountain spirit sensed the entity hovering above her, yet she did not recoil. The mountain remained resolute ... waiting. For she knew why the Night Pegasus had come.

His wings wreathed in glorious light, the Night Pegasus raised his noble head and stepped down from his realm of darkened skies onto the mortal lands below. So pleased was he with this palace of ice, stone, and eeriness, he beseeched Nychta to join him.

"*Fire Prince,*" she whispered, "*I cannot leave my throne. It is not my destiny to step free of my peaks and into the night. Yet, I can recommend another, who has far more credentials than I...*"

On her western face, snow tumbled downward, drawing the Prince's attention to the slightly smaller mountain that adjoined Nychta.

Its peak was jagged and dagger-like, fiercely pitching toward the heavens with all her might. "*I will join you, Prince.*"

The Night Pegasus swept from Nychta and onto the sister peak. The gray stone quivered under his hooves.

"*What is your name?*" murmured the mighty black stallion, his wings ablaze.

"*Eira, my Prince.*"

"*Join me, Eira. Let me free of your throne of rock and ice.*"

Reaching for his sky, the Pegasus brushed a small gathering of nearby stars from the night. They tumbled downward from his muzzle and onto the knife-like peak. The Night Pegasus inhaled and breathed a blast of frozen wind over the glittering stars. Eira leapt free of her mountain seat. With a gust from his glowering wings, the Night Pegasus shaped her.

Stepping out from the dust, light, and ice came Eira. A Pegasus mare as fine as he, her gray coat gleamed like the stars from whom she had been born. Her wings glittered as she stepped up beside her Prince. The night and the stars, the darkness, and the flicker of light.

"*Fly with me, Eira, for we have far to travel tonight.*"

Taking flight with their colossal wings, the pair flew into their sky realm, a king and his consort. As they swept south, the Night Pegasus blazed, and a falling star flew beside him.

CHAPTER
FORTY-THREE

AALTO

The night was long. Blood now caked my wrists, and the muscles in my arms trembled from being wrenched behind my back. But I'd take it all again in a heartbeat. The beating from Narve as his guards held me down. Again and again, if it meant that Destry pulled through this. All through the dark hours, she did not stir, and I counted every single breath she made.

As the light turned meek and gray beyond the cave mouth, Destry finally, *thank the fucking spirits*, took a deeper, steadier breath. She cleared her throat, and a low, pain-filled groan escaped her cracked lips. Slowly, she twisted her head to look up and around her. Her fingers clenched upon the cold stone floor.

"Destry," I murmured.

She turned to face me, her tears leaving clear tracks down her dirtied and bruised face. Fingers clawing, she hauled herself into a sitting position, then dragged her body over to where I knelt as silently as she could.

The guards didn't notice her. Narve was nowhere in sight.

Her first touch on my face set my skin afire. She was alive. I pushed my cheek into her palm, yet she withdrew her hand again, her gaze silently searching mine. Looking for answers I couldn't give her yet. I didn't deserve her pity, not one shred of it.

"I'm getting us out of here." Her voice was hoarse from screaming.

But the ropes binding my wrists to the rock would not budge, no matter how hard Destry grappled with them. Lonan had relieved her of any weapons before dumping her in here like some carcass.

Voices sounded outside, and Destry turned toward it. Rising stiffly and unsteadily to her feet, she crouched before me, a hand braced upon the ground, and she bared teeth. To the man who stepped into the cave and gave her a clipped smile. Narve appeared fresh before us, his face flushed with the cold. "Good morning, Destry dearest. How are we faring?"

Her legs quivering, Destry rose to her full height. With her shoulders thrown back, she looked every bit like the Chieftess she was. Narve retreated a step. Like he had forgotten that Destry matched him for stature. She shifted before me, the skirt of her *holtka* blocking me from view.

"Release him," she croaked. "Release him, and I will go with you willingly."

No, no, no. "Do not bargain for me, Destry."

The Heir Lord tutted. "No bargains will be made today. You will be coming with us. Your transport awaits."

Beyond the mouth of the cave, men shrieked in the cold dawn air. Narve twisted upon the stone and stared. Destry slunk forward. A shuddering boom rocked the stone around us, as a half-ton beast landed outside the cave and unleashed an almighty roar.

I almost wept with joy as Kalana folded her gray wings and stepped into the cave. I had never seen her look so wild, so enraged. Sweat coated her flanks and a fine cut left a red smear over her chest. No sign of her saddle or the wild ward magic that had tried to claim her. The sound of clashing steel echoed off the stone walls, along with the familiar battle cries that I knew off by heart.

The Royants had come.

Narve looked up aghast at the Pegasus.

Kalana tossed her head and bared those yellowed teeth.

"Call off your pet, Thorra," said Narve, barely controlling the quiver in his voice.

My laugh was ghost-like. "She is no one's pet."

Kalana lunged, grasping a mouthful of Narve's tunic, she tossed him outside of the cave as if he were no more than a bag of hay. Even the noise of the guardsmen taking on soldiers couldn't mask the horrendous snap of Narve's leg as Kalana brought her forehooves down onto his flesh and bone.

Destry launched into action with not a single weapon on her. She ran from the cave after Kalana.

I could just make out Kalana stepping back, Narve bleating on the ground, as Destry dropped to one knee and relieved him of *Kathkar*. The lambent stones blazed as she placed the sharpened tip onto Narve's lower lip.

"I remember it all, every touch, every word." That was not Destry who spoke ... but a woman bent on revenge. Her voice was glacial. With expert precision, revealing the promise of the sword skills she could one day possess, Destry trailed *Kathkar's* tip down Narve's throat and abdomen, just as the Heir Lord had done to her with his hands.

All around her, sheer havoc, as my beloved Royants took on the guardsmen. Yet that was all a whirl of motion compared to the utter stillness of Destry. As if Varranar's ice had penetrated her veins, her soul.

"You will *never* touch me again, Heir Lord," Destry hissed. Fury made her voice unshakable, her hands steady, as she twirled *Kathkar*, her light rippling down the sword. "You murdered my mother."

Narve threw up his hands. "That bitch was as good as—"

The dawn sun glanced off steel, as Destry effortlessly cleaved Narve's hands from his wrists with a swift lateral strike.

The Heir Lord's screams came a moment later, agony-filled, like hers had been the night before. Blood stained the golden snow, yet Destry wholly ignored it as she crouched beside Narve. "If Lonan has any mercy in his fucking body, he'll kill you and put you out of your misery."

The Royants surrounded the guards, who dropped their weapons to the pink, dawn-tainted snow. Destry stepped back, her face filled with a coldness I had never seen before. It made me pause and take note, my plans for her crumbling slightly.

Fuck.

Kalana watched Narve like a hawk, her ears snapped to her skull.

"Get out of my sight," spat Destry.

The small group, escorted by several Royants and their Pegasi, walked away, bolstering Narve between them. Yet Lonan was not amongst them. Shep entered the cave, unhurt and armed to the teeth. He stalked forward and cut me free. With a devilish grin, he said, "Platoon Commander, got yourself into a fix, have we? A small group of us flew out as soon as Kalana landed at the stone cabin."

"Lonan?" I asked, rising to my feet, massaging my wrists.

Shep shook his head. "He made off on one of the retired Pegasi as soon as we landed."

We stepped out into the blush-tinted light, the skies free of clouds. Quickly, I scanned the small valley. A cluster of old, saddled Pegasi huddled together for warmth, picketed in the snow at the far end of the valley. Poor, poor beasts.

"Commander, our plans, should we stay and help?" asked Shep in a low whisper, his gaze fixed on Destry's ramrod straight back.

I shook my head, determined. This had to work. I knew what blossomed between Coen and Destry, knew that I would have to try and quash it for my people to accept this. I would have to become something dark, something horrible, if this didn't work. I hated myself for it.

Yet self-loathing was something I wore like a second skin. Ever since I let the woman of my dreams slip away from me. Now she haunted me instead, in vivid dreams of cloud-cloaked mountains and glowing waterfalls. "No, we carry on as planned."

Grier and Nion were flying high above, checking for any further threats.

Then my gaze rested on Destry, who watched Narve disappear from view.

She turned to face me, a flicker of warmth returning to her frozen features, then she walked straight into my arms. I clutched her to me and breathed in deeply. Shep wisely said nothing as I held her.

CHAPTER
FORTY-FOUR

ASHER

The soldiers had roughly constructed a wooden stage beside the royal tent. Three posts stood prominently upon it, each readied with a metal ring and ropes to secure the creatures we had brought south.

Dawn light brushed the posts, the light hazy through the camp kitchen's smoke. The cabin, which now contained not only Olwen, but Orrin and Ebrel, too, stood out starkly against the cream canvas of the tents. Silence pulsed from the structure.

Everything was ready. Meredith was undergoing her final preparations for tonight, a pyre was being built opposite the stage, knives were being sharpened. For when the sun set and full dark fell tonight, the scions would die.

Pherox and I watched from the shadows, our decisions made, united in a brotherhood of blood. My gaze flicked to the royal tent, which flapped open, and a dark-skinned, wool-cloaked woman marched out, tears streaming down her face. The Queen. Who could, apparently, wield water, yet none of us had seen her power.

No one followed her as she wove her way through the tents, heading toward the closest Aarine ruins. Pherox and I shadowed her silently. The royal stopped beside a former watchtower, its primarily wooden build now just fractured planks and cinders. She braced a hand upon what remained and looked across the destruction. Ash twirled with fresh snowflakes.

Pherox inhaled deeply, cataloging the woman's scent. As did I.

More tears fell down her cheeks.

It must feel awful, I thought, to realize that you married a monster.

CHAPTER FORTY-FIVE

ORRIN

I understood why Asher and the Nijinxes let the darkness envelope them, why they surrender to it wholly and make it their world. There was an essence of comfort in it. As much as I could not see, it made me feel like I could not be seen in turn, that I was merely a shadow, a being without form. To harm me would be an impossible feat, that any danger would just slice through the darkness, unable to find purchase on me.

My blindfold of thick hessian obstructed all the light. Yet I could not fully submerge into the inky depths. For I could still hear Ebrel's breath beside me and that of another creature here in this prison with us.

She did not speak, the equine who smelt of crevasse and avalanche, yet I was acutely aware of her and the power radiating from bones. Instinct told me what she was, yet I could hardly believe it to be possible.

The southern king had captured a Unicorn. She was young, a year or so older than Ebrel. I could smell her fear, along with her unwavering resolve.

Like Ebrel and myself, this Unicorn had no intention of dying tonight.

I could no longer hear Ilmari. Her power had fluttered and dissolved around us late last night. Her absence only added to our silence, and we wrapped that about ourselves as if, along with the darkness, it was an extra line of defense that would protect us from harm. It was within an hour or so bound together, that our breathing began to become in sync as a trio, our inhales deep, our exhales calming. In. Out.

Sounds drifted to us, every now and again, and we would flinch collectively. Jaryn commanding his platoons, the wild ward telling the workers to make the stage longer, Asher murmuring to his Nijinx. There was a kinship that I could not understand. A bond between killers.

I could also pick up the soft yet gravelly growls of something else, yet Glentay and its tree residents were too far away for it to be them. The hours slid by, and we found new depths of darkness to cloak ourselves in.

CHAPTER FORTY-SIX

DESTRY

Somewhere upon Serebo, a female was singing. Her haunting, angelic voice lilted across the shimmering ice, caressing the core of our bones as we stood shivering on a precipice. A second melody joined the first, then a third, until Aalto and I were surrounded by wave after wave of alluring song. I couldn't make out their words, if what they sang was our language at all, but I felt compelled to pause and listen.

"We have to keep moving." Aalto gripped my elbow and pulled.

Yet the singing, such wondrous singing. I wanted to wrap myself up in it. Maybe if I stepped closer—

"Destry, Serebo no longer controls the snow sirens. The wild ward does. They will lure you off the cliff faces if you follow their song. Here." Aalto stepped up close before me, his body pressing into mine. Reaching forward, he clasped his gloved hands over my ears.

The singing became muffled and lost its grip. I blinked, dazed.

Inches from my face, Aalto smiled softly. "That's it, focus on the tread of your boots upon the snow, the sound of your very breath, your heartbeat. It helps drown them out." He reached down and gripped my mitt-covered hand in his. "We must keep moving. The glacier is this way."

The glacier. I swallowed and winced, my body not quite recovered from Lonan's beating and Narve's poison the night before. Aalto and

I were alone once more upon Serebo's flanks, her peak hidden high above us. The Royants, with the poor retired Pegasi and Kalana in tow, were flying hard for what was left of Aarine, to stop the wild ward's slaughter. I was worried sick for Ebrel, and prayed to every spirit existing that she would survive. Aalto would not risk Kalana in another wild ward trap, so, restocked, we had pushed upward toward Serebo's largest glacier, Lundakarad. Just the two of us once more.

"It roughly translates to 'snow bear,'" said Aalto, after pinpointing it on the map. "For when it moves down the mountain, it sounds like a roaring bear."

Dusk was drawing closer, and the night was clear. A glance between Aalto and me confirmed this would be our one chance tonight, with such a clear sky and no moon. One chance to smash through the wild ward's grip on the mother of all spirits.

The snow sirens had long fallen silent. We traversed Serebo's southern shoulder, pinnacles of rock and ice cutting the freezing and thin air that penetrated every layer of clothing we wore. My chest felt tight and my shoulders rigid. Warmth began to leach from my fingers and toes until it became hard to grip the snow-covered slabs in front of me.

Aalto reached back to heave me up over a precarious boulder and onto more level ground.

"We need to talk about last night, Destry," he murmured. His cheeks were flushed with the cold, his shoulders appearing even broader beneath all his layers of wool and reindeer skin.

I shook my head, the action making me dizzy. I gritted out, "Later."

He didn't reply, and last night's events hung between us like an iron spider's web, anchoring us together yet trapping us there in time. Aalto bound and bleeding, roaring yet helpless, and Narve.

Narve.

Anger made me want to rage and tear, yet I leashed it harshly, just as I had this very morning when his body had been beneath *Kathkar's* glinting blade. I shoved away the thought of his hands on me and his body hovering over mine. The possessiveness and cruelty he had exuded made me want to retch, curl up in the snow and cry. My light tentatively brushed along my nerve endings in an attempt to soothe. I brushed back against it, and it felt like I was caressing a northern breeze.

I felt no regret at what I had done to Narve. The bastard had deserved it. It was apprehension that clung to my bones as I looked up at Aalto's strong back in front of me. *Kathkar*, a solid weight against my back, pulsed with an ice-hewn power. Aalto had told the Royants not to assist us, to leave just the two of us together again like originally planned. My mistrust of the Commander yawned between us like a void. Coen and Varranar's warning burned in the back of my mind.

But Coen was a long, long way from here. He couldn't save me here this time. I would have to save myself.

Aalto pausing ahead of me, brought me back to the here and now, to this land frozen in time. I drew up alongside him, the last of the day's light revealing what had made him stop.

Lundakarad. It spanned for miles before us, then up and up Serebo's western corrie. The ice glittered in the low-cast light, fractured by snow-capped rock arêtes on either side. Wind tugged at them, lifting flags of white from the chiseled stone. The sky was a deep violet, and stars began to flicker in earnest above our heads.

Our gazes continued to travel upward from the glacial corrie and up the jagged western col, shaped like a series of shark fins, to the summit. Serebo's peak was shaped like a crown for the Queen that she was, her rock fluted seamlessly upward to a notched spire that glittered with crystals of ice.

She commanded our complete and utter attention, her primordial gaze missing nothing and noting everything. As the sun finally set, Aalto and I gazed in awe at the falling star that tumbled toward Serebo's crown.

PART THREE

THE MAGICKED

CHAPTER
FORTY-SEVEN

ASHER

"There were once four sister moons, and they held court of the darkness amongst the stars." Meredith was dressed in a simple, woolen black dress, her feathered cloak gone. She stood upon the stage, pale hands clasped before her as she beheld Jaryn's soldiers and the Nijinxes. Flames from the pyre enameled her body in shadow and light. She wholly ignored the three creatures restrained behind her, their hooded heads hanging low next to their knees.

"One night, a great and furious light blasted into the sister's realm. The mighty fire spirit, Tavaris, had come. The stars watched on as he challenged the sisters to rule the sky. Aurin, the eldest of the four sisters, accepted his challenge, yet she knew she would not win against him. She warned her youngest sibling, Ullko, to flee from the flames of Tavaris, whilst Earth and Amahri decided to remain.

"Tavaris consumed Aurin wholly. Amahri, once blue and lovely, spilled tears into the night sky that fell upon Earth. Merivis, the water spirit, was born. On and on the battle between rock and flame raged, Aurin never giving in, Tavaris never giving up. Their duel sent asteroids into the sky and plummeting at Earth, into the seas that Merivis had created there. Perama, the land spirit, was born.

"Aurin and Tavaris paused in their fighting and saw that beauty had been created from them on Earth. Yet nothing grew or roamed there. And so, from so many miles away now, Ullko sent a gift. Ilmari, the air spirit, was born. Fire and rock now knew that to end their fight would see the life lost beneath them. Tavaris gentled his flames and Aurin embraced them and so our sun was born. As a peace offering to Ullko, Tavaris sent her his purest white flame so that she could shine as the brightest star, even from so far away in the north. To Amahri he also gave a gift, that of light and shape. Together with Aurin, they waned, waxed, and filled her, giving her power over the great seas on Earth. One final gift was bestowed upon a now flourishing Earth, fire and the Night Pegasus.

"All was in balance. Yet Amahri, now the lone moon in the sky, wanted to send her own gift to her sister, Earth. Amahri no longer had liquid water on her surface. She was far too cold to sustain it. So, just like the Night Pegasus that flickered and flew over the magnetic poles, Amahri bestowed a gift crafted of pure moon soul. Mountains and ice. With the help of Perama, Amahri brought a daughter into the world, a queen of sky and snow, ice, and rock. The tallest mountain in the Boreals, so tall Amahri felt she could reach out and touch her ice-crusted peak. That mountain ... was Serebo."

The crowd stilled at the mention of the mountain. The few Northerners here knew the spirit origin tale, yet to the Ilrairians, this was all new to them. Jaryn looked up at Meredith like a man transfixed by a siren's song.

His Queen Consort was a silent presence beside him.

Meredith ran her gaze over the people before her, raking over every face, daring them to challenge her.

"The Lowlanders and the Petish prayed and made offerings to these spirits and their offspring that followed. Yet my ancestors knew that if you challenged their power through our rituals, you could harness the elements and fauna of this world. They succeeded, all those years ago, in ridding the common creatures of speech, so that man could prevail, as we have done today. Yet the Trinitors, with their own depths of magic, were not affected and did not want us to touch the spirits and thought that the wild wards were unfit to wield them. Eight hundred years ago, my great ancestor, Osman, wild ward and royal mage to the late great King Baltsaros Adacus II, were in discussion with the then Trinitor King Colbass, regarding whether the creatures would allow soldiers on their backs."

All the creatures present, the Ilrair Pegasi and the Nijinxes, perked their ears. I moved silently through the crowd, leaving Pherox and the kin swarm to edge closer to the stage. Whatever was about to be said, I wanted to hear every word of it. This wasn't public knowledge. These were closely guarded royal and wild ward secrets. No one really knew why Colbass struck out that day and doomed his species.

"Colbass was a proud creature. He would not agree to the terms, and to show his displeasure, he murdered the king's eldest son and heir."

Lie.

The ties between the wild ward and her servants ran deep within all of us, but I had realized, it ran deeper with me. I knew when she was lying or telling the truth, her wild ward magic flaring in my veins whenever she spoke, glittering gold for truth, brindled white for lies. Meredith clearly had no knowledge of it.

I drew up alongside Coen and his uniformed, mud-spattered colleagues. "Tell it like it really was, Meredith."

Her glance at me was viper sharp, and her eyes appeared to glow in the low light. "Do you contest my knowledge, Asher?"

On the stage, the three equines shifted, their coarse rope bonds moving ever so slightly upon the wood.

"I do. I don't believe a Trinitor King would have done something so rash without being provoked."

Coen half turned toward me, hand on his sword. I ignored him.

Meredith stiffened. "As I said, he was proud, naïve, and rude. His Majesty, King Jaryn, will confirm my words. Colbass killed Ilrair's heir, so just revenge was delivered."

"You mean a curse that gave Baltsaros what he wanted in the end, a biddable and rideable winged creature, when the Trinitor King refused him?"

Soft hisses emerged from the Nijinxes then. Males clicked back and forth between one another.

Meredith gritted her teeth and turned not to reassure the Nijinxes, but to Jaryn for support. The King found me amongst the crowd, his emerald eyes blazing. "You twist the wild ward's words, hunter. Let her speak."

"It makes perfect sense," I continued, not balking from those green eyes. "Dissect the Trinitor down to what you needed, the Pegasus, and disregard the rest of the species. I'm not surprised the great Osman didn't have the curse already prepared for Colbass's arrival. Magic of that magnitude cannot just be doled out right there and then in the court. It would have taken weeks, if not months to prepare." I prowled away from Coen, inching closer to the stage and to Meredith. "It's not enough now, though, is it, Your Majesty? Your legendary aerial cavalry? You want the elements just like the first wild wards did, and the rest of the Trinitor creatures."

Pherox hissed from behind the crowds. The darkness crackled all around us, brushing against every canvas tent and structure. Our darkness, the darkness of Nijinxes and hunters. The Trinitors were no more. Pegasi, Mounties, Unicorns, and Nijinxes roamed the land now.

"Tell me wild ward, when you kill off the elemental spirits here." I gestured to the bound equines in turn. "Ice, air, and forest, what will happen to the Nijinxes?"

Meredith straightened, her fists clenched, and she tightened her magical grip on me. I let her squeeze tight and embraced it. "They will not be harmed."

Lie.

I cocked my head, arms crossed over my chest. "Every element and their offspring are in complete balance with one another, destroy forest, Tellervo and you destroy land, Perama. Kill off Varranar, ice, and you kill off Merivis, water. Kill off Ilmari, air, and you kill off Vaynor and Vaylar, night and day. Iltavorn, darkness, is the father of Vaynor. Kill him, and you lose the Nijinxes too."

The kin swarm tossed their heads in distrust and expanded their wings.

Jaryn stepped forward, his royal guard closing ranks around him. "That is why, hunter, they will be killed when this war is over."

My heart lurched over in my chest and shadows flickered in my veins as I took in his words. *No.* Pherox screeched and the other males took up the call, challenging the King and the wild ward who had offered them sanctuary.

"I won't let you do that." My hands withdrew my daggers, and Meredith bared her teeth.

"Know your place, Asher," she hissed.

"Rein them in, Meredith. I want this over with. Coen, hand her the blade."

Coen took a step forward, a glinting dark dagger in his gloved hand, then he hesitated. The Commander drew himself to his full height, his face solemn. He stared right at Jaryn, his King and his friend. "No."

The word clanged between the two men, but Coen did not balk from Jaryn's furious snarl. I dipped my chin, and Coen's gaze bounced from his King back to me. He gave me the tiniest of nods. My respect for him grew incrementally. *Well, he's a traitor, too, it seems.* The wild ward magic roared in my head and chest, yet, surprising myself with the fact that I could do such a thing, I ignored it. Pherox would not die for this King, nor would Vesperum and her family. Shadows singing in my veins, I launched myself at Meredith.

CHAPTER
FORTY-EIGHT

ORRIN

There was a voice in the darkness now, and it did not belong to the wild ward, as she shared Boreal history to those gathered before the stage. This voice was far older, older than cataloged time, older than thought, wish, or dream. It had ruled before Tavaris and his flames, before night and day had even been crafted.

The voice *was* darkness. The last spirit strong enough to speak. It pressed in on the encampment, snaring Meredith's every word, weaving between its Nijinx wards and dancing in mockery with the pyre.

Iltavorn was here.

The Nijinxes knew it.

So did we.

And a small part of me wondered as the air took on the tang of blood and the yell of men, if Asher knew too.

CHAPTER FORTY-NINE

DESTRY

The star continued to fall, tumbling and flickering as it arced through the sky, dooming itself closer and closer as it neared Serebo's peak. Yet it was the lights that followed that made me wrench the Kottin Mirror from my back. It started as a flicker of green at first, a low crackling blaze beyond the distant mountain ranges.

"They look like they're on fire," whispered Aalto.

The green light spiraled upward, sparking white and purple, then it striated to curtain the entire night sky. My own light danced free from my fingertips, needing no encouragement now.

Hands trembling, I lifted the mirror before me and splayed my right palm flat against the frigid and pristine ice.

"What will you aim for?" asked Aalto, his brown eyes wide with awe and uncertainty.

"Serebo's crown." I took a settling breath, my light flickering over the glass in subtle waves.

"And from there?"

I swallowed and gestured upward to the Night Pegasus. "I hope he knows what to do. A clear night and a falling star heading straight for Serebo? The spirits know we are trying to help them, surely."

The star careened closer and closer, its trail scintillating in its wake. I pressed my fingertips into the ice, nails digging in and unleashed my own light.

Aalto stumbled backward as, just like it had that night in the cave, my light punched through the ice as a meteoric column directed right at Serebo's notched summit. Panting, sweat running down my face, I pressed harder, willing the light further and higher, matching the speed of the star that fell.

Swooping closer into arcs of purple tinged with pink, the Night Pegasus jackknifed and twirled above our heads. He blazed with an intensity neither of us had ever seen. The star tumbled, and my light collided with eons old rock. My knees buckled as the force of the impact reverberated down the column and into my right arm. The pain knocked the air from my lungs, yet still I kept my hands pressed against the mirror. I thought I heard Aalto calling my name.

A lone arc of white light lanced downward and followed the flight of the falling star.

"The star isn't falling," yelled Aalto over the wind. "It's showing the way."

Spiraling upward at the very last moment, the star veered away at such a velocity it sparked brighter than it had before, but it was all the Night Pegasus needed. The white arc slammed into the peak and twinned with my column of light.

I roared, gripping the mirror with all the strength I had left. I felt it then, what we were unleashing and setting free. And I could feel him, too, Fire Prince, the fauna and land called him, lashing his light down to the mountain and drawing strength from my own. It felt glorious to be wrapped in his power again.

The wild ward's curse was like a bed of thorns beneath the snow, brittle yet razor sharp. It bucked and savaged at the power being driven into it.

My ancestors were there too. All the Kivisto women who had carried this spark of light in their bodies, a gift for freeing the Night

Pegasus from his rocky tomb centuries before. I could see their faces in the darkness: wise, strong, and encouraging. *"Nearly there, young one, nearly there."*

Giving myself wholly to the Night Pegasus, I unleashed every last ember of light into the mirror, until only a scrap of it remained. The tiniest glimmer in the darkest corners of my soul. The sky crackled and burned overhead and from the mountain, an archaic daughter of moon soul, a howl began to rise.

CHAPTER FIFTY

ASHER

The male Nijinxes were roaring.

Ear-splitting battle cries that cleaved the winter night air. A cacophony of sound that I hurled myself into and used it to brace myself against. Pherox was the loudest, a creature of unimaginable rage now. He lunged and raked at any soldier stupid enough to get within reach of him or Vesperum.

I could also sense his panic. He couldn't reach me. For Meredith's magic still held them grounded. They could attack, but they could not flee as much as they tried to. One of Jaryn's guards rained punch after punch at my bloodied head as we rolled on the frozen crust of mud, ash, and snow. One of my daggers sat embedded in the guard's left shoulder, the other lay several feet away, blood splattered and useless.

Coen fought alongside me, barking orders to the few soldiers who remained loyal to him. Jaryn was yelling at him, ordering him to submit.

On the stage, the three bound equines yanked and heaved at the ropes, trying in vain to remove their hoods. I heaved myself upright, dodging another punch and drove my right fist into the guard's left cheek. He staggered backward, clutching his face. Shadows fought to break rank from my body, but I reined them back. *Not yet, not yet.*

"The spirits can claim any creatures they wish as their scions," a coarse and otherworldly male voice sounded in my head, and I froze.

I knew that voice, deep within my blood and bone. The giant pyre beside the stage snapped out, followed by every torch and candle in the encampment. The fighting and struggling ground to a halt. *"It is a bond bound by blood. And I, huntsman, claimed you."*

Iltavorn.

His was the darkness that enameled my bones alongside the wild ward magic. It was his shadows that pulsed in my blood and sought to break free into the world. My eyes adapted in nanoseconds to the gloom. I turned on my heel and sprinted for my thrown dagger. Darkness seeped into every pore of my skin now, snuffing out the tendrils and embers of the wild ward magic as it went. I heard Coen curse and break into a run as he finally began to see through the darkness and saw what I was running toward.

Not Vesperum.

Not Pherox.

I leapt into a forward roll, plucking my fallen dagger, and then I was up again, racing for the wooden stage. Darkness prowled through every sense now until it could have been midday. I saw it all so clearly. Jaryn marching for Meredith. Pherox rearing. The eerie glow of scorching blue light from beneath the Unicorn's blindfold.

I sprang onto the wooden stage. The Mountie was closest to me. In one strike of my dagger, his hood was off, another strike, so were his hobbles. What followed was the most ear-splitting stallion's roar I had ever heard.

The Nijinx males threw up their heads as they sensed the pure male power in their midst.

Orrin.

The Mountie bared his teeth centimeters from my face. We no longer had our mental connection, not since Gracien's death. His golden gaze locked onto mine. I had broken him, and now I was freeing him. Orrin wheeled away from me. His gaze now fixed on the cause of all this harm, all this hurt.

I was forgiven.

The Pegasus was next, another two dagger cuts and she was free. Her haunting cry joining Orrin's as she leapt, not for the skies, but for Meredith, who tailed me, and it was darkness that gave her flight.

Then, at last, at last ...

Iltavorn curled around my neck, my chest, gilding my skin with dark armor. *"Set her free, hunter."*

The screaming and yelling had restarted again, everyone's sight now adjusted to the night-filled encampment. Yet it did not deter me as the rope and hessian fell away to fully reveal the creature stolen from the heart of Serebo's lands.

Doleful, summer-blue eyes burned in the night. The young mare stepped backward, lifting her head higher, and my gaze roved upward to that pale, twisting, spindled horn. She reared upon the stage, forelimbs raking, and her powerful muscles quivered under a pelt crafted of the purest ice.

The sound of it came a second after she unleashed a barrage of blue-tinged light toward the heavens, like an ice shelf cleaving itself free from a glacier. She landed back on all fours gracefully, like a highland dancer. A heartbeat passed. I looked upward, as did everyone else, to see what, *who*, she had summoned to our plight.

The Night Pegasus had heard her call.

Only the second time he had been seen this far south, the Fire Prince crackled in the heavens, lashing light in every direction.

Her breath steady and measured, the Unicorn looked at me. I blinked, finding my hand stretching out toward her. A creature so pure, nothing tainted her. Neither pride, envy, nor hatred could find purchase on her, just cool and calm understanding. A being of infinite patience, for that is what she had, an eternity of observing and keeping Serebo's secrets from the world. I felt the warm air of her whicker over my hand as she placed her muzzle into my gloved palm.

A second passed, and the moment melted away like a late spring snow. The mare backed up and fixed her cool gaze upon the Nijinxes beyond the stage. Not an ounce of fear flickered over her body, as she charged at the soldiers penning the kin swarm.

Darkness and light, ice and fire, air and forest, all working to drive out the wicked forces that choked their home. Human greed and wild ward magic. Even if the wild ward's power ... made me what I was now, I gladly stepped onto the path Iltavorn was carving for me, as the night spirit continued to snuff out her magic within my blood. The brindled gold web over me was smothered out, replaced with something purer and older.

Jaryn screamed at his men, and the Nijinx males screamed back.

Snarling, I threw myself into the fray and unleashed shadows from my hands.

CHAPTER FIFTY-ONE

ORRIN

I galloped toward the wild ward. Jaryn had loaned her a small unit of soldiers, soldiers who now tried in vain to protect her from the equines who were hell-bent on destroying her. She still held the Nijinxes on the ground, and Jaryn's troops penned them tighter and tighter with spears and swords until squeals of beastly pain began to rise in the night air.

My pace picked up in earnest, and I flew over the charred and muddied ground. I sensed the Unicorn galloping as well, eating up the distance between her and the troops that cut into the Nijinx kin swarm.

Then I spied her, her face pale in the darkness.

The wild ward.

An ear-splitting horn blast careened through the camp. I thrust up my head, my skin trembling as Ebrel whinnied with happiness. An answering whinny floated down to us as Kalana and the Royants smashed into the flanks of Jaryn's remaining men.

I backed up a step, then two ears pinned to my head as the wild ward ran from the camp, shrouded by her soldiers. Jaryn and his royal guard followed suit. I snapped my teeth in frustration yet held my place. Her life was not mine to take. There was only one thing that could rightfully end her now.

I shifted my focus to the Nijinxes. Ebrel ran for my side, and we plowed into the men holding the dark creature's captive. Asher was there, a twirling vision of death as he cut down any soldier who got within striking distance of his Nijinx brother. Shadows arched from his hands. When he struck, soldiers died.

Iltavorn pressed in all around us, guiding us to any weak spots within the soldiers' circle. I struggled to remain upright and whinnied to Ebrel as the ground beneath our hooves rumbled, and dead sections of heather and gorse snapped free from their mother plants and fell to the trembling earth.

My gaze ripped to the distant moorland on our left and the faraway rock spires. The dwellings of the moor spirit.

"Fall back!" I yelled as the ground itself began to rip apart. Heather and grass tore, revealing frozen earth and splitting slices of rock.

The soldiers screamed and ran for what remained of their forces. Jaryn and the wild ward tried to run. The Royants doubled back and leapt for the skies.

The gigantic breach in the moorland turned and split northward. Water churned upward and frothed in the blackened fissure. I felt a feather-light touch down our spines, and I pressed Ebrel closer to my side. The mare leant into me, whickering softly.

Dancing across the winter skies, I felt Ilmari smile. Then I realized she did not quake in fear, but in amazement and relief. From the north in quick succession, three colossal *booms* swept out across the land. The world fell deathly quiet in their wake.

I inhaled sharply as I felt the barrel of power gather momentum and hurl southward. Destry and the soldier had done it. It was only then did the King of Ilrair care to look down at the roots of heather that clutched his boots, trapping him and his remaining soldiers to the earth.

The ground, which now ripped anew once more, as a wave of magic swept over Harracombe and Aarine. Ilmari carved herself into fractions of spirit, spreading herself thin to protect her wards, the Pegasi that still believed in her, who knelt only to her, the Queen of the Air.

As the magic plowed through the Anduns, leaving her sparking touch on every living thing she swept by, did I sense who this was. She who had left her mighty throne, the only thing strong enough to take on the wild ward magic that had choked and damaged her homeland.

Serebo.

Untainted, untamable, pristine, and primitive, the mountain spirit angled herself into an almighty dagger that tore toward Jaryn and the wild ward beside him. With her sister spirits, Ghel and Bronzo, on either side of her, Serebo was an unshakable force that no mortal could ever dream to control.

The cut in the land yawned wider, unleashing a spirit that pummeled every inch of coastline and set frozen kisses upon the land every winter in apology. Merivis, the water spirit, rose and peaked, as Serebo swept up from under her, creating an inland tsunami that grew and grew, higher and higher.

Jaryn and the wild ward screamed in fear.

Only by working together could the spirits survive this. Now free from her prison of magic, Serebo was going to do exactly that.

The wild ward wrenched her magic away from the Nijinxes, leaving them confused, lost, and gasping. She hurtled every ounce of her power into defending herself. The crackling, brindled magic snapped upward, as the wave caught itself upon the jagged rock and earth, as if it were an ancient reef. Casting a dark net around Jaryn, she hurled him far from the wave's path to safety.

The wave crested an unimaginable wall of sparkling blue and hissing white. Then it plunged, fracturing apart the wild ward's magic and body as if they were no more than lifeless branches. The wave devoured her screams as it crashed back down into the earth, rippling outward until the water settled into a new, vast inland lake.

Only wingbeats and ragged breaths could be heard now.

A palomino Pegasus landed beside Jaryn, and I snarled in frustration as a staggering and bleeding Coen hurled the King onto his mount and they both took flight south, followed by the Queen on her Pegasus.

Equines and humans looked on as the Night Pegasus burned the night sky above our heads.

CHAPTER
FIFTY-TWO

DESTRY

Only flickers of light resided in me now, mere scraps compared to what I'd possessed before yielding it over to its rightful owner. I had given nearly every drop back to the Night Pegasus, to free Serebo from her cursed cage. And I had been glad to do it, proud even. The almighty boom of her prison cleaving open had knocked Aalto and me off our feet, and on a keening wolf-like howl, the mountain spirit had raced south with her sisters to splinter the wild ward magic apart.

The spirits and their scions were now free once more.

I blinked, my body feeling like I had been run through with a dozen swords as I lay gasping on the snow-covered ledge. The stones beneath the snow dug into my back like razors, and I was so utterly cold like the ice of Serebo had infused with my very blood. The Night Pegasus still flared in the sky above in gentle curtains of flickering emerald. Lying shattered into several pieces beside me was the Kottin Mirror.

Readying my body and my mind, I dragged myself onto my knees and then Aalto was there, gripping my elbows and hauling me against his chest.

"You did it," he whispered into my hair. "You *did* it."

I let him hold me, not having the energy to push back away from him.

Tenderly, he brushed snow from my shoulder. "Your light?"

I held up a bare, shaking hand, my nails cracked and bleeding. A faint violet glow twined around my fingertips.

A flash of relief coated Aalto's handsome face, followed by a beat of silence and despite the exhaustion eating away at my bones, unease coated my already sweat-soaked skin. "Aalto? Are you ok?"

With both hands, he cupped my face and silently implored me with his gaze. My grip changed to clasp his hips, ready to shove him away if needs be. Anxiety rolled off him in waves. He looked down, then back up at me, shaking his head. *Kathkar* sent a pulse of chilled magic down my spine. A warning.

"Aalto?"

"My ..." He took a steadying breath and lowered his hands. "My true name ... is Rekorious Neimi."

I tensed and searched his face. The knowledge he had just shared, clattering in my mind. My throat constricted as I felt the first waves of rage take root in my torso. *"Why?* Why did you lie to me?"

His right hand moved up to clasp the back of my neck and his voice was earnest, desperate. "I had to. I couldn't trust you yet, despite ... despite this *need* between us, and we had this monumental task. I didn't want to jeopardize it and distract you. I didn't want you to see me as your enemy."

Ice clung to my lashes, despite my tears. He had lied to me, and I could appreciate his risks, that he had been an Ilrair cavalry commander whilst rebelling as a Petish warlord. Yet after everything, after *Narve*, he still hadn't told me. I would have gladly gone with Narve to free this man.

I shoved myself away from him, despite the heat that poured from him, despite the attraction I had once felt for him. Shivering and shaking, I appraised him, my heart pounding against my ribs.

"There's ... one more thing." He stepped forward and I retreated, drawing *Kathkar* from its scabbard.

"What?" I snarled. Ice magic, *truth* magic, flickered from the hilt and up my arm.

He took a haggard, frozen breath. "Lochlan, your father, had promised you to the eldest Niemi son the moment you were born in order to strengthen ties between the clans."

The eldest son. I gaped at him, my knees quivering. "I'm betrothed ... to *you?*"

Aalto—no, *Rekorious*, nodded, his gaze unflinching. A warrior preparing for battle. "You were destined to be mine, Destry." He stalked forward, and before I could run him through, he struck out and grabbed one of my wrists.

I glowered at him. My heart was frozen in my chest. As much as I loved and respected my father, part of me felt utterly betrayed that he would have organized this. *"No."*

His smile faltered then. "What did you say?"

I wrenched my arm from his grip and stepped back, angling *Kathkar* in front of my torso. "I said *no.*"

A cool calm washed over Aalto's handsome face, his mask slipping, and he followed me. "You do not wish to marry me, Destry?"

"It's your only claim to the Petish throne, marrying me. You all thought I was dead weeks ago, and you had every right to march into Petowin with your army and rule it." What remained of my light circled about my head, my hair lifting and curling around me. "But I wasn't dead, was I? So, you tracked me down, brought me here, alone, to give you every possible chance to sway my decision. To be seduced by *you.*"

I barely recognized my own voice. It had gone guttural and glacial, just like it had with Narve. My sword trembled within my two-handed grasp, but I didn't back away from him.

Rekorious breathed deeply through his nose, his lips set into a grim determined line. "Clever, wild thing, aren't you?"

He pressed forward, within easy reach of *Kathkar's* cutting edge. His voice dropped an octave, his dark gaze capturing mine. "Would it be so bad, Destry, to be married to me?"

"I'm done being a pawn played by men. I am fucking *done*," I snarled. "Every kind thing you have done to me, for me, has been a lie." I pointed to the river fish embroidered on my cloak. "Your mother had sewn the Neimi sigil onto *my* family's cloak as if this was all settled and decided."

For a second, hurt flashed across his face, then it was gone, replaced with cool, calm contemplation.

No, I would not marry this man. No more betrothals, no more being tossed and cleaved from ruler to ruler. *No more.*

I thought about the Commander who had shown me any real tenderness, who had wiped blood from my face, and had cradled me after saving my life, who had been haunting my dreams ever since I had left Saltfen. The man whose warning now rang true. *Coen.*

I twirled *Kathkar,* the length of the sword glowing a delicate, faint blue. Rekorious' gaze widened as he took in the magic imbued into the weapon. He rolled his lower lip with his teeth and quirked an eyebrow. "You're walking off this mountain with me, Destry Kivisto, and you're going to be my bride whether you like it or not."

I snarled then, utterly enraged at his entitlement. "I will do no such thing."

The lambent stones in *Kathkar's* hilt flared brightly as I swung and brought the blade down against his unprotected torso.

EPILOGUE

COEN

I stood at the northern edge of Harracombe Moor, the winter wind ripping and tearing at the leather of my rider's coat. Hestian was a golden, white-winged behemoth at my back, his warm breath billowing in the frigid air.

"Tell me, *traitor*, why I shouldn't just slit your fucking throat right here and now?" I snarled, my gloved fists crossed over my chest. "If Jaryn had found you first, you would already be *dead*."

Those familiar copper eyes silently implored me, but the soldier standing across from me ground his teeth. "I'll tell you everything."

I stepped closer, rage rippling over my body. "You better fucking had, *Farrow*."

The Sergeant had enough of a backbone to not cower from me. It was taking all my sheer will and experience as a commander to not kill him already. He had jeopardized everything. *Everything*. Then he had the fucking audacity to come crawling back.

Guilt curled a gnarled fist over my heart, as the thought of Destry flickered through my mind. I had thought of no one else, of *nothing* else, after Aalto had taken her. She haunted my dreams, the wildness of her capturing my every waking moment. I should have gone after her that night. Even her scent, which reminded me of sweet, alpine flowers, followed me everywhere.

It had all gone to shit. Jaryn's madness, the fire and Nijinx siege on Aarine, the execution of the wild ward, the shadow-wielding hunter that was now at large beyond Glentay with his band of Njinxes. And *Destry* ... whom I had threatened and treated like an utter scrap of human existence, all because I hadn't known the truth. Then I had saved her life, and she had saved mine. I would be a drowned man if she hadn't plunged into the lake that night. Hestian would have been dead too. Then Thorra had arrived and had gotten inside her head. I should have never left her alone with him.

I should have gone after her.

Jaryn was my oldest friend, and all of this had been for him, all that I had done ... despite his madness, I had saved his life and had unceremoniously dumped him and Amadea on the outskirts of Ilrair last night.

Amadea had gripped the lapels of my rider's coat with a ferocity that matched the fury on her face. "Do the right thing, Silvano. For all our sakes."

The Queen had called me a snake, just like Jaryn and all the others in his rotten court. Yet now it felt like the reptile was devouring me whole, constricting my chest tighter and tighter, until I could make this right. Regret and guilt coiled around my heart and waited there.

Destry. She was hundreds of miles away to the north, yet I could feel her here, even now. I couldn't get the night I had saved her out of my head. Her face had been filled with such gut-wrenching relief upon seeing me. Relief and awe, just like I had felt when she had pulled me out of the lake. She had come for me when no one else had.

I blinked at the memory, and Farrow swallowed harshly. "I've been Thorra's spy since I joined this platoon six years ago. I had originally petitioned to join the Royants, but he approached me and proposed I join Bromtide. Everything Bromtide has done, I reported to Thorra."

My jaw clenched and Farrow tensed.

"He ... Thorra ... he's not who you think he is, Commander."

I stalked forward, my face inches from the Sergeant's. "Then who the *fuck* is he?"

"The Petish warlord. Rekorius Neimi."

Shock washed over me for all of a second before it was replaced with an ice-cold fury. "You've been relaying every military detail of ours to the most powerful Petish warlord since Lochlan Kivisto, and you think that gives you a right to still be breathing in my presence?"

Farrow dropped to his knees in the snow. "Only because I can be of use to you now. I can't go back north and join him."

"Why?" I snarled

"Thorra needed Destry back in Saltfen. I smuggled a small lambent stone into her room to elevate her powers, then I orchestrated Destry, revealing her surname to me during our training. She didn't know the guards were listening. Our agreement was they would only threaten her, to give Jaryn an incentive to move her back north earlier than planned. I didn't realize they were going to try and fucking *kill* her."

My blood was a dull roar in my head.

"If Rek ... I—I mean Thorra, finds out I nearly got her killed, he'll rip out my throat. If Destry doesn't get to me first."

I lunged down, grabbed the collar of Farrow's coat and hauled him back to his feet. "You want to thank whatever gods you pray to that I was there that night, you useless piece of shit."

Farrow loosed a breathless, shaky laugh in my face. "It worked though, didn't it? You flew north the next morning."

"I swear to the Lady herself, if Thorra doesn't kill you, I will, Taneli Farrow." I shoved him away, sending him flying onto his back in the snow. Hestian pranced forward, wings arching, and he placed a lethal forehoof on the soldier's panting chest, pinning him to the ground.

I stood beside my Pegasus and glared down at Farrow. Barely recognizing the ice in my voice, I said, "You're going to tell me everything Thorra has planned. For Petowin, for Destry, all of it. And if I discover you've double-crossed me, I will kill you and leave you in an unmarked grave in the middle of fucking nowhere. Do you *understand?*"

"He—he—he is betrothed to her, Silvano," said Farrow earnestly, his gaze bouncing between Hestian and me.

"What?"

Hestian released a low, threatening rumble from his golden chest.

"Destry's father promised her to him after she was born, but when everyone thought that she had died, the Kivisto bloodline with it, Rekorious was free to ascend to the Petish throne." Farrow sucked down a harried breath. "But ... but now she's alive—"

"The only way he can claim it ... is by marrying her?"

The traitor nodded. "He's been hunting for her since she fled Aarine, but Bromtide got there before he did."

I stood tall before Farrow, rolled my shoulders, and cast my gaze northward. Destry had been plucked from one man's cage and thrown straight into another. She may have used her light to grant the spirits their freedom, but she had forfeited her own in the process.

Fuck, maybe she would *want* to marry him. But if she didn't and he forced her ...

Thorra was a changed man, ever since Amadea. The Queen had nearly died because of their love for one another. Now, it seemed, his heart had been fully ripped out, and he was bound by duty to his people, his family, ensnaring Destry in the process.

I dropped to one knee on the snow, and I looked at Farrow with a face that promised death. "Where is she?"

EPILOGUE PART TWO

ORRIN

A tiny, pale-white alpine flower had bloomed beside the plinth upon which I had first met Ebrel. Snow clustered around its fragile green leaves, yet still, it reached for the pre-dawn light, the delicate petals angling to the east. Awaiting the rising of the sun. Dawn wasn't far away.

I inhaled deeply, my hooves planted firmly into the packed snow and earth beneath me. The forest at my back murmured across my pelt and my mind. *Home*, it whispered. *Our King is home.*

Faintly, I could hear a small flock of roe deer in the valley below, their sing-song voices filtering through the fog that clung to the lower altitude. Free of the wild ward. As were the wolves, the bears, the foxes, and little creatures. Arching my neck, my blond mane cascading over it, I took in Glentay. My family's home for generations. A family who had battled a curse and had let love prevail, despite loss and hardship, war and grief. Love had won.

The Breccan River, far below, rumbled in agreement, as did the northern sky and the silent stars. The song of the wilds filled my head and my heart. I reared. From my lungs came a stallion's roar, a decree that as long as my heart pounded in my chest, I would forever protect this place. My cry rang out over the trees and mountainsides as the first rays of dawn pierced the horizon.

SPIRITS OF THE BOREALS

Elemental Spirits

Darkness: **Iltavorn.** Mortal scions can wield shadows, Nijinxes are also his scions.

Fire: **Tavaris.** Mortals can wield truth magic with his power. No current bloodline has this gift.

Water: **Merevis.** Scions are Orca.

Land: **Perama**

Forest: **Tellervo.** (Son of Perama). Scions are Mountain Horses.

Ice: **Varranar.** (Son of Merevis) Mortals can wield truth magic with his power. Truth Keepers and one female bloodline currently have this gift.

Air: **Ilmari.** Scions are Pegasi.

Night: **Vorna.** (Son of Iltavorn)

Day: **Vayla.** (Daughter of Tavaris)

Northern Lights: **Night Pegasus.** *Fire Prince/Wings of Fire* (Son of Tavaris). Only one female bloodline currently acts as his scion and they can wield his light.

Southern Lights: **Corapesi.** *Painter of Light*, (Daughter of Tavaris)

Mountain Spirits

Serebo: Scions are Unicorns. Her peak is protected by varki deer, ibex, and snow sirens.

Ghel: Serebo's younger sister.

Bronzo: Serebo's younger sister.

Nychta: Not yet discovered by mortals.

Eira: Nychta's younger sister (Consort to the Night Pegasus, when she flies with him, her form is that of a falling star.)

<u>Sister Moons</u>

Amarhi: The Moon

Aurin: The Sun (Claimed by Tavaris)

Ullko: The North Star

Earth

PLAYLIST

Skydance by Kim Planert
Where the Light Goes by Josh Kramer
Stars Are on Your Side by Ross Copperman
Pegasus by Meduza, Eli & Fur
How to Help by Harrison Storm
Sweet Nothing by Calvin Harris, Florence Welch
worship by LACES
moved by LACES
Are You With Me by nilu
Among Trees by Krale

ACKNOWLEDGEMENTS

They say it takes a village to raise a little one, and I think the same could be said for bringing a book into the world. I give my thanks to the beautiful souls who helped me craft Night Sky Burning into what it is today.

Firstly, to Kara Douglas, Hannah Sears, Kelsey McCullar and Lorna, my beta readers, who offered such amazing support and comments.

Special mention to Lucile, who is still my number one hype queen to this day, I'm going to really try to write a HEA for you.

To Claire Butler, who held my hand during those first steps into the world of being an indie author. Your wealth of knowledge and helpfulness is truly special, and I can't thank you enough. Hopefully, we get our writer's weekend retreat someday.

To my wonderful editor and beta reader, Melissa Smith, you took the raw magic of NSB and created something so special. Thank you so much.

To the Cottesloe Vet Nurse Crew, working with you was such a privilege and I miss you all so much.

To David Gardias, for taking my crazy book cover dreams and making them a reality.

To Tiny, for keeping me humble, present and sane.

To Nana, who read that first Pegasus v.s Unicorns story I wrote when I was twelve, thank you for believing in me. To Grandma, for the crochet and patchwork skills and to Grandad, who instilled in me the love of miniatures and making small moments of magic. I miss you all so much.

To my parents, I'm so blessed to have you both in my life, and I would not be where I am today without you. I'm sorry Australia is so bloody far away.

To Nora, my darling girl, you are unconquerable and as wild as the northern sky. I love you so much.

And finally, to my husband, Rob. Bear's, this book is a testament to all that we have lived through, all the adventures we have seen and the darkness in which we held each other. My heart fully belongs to you, and I can't imagine walking this life without you by my side.

Asher and Destry's stories continue in Book Two of The Trinitor
Chronicles

DAWN SKY RISING

The truth will be carried on white wings.

Releasing September 2025

CHAPTER
FIFTY-THREE

ABOUT THE AUTHOR

Hayley is a Western Australia based indie author with a passion for horses. An experienced veterinary nurse, Hayley focuses on writing fantasy and romance. She lives in a little country town with her husband, two young daughters, a cheeky Labrador and probably to many chickens. She loves to curl up with a strong cup of tea and a good book. Some of her favourite authors include Ali Hazelwood, Sarah J Maas, A L Rojo and Claire Butler.

If you loved this book, please consider leaving a review on Amazon or Goodreads. Reviews are incredibly important, especially to us indie authors, and we appreciate them so much. Thank you!

If you wish to connect, you can find me on IG and Threads @h.a .walkerwrites

Website is currently in progress!